GOLDEN TERRACE

VOLUME II

CANG WU BIN BAI

TRANSLATED BY

E. DANGLARS

ISBN 978-1-956609-96-7 (paperback)

Translation by E. Danglars
Editing by Molly Rabbitt
Proofing by Lori Parks
Cover Art by Qing Meng Huan Tu

Published originally under the title of 《黄金台》
English edition rights under the license granted by 北京晋江原创网络科技有
限公司 (Beijing Jinjiang Original Network Technology Co. Ltd) through
Wuhan Loretta Media Agency Co., Ltd.

Printed in the USA

Published by Peach Flower House LLC 2022
PO Box 1156
Monterey Park, CA 91754
Visit www.peachflowerhouse.com

Learn how to pronounce the character names here!

https://www.peachflowerhouse.com/

pronunciation-guide/golden-terrace

CONTENTS

CHAPTER FORTY-FIVE

A servant came urgently to knock on the door of the main room. Inside, Yan Xiaohan was startled, and Fu Shen, seeming to sense something, also moved, then was gently embraced by Yan Xiaohan, who said vaguely, in a low, hoarse voice, "It's all right, sleep."

He put on some clothes and got up. With disturbed weariness all over his face, he went to open the door. "What is it?"

The servant was smiling brightly. "A joyous occasion! Prince Qi Manor just sent someone to bring news. At three o'clock this morning, Princess Qi gave birth to a little commandery princess. Mother and daughter are both safe and sound."

This really was a joyous occasion for the Fu family. Princess Qi had given birth to the eldest daughter of the first wife before any of the other concubines could give birth. While this wasn't a son, it was the first child of Prince Qi Manor, and in the future would presumably be a carefully cradled royal pearl. Yan Xiaohan woke up a little and told him to go reward the person who had brought the news, then to go pass on a message to the accountant to give the manor's servants an extra half month of wages. After making the proper arrangements, he closed the door and turned around, but he saw that Fu Shen had entirely woken up at some point and was holding himself up in bed, trying to sit up.

The quilt had slipped, his belt was loose, and his lapels were wide open, revealing a smooth, sturdy chest and muscles flashing in and out of sight. Worst of all was the speckling of red marks on his collarbones, floating down like fallen red petals to his chest, irrefutable evidence left behind by a night of bliss. And the little siren who had enjoyed conjugal love with him had been unusually ardent and clinging—and had even sucked a mark onto the prominence in his throat!

Fu Shen pulled himself up but couldn't manage to sit upright. His whole "waist" seemed to have been pulled out of his body. He frowned and put a hand to his back. The movement was a little exaggerated. Yan Xiaohan immediately came over and, as if guarding against thieves, pulled up the quilt and wrapped Fu Shen up tightly and set him down. "Don't get up. Just lie back."

Luckily Fu Shen had just woken up and hadn't yet taken the time to recall what had happened last night. He had only vaguely heard something about "Princess Qi;" forcing his eyelids to open, he asked, "What about Princess Qi?"

"Congratulations, you're an uncle." Yan Xiaohan's dry, warm palm pressed against his forehead. "Princess Qi has given birth to a daughter. They just sent someone over to announce the good news."

Fu Shen was immediately energized. "How is my sister?"

"Don't worry, mother and daughter are both safe and sound." Yan Xiaohan hung up his outer clothes and also lay back in bed, taking half of his quilt. With the two of them sharing one set of bedding, it seemed that the warmth and tenderness could make a person leap into dreams as soon as they closed their eyes.

"It's still early. Go back to sleep. You can go to Prince Qi Manor to congratulate them when you wake up."

The low whispers could only be heard between the two of

them. The little universe surrounded by these bed curtains contained a particular kind of intimacy. In fact, there would be something different from now on.

Yan Xiaohan pulled Fu Shen over and massaged his back. From soreness and numbness, the muscles gradually recovered sensation, and the absurdities all appeared at the same time. By the weak light coming in through the window, he bent his head and looked at his chest. "Yan Menggui, were you born in the fucking Year of the Dog?"

Quiet laughter flowed past his ear, bringing with it a limpness that made the heart itch. The contented sigh carried even more insatiability. "Jingyuan."

"Hm?"

"Jingyuan."

Fu Shen pulled a long face. "Go fuck yourself."

"No." Having had his wishes fulfilled, Yan Xiaohan was now one big demonstration of being spoiled by the certainty of favor. He maliciously spoke an obscenity into his ear: "I only want to fuck you."

Fu Shen expressionlessly slapped him. The skin-to-skin contact made a crisp sound, but there was only the slightest sting. Yan Xiaohan knew that this was an indulgence he would never speak aloud, a small punishment to prevent future offenses, holding back his strength even if he hit him, just like last night, when he had knit his brows and panted but hadn't once told him to stop.

He involuntarily hugged him close, with a force that seemed as if he wanted to fuse their blood and bones together. "Jingyuan, I appreciate you going to the trouble."

"Stop showing off," Fu Shen said coolly. "Why didn't I see this compassion when you were tormenting me last night? Next time, before pretending to be sorry in front of me, at least hide your wagging fox's tail."

"So there'll be a next time?" said Yan Xiaohan.

"… No," said Fu Shen, "scram."

3

When he woke up again, the other side of the bed was empty. There was full daylight outside and the twittering of birds. Yan Xiaohan must have massaged his back for a long time. Fu Shen could finally sit up stiffly. He performed a close inspection and was almost frightened by the love bites and bruises on his body. It was honoring Yan Xiaohan beyond his deserts to say he had been born in the Year of the Dog. He truly lived up to being part of the Feilong Guard—in this miserable state, he simply looked as though he had been in the North Prison's interrogation department.

He definitely couldn't go out and see people like this. He vaguely remembered Yan Xiaohan saying there was ointment by the bed, so he reached out and pulled open a drawer to rummage around. He didn't find a medicine bottle, but instead he turned up a small sandalwood box.

The box wasn't locked, and Fu Shen didn't think too much of it. His hand moved faster than his brain. He lifted the lid.

Two morning calm flower jade pendants lay side by side on deep red brocade, one bright and clean as new, one broken and then inlaid with gold, just barely restored to its original form.

By a great coincidence, Fu Shen recognized both of these jade pendants. One he had gifted, and one he had broken.

He had already learned about Caiyue. At the time, he had felt a surge of emotion, hard to subdue. He had already thought that was the upper limit of heartache, not expecting that another grip on his heart would now be added.

No matter what aspect you looked at it from, Yan Xiaohan certainly didn't have a weak or passive character. He couldn't even be called good and honest. Only when it came to Fu Shen was he so careful that he feared to make a single move.

When it came to his own bad habits, Fu Shen could pick out a whole list with his eyes closed: bad tempered, peremptory, ruthless when he ought to be lenient but indiscriminately nice when he ought not to be lenient. As a teenager, he had moreover been ridiculously naïve. Strictly speaking, it wasn't as if he had been entirely without blame in the situation back then, but in the long run, it had been Yan Xiaohan losing sleep over it, being tormented.

What had he ever done to deserve to be treasured like this?

While he was lost in thought, light and steady footsteps came from the passage. Shortly, they had reached the door. Yan Xiaohan opened the door one-handed, carrying a purple-gold hair-binding crown. He walked in and said, "Jingyuan, are you awake?"

Fu Shen got up as though nothing were the matter. "Yes. What do you have there?"

Yan Xiaohan put the crown on a small stool and brought Fu Shen's outer clothes, freshly perfumed, to the bedside. While helping him arrange them, he said, "Aren't you going to Prince Qi Manor today? I just had them put together some gifts and find a crown for you while they were at it. You can't be dressed too plainly when going to pay a congratulatory visit."

Fu Shen's waist was still sore. He leaned against him idly and suddenly said, "Come with me when I go."

Yan Xiaohan's hand shook. He nearly fixed the crown crooked. He repeated in astonishment, "Come with you?"

Visiting relatives together was a thing that only a genuine husband and wife would do. Though he and Fu Shen were husband and wife in name and now in fact, in the eyes of outsiders, theirs was only a false marriage. Princess Qi probably wouldn't recognize him as a "family member." Why did Fu Shen suddenly want to bring him along? Didn't he know what that meant?

"You're going to Jingchu with Prince Qi next month. You can say hello first," Fu She said. "You're family, you should get to know each other ahead of time."

Family…

Yan Xiaohan gently put his hands on his shoulders. In the not very clear bronze mirror, Fu Shen saw a helpless expression flash over his face.

"What?" he said with a careless smile. "A newborn niece, and you as an aunt don't want to go see her?"

Yan Xiaohan could clearly sense a change in Fu Shen's attitude. He didn't know whether it was the influence of last night's marital intercourse, but Fu Shen seemed to have thoroughly accepted him, and entirely opened his arms to him. Before, while Fu Shen had also yielded and indulged on many points, he had very rarely taken the initiative to ask him to do anything, and the progress of their relationship had been limited to between the two of them, unknown by outsiders. But now, he seemed to have at last been admitted by Fu Shen into the scope of his "people."

Yan Xiaohan surreptitiously took a deep breath, attempting to calm his chaotic heartbeat. "If you and I go visit together, aren't you worried Prince Qi will misunderstand?"

"Misunderstand what?" Fu Shen froze. Then he understood and flippantly pinched his cheek. Unable to suppress a smile, he said, "Our Lord Yan is pretty and virtuous, gentle and likable, naturally presentable and fit for social occasions. Don't be scared, I'm not planning to keep you like a mistress in a love nest."

"I can't…" Yan Xiaohan knew that he had made a slip of the tongue and immediately stopped.

Fu Shen's expression gradually turned serious. "What are you trying to say? Finish what you were saying."

As soon as his grandeur came into play, Yan Xiaohan immediately shrank. Seeing him like this, what was there for Fu Shen not to understand? He felt affection and anger, and a sliver of dissatisfaction at expectations not met. Therefore, he said with a cold laugh, "Wonderful. Since when has the mighty Imperial Investigator and commander had a problem with feeling inferior?"

He was too skilled at seizing the crucial point, hitting the target at the first strike. Yan Xiaohan was briefly struck dumb, then finally said, roughly, "Jingyuan, I'm covered in muck myself, I can't…"

Fu Shen hit the table with a bang and sternly said, "Yan Xiaohan! Just try saying it and see what happens!"

He had just made him "finish what he was saying," and now he wasn't letting him speak. It really was a little unreasonable. But Yan Xiaohan knew that he had already understood what he meant.

He couldn't from his own selfish interests stain Fu Shen with dirty water; the Marquis of Jingning's clean name up to now couldn't be tarnished by a crafty sycophant like him.

Though it sounded absurd, that was indeed what he thought.

Fu Shen hadn't been wrong to say he felt inferior. With such an undesirable background, censured ever since childhood, growing up in such surroundings, one would either be deranged or willing to degrade oneself. Yan Xiaohan's current state already amounted to the outcome of utmost restraint.

In fact, Fu Shen knew very well that Yan Xiaohan's sticking point lay in "making too much of himself," and Fu Shen had been unable to give him an adequate sense of security. The difference in their positions was too great; the more you cared, the more worried you would be about personal gains and losses. While he couldn't keep himself from wallowing in it, he also couldn't keep himself from knowing that every bit of intimacy was stolen time.

Living in this world, it was one thing not to be able to recklessly pursue your heart's desires; Yan Xiaohan also had to burn up his heart's blood like this. Born to the life of a treacherous official, he didn't have the disease of the treacherous official. Thinking about it like this, he was rather pitiful.

Fu Shen said, "When His Majesty arranged the marriage between us, wasn't he planning on making you half a member of the Fu family by force, to pave the way for you to legitimately take over Beiyan's military authority in the future? That being the case, shouldn't you be dedicating your efforts to making that reputation a reality? Why are you dodging and hiding instead, not daring to see people?"

Every word struck to the heart.

"Jingyuan." Yan Xiaohan's expression looked as though he had stabbed him in the chest. He closed his eyes and earnestly said, "You know I'm not doing this for military authority."

"Right, you're doing it for me," Fu Shen said. "But when I want to be with you openly, you don't want it."

Yan Xiaohan also got angry. "You think this is what I want? I... A spotless national hero getting mixed up with the court's dog—are you going to tell me that sounds good?!"

"Fine, I understand." Fu Shen laughed coldly, extremely angry. "After all this talk, in Lord Yan's heart, I'm less important than a false reputation."

Yan Xiaohan choked. Shortly, he sighed, his anger departing as quickly as it had come. He didn't want to argue with Fu Shen today. Conciliating, he said, "Jingyuan."

"Do you think now that being with me will sully my reputation?" Fu Shen wasn't taking the kindness, however. He suddenly raised his voice. "You've even sullied my person, why didn't you think then that it would come to this?!"

Yan Xiaohan said nothing.

Ancestor, I beg you, don't shout.

"Yan Xiaohan, I'm going to leave the conversation at this today. A marriage was arranged between us by the emperor, our wedding presided over by the Ministry of Rites. We were legally married and bowed to heaven, earth, and the ancestors on Golden Terrace. Last night we engaged in marital relations, and a hundred years from now we'll fly on cranes to the Western Paradise together, and you will be buried with me." With rare solemnity, Fu Shen said, "Husband and wife are one. There is no discussion of worthy or unworthy. Even when you go out this door, you can still openly call me your husband."

The rims of Yan Xiaohan's eyes burned. He was both moved and amused.

He couldn't cry, and he couldn't laugh. A hundred thousands of words came to his lips and all turned into a sigh. "To hear you say that, even if I should die on the spot, I would have no regrets. It's only that rumor and gossip kill invisibly. It's enough that my reputation alone is burdened. Listen to me, don't pay with your reputation as well. It isn't worth it."

"Didn't you understand what I just said?" Fu Shen said categorically, "Having you is enough. What would I want with an empty reputation?!"

CHAPTER FORTY-SIX

"CAN..." YAN XIAOHAN ACTUALLY TRIPPED OVER HIS WORDS, stuttering, "Can you... say that again?"

Fu Shen looked at him in great exasperation. Finally, after a long time, he sighed and reached his arms out to him. "Come here."

As if he didn't dare to use strength, Yan Xiaohan hugged him loosely. "Say it again."

Some words could be blurted out perfectly naturally, but if they were said again, they would change in flavor. Fu Shen was for once a little embarrassed. He blushed. "Go on, don't fool around."

Yan Xiaohan hugged him a little tighter. "Say it again."

"Have you been possessed by a myna bird spirit?" Fu Shen twisted cleverly, slipping out of his hands. "Stand aside, we're in a hurry to go see our niece, don't make trouble."

Lord Yan's arms were left empty. Disappointment showed clearly in his manner. Fu Shen carried on straightening his lapels and cuffs, then suddenly said, "Don't reproach yourself. I must have spent three lifetimes accumulating merit to have received the blessing of meeting you."

No sooner had he spoken than he was pushed down by Yan

Xiaohan onto the soft bedding. His strained back let out a sound suggesting it wasn't up to bearing heavy burdens.

Yan Xiaohan looked down on him from on high, a crafty smile flowing through his eyes, like radiant stars sprinkled over a pitch-black sky. Fu Shen suddenly thought that perhaps Yan Xiaohan really was a fox from deep in the mountains who had cultivated a human form, every bit of his countenance exquisite and beautiful, yet there was nothing feminine about it. The corners of his mouth were seductive, and so were the slightly curved corners of his eyes. Even his slightly curled eyelashes made an arc that looked ready to be kissed.

Like a sigh, he said, "So long as you feel as I do."

Fu Shen, held down like prey caught by a wild beast, unexpectedly didn't feel awkward. Perhaps because he knew in his heart that this person wouldn't hurt him no matter what, he even felt at leisure to raise his hand to pinch his cheek. Even his fingertips were gentle. "I really don't understand it. Look at you, wealthy and handsome, in a high position with great power, boundless future prospects—how could you still think no one would like you?"

"Surrounded by gems, it's easy to know your own vulgarity." Yan Xiaohan squeezed his hand and affectionately nuzzled his cheek. "It's because you're too good."

Not only in external things like family background and position—what made it really hard to compare to Fu Shen were his mind and character. Yan Xiaohan had been contemptuous, doubtful, but having weathered the elements, he knew that he could never do what Fu Shen did. An upright gentleman was like the splendor of the moon. You might not be able to meet one in a whole lifetime. He had only watched from afar, never daring to entertain the extravagant hope that the moon in the highest heavens would one day land in his embrace.

Fu Shen laughed in spite of himself. "Just which one of us has bewitched the other? ... All right, get up, we still have to go to Prince Qi Manor to congratulate them. I'll remember this and settle the accounts with you when we get back."

Yan Xiaohan said, "There are still accounts to settle?"

"What did you think?" Fu Shen smiled slyly. "If I don't give you a severe seeing to, I don't think you'll remember who has the final word in this house."

Yan Xiaohan didn't respond.

Prince Qi Manor.

Prince Qi Sun Yunduan, hearing that the uncle had come, quickly went to the front hall himself to welcome their guest, not expecting that he would first come face to face with Yan Xiaohan. He froze on the spot. "Lord Yan, Marquis Fu."

"Congratulations, Your Highness," Fu Shen said, cupping his hands, "on the happy occasion of the birth of your daughter."

Prince Qi automatically returned the salute and recovered from the head-on attack. Putting a smile on his face, he said, "Thank you. Please come in and sit down, both of you."

Fu Shen had in fact had little contact with Prince Qi. In his position, it wasn't a good thing to get too close to anyone, so even though Prince Qi was his relation by marriage, they still didn't visit each other regularly. The two of them were unusually distant when they met.

At this time, his foresight became obvious. After all his time in the palace, Yan Xiaohan had long ago developed the ability to speak to everyone in their own language. Seeing that Fu Shen didn't speak, he understandingly took over the subject of conversation.

Prince Qi was quite respectful toward Fu Shen; when it came to Yan Xiaohan, only dread remained to him. The Feilong Guard were His Majesty's personal guards, and Yan Xiaohan was naturally His Majesty's man. Though he didn't know why he had taken the unprecedented action of coming to visit with Fu

Shen, it obviously wasn't for the sake of delivering congratulations. Prince Qi had already been worried about Emperor Yuantai arranging for the two of them to go to Jingchu together; now he let his imagination roam even further, involuntarily slipping into official jargon as he spoke.

One was focused outward and one was focused inward, the apportionment of work evident as they tacitly cooperated, and Fu Shen didn't care now for the dignity and self-respect of a "husband." Carefree and unhurried, he looked at the wrinkly little baby, then asked about Fu Ling's condition. He looked back and—wow—in the cool spring breezes of the third month, His Highness Prince Qi had started to sweat.

He glanced at Yan Xiaohan with a smile, indicating for him not to go overboard.

Yan Xiaohan understood his signal perfectly. In a few words, he turned the subject to household chatter. Fu Shen didn't lose time interjecting: "We're all family, so we won't stand on formalities. In the trip to Jingchu next month, I'll rely on Your Highness to put up with and look after this fellow for me."

Prince Qi couldn't work out right away what kind of "looking after" he was talking about. He was stuck. Then he forced a smile and said, "You overstate matters, Marquis Fu. In these distant travels, it ought to be me relying on Lord Yan."

"This fellow"... Without a vast difference in position, what man would be willing to acknowledge himself in the position of a "first wife?" While Great Zhou permitted marriage between men, the country still belonged to the "husbands." Prince Qi guessed that when he had arranged this marriage, Emperor Yuantai had intended to have Fu Shen in the role of the "wife." In saying such a thing in front of him now, did Fu Shen mean it to be an insult to Yan Xiaohan's dignity, or a slap in the face to Emperor Yuantai?

When his doubtful reaction appeared before the two of them, Fu Shen felt rather regretful, while Yan Xiaohan could hardly resist feeling delight at his suffering. He gave a dry laugh and said, "Your Highness and the princess have both had it hard, and we've taken up a lot of your time. We'll be taking our leave now."

Prince Qi wanted them to fuck off as soon as possible. He delivered a few hypocritical civilities and finally got the two great divinities out the door. When he returned inside, taking no care for his deportment, he plopped down and gave a weary sigh.

Just then, Fu Ling woke up and said in concern, "What's wrong, Your Highness?"

"Your big brother, is he…" Prince Qi hesitated, then haltingly asked, "… really a cut-sleeve?"

Fu Ling immediately said, "Of course not! If he'd really been of the Longyang proclivity, that would have saved trouble. What need would there have been for him to wait for His Majesty to arrange him a marriage and let that court lackey bully him?!"

Seeing that she was truly angry, Prince Qi quickly restrained her and soothed, "Don't be angry, don't be angry, I was only asking. It's just that they came together to visit today, and Marquis Fu said something suggestive, so my thoughts went astray."

Fu Ling thumped on the bed hatefully. "It must be that horrid Yan forcing him!"

Yan Manor.

Fu Shen changed clothes and let down his hair. He asked casually, "What do you think of Prince Qi as a person?"

Yan Xiaohan coiled a strand of hair around his finger, thought about it briefly, then said, "Sticks to established practices, overcautious in small matters."

"Yes," Fu Shen said, "and he has his father's excessive suspicion. Come to think of it, that niece of mine doesn't look like her mother, but she looks quite a lot like Prince Qi, the chin and the eyes are identical… Huh?"

He suddenly stopped talking and reached out to pinch Yan

14

Xiaohan's chin and examine it from all angles. "I've just realized that your chin is also a lot like theirs."

Yan Xiaohan responded with nonsense: "Don't they say that marriages are predestined? We were meant to be family."

Fu Shen laughed. "So now we're 'family' again? Who was it pitching a fit just now, unwilling to go out and see people dead or alive?"

Yan Xiaohan, trying to get out of it, kissed him on the lips. "A great man can afford to be broad-minded, Lord Marquis. Don't squabble with me, hm?"

"Hey, how pathetic." General Fu was hardhearted, remaining unmoved. "Let's have none of that. I'll make sure to give you something to remember today."

He casually grabbed a book off the small bedside stand and tossed it to Yan Xiaohan. This was a thin volume with an indigo cover whose label said the name of the book: *Essays from the Xuemei Temple*.

Yan Xiaohan was bewildered. He casually flipped open to a page and took a cursory glance through it, then was instantly awed by the words "the nation belongs to all, tyrants are traitors to the people" written in the essay.

"I'm not mistaken?" He flipped back to the cover and looked at the name of the author. "There's a banned book hidden in the home of the Feilong Guard's Imperial Investigator? Lord Marquis, where did you get this?"

"That's none of your business," Fu Shen said. "I'll just ask you, last winter after I returned to Beiyan, the Feilong Guard conducted a case at the Kuangshan Academy, yes or no?"

Yan Xiaohan thought back to it. "Here I was thinking this wise gentleman seemed familiar. It turns out it was him."

"This former wise gentleman was the respected teacher who instructed Gu Shanlü, Imperial Censor Gu. I owe Imperial Censor Gu a favor for the Eastern Tartar diplomatic mission case. While his teacher has violated a prohibition, his crime doesn't merit death. Having spent this long in prison, he's suffered enough," Fu Shen said. "So I wanted to ask you to inter-cede. Can you be magnanimous and release this old gentleman?"

Yan Xiaohan's eyes slowly turned cold.

"Jingyuan." He cast down his eyes to look at the writing on the page. "Have you really forgotten, or are you deliberately reminding me?"

Fu Shen said, "What did you say?"

"The Jin Yunfeng case." Yan Xiaohan raised his eyes. His gaze unexpectedly seemed to have been dipped in snow and ice. "What, after seven years, you still want to test me with a case just like that? Aren't you afraid I'll revert to my old ways and stab you in the back again?"

Ordinarily, had anyone dared to speak to him like this, Fu Shen would have boxed their ears for them by now. But today he was extraordinarily calm and collected. He didn't get angry, only evenly said, "You're overthinking it. I wasn't trying to test you, I only wanted to ask for something. Can't I?"

Yan Xiaohan said irritably, "No, you can't ask for something on behalf of another man."

Fu Shen nearly lost his temper. Forcing himself to hold back, he said, "It's give and take. I'll compensate you."

"How will you compensate me?" said Yan Xiaohan.

"I've given you two morning calm flower jade pendants," Fu Shen said. "If you help me with this, those two jade pendants will act as vouchers, each one representing a favor. If you command, I will be sure to comply. What do you say to that?"

As if a bolt of lightning had struck his head out of the blue, Yan Xiaohan went rigid.

His consciousness seemed to float out of his body. He vacantly listened to himself numbly ask, "Apart from the one you sent me last year, the other one... Which do you mean?"

Fu Shen quoted his words back to him. "The Jin Yunfeng case. What, after seven years, don't you remember?"

He knew everything.

The slack gaze gradually focused. Fu Shen's image came

clear in his eyes bit by bit, then was carved in perfect lifelike detail at the bottom of his heart, like the descent of a hurricane, sweeping away all past wounds with unmatched force. The regret and dejection shut away from the sun were at last lit up by bright light, then instantly dispersed like clouds breaking up before a strong wind.

To be struck dumb several times in one day was an unprecedented experience for Yan Xiaohan. In this instant, he suddenly understood the reason behind all of Fu Shen's words and actions since this morning.

Fu Shen had given himself to him, and he was also offering up his whole heart with both hands.

There was no question of who was first and who was last, or who didn't deserve whom. This was a predestined opportunity, ordained by fate; they were a match made in heaven.

Yan Xiaohan's breathing suddenly became rapid. When he opened his mouth, his voice was as hoarse as though there were grit in his throat. There was even a fine tremor in his voice. "Then it's settled?"

"Yes." Smiling, Fu Shen repeated, "If you command, I will be sure to comply."

CHAPTER FORTY-SEVEN

A TRAVELER'S PAVILION IN THE CAPITAL'S OUTSKIRTS.

The mountain flowers were in full bloom and the willows were rustling, but sadly those leaving from the pavilion and those seeing them off were few. Among them was an old man whose hair and beard were all white and who had a weary look. This was Ceng Guang, who had been recently released from the imperial prison.

With the support of his student Gu Shanlü, he faced the man sitting in the wheelchair and, tottering, bowed deeply.

Fu Shen quickly reached out to indicate for him to get up. "There's no need for this, Mr. Ceng."

Ceng Guang said, "Had you not stepped in to uphold justice, my poor old bones would have rotted in the imperial prison. One must extend gratitude for a life saved."

"Certainly not," Fu Shen said, smiling. "Heaven helps the worthy like you, and you have a good student in Officer Gu. I only said a few words. The one who really did the work was the one at home. I truly do not dare to take the credit."

Fu Shen had heard of the Kuangshan Academy case, and he had known a few things about Ceng Guang himself. As a child he had become famous in his village for being a prodigy.

After passing the imperial examinations, he had been assigned to be the local magistrate in a certain prefecture, but he had been suppressed by his superiors and had never been transferred or promoted. Ceng Guang had a temperament as potent as flame. He had resigned from office and left, returning to his hometown, no longer setting foot in government halls. He had concentrated on scholarship for many years, his essays becoming famous throughout the country, but his words had been violent, pointing out the social ills of the day, often classified as a departure from the classics and a rebellion against orthodoxy. Last winter, because the view that "the nation belongs to all" put forth in *Essays from Xuemei Temple* had been reported by designing people, disturbing the court, Ceng Guang had been thrown in prison on the charges of "disrespect to the court" and "spreading fallacies to deceive the people."

Kuangshan Academy had always been prone to inciting disturbances while rarely doing anything in fact. After Ceng Guang had gone to prison, the academy's hundreds of students had scattered like birds and beasts, and his relatives and old acquaintances had avoided him like poison. Gu Shanlü alone had gone to intercede on his behalf, but his position was too lowly for his words to carry much weight, and his actions had produced few results.

But perhaps because Ceng Guang's life wasn't meant to end now, or perhaps because there was some obscure divine will, his article had suited Fu Shen's tastes, and Fu Shen had had some impression of him. Besides that, the Kuangshan Academy case had just happened to take place on New Year's Eve last year, so it had been put off until this year. When the year had turned, it had been quickly followed by the Vast Longevity Festival. Only when Fu Shen had struck up a conversation with Gu Shanlü had he learned that Ceng Guang was his teacher. Fu Shen had already known the truth of the Jin Yunfeng case then, and he had been looking for a reason to explain it fully to Yan Xiaohan;

by coincidence, he had just happened upon the Kuangshan Academy case.

It wouldn't be an exaggeration to say that Fu Shen and Yan Xiaohan were vital to his fate. Had these two gentlemen not insisted on playing a romantic game, old Mr. Ceng would have been squatting in prison indefinitely.

After Yan Xiaohan had agreed to Fu Shen's request, he had originally planned to fake Ceng Guang's death to let him escape, as well, but then on the fourth day of the fourth month, a sudden snow had fallen in the capital; the whole city had been silvered and dressed in white, disturbing even Emperor Yuantai deep in the palace.

Since fainting during the Vast Longevity Festival, Emperor Yuantai had been in ill health; court assemblies had been changed to once every three days, with Yinghua Hall assisting in affairs of state. The Court of Imperial Physicians had tried all kinds of treatments, but there had been no improvement. It was only when this heavy snow fell that everyone had a sudden realization: perhaps His Majesty had acted in defiance of the natural order, bringing down a warning from heaven upon himself, commanding him to examine his conscience?

It wasn't only the ministers who thought this; even Emperor Yuantai himself believed it. Sick as he was, he went in person to the Imperial Ancestral Temple to worship. Yan Xiaohan had struck while the iron was hot, finding an opportunity during an audience with the emperor to mention the Kuangshan Academy case. As expected, his words had moved Emperor Yuantai's heart. The next day he had issued a merciful decree, granting a general pardon.

Now Yan Xiaohan had already gone south with Prince Qi, and Fu Shen had deliberately come to accompany Ceng Guang, not just to give him a sendoff, but also so he could brag about Yan Xiaohan's contribution in front of these literary folks.

The words "the one at home" hit Imperial Censor Gu so

hard that he saw stars. He pursed his lips as if he had a toothache.

"No matter what, it is because the Lord Marquis and Lord Yan devised a means of rescue that my teacher was able to escape death." He also saluted Fu Shen. "You are two virtuous and righteous people and have my undying gratitude. I must do something to repay this debt of gratitude."

Fu Shen joked, "When my humble wife heard before leaving that I was going to give Mr. Ceng a sendoff, he particularly asked me to pass along a message: there is no need to repay the debt. He only hopes that in the future the two of you can be merciful in your words, not criticize 'the court's dog' so often. That will be tough to satisfy him."

The empire's scholars had always denounced the Feilong Guard by word and brush, abhorring them, especially old gentlemen like Ceng Guang. He had thought that Fu Shen had seen an injustice and engaged in a lengthy battle of wits and courage with the Feilong Guard in order to rescue him and let him see the light of day. He'd never expected that the Marquis of Jingning's every other sentence would be about that court lackey, even giving him all the principal credit—had the world changed altogether while he had been in prison? If a person was devoted to goodness and not killing innocents, could he still be called a Feilong Guard?

Imperial Censor Gu saw more clearly than he did. Seeing that his teacher was still shocked and perplexed, he gave Fu Shen a helpless smile and said, "Then please pass along mine and my teacher's thanks to Lord Yan for lending a hand, Lord Marquis."

Seeing that he was very willing to go along with it, Fu Shen nodded in satisfaction. "Of course."

It was getting late. Gu Shanlü helped Ceng Guang into a carriage and bade farewell to his teacher. After watching him recede into the distance, he said goodbye to Fu Shen and returned to the city on horseback, while Fu Shen got into a carriage and headed in another direction, toward the villa on Mount Changle.

It was a perfect spring day, with the warm, damp scent of grass in the wind. It was a perfect time for a springtime outing. Sadly, while the flowers were before his eyes, the one who would scruple to pick the flowers wasn't.

Now Yan Xiaohan had gone to Jingchu, there was no point in Fu Shen staying in the manor in the capital alone, so he had simply moved to the villa to convalesce again. Yu Qiaoting and Xiao Xun had long since returned with their people to Beiyan, and now only a small number of servants to do the rough work remained in the manor. He was only too glad to be idle. He floated lazily through the days. But that night, a tightly covered carriage suddenly stopped at the manor's gate.

The carriage's curtain was lifted aside, revealing a big box. In the firelight, the cold light of black iron seemed to flash at the corners of the box.

Outside of Jingzhou, in the wilderness.

This place was about a two-day trip from Jingzhou. Prince Qi's party had left the Heshan post station in the early morning, originally intending to reach the next post station that evening, but a strong rain began and the river rose dramatically, flooding the road they were to have taken. They were forced to change their route, but the rain became stronger and stronger, almost to the point that it was impossible to advance.

The rain was misty, and the sound of it filled the space between heaven and earth. They nearly lost their way. At last, they fortunately found a dilapidated temple in the wilderness that could still shield them from the elements. Yan Xiaohan oversaw the bedraggled Prince Qi's dash into the temple's main hall. He saw that the divine statue was destroyed and dust and spiderwebs were everywhere, but the building was still holding on; he breathed a sigh of relief.

The attendants braved the rain and found half of a broken gate in the rear courtyard to serve as kindling. They started a fire.

With a fire and hot water, the panic of rushing through the rain gradually faded. Yan Xiaohan methodically ordered people to gather up their bundles and dry provisions and prepare to spend the night, and arranged the night watches. His figure standing against the light at the door was inexplicably comforting. While Prince Qi was a pampered child of royalty, he was still pretty good at roughing it. After changing out of his wet clothes, he was still in the mood to hold a container of hot water while walking deeper in to examine the dust-covered divine statue.

Seeing this, Yan Xiaohan walked over and said, "Your Highness?"

"Lord Yan," said Prince Qi, "do you know what god is worshipped in this temple?"

Yan Xiaohan narrowed his eyes slightly and took a close look. He could only distinguish that the clay statue had a tall wooden hair coil and long eyes and brows. It seemed to be a female immortal. He humbly said, "Please enlighten me, Your Highness."

"The better half of the plaque at the door is damaged, but you can still make out what it says," Prince Qi said, pointing it out to him. "It's a Fan Immortal."

Yan Xiaohan had grown up in a Buddhist sect, but he had never heard of a "Fan Immortal" whose name used a character for "Buddhism." Involuntarily doubtful, he said, "What kind of divinity is that?"

Prince Qi said, smiling, "'Fan Immortal' is another name for a fox immortal. In fact, this temple is consecrated to a fox immortal."

Aren't they afraid of worshipping woodland spirits and monsters instead of worshipping Buddhas and Bodhisattvas? Yan Xiaohan thought, but what he said was, "I suppose a fox immortal must have worked a miracle here, causing the people to build a temple to worship it."

Prince Qi said, "The records of the ancient say, 'No village will rise without a fox spirit.' It's normal for common people to worship fox immortals. Since there is a fox immortal temple here, I suppose it won't be too far from a village."

Yan Xiaohan nodded, then said to him, "Your Highness is of true imperial stock. Monsters and ghouls will automatically avoid you. You need only rest, worry not."

Because of the strange phenomenon of the heavy rain earlier that day, Prince Qi was ready to trust in these tales of gods and spirits, though from Yan Xiaohan's manner, while he had these soothing words ready to hand as soon as he opened his mouth, he actually didn't believe it himself.

But it was precisely that courage that made him think that this dilapidated temple wasn't all that unendurable. Compared to a crafty sycophant who could at a stretch be counted as his brother-in-law, ghosts and spirits were still a little scarier.

Because it was pouring rain outside, shortly before evening, it was already so dark they could hardly see anything. They had brought sufficient dry provisions and drinking water and weren't afraid of staying the night. What Yan Xiaohan was most worried about was a sizable lake not far from the temple. While the fox immortal temple stood on high ground, he was still afraid that the torrential rain would cause the water level to rise and flood in the middle of the night.

While he was lost in thought, there was a splashing sound in the distance, as if something was wading wildly through the water. The sound came closer and closer. Yan Xiaohan focused and listened closely. As expected, shortly after, a figure wearing a bamboo hat appeared in the rain, charging toward the dilapidated temple they were in.

In an instant, that person was right in front of him. The bamboo hat covered his face. He wore a black robe without design or ornament and had a long cloth pack on his back that seemed to contain a sword. He sat astride a horse that was all skin and bones. Dripping wet, he loudly called to Yan Xiaohan, "Friend, the rain has made the road slippery and hard to travel. Allow me to temporarily take shelter here with you. Thank you, thank you!"

With a clank, Yan Xiaohan's sword came out of its sheath and blocked the horse's way, glinting with cold light. The man was startled into quickly reining in his horse and nearly fell off. Yan Xiaohan's slightly cold voice spoke through the rain, a little indistinct. "Sorry, I can't allow that."

The man froze, then shortly afterward cried out in disbelief, "What did you say?"

"I said, go find somewhere else," Yan Xiaohan said immovably. "There's no place for you to rest here."

Prince Qi was inside. Who knew where this person came from? Even if he got soaked to death innocently in the rain, he still couldn't let him in.

The man tried reasoning with him. "Big brother, we're both wanderers brought down to miserable straits. In this wilderness, where do you want me to find another place to get out of the rain? Make an exception. I'm not going to do anything. I'll leave as soon as the rain stops. Or I can pay you…"

He motioned reaching for his wallet. Yan Xiaohan still said unfeelingly, "No."

"Why are you still not convinced?" The man didn't even get out his money. He said irritably, "Did your family build this temple? Or did the great immortal inside the temple hire you to be a watchdog? How much are your monthly wages, I'll double them!"

Yan Xiaohan was silent.

Without knowing it, he'd hit him in a sore spot.

Yan Xiaohan's eyes turned slightly cold. His fingers gripped the hilt of his sword, and his wrist lowered. The rain formed a silver thread like flowing light at the tip of the sword—

CHAPTER FORTY-EIGHT

RAIN POURED DOWN THE BRIM OF THE BAMBOO HAT AS IF VEILING the man's face. He glimpsed Yan Xiaohan's slight motion, and his eyebrows rose. He reached behind him to feel for the long cloth pack on his back.

Just then, a shout like the call of nature came from the hall, interrupting the animosity between the two of them.

"Yan—" At the crucial moment, Prince Qi called out, "No need to block his way, let him in."

Before Yan Xiaohan could answer, the man drew back his hand as quickly as when he had been feeling for his wallet and clamored, "You hear that? You hear that? The great immortal has spoken. Do not get in my way, let me in!"

When this person spoke, it was like ten myna birds all clamoring into your ears in unison as he made a racket in his hoarse voice. Yan Xiaohan was awfully annoyed and very unwillingly put his sword away. When the man jumped off his horse, his sensitive ears suddenly caught a crisp sound, like metal knocking together. It was a bang with a distant echo that lingered uninterrupted for a long time.

He immediately looked up and fixed his eyes on the man, who candidly came toward him, meeting his gaze, the mouth beneath his bamboo hat curved into a slightly flippant smile. When the two of them brushed shoulders, Yan Xiaohan suddenly reached back; grabbing and yanking, he swiftly snatched away the cloth bundle on his back.

The man's reaction was also very quick. Almost at the same time as Yan Xiaohan acted, he grasped the other end of the bundle. As he moved, his bamboo hat slipped back, revealing the plain, unremarkable face beneath it. Grouchily, he asked, "What are you doing?"

"Surrender your sword," Yan Xiaohan said expressionlessly.

The man's expression was bewildered. "Surrender my sword? What sword?"

Yan Xiaohan's gaze moved downward onto the cloth bundle both of them held. When the man saw this, he immediately laughed easily. "You mean this? This isn't a sword."

"Open it."

The young man shook his head. There was a deliberately assumed elderly exasperation in his manner. Putting on an act, he said, "Well, if you really want to see… then all right."

Yan Xiaohan skeptically watched as he undid the cloth bundle in a few rapid movements, unwinding round after round of cloth strips, revealing a blackened, almost yard-long—

Club.

Yan Xiaohan had no words.

Very innocently, the man said, "I told you it wasn't a sword. You insisted on looking."

The attendants in the room who had witnessed this scene all covered their mouths and lowered their heads, struggling to hold back laughter. Yan Xiaohan at least managed to keep his cool. Flatly, he said, "Give it here. You can't bring it in."

You had to bow your head beneath a roof. The man didn't insist. He eased his grip. Before going in, he only quietly muttered, "Petty. Won't even let a club get past him."

Yan Xiaohan, repeatedly exercising patience, at last condescended to let him in. At the same time, he felt a faint sense of strangeness. That man seemed very young, but there was an old drifter's unconstraint about him and an indiscernible slickness in his direct gaze. Yan Xiaohan's repeated attempts to sound him out were deflected without leaving a trace. He seemed to have determined in advance that he would succeed in entering this dilapidated temple, so even when Yan Xiaohan had drawn a sword on him and barred his way, he hadn't been really angered. Instead, from beginning to end, he had taken every opportunity to mock him.

This manner of speaking, keeping within the bounds but drawing blood with every prick, was really very familiar.

He shook his head, thinking that perhaps he really had lost his mind. It was probably because he had ushered in a prolonged separation right after getting a taste of sweetness that he couldn't resist thinking of Fu Shen no matter what he saw.

Compared to the evident detestation on Lord Yan's face, Prince Qi and the attendants were all very friendly and welcoming toward the young man they had met by chance. While Yan Xiaohan had briefly been lost in thought and taken his eyes off him for a moment, the man had already sat down by the fire. While stretching out his limbs and warming himself by the fire, he talked in an endless assured stream. The inexperienced Prince Qi was listening with great interest.

"… My surname is Ren, my given name the single character Miao, the one consisting of three 'water' characters. My fortune lacks water. I come from Yanzhou. I started traveling up and down when I was sixteen, doing chivalrous works everywhere… Parents? My late parents died early deaths. I grew up on public charity.

"I lived in the capital for a while, working as retainer and guard for a merchant." He smiled awkwardly. "Sometimes I also helped out the neighbors, and so… I took a liking to that family's young mistress."

Yan Xiaohan sneered inwardly, but Prince Qi was particularly fond of this kind of love story, which was more moving than a novel or an opera. He pursued with interest: "And then what?"

Ren Miao drank a mouthful of warm water and continued: "Their business in the capital failed, so they let their house, packed up, and returned to their hometown in Jingzhou."

Prince Qi sighed with feeling. "Too bad, too bad."

"It's not too bad," Ren Miao said with an easy smile. "Haven't I come to find her?"

Saying so, he turned his head to take a glance at Yan Xiaohan, a glance that bewildered Lord Yan. *You carry on chasing the one you love,* he thought, *what are you doing looking at me? Showing off that you have a beloved?*

Prince Qi asked, "What is that family's name? What is their business? Are you certain she's in Jingzhou? What if they've gone elsewhere?"

"Their surname is Meng. They're cloth merchants," said Ren Miao. "Leaving the capital to go to Jingzhou was arranged by her family elders. As an unmarried woman, there was nothing she could do. She could only send a maid to bring me a letter in secret."

Prince Qi said involuntarily, "You mean that… your feelings are mutual?!"

Ren Miao said, "Naturally. Otherwise, if it were only my own wishful thinking, what would I be doing coming all this way to chase after her? Though she hasn't said as much openly, she must be looking forward to seeing me. I can't let her down."

Once these words were spoken, the listeners all paused, especially those who were married; they were deeply touched. Yan Xiaohan had been rather prejudiced against him, disliking his nonsense and slippery tongue, but his heart was moved by this unexpected "can't let her down." The longing he was using all his power to control, like water breaching its banks, uncontrollably overflowed in his heart and his eyes.

After a long silence, Yan Xiaohan said, "Enough, don't stain the young lady's pure reputation here."

Ren Miao turned his head to give him another look and defiantly said, "Big brother, you look very imposing to me. I suppose you're already married?"

Yan Xiaohan gave a cold and restrained nod and asked, "You come from Yanzhou. Have you heard of the Beiyan Cavalry's commander, the Marquis of Jingning Fu Shen?"

"Of course I have, who hasn't heard of him?" Ren Miao said carelessly. "You aren't trying to tell me you're married to the Marquis of Jingning? Forgive me for being blunt, big brother, but you'll burst from blowing that much hot air, hahahaha…"

There was silence.

"Why are you all looking at me?" Ren Miao asked awkwardly.

Yan Xiaohan forced his emotions to calm and said, "I was saying, since you were in Beiyan, why didn't you enlist in the Beiyan Cavalry and win military honors for yourself, then grandly take this Miss Meng of yours to wife? If you go to Jingzhou now, even if you come to the door and make a proposal of marriage, they might not be willing to give you their daughter."

"Joining the army is no good." He shook his head and said, smiling, "I'm an unambitious man. I don't want to have a distinguished career. I only want to live out my life with my beloved in peace and quiet. I can earn food and clothing with my own abilities now, enough to keep a family. If I joined the army, I don't know whether I would come back alive. If I cast her out into the world all alone, I wouldn't be able to close my eyes in death."

This person had simply been sent by heaven to jab at Yan Xiaohan's weak spots, each jab hitting its mark. Yan Xiaohan was about to start throwing up blood from his jabbing. Not giving up, he asked, "How do you know this Miss Meng doesn't want a phoenix coronet and an embroidered cape, to receive a noble title after your death, and only wants to live in poverty with you?"

Ren Miao bent his leg. A somewhat bashful but sentimental

smile appeared in his eyes. As if to himself, he said, "She isn't that kind of person. Or else, when there are so many people in the world, why would she have fallen in love with me out of all of them…?"

This warmth that couldn't be concealed was nearly scalding to the eyes. Yan Xiaohan felt half frustrated, half bitter. What Ren Miao was speaking were the deepest regrets and unattainable desires in his heart. But he and Fu Shen were a noble and a minister in a high position. Even if they weren't attached to power and position, how could they cast everything aside without a thought, just up and leave?

The passing years were weighed down by "compulsion." Bobbing in the mundane dust, they might well be weighed down until they were past their prime.

Ren Miao shot a glance at the blank-faced Yan Xiaohan. The light in his eyes flashed, and he unhurriedly changed the subject. "Where do you all come from? Are you also going to visit family and friends?"

Yan Xiaohan didn't speak. Prince Qi braced himself and undertook answering, saying, "Yes, we come from the capital. We're going to visit family in Jingzhou."

He didn't elaborate, and Ren Miao tactfully didn't follow up. He only said, "What a coincidence. Maybe we'll meet again in Jingzhou City. I'll have to treat you all to a meal then."

At nightfall, the force of the rain slackened slightly. Ren Miao had dried his clothes beside the fire and, opting for shamelessness, asked them for a meal. After eating and drinking his fill, he picked up a pile of straw and built himself a makeshift bed in a corner and went comfortably to sleep. Yan Xiaohan had arranged the night watches. Passing by that corner, he kept his footsteps very soft, but Ren Miao, who ought to have been dreaming, twitched the tips of his ears. His eyelids rose as well.

Their gazes just happened to meet.

Instantly, an indescribable shudder entered the top of Yan Xiaohan's head. Countless fragments quickly flitted through his mind. He had a distinct sensation, but he couldn't catch the illumination that flashed past and then was gone.

Seeing that it was him, Ren Miao closed his eyes as though nothing were the matter.

Yan Xiaohan was full of doubts, and he was still concerned about the force of the rain outside, so he didn't sleep very soundly that night. In the small hours of the morning, the sounds of dull thunderclaps came from above. He woke with a start from his shallow sleep. As soon as he opened his eyes, he found that someone was already standing at the door.

All the hairs on the back of his neck were standing upright. His first reaction was to go for the sword next to him, but the person turned and walked toward him. "Awake? I was just going to wake you. Get up and take a look. I keep thinking there's something wrong with this thunder."

Only in this half-reclining posture did Yan Xiaohan discover that Ren Miao was actually very tall, and his legs were particularly long. When he wasn't being flippant, his face unexpectedly looked very steady and dependable.

They went out the door of the temple. The rain was already very light, but the dense clouds in the sky had yet to disperse. Instead, they were gathering thicker and thicker, with lightning flashing through them and thunder rumbling, and the lightning and thunder were right above their heads. Every time the lightning tore through the sky, even the dilapidated temple shook faintly in time to it.

"This place is on very high ground. While it won't be flooded, it'll be bad news if it gets struck by lightning," Ren Miao said. "Da-ge, why don't you wake them up, go somewhere else…"

Before he could finish, silver-white lightning accompanied by crushing thunder, like the galaxy itself, struck right at the roof of the fox immortal temple!

Ren Miao: "Just what I was saying!"

Yan Xiaohan swept into the temple like a tornado and pulled up Prince Qi. He said loudly, "Everyone get up, run!"

The next moment, something tightened over the back of his neck, and he and Prince Qi with him were yanked away by a powerful force, thrown clear of the incense table!

Almost at the same time, snow-bright lightning pierced the ceiling, shattering the hall's divine statue with a rumble. The ceiling beam snapped and came crashing down in the place where Yan Xiaohan had just been standing.

Everyone was dumbfounded.

CHAPTER FORTY-NINE

PRINCE QI SAT UP DIZZILY. "WH-WHAT'S GOING ON...?"

Yan Xiaohan, meanwhile, was looking suspiciously at the person behind them.

Ren Miao held his club in his left hand, frowning as he flexed his right hand. He seemed to have twisted his wrist with the sudden exertion of strength. Noticing Yan Xiaohan's gaze, he raised his head and smiled apologetically. "I'm sorry, I was anxious. I hope I didn't hurt you?"

That club of his had been next to Yan Xiaohan before. The two of them had just been standing at the door together, and Yan Xiaohan had gone to save Prince Qi, while Ren Miao had gone to get the club. The distances to the two places were about equal, but he had still been able to push away Yan Xiaohan and Prince Qi before the ceiling beam collapsed. Never mind his frightening strength, that speed coming and going alone wasn't something an ordinary person was capable of.

His movements and reactions were even faster than Yan Xiaohan's, but in that case, why, when he had come in, had Yan Xiaohan easily been able to get close to him and snatch his bundle?

Either his skills had suddenly erupted at the moment of

danger, or else… he had been deliberately playing weak to take them in.

The divine statue had been charred black by the lightning strike and broken to pieces. Ren Miao walked over and prodded it with the club. He said, "It isn't safe in the temple. Who knows whether…" He remembered his crow's mouth prediction from earlier and swallowed the rest of his words. "Forget it," he said, "let's just get out."

Yan Xiaohan silently helped Prince Qi out.

Strange to say, after they went, the thunder gradually quieted and the dense clouds parted. After that great bolt of lightning had come down, even the rain stopped bit by bit. Everyone raised their heads and looked into the sky, doubtful and confused and with an inexplicable reverence. There was even someone who knelt on the spot and silently recited Buddhist scripture.

Prince Qi hadn't panicked in the face of death. He fixed his clothes and hair and bowed deeply to Ren Miao. He said, "Thank you for coming to the rescue."

Ren Miao was leaning on his club with one hand. He used the other hand to cover his head with his bamboo hat and carelessly said, smiling, "There's nothing to it. If you hadn't taken me in to begin with, this wouldn't have happened afterward. When it comes to predestination and coincidence, who can rightly say?"

Yan Xiaohan said, "Are you leaving?"

Ren Miao picked up his horse's reins. "The rain has stopped, and the temple has been destroyed. If I don't go now, am I going to wait around for the next wave of bolts of lightning from the heavens?" He mounted nimbly and saluted everyone. Loudly, he said, "Everyone, we will meet again one day. See you in Jingzhou City!"

Having said this, he spurred his horse and headed off, leaving with a swagger without so much as a look back.

Prince Qi said, sighing, "What a miraculous encounter."

Yan Xiaohan narrowed his right eye imperceptibly. The doubts in his mind hadn't disappeared. He watched that tall, slender figure disappearing into the distance. He kept thinking that this wasn't over yet.

Early the next morning, they arrived exhausted at a nearby village to borrow shelter from the local commoners. This place was called Xishan Village, falling under the jurisdiction of Jingzhou's Kuangfeng County. Its ways were rustic. With guests arriving from outside, the village head and clan elders welcomed them enthusiastically, not only finding them a place to stay but also having their families bring all kinds of foodstuffs.

Prince Qi couldn't hold out and fell asleep. Yan Xiaohan took a nap. He was still concerned about last night's events, so after waking up, he went to ask the locals about the fox immortal temple outside the village.

There were elderly people who still remembered that temple. They said that a fox immortal had worked a miracle, warning the villagers in advance of a flood so they could avoid it but, having revealed the designs of heaven, the immortal had incurred a heavenly tribulation and been struck dead by lightning. The locals had built a temple to worship the fox immortal. But it seemed that the immortal had worked no more miracles after this, so the temple had gradually fallen into disuse.

That bolt of lightning last night had evidently been outside of human power, but it had precisely struck the divine statue; that was too much of a coincidence. Could it really have been some warning from heaven?

The legend said that the fox had incurred a heavenly tribulation by revealing the designs of heaven. Then what "heavenly design" had that bolt of lightning been foretelling?

He was just lost in thought when a knock suddenly came from the door. Someone in the courtyard said, "Is there anyone there? I'm just passing by. I wonder if I could stay the night here?"

There was a creak as the door opened wide. Beside the door, Lord Yan's expressionless cold face appeared.

"Hey!" Ren Miao lifted his bamboo hat and said in surprise, "It's you again! Well met, well met!"

There wasn't a single sign on Yan Xiaohan's face that he thought this meeting would go "well." He coolly said, "Well met."

"It's fate. Ineffable." Sighing with emotion, Ren Miao tied his horse up in the courtyard and familiarly walked inside. "I've been riding half the night. I'm dead beat. Big brother, do me a favor, lend me this room of yours and let me sleep."

Yan Xiaohan didn't budge and didn't yield. He said, "No."

"What?"

"I'm a married man," he said. "It's inappropriate for me to stay in a room with someone else. Why don't you go pick somewhere else to stay?"

"Wait, what?" said Ren Miao. "I'm a full-grown man. What am I going to do to you? Are you that afraid of your... wife?"

Yan Xiaohan said, "My wife is a man. Forgive me."

Ren Miao was silent.

"All right, all right." He waved a hand helplessly. "I'll go find somewhere else... Honestly..."

Unable to express himself, Ren Miao left. Yan Xiaohan walked out the door and went to where Prince Qi was staying. Seeing that he hadn't woken up yet, he told the subordinates and attendants to be on the alert and protect Prince Qi, while he himself took a turn throughout the whole village. He saw that Ren Miao had been put up in the woodshed of the house next door. Then he went around behind the village. Farmers were working in the paddy fields in the distance, children were frolicking, women were gathered by the water washing clothes and rinsing rice. It seemed as ordinary and quiet as could be.

Perhaps he was being paranoid, but that bolt of lightning that had nearly fallen on his head clung to his mind like his shadow. Yan Xiaohan wandered around aimlessly. By the time he realized that he had taken a wrong turn, he was already standing in front of the village's memorial hall.

The memorial hall was an important place. It would be violating taboo for an outsider to barge in. Yan Xiaohan had turned, about to go, when his overly sensitive ears caught a trace of unusual noise. There seemed to be people having a whispered conversation behind the building. A few words had just happened to leak out and be overheard by him.

"… With these outsiders here, tonight's sacrificial ceremony…"

The voice came closer and closer. Yan Xiaohan had a thought. He leapt as lightly as a swallow, just like a floating sheet of paper. He silently climbed up to the eaves and disappeared in the shadow beneath them.

The village head he had seen that morning walked out from behind the building with a lean young man. He was saying, "… Guang Ping and the others can't wait until the fifteenth, we'll do it tonight. Have the women add some drugs to the food to knock them out. Tomorrow we'll drag them out. All we need is for them not to get in the way. To my eyes, those people all seem to be dressed in top-grade silks. We'll be able to turn up quite a lot of nice things in their luggage…"

Yan Xiaohan understood that these people were planning to drug them and do some pilfering, but he didn't understand what was meant by the "sacrificial ceremony." This seemed to be a ritual that only people belonging to this village could participate in, but even if they were offering sacrifices to ghosts and gods, what was there about it that couldn't be revealed to others?

Then there was that bit about "can't wait until the fifteenth." What did that mean?

When the two of them had gone into the distance, Yan Xiaohan leapt down from the roof, landing as lightly as a cat. He stood up straight and was just planning to slip away without anyone being the wiser when he stopped in his tracks and abruptly turned his head, just happening to meet a pair of black eyes at the end of a corridor.

The memorial hall was dark to begin with, and that person

was hidden behind a corridor pillar, only a pair of pitch-black eyes like drops of ink showing. He didn't speak, either, only stared fixedly at him.

A chill instantly went up Yan Xiaohan's spine, and he broke out in cold sweat.

He steadied his steps and met his eyes as calmly as possible. The thought flashed through his mind to simply kill this witness to avoid a disturbance.

He had one hand behind his back. The knife hidden in his sleeve had already slid into his palm. Just then, the person suddenly leapt up from behind the pillar, gave him a last look, and turned to run off with a patter—this turned out to be a small child young enough to have loose hair.

With Yan Xiaohan's skills, if he only wanted to, killing that child on the spot wouldn't have posed any difficulty. It was just that when he ought to have struck, his practically nonexistent compassion suddenly acted up. Ultimately, he didn't toss the knife in his hand.

Everyone said that after getting married, a person steeped in iniquity would develop some scruples and become more restrained in conduct. Yan Xiaohan hadn't experienced it before, but now he vividly sensed that there was another force outside of the urge to kill stopping him. Involuntarily, he thought of Fu Shen. If he were in this situation, what choice would he make?

Children were innocent. What need was there for ruthless slaughter?

He always thought too highly of Fu Shen. This misapprehension made him soften his heart and stay his hand, and it brought about a series of unforeseen consequences for him.

Supposing that Fu Shen really had been present, he certainly would have first knocked the child unconscious, then woken him with a slap. Threats and bribes would both be fair game—on being discovered doing something bad, even if you didn't kill the witness, you still had to make certain they would keep their mouth shut. How could you just let them go?

Yan Xiaohan returned to the house where they were staying as though nothing were the matter. He woke Prince Qi and instructed him and the others not to touch any food or drink given to them by the village's people and to set out for Kuangfeng County after noon.

The group busied themselves for a while hitching their horses and stowing their luggage, getting everything cleaned up. Yan Xiaohan pretended to be in a hurry to get under way. He said goodbye to the village head and gave him some money. With money, you could command ghosts and demons. The village head had been a little suspicious to begin with, but seeing the money, he forgot everything and agreed at once.

Yan Xiaohan accompanied the party part of the way. When they had completely left the boundaries of Xishan Village, he told Prince Qi and the others to go on ahead, while he turned his horse's head around and silently returned to the forest outside of Xishan Village.

Only on leaving the village had he remembered that Ren Miao was staying in the house next door. In the dilapidated temple, even Yan Xiaohan's footsteps had woken him. It didn't make sense that he wouldn't have heard them making such a big fuss packing up, wouldn't even have shown his face.

Ren Miao had saved his life, after all. Yan Xiaohan felt indebted to him; he ought to help him out when it was necessary. He thought to himself that once he had worked out what this sacrificial ceremony was, he could bring him along on his way out.

Half a day later, dusk had fallen. Night was approaching. Scattered lanterns were lit in the village. Yan Xiaohan, hiding under cover of dusk, followed the road from that morning to slip into the village's memorial hall.

The village head and the clan's elderly people were all gathered outside the memorial hall. In the inner courtyard were three flat carts, decorated with fresh flowers and streamers of silk. On each cart lay a person in plain white clothes. It was dark, and

Yan Xiaohan couldn't see those people's faces clearly. He didn't know whether they were dead or alive. He only heard one clan elder in the courtyard say, "Everything has been prepared appropriately. We should be on our way."

Some young and middle-aged people came forward to push the carts. The whole party picked up white paper lanterns and slowly went out. This scene seemed to be a funeral for the dead. With dusk just on the point of ending but not yet ended, it seemed exceptionally somber and strange.

Yan Xiaohan wanted to follow them to investigate what was going on, but when he looked down, he saw that the child from before had once again popped out from somewhere. He was talking in the direction of the eaves where Yan Xiaohan had been hidden during the day. His mouth opened and closed, but he didn't make any sound.

It turned out that he was mute.

No one appeared. A confused expression appeared on the child's face. He repeated himself a few more times. This time, Yan Xiaohan finally saw the shapes his mouth was making. He was saying, "Are you there?"

Perhaps because the compassion he had felt that morning had yet to fully fade, Yan Xiaohan, looking at that child, felt that there was no malice in him, and moreover a child couldn't constitute a threat to a grown man like him. He pondered briefly, thought that he couldn't give up a lead that had come to his door like this, and stepped out from his hiding place. He took a knife in his hand and calmly asked, "Are you looking for me?"

The child turned his head abruptly, looking like a pale little ghost. Seeing him, he urgently made two gestures with his hands, indicating for him to follow. Yan Xiaohan didn't know what he wanted to tell him, so he let him lead the way. The two of them took turn after turn and came to a compound behind the memorial hall.

The child led him in front of a building and pointed to the door so he would enter.

41

Yan Xiaohan asked quietly, "Aren't you going in?"

The child shook his head forcefully and showed him the traces of bruises on his arms. He made a "hit" gesture.

Yan Xiaohan understood. This must be some important secret place for the village. Ordinary people couldn't enter without authorization, or else they would be beaten, like this child.

He nodded and said, "Thank you."

The child took a step back. Yan Xiaohan cocked an ear to listen, determined that there was no one in the building, then gently pushed open the wooden door and stepped inside.

CHAPTER FIFTY

IT WASN'T COMPLETELY DARK INSIDE. THERE WAS A BIT OF FAINT yellow light glowing all around. There was no one inside, and no frightening scene. Yan Xiaohan took a few steps inside. His nostrils flared as he suddenly smelled an unusual sweet scent whose source he didn't know.

He froze briefly. Then an indescribable joy surged up to the top of his head, so hard he was instantly dizzy, his footing becoming unsteady. Then that sweet scent suddenly became denser. Like hot oil ladled over a fire, making the flames explode, the heat rising. All the blood in his body began to boil. Visible blood vessels crept over his eyes. A raging fire seemed to be burning in the pit of his stomach. His lower body reared its head in an immediate reaction.

With a clang, the knife in his hand fell to the ground.

His body was like a damaged cage on the point of breaking, unable to contain the agitation and endless, inexhaustible lust. Yan Xiaohan bit the tip of his tongue and staggered toward the door, but the door that had just opened at a touch had now been tightly locked from outside. All his muscles convulsed constantly, his fingertips trembling too hard to obey his commands. His body was at the highest pitch of excitement, but he didn't even have the strength to break down the door.

A trap from start to finish. The "mute child" who had led the way had been a snare arranged for his benefit.

The sweet scent enveloped him like something living, twining, wandering over his limbs and his whole body. The darkness before his eyes became flash after flash of grotesque and marvelous dream. With the last thread of clarity set on fire by the flame of desire, Yan Xiaohan suddenly remembered during the major case of the murdered Jinwu Guard, while inspecting the white dew powder, how a whole courtyard of Feilong Guards had been affected. Shen Yice had said that that drug would give a person an experience "more blissful than bliss itself."

Why would there be white dew powder in a remote mountain village over a thousand li from the capital?!

But this bone-chilling thought didn't last long. Soon, he could no longer think about it. His thoughts were chaotic and jumbled, now flying up to the clouds, now seeming to have been dropped into fog. Yan Xiaohan at last slid slowly to the ground with his back against the wall, and closed his eyes, his chest undulating violently, the sound of his breathing becoming more and more urgent.

He gritted his teeth, holding back the moans that wanted to slip from his mouth. Savage veins rose on the backs of his hands. Big beads of sweat trickled from the hair at his temples to the corners of his eyes. But at the moment he was defeated by desire, he finally couldn't resist. Shuddering, he called out, "Jingyuan."

Meanwhile, at the other end of the village.

Ren Miao woke up and found that everyone had taken off. He was so hungry his legs were weak. His head spinning, he went to the kitchen and found a bun and nibbled on it, washing it down with cold water. When he was finished eating, he patted the crumbs off his hands and went to Yan Xiaohan's courtyard to get his horse. He was just about to follow their party to Kuangfeng County when, for some reason, his heart suddenly lurched.

It was hard to describe this feeling. It was like a premonition, and it also seemed to be an inexplicable tremor coming from a string obscurely tied to him.

He looked around suspiciously and, hesitating, walked a few steps further into the town. When he had just left the rear courtyard, he saw a child who didn't even come up to his hip come out from behind a building.

The two of them saw each other. Both froze. Before Ren Miao could move, the child turned in a panic and ran off.

It was all right before he ran, but once he did run, it immediately seemed like he had a guilty conscience. Ren Miao was in fact much faster than Yan Xiaohan. He casually picked up a small stone off the ground and tossed it easily with his fingertips. There was a whizz as it soared through the air, and the child was hit in the back of the knee, falling face-first into the dirt with a thump.

Ren Miao reached back and pulled out the club he wielded with such facility and picked the child up with it, then shook him in the air. Thinking he was being genial, he said, "Why are you running?"

The child shook like chaff being sifted. Ren Miao said, smiling brightly, "Go on. You acted like you'd seen a ghost when you saw me. What shameful things have you been up to?"

The child couldn't speak. Tears quickly welled up in his eyes. He looked rather pitiful. But this stone-hearted man wasn't moved in the least. Seeing that he didn't answer, he walked over to the nearby well carrying him and dangled him over the mouth of the well. "You won't talk? Then you can go down there and wait. There's no one in the village now, anyway, and by the time they get back, you'll most likely have dissolved…"

The child stared blankly at him, then looked down at the

pitch-black mouth of the well beneath his feet. He burst into tears.

"Will you be good now?" Ren Miao said in satisfaction. "Where have they all gone? Point the way."

The child wailed. Ren Miao's original intention had been to ask him where the villagers had gone, but he didn't hear him clearly and thought he had been found out by Yan Xiaohan's accomplice, so he led him all the way to that house, sobbing.

Ren Miao shook him off the club, then took a rough measurement of the lock on the door. Then, without another word, he brought the club down on it. A sharp wind was accompanied by an earth-shaking boom. The heavy brass club smashed the lock to pulp along with half the door.

The mute child was dumbfounded. He suspected this blackened club of being some peerless divine weapon that could break gold and jade.

When the door broke, the sweet smell inside escaped. Ren Miao raised his sleeve and held his breath. On the principle of *better you than me*, he grabbed the child and tossed him inside.

A half-grown child couldn't bear so much dense white dew powder. He was instantly knocked unconscious. Seeing this, Ren Miao was even more loath to act rashly. He stood upwind covering his nose. Only when most of the smell had dispersed did he cautiously walk in over the broken door.

As soon as he walked in, he saw the person curled up in extreme pain in the corner.

Moonlight like white silk flowed in through the broken doorway, lighting up the disorder covering the ground. Yan Xiaohan had been disturbed by the boom. Reacting sluggishly, he raised his head. His blood was about to boil away from how hard he was trying to endure. From the neck down, his skin was unusually warm and flushed. His eyes were unfocused, and cold sweat was constantly rolling from the hair at his temples, pouring over his cheeks and lining the bright red rims of his eyes, making his face look tearstained.

The newcomer had his back to the light, his face hidden in the night. The tall, slender figure unexpectedly accorded with his memories. He thought he was seeing an illusion. Dazed, he said, "Jingyuan..."

Ren Miao silently uttered several profanities and strode toward him.

But before his hand could touch Yan Xiaohan, the latter gave a sudden start, as if he had suddenly recognized his face, and also as if the night wind had awakened his reason. His slack gaze focused again. Somewhere he found the strength to wave away his hand.

"Stand back..." Panting, he hoarsely said, "Don't touch me..."

He had at some point gotten back the knife he had dropped on the ground. There was a bit of silver light between Yan Xiaohan's fingers. He raised the knife and stabbed at his own right arm.

In a flash, Ren Miao finally understood what the scene before his eyes meant. He immediately raised a hand and jabbed at the acupoint in Yan Xiaohan's wrist and wrestled the knife out of his hand. With his other hand, he aimed a slanting chop at the side of his neck. Yan Xiaohan's head fell sideways; he had lost consciousness instantly, falling limp into his arms.

That knife had nearly stabbed him in the heart. Ren Miao let out a breath of relief and wiped away the sweat on Yan Xiaohan's face. He bent down, ready to carry Yan Xiaohan away over his shoulder. Unexpectedly, as soon as their bodies touched, he felt something poke his shoulder.

"What the fuck..."

Awkwardly carrying him over his shoulder, he left the room and threw Yan Xiaohan onto his horse's back, then leapt up onto the horse after him, hugging him in front of himself. He spurred on the horse and went racing in the direction of Kuangfeng Town.

In Kuangfeng County, the Joyful Journeys Inn.

The old doctor Ren Miao had dragged out of his house finished taking Yan Xiaohan's pulse, pinched his beard, and said with an attitude of having seen it all, "It's not a serious illness, he's just taken too much of this drug. There's no need to be anxious, go to the pleasure district and find him someone to relieve it. Once the effects of the drug are played out, naturally he'll be better."

Ren Miao asked, "What drug has he taken?"

"Autumn night white." The old doctor shook his head. "I've seen many patients like this, they're just out for some pleasure… This drug forms an addiction as soon as it's taken. It'll be hard going in the future!"

And just what the fuck was autumn night white supposed to be? Was it the same thing as white dew powder? Why was it also addictive?!

There was no time to make detailed inquiries about all these questions. The critical matter lay in bed. Ren Miao didn't have time to listen to the doctor sigh about the decline of public morals. His head aching, he said, "Enough, I understand. So… we'll leave it at this for tonight. Tomorrow I'll bring him to you to be examined."

The old doctor took his fee and tottered out. Ren Miao looked at Yan Xiaohan, laid out on the bed with his brow tightly furrowed, in unbearable pain. He sighed wearily. He sat at the table and took a small bottle of lotion from an inner pocket and carefully applied it to his face while looking in the mirror. In the time it takes to drink a cup of tea, he slowly peeled a human skin mask from his face.

The bronze mirror reflected the cold and handsome countenance of the young general.

He put the mask in front of the mirror, got up, and walked over to the bed. He raised a hand and flicked the acupoint on

Yan Xiaohan's chest. The person he had knocked unconscious before coughed twice, then slowly woke up.

Fu Shen sat down on the edge of the bed and raised the hem of his clothes, revealing a pair of black boots that went up to mid-thigh. These boots were a product of the Beiyan Army's armaments department. At the tops of the boots, the knees, and the ankles there were specially made mechanical clasps. At the calves were six black iron braces, and the soles were pieced together from iron plates, all linked together with ingenious gears. Once you had put them on, there was no need for your feet and legs to take weight; from the knee down, walking would be entirely carried out by machinery instead.

This was a transportation tool that the armaments department had developed especially for him after he had been injured. Even a real cripple with absolutely no sensation below the knee could still walk as normal after putting on these boots, never mind a half-cripple like Fu Shen, who had mostly recovered. At the villa, he had received the boots delivered by people dispatched by Yu Qiaoting. He had thought that he didn't have anything else to do, so he might as well go tease Yan Xiaohan. He had gotten excited, so he had changed his appearance and adopted a false name and gone to chase him to Jingzhou.

He really ought to thank the skilled craftsmen of the Beiyan Cavalry and his own sudden flash of inspiration. It was fortunate that he had come chasing after him, or else after this mission was carried out, his household would have been broken up.

He undid several clasps and stepped out of the boots. He took a towel from the basin next to him and wrung it out, then plastered it to Yan Xiaohan's face. "That's enough. Why don't you wipe away those tears? It's a pitiful sight."

A scalding hot, trembling hand grabbed his wrist.

Yan Xiaohan suspected he had gone completely mad. He was staring at him fixedly in disbelief, not even daring to blink, as if afraid that he would vanish the next moment. He whispered, "Jingyuan…"

"Yes." Fu Shen finished wiping his face, then wiped his neck and hands. Gently, he said, "It's me."

"Am I dreaming...?"

Fu Shen tapped maliciously on a certain unspeakable spot, drawing a shudder from him, and said with a smirk, "A spring dream, I suppose?"

Fu Shen wasn't actually angry at Yan Xiaohan, only a little afraid after the fact when he remembered his decisive strength as he waved the knife at his own arm, with some inexpressible heartache mixed in. He had developed a hatred against all of Xishan Village. Supposing no one had rescued Yan Xiaohan, he would have spent a whole night in that awful place. After getting out, he probably would have been ruined. If he had struggled free and run away, relieving the effects of the drug would have been a big problem. Fortunately, it was Fu Shen who had come in time, and it was Fu Shen who was with him now. A wretched thing like this between husband and wife could with a stretch amount to a love game.

"How did you..."

Fu Shen lowered the bed curtains on both sides, turned, and got into bed. As he undid his belt, he said, "Are you still engaging in idle chat with me at a time like this?"

His fingertips inadvertently touched Yan Xiaohan's exposed skin. He seemed to have been burned. His whole body trembled. Then some invisible cage broke with a rumble. The beast uttered a long cry. There was a tightness around Fu Shen's waist as he was embraced and borne down onto the pillow. Wild, scalding kisses rained down on him like a flood.

"Jingyuan, I'm going to lose my mind..." With his reason in its death throes, Yan Xiaohan spoke into Fu Shen's ear, his heavy panting breaking his sentence into three parts. "So if I hurt you... make sure to push me away..."

Fu Shen turned his head and kissed his face and raised a hand to knead the sweat-soaked back of his neck. Quietly consoling, he said, "It's all right. Don't be scared, I'm here."

CHAPTER FIFTY-ONE

THE NEXT DAY NEAR NOON, YAN XIAOHAN MISSED A STEP IN HIS dreams and abruptly woke with a start.

He was lying flat in the bed at the inn. His vision was filled with a plain gauze canopy. The quilt was tightly tucked under his chin. He wasn't naked. He was still wearing his inner robe.

Yan Xiaohan, his gaze slack, stared up blankly for a long while, then finally remembered amid a fierce headache everything that had happened last night. First he had fallen into a trap, then he had been rescued and taken away. Midway he had been unconscious for a while. When he had woken up, Fu Shen had appeared at his bedside. There had followed a lengthy sequence of sensual abandonment and lovemaking. He had been on the brink of losing control. Many details were confused and unclear in his memory. The only thing he couldn't forget was the elation that made one tremble, running almost bone-deep.

Wait. Fu Shen?

He automatically reached out to feel the bed beside him. The other side of the bed was already cold, completely empty. Yan Xiaohan's heart instantly seemed to have been pinched. His face turned ghastly pale. He lifted the quilt and staggered out of bed. Not even putting on his shoes, he dashed out barefoot.

Where was he?!

Had he had a preposterous dream, or had it really happened? How could Fu Shen suddenly have appeared here? Also… the person who had entwined with him even unto death last night, who had that been?

He had been overstimulated by the drug. His brain was still numb, his memories and thoughts a mess. There were many obvious clues he hadn't even noticed. He was so panicked that he bristled. Caring for nothing, he pulled open the door and charged out into the corridor.

Fu Shen just happened to be coming up the stairs holding a paper bag. The two of them came face-to-face on the landing. He wasn't wearing a mask. That completely uncovered sharp and handsome face struck Yan Xiaohan's eyes without warning.

"You're awake?" He raised his eyelids and switched the paper bag to his left hand, and as calm as anything, asked, "Why have you run out without your shoes?"

The rims of Yan Xiaohan's eyes quickly reddened. He threw himself at him and hugged him fiercely.

"Hey, not so hard…" With his free hand, Fu Shen patted his slightly trembling back. "You're going to snap my back."

Having said this, he shut his mouth, feeling that there seemed to be something off about these words.

"It really is you…" Yan Xiaohan whispered. "I thought that… I've been a complete fool…"

The surname "Ren" was pronounced like "ren," person; three water characters made up "miao." "Ren Miao" were in fact the radicals of the two characters of Fu Shen's name. Then there were his deeply hidden skills, and even the so-called "Miss Meng." With so many obvious and easy clues laid out in front of him, Yan Xiaohan had still looked without seeing like a blind man.

If he hadn't ended up in a dangerous situation last night, forcing Fu Shen to reveal his identity, how long would it have taken him to recognize this spouse who kept him company day in and day out?

Fu Shen couldn't help laughing. "You haven't been very clever."

He stroked Yan Xiaohan's back again and again, as if he were holding a big child. When he was a little calmer, he took his icy hand and led him back into the room and pressed him down onto the bed. "The floor is cold. Get a hold of yourself, sit back down. I'm going down to get someone to prepare medicine and get a waiter to bring some hot water while I'm at it."

Seeing Yan Xiaohan's dazed, completely lost expression, Fu Shen felt uneasy. He drew close, bent his head, and kissed his cheek. "I'll be back right away," he emphasized.

Physical contact was more useful than words. A bit of life finally appeared in the dead ashes of Yan Xiaohan's eyes. The roots of his ears reddened slightly. He tenderly touched Fu Shen's cheek with the back of his hand. "All right, go on."

He seemed to finally wake from his disjointed nightmares. The numbness brought on by intense stimulation was gradually replaced by pain. The sequence of events came together into a line in his mind. His intellect, in shattered pieces all over the ground, was picked back up and stuck back together, then once again toppled with a crash from the attack of countless vivid and intimate fragments like raging waves.

Yan Xiaohan was stunned.

All the things he hadn't dared to do on their wedding night out of concern for Fu Shen's health, he had done last night.

It was an open question whether Fu Shen's knees could handle it.

There was a rumbling explosion in his mind like sudden thunder and lightning. He abruptly stood up, blatantly remembering something he had been taking for granted since waking up—Fu Shen could stand!

The door opened with a creak, and Fu Shen walked in.

Before he could open his mouth, he was caught by Yan Xiaohan. "Jingyuan, what's going on with your legs?"

"Oh, you've finally remembered?" Fu Shen lifted the hems of his robes and showed him the specially made black boots. "Beiyan's armaments department made them for me, with gears in place of joints. When you put them on, you can walk as normal even with injured legs."

His legs were straight and long to begin with, and the iron plates in the soles raised him another few inches. Standing, he was about the same height as Yan Xiaohan. The tight black boots and three sets of silvery black clasps made his waist look even narrower and his legs even longer. His bearing was upright. He was practically a living "temptation."

Yan Xiaohan coughed uncomfortably. As soon as his thoughts went astray, his headache became more intense. Holding back, he said, "Last night, no, the night before that, the rain was so heavy, did you spend all day traveling in the rain? On dark and rainy days at home, you're usually in too much pain to sleep, did…"

Fu Shen stopped his mouth. "I brought medicine, mixed by Du Leng. Taking it numbs the calves, leaving no sensation. Anyway, I don't need my calves to walk. It's really all right, I'm not lying."

"If there really is such a magical medicine, why didn't you take it before? Why wait this long?" Yan Xiaohan wouldn't be taken in. "Don't try pulling one over on me."

Fu Shen was at a loss for words, then said in surrender, "Fine, there's just one thing, actually. When I found you yesterday, I said I was especially sleepy, do you still remember? Taking this medicine makes me sleepy. By the time I woke up, Prince Qi and the others had all cleared out."

"My fault," Yan Xiaohan said wearily, rubbing his temples. "If I had recognized you earlier, I wouldn't have made you suffer so much for nothing."

Fu Shen was particularly unwilling to listen to this kind of talk. He was just about to erupt. But seeing Yan Xiaohan's haggard appearance, he held his nose and contained himself. "Don't worry about me, think of yourself first. I went to speak to the doctor this morning. There's no doubt that the drug you were given is white dew powder. It forms an addiction after a single use, and giving it up is very difficult. Send word to Prince Qi, give up on this assignment and return to the capital with me to get treatment, all right?"

"Why would there be white dew powder here?" Yan Xiaohan asked. "The white dew powder in the capital was brought by Daoist Chunyang. Could the source of white dew powder be here?"

Fu Shen said impatiently, "What do you care whether it's white dew powder or black dew powder? An addiction to this thing is a disaster, you know that better than I do. Wait until you're better, then you can pay attention to other people's lives and deaths!"

Yan Xiaohan shook his head. "Jingyuan, if you were in my position, you would also keep investigating."

"Bullshit!" Fu Shen's anger soared. "How is this happening to you any different from it happening to me? Will everyone in the empire die without you or what? How can you be so stubborn?!"

Only after scolding him did he remember that the doctor had said, because of overstimulation to the brain from taking white dew powder, when the effects of the drug had faded, the person who took it would experience forgetfulness, disordered thinking, confusion, depression, and other such symptoms. He couldn't rush him or scold him, only quietly stay with him and help him gradually break the addiction. It was work that would require a long, constant trickle of effort over time.

For Fu Shen, it was like making an old ox pull a rickety cart.

Yan Xiaohan didn't have the strength to quarrel with him. It wasn't that what Fu Shen was saying was unreasonable, it was just that he wasn't receptive to anything now. It was as if he had a watermelon sitting on his shoulders. Even thinking had become difficult and painful. Of course he knew that silence would only make the atmosphere between the two of them worse, but surging emotional weariness and physical exhaustion, as well as gloom that no one could answer for, were filling his chest. He really couldn't gather the strength to try redeeming anything again.

Fu Shen stood, frowning. Just as Yan Xiaohan thought he was going to slam the door and leave, the black boots stopped in front of the bed. "Forget it, you don't have to go back. I can't control you."

It was as if his heartstrings had been inadvertently plucked. Yan Xiaohan raised his eyes to look at him, his reaction sluggish. Astonishment was like a distant tide, whose faint tremors could already be felt even though it had yet to reach the shore.

Fu Shen idly pinched the tip of his ear. His doting intent was all in evidence. "If you don't return to the capital, then you'll have to be good and stay with me. Don't run around, take your medicine like you're supposed to, get your treatment like you're supposed to. Do you agree?"

Yan Xiaohan's expression was blank. He nodded automatically. So Fu Shen bent down and kissed the center of his brow. "It's all right, don't be scared. Do what I say. I'm here to take care of everything."

There was a strange, calming steadiness about him, perhaps an aura refined by years of commanding soldiers; it made Yan Xiaohan think that even if he was watching the world collapse, if Fu Shen were there, he would still be able to create a peaceful spot.

In fact, Fu Shen was also possessive, but it wasn't obvious. When Yan Xiaohan was lively and frisky, he seemed cool and indifferent. Only at times like this would it all erupt. The only thought in his mind was that, whether in the capital or in Jingzhou, this man had to stay where he could see him. As for Prince Qi and the assignment, they could go fuck themselves.

Just then came the waiter's knock on the door. "Sir, the hot water is here!"

After the hot water, a table's worth of food was also brought in. After Yan Xiaohan had bathed and came out wringing his half-dry hair with a towel, he saw a dish of dark brown broth on the table. It had a piercing medicinal smell. He couldn't resist asking curiously, "What is this?"

Fu Shen served him a bowl of it and candidly said, "The restorative broth I specifically ordered. Isn't your back sore?"

Hearing the word "restorative," a suspicious redness came over the roots of Yan Xiaohan's ears. He was wearing only an inner robe that revealed the skin of his chest and neck, so the redness was particularly obvious. The sight of him nearly dazzled Fu Shen. While casting half-inadvertent glances, he thought that his slightly embarrassed appearance was both pitiful and adorable.

He picked up the broth and tasted it. He thought that the flavor was just bearable. He picked up a robe from beside him and gave it to Yan Xiaohan to put on and called him over to sit down and eat.

Their roles seemed suddenly to have been reversed. Before, it had been Yan Xiaohan taking care of Fu Shen in matters big and small, and now it was Fu Shen showing so much meticulous consideration.

Especially since, coming from a man who was normally rough and ready, this kind of meticulous consideration seemed particularly rare and precious.

An indescribable feeling welled up in Yan Xiaohan's heart. It wasn't entirely sweet; there seemed to be some portion of unspeakable bitterness in it. It ought to have been him taking care of Fu Shen, but in the end he had instead made him run around in the rain, waited to be rescued by him, used him to relieve the effects of the drug, and he was making him exhaust his mental efforts on him.

Self-hatred grew as wildly as weeds. Suddenly, white steam

was curling up in front of him. He focused and saw that a bowl of broth had been placed in front of him.

He automatically reached out to take it and saw Fu Shen take up the bowl by his own hand, raise it, and clink it against his. With soaring valor, he said, "Cheers."

Yan Xiaohan was silent.

CHAPTER FIFTY-TWO

AFTER EATING LUNCH, FU SHEN SAW THAT YAN XIAOHAN'S energy was failing, so he coaxed him into taking an afternoon nap. Only after waking up did the two of them go out to see the old doctor who had examined him the day before.

Kuangfeng County wasn't to be compared to the county towns on the capital's outskirts. There were only a couple of well-known medical halls in the county town. Fu Shen's human skin mask had been applied by Du Leng. Once it had been removed, it couldn't be put back on. When he had gone to see him in the morning, the doctor hadn't recognized him at all and had even asked curiously, "Why didn't that young fellow from last night come? Did he entrust the patient to you?"

The plain and unremarkable face of "Ren Miao" was truly too different from his own face. Fu Shen had to brace himself and blurt out a lie: "Yes, he had something else to do. You can just tell me anything you need to."

They walked to the medical hall. While Fu Shen was wearing a bamboo hat, that did nothing about Yan Xiaohan next to him; they were still stared at wherever they went. The old doctor's gaze was even more merciless. Seeing the two of them walk in together, he hit on the truth at once: "I suppose you two are married?"

Even Yan Xiaohan was startled. Fu Shen asked, "How can you tell?"

On the surface, this was a question, but in reality it was an acknowledgment. The old doctor had Yan Xiaohan sit down. While feeling his pulse, he said, "Apart from medicine, I've also studied physiognomy in my time. The two of you have the look of a husband and wife. Your fortunes are good, your stars aligned. Your road to happiness has been strewn with difficulties, but in the future there will be blessings."

Hearing him say this, a bit of a smile appeared involuntarily in Yan Xiaohan's eyes. He said, "Thank you for the auspicious words."

The old doctor concentrated on feeling his pulse. Shortly, he put away the wrist cushion and said to Yan Xiaohan, "I said this morning to this young gentleman that taking autumn night white causes addiction. It cannot be cured with medicine. You must get rid of it yourself. You're still young, in your physical prime. Though the drug has worn away some of your vitality, you'll be all right after a period of recovery. Moreover, I hear that you took it by mistake and intend to stop taking it. As long as you can resist the allure and endure some pain, in about a year you can rid yourself of it."

Fu Shen, frowning, asked, "Is getting rid of the addiction very painful?"

Yan Xiaohan understood what he had left unsaid. Pressing his hand, he gently consoled him: "It doesn't matter. As long as I can rid myself of it, a little pain is nothing."

The old doctor shook his head. "Autumn night white is like taking out a loan with interest. If you borrow money and spend as much as you like, when it comes time to pay, it'll mean tearing out your tendons and peeling off your skin. I advise you to prepare yourself. When the craving flares up, it's not something the average person can endure. If it were really so easy to get rid of, how would the streets have ended up full of sickly wrecks who had brought their families to ruin?"

Bearing suffering wasn't a big deal for Yan Xiaohan. Since entering the palace, he had constantly been wading through mountains of swords and seas of fires; the staunchness of his temperament went without saying. It was only that Fu Shen couldn't stand to see him tormented, so he asked, "Is there some way to alleviate it?"

The old doctor looked him over and slowly said, "It isn't that there's absolutely no means of resolving it, only..."

"Only what?" said Fu Shen.

"Only you'll have to put some work into it," said the old doctor.

"What do you mean?" said Fu Shen.

"According to what I observed, after taking the drug last night, this young gentleman's sexual desire was aroused to an uncontrollable point," the old doctor said. "This is precisely where the effects of autumn night white lie. First, it raises a person's spirits, as if they have been dropped into a paradise. Second, it makes a person's vital energy and blood surge and their sexual desire flourish. So my thought is, since the two of you are lovers, when his drug craving acts up, you might perhaps try that means to alleviate it slightly."

Fu Shen was dumbfounded. "... Will that work?"

"The effect of autumn night white is nothing but making a person experience satisfaction and joy," he explained carefully to Fu Shen. "Worldly happiness can be roughly separated into three types. The first type is the happiness of food and drink. When one is hungry and eats one's fill, that is satisfaction. The second type is the happiness of the conjugal bed. When a couple is mutually attached and comes together in harmony, that is delight. The third type is the effect of drugs. When the drug captivates a person's mind, that is bliss.

"While the bliss of autumn night white far surpasses food and drink or sexual intercourse, perhaps they can be used to make up for it somewhat. For instance, if someone is addicted to sweets and you wish them to break the habit of eating candy, of course it will be hard for them to bear giving up candy all at once. You need to consider how to gradually reduce the amount over a long period of time, and only then can they become just like an ordinary person."

"I understand." Fu Shen nodded. "Give him something sweet when the craving acts up, and he won't feel so bad."

"That's it exactly," the old doctor said, twiddling his beard. "But there is one thing you must bear in mind: seeing him in pain, you must under no circumstances let him touch autumn night white again. Softheartedness must be avoided at all costs."

This time, Fu Shen didn't answer at once. Instead, he turned his head to glance at Yan Xiaohan.

Yan Xiaohan smiled comfortingly at him. His features looked weary but unusually gentle. "What are you looking at me for? Are you afraid you can't be ruthless enough?"

"Right," Fu Shen said with a sigh, standing up while holding his hand. "Are you the one being treated, or am I?"

The two of them left the medical hall carrying a bag of medicinal ingredients for invigorating Yang and strengthening the kidneys. Yan Xiaohan left a verbal message for Prince Qi at a local money shop they were using as liaison, notifying him of the lead of white dew powder appearing in Xishan Village and telling his party to proceed to Jingzhou while Yan Xiaohan stayed for a few days to investigate.

While they had the leisure for it, the two of them strolled around the county town. The fourth month was a good time, when spring warmed up and the flowers bloomed, and in the south it was especially wet and warm. Kuangfeng County abounded in all kinds of fresh fish and fresh lotus roots, with a distinctive flavor different from the capital. Though Yan Xiaohan's drug addiction had yet to be resolved, when it wasn't acting up, he was no different from usual. He concealed his dullness and low spirits very well and roamed hand-in-hand with Fu Shen; he didn't feel that this time was hard to get through.

Only after asking around in many ways did the two of them work out what exactly this so-called "autumn night white" actually was.

It originated from a flowering, fruit-bearing plant. It was said that an emperor of the previous dynasty had received it as a gift from Chang'e while traveling through the Palace of the Moon in his dreams. It often came into full flower on autumn nights, from which it took the name "autumn night white." The flowers were pure white as snow. When the fruits were ground, they became the color of cow's milk. Consuming them made a person's body warm and intoxicated them. The crudely processed juice of the autumn night white fruit assumed the form of light brown filaments, which could be inhaled with an opium pipe. Refined autumn night white, meanwhile, assumed the form of brown half-transparent lumps, something like amber. It was purer, and its effects were stronger. After it was ground down to powder, it only needed to be heated slightly over a fire to release a bewitching sweet smell. This type was the "white dew powder" that Yan Xiaohan and his people had discovered in the capital.

There were many local households who grew autumn night white, and crude autumn night white filled the streets. Because this drug had aphrodisiac effects, much of it was sold as a tie-in in the pleasure district. Brothels that sold autumn night white all hung white flower-shaped lanterns outside their doors as signs. Refined autumn night white, meanwhile, was an extremely rare product. The common saying about it was that "autumn white is worth its weight in gold."

The sheer luck among the misfortune was that what Yan Xiaohan had encountered in Xishan Village was only the village's crude autumn night white. There had been many impurities when it was burned, and the dose hadn't been very large. If he'd really had the terrible luck to run into refined white dew powder, having been locked in that room for so long, never mind getting up to seek medical treatment, he would probably be a husk of himself by now.

The deeper the two of them went into the town, the more frightening scenes they beheld. That case of the Jinwu Guard in the capital had put everyone in a state of anxiety. The Feilong Guard had strenuously investigated "white dew powder," doing their best to turn Qingxu Temple upside down. But in Kuangfeng Town alone, as Fu Shen and Yan Xiaohan walked, they saw no fewer than ten pleasure houses with flower lanterns hanging at the door, never mind the countless instances of home-made autumn night white being illicitly traded among the people.

In a street separated only by a wall from the twittering of orioles and swallows, the gold powder and red sleeves, there was even an unkempt beggar with festering sores on his body, still clasping an opium pipe, unwilling to let go.

This scene was both extravagant and enchanting, and also inexplicably bleak and strange. The sight of it made Fu Shen bristle. Bewildered, he said, "That's just bizarre. Is it really worth ruining yourself like this for the sake of some lousy drug?"

Under cover of their sleeves, Yan Xiaohan squeezed his hand and said, "You haven't taken the drug, so you can be reasonable about it now. There is so much bitterness in a human life. Once they have experienced bliss, naturally it's hard to endure the pain and difficulty of the human world again."

Fu Shen, rather displeased, said, "So what about you? Are you also planning to leave the mortal world and ascend to heaven?"

"No." Yan Xiaohan turned and looked at him. His gaze was tender and steady. With a smile, he said, "The greatest bliss I have known in my life was when I knew that you loved me, too."

Fu Shen said, "… If that's all you have to say for yourself, let's go!"

Like an evil despot who had been teased by a woman of good family, he shook off his hand and slithered away. Shortly, he stopped up ahead, waited for Yan Xiaohan to slowly catch up, and once again took his hand.

That night, the two of them ate and bathed. Everything was as usual. Yan Xiaohan's condition remained stable. There were no signs of the craving acting up. Fu Shen uneasily asked him about it several times. This was his first time dealing with such a thing. Though his expression looked calm, he couldn't avoid feeling anxious. Seeing him shifting around as if there were nails under his ass, Yan Xiaohan simply pulled him into his arms and held him. "Weren't you the one who told me not to be scared? Why are you in such a panic now?"

"Isn't that obvious?" said Fu Shen. "I'm scared, too."

"Scared of what?" said Yan Xiaohan.

"Scared I won't be able to satisfy you," Fu Shen said sarcastically.

Yan Xiaohan buried his face against the side of his neck. There was muffled laughter.

He laughed and laughed, then suddenly exclaimed softly.

Fu Shen immediately said, "What is it?"

"Nothing, don't be nervous." Yan Xiaohan took his hand and pressed it against his chest, letting him feel his slowly quickening heartbeat. "It's acting up... Ah, it's still tolerable."

But soon he could no longer stand it. Following the intense throbbing, an itching pain like ant bites emerged where his heart was, then spread throughout his body. Yan Xiaohan's arms and legs began to tremble uncontrollably. His muscles twitched. His body pitched forward involuntarily and was deftly caught by Fu Shen.

He felt the person in his arms shaking incessantly and quietly asked, "What do you feel now?"

Yan Xiaohan hugged him as if clinging to his last hope for survival. His teeth were chattering. Indistinctly, he said, "... Cold."

Fu Shen kept one arm around him while the other hand wandered tantalizingly over his whole body. Like a dragonfly skimming the water, his fingertips brushed the nape of his neck, his waist, and other sensitive areas, then burrowed into the lapels of his robe, lingering over the clammy skin. Dense kisses fell on Yan Xiaohan's neck and ears. He seemed to be comforting, yet also enticing. In an erotic husky voice, he said into his ear, "It's all right. I'll warm you up soon."

The kisses had changed in nature at some point, poignantly blazing into a prairie fire, burning so hard that his palms were scalding hot, his blood boiling. The assault on his mouth was dizzying, as if he were immersed in a hot spring with steam curling up. An inexpressible warmth rose from the bottom of his heart.

Yan Xiaohan had been right. The traces left in his body by the autumn night white in fact couldn't compare to the obsession Fu Shen had carved into his bones over the past seven years.

Fu Shen had lit a cluster of flames in his belly, flourishing as they burned, but he wouldn't leave it at that. His callused hands, neither slender nor soft but unusually clever, stroked all the acupoints on Yan Xiaohan's body one by one, rubbing with moderate force, easing his stiff muscles like a massage.

The soothing pleasure was like a few drops of timely rain falling during all-consuming, scorching thirst. Though it wasn't enough to extinguish the pain, it let him keep hanging on.

When he wasn't so tense and had relaxed slightly, Fu Shen grabbed a pillow and put it under him. He had meant to have Yan Xiaohan lean against the head of the bed, but instead Yan Xiaohan kept hugging him, unwilling to let go, so Fu Shen could only laugh helplessly, undoing his belt while he teased, "So clingy. Do you have to be holding me?"

Accompanying the kisses and whispers that lingered bone-deep, those hands that had held swords and reins, that had been stained with blood and with the harsh weather of the north, easily lifted him up to the clouds.

The insistent restlessness temporarily eased because of this bit of sweetness. Yan Xiaohan's panting breaths calmed. With difficulty, he found a drop of clarity. Remembering what the old doctor had said about "giving up sweets," he felt that in fact there was some sense in it, but it would depend on the person. If he had done it himself, the effects certainly wouldn't have been as striking as Fu Shen doing it.

But Fu Shen suddenly released him and turned to search outside the bed. He stuffed some incense into the incense burner by the bed.

Yan Xiaohan, eyes fixed on his movements, asked half a beat late, "What did you put in there?"

"Just a bit of harmless aphrodisiac." Fu Shen's lips curled, his overly cold handsomeness softened by the smile, becoming an even more enchanting attraction than the faint fragrance. The gauze bed curtains floated down gently. He slowly opened his own clothing and drew close to kiss Yan Xiaohan's lowered eyelids. "Come on, this time I'll give you something sweeter."

The incense curled up around them. Only halfway through the night did that incense burner finally go out.

Yan Xiaohan turned and embraced Fu Shen, who was fast asleep from exhaustion, and pressed a kiss to his slightly furrowed brow. His heart was filled with many emotions. He had thought that the old doctor's remedy was only a psychological comfort. He hadn't thought that the Lord Marquis would be able to come up with so many tricks and artifices to alleviate his addiction.

CHAPTER FIFTY-THREE

IT WAS SAID THAT WHEN AN ADDICTION TO AUTUMN NIGHT WHITE formed, the first three days were the most dangerous and difficult. Yan Xiaohan had believed the old doctor's horror stories and had prepared himself to walk up a mountain of knives and be dropped into a pot of boiling oil, not expecting that with an "omnipotent" Marquis of Jingning at his side, the memories that ought to have been grim and frightening would be enveloped in sweetness, not seeming all that painful.

It was only that when the craving flared up, he became muddled. Though he had repeatedly admonished himself ahead of time not to make excessive demands, more often than not, when his head cleared, he would find that Fu Shen was already spent from the exertion.

After a few days, Yan Xiaohan felt the condition of being insensitive to all outside things and in total chaos slowly recede, so he brought up wanting to return to the fox immortal temple and Xishan Village to have a look.

Fu Shen was sleeping until midmorning every day now and drinking comprehensive restorative broth like water. Hearing him, he languidly said, "What did you promise me before? You've forgotten it in the blink of an eye."

Yan Xiaohan pursed his lips. "The sooner we take care of it, the sooner we can leave. It can't be put off forever."

Fu Shen scoffed and reached out to take hold of his chin. "Don't act like I've been bullying you. Who's the pathetic act for?"

Yan Xiaohan grabbed his hand, brought it to his lips, and kissed it. Confidently, he said, "For whoever's heart aches watching it."

Fu Shen said, "I spoil you."

Yan Xiaohan wasn't in a hurry, and he didn't argue. He only watched him, gentle and soft as water. Fu Shen wasn't worried about him wrangling; what he was worried about was him using his beauty as an enticement—especially this distinctive flavor of the sickly beauty. He couldn't keep up his cold attitude for long. Relenting, he said, "Fine, fine, if you want to, we'll go. It's all up to you."

The proud words "who has the final word in this house" had been resoundingly spoken, but now this "master of the house" had drunk his prestige down along with restorative broth.

Xishan Village was close to the mountains and the water. It ought to have been a paradise, carefree and peaceful, with scenes out of a painting. Who could have thought that so many dark secrets would be hidden in this village with hardly more than a hundred residents?

The villagers here were very guarded against outsiders, and Yan Xiaohan and Fu Shen were too noticeable. Neither of them was skilled in disguise. They could only squat in a little forest on the hill behind the village, observing from a distance across the river. The two of them waited from nightfall to sunset, watching a whole day's worth of women washing rice, and apart from two turtledoves Fu Shen brought down with stones out of boredom, they came up with nothing.

"This won't do, Lord Yan," Fu Shen said. "We could squat here until we died without seeing anything. Why don't I just go down and grab someone for you to have a go at interrogating?"

Yan Xiaohan didn't answer. He seemed to be lost in thought.

Fu Shen reached out and patted him on the arm. "Menggui?"

"Hm?" He seemed to have been abruptly pulled back from some scene. His vague gaze collected into a single thread. He focused and said, "What did you say?"

Fu Shen wasn't taking anything else seriously, only keeping a close watch on him. He acutely noticed that something was off about Yan Xiaohan and grabbed his wrist to check his pulse. "What's wrong?"

Yan Xiaohan for some reason dodged him. Fu Shen was used to cooperation from him. When he came up empty, even if there had been nothing wrong to begin with, there was instantly something wrong now. "What are you hiding from me? Give me your hand. Let me see."

The hand hidden beneath Yan Xiaohan's sleeve was trembling uncontrollably, and it was intensifying. Enduring it, he said, "It's all right."

"All right my ass," Fu Shen said coldly. "You're shaking like chaff, and you're still lying through your teeth."

He silently recited *He's sick, don't squabble with him* three times, suppressing his anger. "It's the craving flaring up again, isn't it."

Yan Xiaohan's face was pale. He didn't deny it.

Fu Shen looked around but saw that the trees were luxurious and there was dusk all around. The whole forest was quiet, without trace of human speech. There was only the breeze and the chirping of birds. He blushed in spite of himself. Sighing, he said, "You really know how to choose a spot…"

Yan Xiaohan absolutely couldn't imagine Fu Shen, with his upbringing and background, condescending to do such a thing out in the wilderness. On hearing the intention revealed by his words, he quickly said, "No way! Don't mess around."

Fu Shen asked, "Can you hold out until we get back to the county town?"

Perhaps it was the craving making mischief, and perhaps it

was that his remorse and self-reproach had lately accumulated almost to the limit of what he could contain; Yan Xiaohan's thoughts took a wrong turn somewhere. He retreated further and dully said, "Jingyuan, you don't have to force yourself…"

This gesture of retreat was more injurious than anything he could have said. Fu Shen nearly lost his temper with him. "Force myself?" he repeated.

"Oh, very well." He pointed at Yan Xiaohan and gave several bitter laughs. "I keep coming up with new ways to treat your illness, and you keep coming up with new ways to annoy me, is that it?"

Fu Shen irritably paced a little way back and forth along the forest path, restraining himself again and again, but finally he couldn't keep it up any longer and roared furiously, "Yan Menggui, I'd love nothing better than to hold you in both hands and treat you like a treasure, and when it comes down to it, you think of that as 'forcing myself?' Was your conscience eaten by dogs?!"

He was a person who had come off the battlefield. When he was truly angry, there seemed to be blood and the cold gleam of weaponry in his voice. A grandeur like Mount Tai bore down. But when he hurled this reprimand full in the face at Yan Xiaohan, the latter felt a bit of sickly ease.

This is unfair to him, he thought.

He knew that Fu Shen loved him, but ordinary pampering and indulgence was one thing, and the eldest young master who had never done his own laundry lowering himself to yield to him was another. Husband and wife were birds in the forest, each flying their own way when disaster befell; there was nothing wrong with this saying to begin with. When a person had fallen into an abyss, did he really have to drag along another person who had sunk with him in order for his love to be called as deep as the sea?

When he was finished yelling, Fu Shen's anger had yet to disperse, but his mind had calmed down. Yan Xiaohan's eyes were misty and uncertain, seeming to contain both sadness and happiness. Fu Shen knew that he was being impacted by the drug to some extent, that when he was in low spirits, feelings of hatred and loathing would grow as rampantly as poisonous weeds. Fu Shen not only had to satisfy his body's desires, he also had to keep a constant watch on his changing moods.

The only thing he didn't understand was, why did Yan Xiaohan always think of himself as a burden?

When he thought this, he asked the question aloud. Yan Xiaohan seemed not to have expected him to be so direct. He froze for a moment, then said, "I was poisoned because of my own carelessness, but it's led you to have to tax your ingenuity. Your legs haven't healed yet, you ought to have been in the capital recuperating, but instead you're running around all over the place for my sake... It's because I couldn't take care of you properly. Instead, I've been a burden on you again and again."

Fu Shen picked up: "According to your own reasoning, no one owes anyone, so why do you have to take care of me properly?

"Yan Xiaohan, do you think I married you for your great wealth, or for your lofty position of upper third rank official?" He said with a sneer, "Here's how it should be—clearly, as a cripple without position or power, I'm the one who ought to be a burden on you, right?"

Yan Xiaohan couldn't stand to hear him say the word "cripple." All his thoughts halted for a while. He said seriously, "Don't talk nonsense."

It was like a ladleful of water poured over a fire. Fu Shen's sneer stiffened on his face. He was simply at his wit's end.

"You..." His anger was getting to be a little too much for him. He wanted to string Yan Xiaohan up and give him a beating, clear his head a little. Holding back, he said, "Forget it, don't talk about these useless things. Let's see to your craving first."

But Yan Xiaohan stood still, maintaining his stubborn *you can talk yourself blue in the face, I'm going to stand my ground* attitude. "It's all right, I'll deal with it myself, and it will pass. This is an unsuitable place."

Fu Shen suddenly said, "Menggui, the day you were drugged, do you still remember what you were doing when I found you?"

For some reason, his tone had instantly softened; it could even be called kindly. Yan Xiaohan knit his brows and pondered briefly. He really couldn't remember. He shook his head.

"I remember. Every time I've closed my eyes these past few days, it's been the only thing I could see. I might not be able to forget it for the rest of my life." Fu Shen lowered his eyelids. "I was still 'Ren Miao' at the time. As soon as I came near you, you pulled out a small knife and tried to stab your own arm.

"Tell me the truth. If it really had been someone else that day, what would you have done?"

Yan Xiaohan looked into his eyes. The answer was practically self-evident—

That knife would have gone right in.

Fu Shen walked up to him and gently stroked his face, as if wiping away nonexistent tearstains. "Whose sake do you think I came all this way for? I've said this so many times I'm about to get calluses on my lips. Menggui, I haven't even had time to love you. How could I think you were a burden?

"If you absolutely need a reason," he said, his tone bantering but his manner exceedingly solemn, "if you can preserve your chastity for me, then I can let you do whatever you please, give you whatever you want. Do you understand?"

Ever since being dosed with autumn night white, Yan Xiaohan had felt that a big hole had opened in his heart, connected to an abyss. In that abyss lived all his fantasies, obsessions, and desires; it seemed that it could never be satisfied. When he was lucid, he could control himself, but when he wasn't lucid, he couldn't distinguish whether this was a loss of control brought about by the drug or his own hideous true colors.

But now, Fu Shen had jumped into that abyss with righteous

purpose and no thought of looking back, and what met him wasn't the bite of a vicious beast but a wounded yet slowly healing heart.

Yan Xiaohan finally realized that his satisfaction did not lie in the moment he could spread his wings and keep Fu Shen safe in his embrace but in the moment when, just as he was about to stumble and fall, a pair of hands reached out of nowhere to hold him up.

He bowed slightly and picked Fu Shen up. He pressed him against the nearest tree and stopped his parched mouth.

A cool breeze blew by. The leaves rustled.

When night had completely fallen, two immaculately dressed men at last walked out of the small forest. One of them was clearly faltering in his stride, shaking once for every three steps. The other man couldn't stand to watch this. He picked him up and placed him on horseback.

The two of them were just about to leave when an uproar suddenly came from Xishan Village in the distance. A woman's wails pierced the night sky. Lamps lit up in many houses, one after another. A number of people opened their windows and raised their voices to ask: "That's Tian Cheng's missus. What happened?"

Fortunately it was already late and the villagers had shut up their houses. They had to yell to talk, so the two people on the slope could also get the gist of what they were saying. Someone answered, "Tian Cheng's dying, he has to be brought to the memorial hall and sent off tomorrow night!"

The woman gave a heartrending wail. "Everyone, aunts and uncles, he can still be saved, I'll take him to town to see a doctor! Don't take him to the memorial hall… I'm begging you…"

A gruff-voiced man said loudly, "You can't! You can't go to the county town. Are you going to drag down the whole village for one person's sake?"

Fu Shen and Yan Xiaohan's eyes met without prearrangement.

There really was something fishy going on in this Xishan Village. How would it drag down the whole village if a sick man were taken to the county town to see a doctor?

An ominous premonition suddenly flitted through Fu Shen's mind. "Could it be… plague?"

CHAPTER FIFTY-FOUR

AFTER THE SICK MAN WAS BROUGHT TO THE MEMORIAL HALL, QUIET was restored to Xishan Village. Running the risk of being chased and bitten by all the village's dogs, Yan Xiaohan and Fu Shen snuck into a courtyard and spent ages eavesdropping, putting together a rough sequence of cause and effect. It was said that the sick man had been infected with a foul disease that couldn't be treated. Everyone in the village thought that this was an inauspicious omen, and they had to hold a sacrificial ceremony by the river tomorrow to drive out evil.

Fu Shen's waist was sore, and his back hurt. He was tired and sleepy. He almost didn't hold out. He staggered forward; Yan Xiaohan opened his arms and caught him in an embrace and simply didn't trouble him to walk for himself again. He carried him right out of the village. The two of them spurred their horse and returned to town and asked a waiter at the inn for hot water and food. When they had washed themselves clean and eaten their fill, General Fu lay in bed resting his waist, while Lord Yan very obediently and conscientiously sat on the bedside and pulled his legs over his own knees to massage and relax them.

"What kind of plague do you think this 'foul disease' is?" Fu Shen asked. "If there really is a plague, this village is really being too bold. Once the scope of the disease expands, one village dying off will be the least of it."

"Concealing it and not reporting it is only natural." Yan Xiaohan rolled up Fu Shen's pant legs and pressed on the acupoints on his calves. "Think about it. The local official won't even report to the court that autumn night white is spreading unchecked in his jurisdiction. If he found out that a strange illness suspected of being plague had appeared time and again in Xishan Village, what would he do?"

Fu Shen raised his eyebrows. Yan Xiaohan said, "Better to kill by mistake than to let anything get away—regardless of whether it is or isn't plague, only by annihilating it all can future troubles be eliminated forever. The villagers all know that if this gets out, their whole village might not get out alive. That's why they're desperately covering it up, not daring to report it to the authorities."

Fu Shen smacked the bed. "What kind of rotten official is this? It's a disgrace!"

Yan Xiaohan smiled without speaking.

Fu Shen shot him a sideways glance. "Hey, how strange. Where have your sulks and childish temper gone today?"

For Yan Xiaohan to be able to guess the local official's line of thought at once, he himself couldn't be particularly upright. If Fu Shen had said something like this before, he couldn't have helped being slightly stung. Now, however, it was as if he really had set down many years of ill feeling, become open and candid, with rather the attitude of being indifferent to favor or humiliation.

Smiling, he said, "If I go into another sulk, will you be able to take it?"

It was as if Fu Shen had built an incomparably steadfast wall in his heart. He knew that he possessed all of this man's love and tolerance, enough to make him look down on all creation in his vicinity. Once a person had confidence, naturally he could straighten his back and raise his head, no longer be constrained by gains and losses.

"Amazing…" The muscles of Fu Shen's legs tensed instantly. "Hey, where's that hand going?"

"Relax," Yan Xiaohan said good-naturedly. "Why squeeze your legs together so tightly? Open them up a little… I'm not doing anything. Aren't your legs sore? I'm giving you a massage."

Fu Shen was rendered speechless by his flirting. He simply put him out of sight and out of mind, closing his eyes and letting him get on with it. In his mind, he slowly organized the events of recent days. First there had been the rapid string of homicides in the capital, then the grain tax revenue falling short in Jingchu, Yan Xiaohan being dosed in Xishan Village, the rampant spread of autumn night white in Kuangfeng County… The crux of all these events lay with the previously unheard of "autumn night white."

The questions they needed to find answers to now were: First, what secret was Xishan Village hiding? Second, was the shortfall of tax revenue in Jingchu connected to the catastrophic spread of autumn night white? Third, by what channel had autumn night white entered Jingchu—and had it been deliberately introduced or grown naturally? Was autumn night white blooming everywhere a situation limited to the area of Jingchu, or had it spread to other places?

At the outset, Fu Shen had only had a surge of excitement and wanted to discreetly accompany Yan Xiaohan while he carried out his mission. He hadn't expected them to run into a vexing problem that would make it difficult for him to stay out of it even if he had wanted to. He couldn't tell whether he had purely picked up some bad luck, or whether he had been destined from birth for a hard life.

As he thought this, sleepiness gradually arose, and without noticing it, Fu Shen fell deeply asleep. Yan Xiaohan heard his breaths gradually become slow and even, then softly put his legs back onto the bed and pulled up the quilt to cover him. He was just about to straighten up and go wash his hands, but before he could straighten, Fu Shen woke up.

He couldn't have been called entirely awake. He hadn't even fully opened his eyes. Fu Shen seemed to be in a daze, but he clearly knew that he was leaving. He reached a hand out from under the quilt. "Where are you going?"

Yan Xiaohan took his hand and put it back under the quilt. He wanted to laugh a little, and at the same time his heart was impossibly soft. He bent down to kiss the center of his brow and softly said, "Sleep, I'm going to wash my hands."

Hearing this, Fu Shen closed his eyes again, but this time he wasn't asleep. Shortly, the lamp in the room was extinguished, and the curtains were pulled down. In the dark came the rustling of fabric, followed by the bed beside him dipping slightly. Yan Xiaohan got into bed and very gently pulled him into his arms. Fu Shen, his eyes closed, drew a fingertip along the back of his hand and heard Yan Xiaohan quietly sigh into his ear and say, "You wake at the slightest noise. You're going to overtax your nerves like this."

Body heat and scent were the best soporifics. Fu Shen's sleepiness surged up once again. This time, not even Yan Xiaohan chattering into his ear could disturb him. He rolled over, put a hand on Yan Xiaohan's waist, rather carelessly slapped him a couple of times, and indistinctly said, "Sleep."

Yan Xiaohan laughed in spite of himself. He thought to himself, how could this person be like a child who started searching for his mother as soon as he opened his eyes and would make a fuss if she left? He pulled the quilt higher, covering their shoulders, and quietly answered, "Yes. Let's sleep."

The next morning, the two of them once again went up the mountain behind Xishan Village. Today there was a woman by the river constantly wiping away tears. The women around her came up one after another to comfort her. Presumably this was the sorrowfully weeping "Tian Cheng's missus" from last night. Fu Shen had recovered his energy today. He was spinning that club in his hands. "Keep an eye on her and lend a hand when the need arises. Perhaps we can get some truth out of her."

Yan Xiaohan said, "Yes, sir."

General Fu's club nearly slipped from his hand and went flying.

The day passed quickly. The sun sank into the west, the weary birds returned to the forest, and the villagers hard at work in the fields trickled back home. Yan Xiaohan and Fu Shen stood halfway up the mountain, perfectly able to overlook the whole village.

The scene from the other night repeated itself. First a number of lights lit up in the direction of the memorial hall. Then everyone left their houses carrying lanterns and gradually congregated into a band of light that zigzagged forward along the village's little street, heading toward the river.

By the lantern light, a festooned cart could faintly be seen among the crowd. A white-clothed man who may have been dead or alive lay in the cart. This scene sent a chill up Yan Xiaohan's spine as he remembered the rather strange procession he had seen in the memorial hall the other day, which had seemed like a funeral.

Warmth suddenly came from the back of his hand. Fu Shen was holding his hand. Seeming absent-minded, he casually said, "Don't be scared."

That night, a person had charged alone into the depths of the village and brought him out of the nightmare, taking him into a gentle romantic dream.

Yan Xiaohan quietly rotated his hand and laced their fingers together. "Right. I'm not scared."

Fu Shen hissed as if he had a toothache. The two of them had done so many intimate things, but he was stung by this manner of holding hands like small children. But out of some unknown considerations, he didn't struggle free. He let Yan Xiaohan hold his hand like this, until the villagers had come to the riverbank, placed the festooned cart in an empty space by the river, and laid out an offering of fruit.

A gray-bearded elder walked out of the crowd. First he solemnly kowtowed three times in the direction of the rapid river. Then, trembling, he took a yellow talisman from his sleeve, recited an incantation, then placed the yellow talisman over an incense candle and lit it on fire. When the talisman had turned into a handful of flying ashes, he rang a bell and began to pray in a loud voice. Fu Shen heard him vaguely. The prayer seemed to be requesting that some deity be generous, send the sinner beyond, bless the village with favorable weather and keep a plague from forming.

Fu Shen said in astonishment, "The current dynasty abolished live sacrifices to the River God long ago and instituted sacrifices to the Water Official and the Dragon King. How can these ignorant people still dare to sacrifice people to the river?"

He was speaking of the previous dynasty's old custom. Previously, whenever there were rains and floods, the common people would think that the River God was angry and could only be calmed with a sacrifice. A good portion of them used pigs, sheep, and other domestic animals. Furthermore, there were those that used virgin boys and girls or even beautiful young women as sacrifices. Countless innocent women and children had met their deaths in this way. When the current dynasty had been established, its first emperor had commanded the abolition of the old custom. All the River God Temples were knocked down and live sacrifices were absolutely prohibited. Common practices had been completely remade.

Who could have thought that today, hundreds of years later, in this remote place, the nightmare would reappear, past events be reenacted.

Yan Xiaohan held him back. "Wait, don't get frantic. The River God is only concerned with favorable weather. I've never heard that he also concerns himself with plague. Also, they say that the old sacrificial practices used virgin boys and girls for sacrificial objects. The person in the cart seems to be a man. This isn't necessarily a sacrifice to the River God. For now, let's watch and see what happens, see what he's going to do next."

When the old man had finished reciting the prayer, two firmly covered-up men lifted the white-clothed person off the cart. They pulled out several strands of rope and bound him hand and foot. Instantly, a woman among the crowd gave a mournful, heartrending wail. Ignoring the crowd holding her back, she threw herself forward to tear at the two men. "Let me die! Let me die in his place!"

The village head indicated for several women to come forward and pull her away. The woman collapsed entirely and lay prostrate on the ground, sobbing and cursing, but all the villagers seemed to be turning a deaf ear on it. The two men lifted the white-clothed person and threw him into the racing river. Following an aged and raspy "a gift to the true immortal," everyone knelt in unison and devoutly kowtowed thrice in the direction of the river.

Fu Shen's expression was grim. With his eyesight, he could even see that when that man had been thrown into the river, his hands and feet had still been constantly struggling. He quietly said, "This river flows into the little lake behind the fox immortal temple. Let's go there and look for him. We might still be able to save him. Come on."

But Yan Xiaohan said, "If the husband dies, the wife might not live through the night. I'll go fish him out of the lake, and you follow her. If it's too late to save her husband, we still need a living witness."

Fu Shen muttered to himself briefly. He seemed rather uneasy. Yan Xiaohan knew what he was worried about and soothingly said, "Don't worry, I'm a decent swimmer, and if anything goes wrong, I'll be sure to save myself. I'm not about to risk my life for the sake of a stranger."

"You must be careful. I couldn't take a repeat of that bolt out of the blue last time." From his sleeve, Fu Shen took out the small knife Yan Xiaohan had attempted to injure himself with and tossed it to him. He said, "I'll bring that woman to the fox immortal temple."

Yan Xiaohan took the knife and twirled it through his fingers as if doing a trick. He leapt onto his horse and laughed into the wind. In the dim night, his face seemed to be glowing. "Fine, then we'll see each other at the fox immortal temple."

CHAPTER FIFTY-FIVE

AFTER SEVERAL DAYS AWAY FROM IT, THE FOX IMMORTAL TEMPLE still stood on the slope of a hill the same as before, only looking more dilapidated. In the night, it was like a ruin. The river, meanwhile, flowed behind the hill into a broad body of water.

There was no wind or rain tonight. The moonlight was bright. The rocks on the shore of the lake were craggy, and the lake was calm and waveless, giving off an indescribable feeling of grim cold. Yan Xiaohan dismounted and stood still beside the lake for a long time, watching the dark blue lake and letting his mind wander. Finally, he realized what was strange about this place.

When it had been pouring rain that night, they hadn't approached the lake to look at it closely. And Prince Qi and Yan Xiaohan, along with the whole party, were all northerners, not very familiar with the scenery of the south, so they hadn't noticed that something was off: this lake was located in the countryside, with running water flowing into it, but not a blade of grass grew beside it, and there were no reeds or aquatic plants, no water birds perching. There were even very few fish and shrimp. The whole lake was like a pond of stagnant water, without a drop of vitality.

And connecting that to what the villagers had done tonight, Yan Xiaohan suddenly came up with a frightening guess.

Soon, the sound of splashing came from the water. Yan Xiaohan looked closely. As expected, there was a white figure bobbing in the middle of the river.

The Xishan villagers lived next to water. They were all excellent swimmers. Perhaps because his wife had charged in midway to obstruct the proceedings, the ropes holding the man hadn't been tied tightly. They had loosened somewhat after entering the water, which had kept him from drowning up to now. He was holding on with a single breath, floating toward the lake along with the water.

Yan Xiaohan took off his outer robe and dove into the water unburdened. He swam all out to the center of the river, used the blade between his fingers to cut several ropes, then knocked out the man still struggling wildly with a punch and dragged him behind himself, floating in the water, and swam for shore.

He had been just in time. While the man had inhaled water, he was still breathing. Yan Xiaohan tossed him onto the shore. Seeing that he was only going to be coughing up water for a while, without the strength to run away, he turned and dove back into the water and swam toward the lake.

It was already well into the night and even darker in the water. Yan Xiaohan could only see clearly about a foot away. He held his breath and sank down, feeling the flowing rhythm of the river when it converged with the lake, and continued probing in the direction of the depths at the center of the lake.

He swam and swam, then felt that he seemed to have touched something. At first he thought it was a fish. Then the thing kept poking him from behind, this way and that. He reached behind impatiently to grab it. The sensation was soft and slippery. He pulled it close to take a look. It was as white as a young lotus root and branched at the end—

It was a human hand.

He'd just come here and already he was holding hands with

one of the lake's tenants. Lord Yan nearly passed out on the spot. He almost thought that his craving was acting up and he was hallucinating again. He spat out a stream of bubbles, feeling that after the scare he'd just had, the air in his mouth wasn't enough to sustain him through another fright, so he decisively gave up on it. He kicked in the water, turned over, and swam upward.

Shortly, a big spray of water bloomed on the lake as Yan Xiaohan broke through. As soon as he let out a breath, he heard the clop of horse's hooves from the shore.

Fu Shen didn't wait for the horse to come to a full stop. He leapt off the horse and quickly walked over to the lakeshore. "Menggui!"

Yan Xiaohan waved at him, showing that he was all right, then swam back from the lake into the river to rinse himself repeatedly in the clean water. He didn't have an obsession with cleanliness, but no one who had spent this long flopping around soaking in corpse water could well have avoided feeling revolted. Fu Shen followed him, going around the lakeshore to the riverside. He reached out to pull out the sopping wet Yan Xiaohan. He snatched up his outer robe and covered him with it. Bewildered, he said, "What were you doing messing around in the lake?"

Yan Xiaohan clung to his hand. "I'm not telling you. You won't let me hold your hand."

Fu Shen laughed disapprovingly. "It's always something with you."

The wind was strong by the water, and Yan Xiaohan was soaking wet. With the wind blowing on him on top of the scene at the bottom of the lake just now, all the hairs on the back of his neck stood on end. He shivered. Fu Shen, seeing this, took off his own outer robe and gave it to him. Unexpectedly, Yan Xiaohan still had a death grip on him, unwilling to let go. Fu Shen struggled and couldn't get free. Exasperated, he said, "Still not letting go?"

"No." Shivering, Yan Xiaohan said stubbornly, smiling, "I'm very scared. I need the Lord Marquis to give me a hug."

Fu Shen looked at this trembling "poor little boy" with too many thoughts to express. "I hope you're scared to death."

Despite this, he still reached out to embrace Yan Xiaohan, shielding him from the wind with his own body. The two of them left the lakeshore as if glued together and went to look at the place where their horses were tied up. There was an unconscious woman in mourning garb lying facedown on the horse's back. Yan Xiaohan shot a glance at the man he had knocked out, then turned his face away, pretending he hadn't noticed the rough methods identical to his. "Move them into the fox immortal temple?" he proposed.

They each carried one of the people into the fox immortal temple. Fu Shen found some splintered wood in the backyard and built a fire, pressing Yan Xiaohan down in front of it to dry out. Yan Xiaohan told him a bit of what he had seen at the bottom of the lake, originally intending to scare him, not expecting that Fu Shen's tolerance would be much higher than his. Hearing about it, he only frowned. "According to the villagers' habits, I'm afraid there won't be just one corpse at the bottom of the lake. How many people are there in the village? How can they afford to throw so many people away?"

Yan Xiaohan said, "It can't have started too long ago. My guess is that it may have been roughly around the time white dew powder spread in the capital."

"Be more precise," said Fu Shen.

"First," said Yan Xiaohan, "Daoist Chunyang entered the capital and took up lodgings at Qingxu Temple roughly three and a half years ago, or in other words the twenty-second year of Yuantai. Second, the shortfall of tax revenues in Jingchu. These were accounts that ought to have been settled in winter of last year, but they've been pushed back to this spring. If the reduced yield was caused by the proliferation of autumn night white, then prior to the autumn of the twenty-fifth year of Yuantai at least, autumn night white had already appeared here."

Fu Shen said, "How are the grain taxes and autumn night white connected? Your second point seems a little arbitrary."

Yan Xiaohan explained: "While Jingchu doesn't contribute as heavily to revenue as places like Jiangnan and Jiangxi, last year there was neither drought nor flood, nor the manmade calamity of war here, but the grain taxes went down by twenty percent out of nowhere. That doesn't make sense. You saw it yourself in Kuangfeng County—it's easy to get addicted to autumn night white, and the price of it is high. Users often bring their families to ruin and become riddled with disease. Couldn't this have resulted in a portion of farmers going bankrupt?

"Besides, autumn night white itself creates huge sudden profits. Supposing someone made a big profit off it and everyone else followed their example, left farming to plant autumn night white instead, that would also lead to the current situation. It would be easy to verify this point. Another time we'll take a tour outside of Jingzhou City and see what's actually growing in the fields."

Fu Shen nodded, indicating that he understood and that Yan Xiaohan could continue.

"Third, according to what Yi Siming said, white dew powder appeared in the capital around autumn and winter of last year. That was just after you were injured in Qingsha Gap and His Majesty arranged a marriage for you and me. Daoist Chunyang had been lying low in the capital for years without acting. In order to take revenge on your behalf, just as the properties of autumn night white were proven in the south, he brought the drug to the capital."

He paused and summarized: "From the clues we have now, it appears that autumn night white first spread in the south, then was brought to the capital by Daoist Chunyang. I think there will be no objections to this."

"You're making assumptions again," said Fu Shen. "According to your line of thought, autumn night white has

88

existed all along, but those who had it kept it hidden and wouldn't bring it out. Later, at some juncture, it became popular in the area of Jingchu, and was brought by Daoist Chunyang into the capital to do harm. Since autumn night white is so profitable, why didn't they bring it out earlier and fill up all their coffers instead of clinging to their integrity and only using it after I was injured?"

"I'm not making assumptions." Yan Xiaohan shook his head and reminded him, "Jingyuan, don't forget what we guessed at the beginning about the identity of the person behind this."

Coming from someone else, holding a weapon and holding back from using it might be strange, but what if that person belonged to the Beiyan Cavalry?

Absent profound hatred and resentment, being pushed past endurance, how could he turn the butcher's knife facing foreign enemies around and aim it at the empire that he had defended with his flesh and blood?

Fu Shen could go to his death without perpetrating a traitorous attack like this, but former subordinates of the Beiyan Cavalry in fact might.

Yan Xiaohan guessed that he would be feeling unhappy and spread his arms to put them around his shoulders. Fu Shen considered briefly, then said, "There's something else that puzzles me: if autumn night white appeared in the south before it did in the north, then the juncture wasn't my injury, but some other, prior event."

This question stumped Yan Xiaohan. He frowned and muttered, "Last summer... What happened that impacted the south?"

Their eyes met. A scene that had made a profound impression flashed simultaneously through their minds.

Yan Xiaohan said, "In the sixth month of last year, the two of us argued in the morning court assembly and were each docked half a year's salary by His Majesty."

Fu Shen picked up: "It was over the court planning to send

army supervisors to all the borders, and someone being flattering and saying that it would be most suitable to assign this work to your Feilong Guard."

Past events were still clear in their minds, but they were like something from another lifetime.

Who could have thought that the pair of enemies who had thrown the court into disarray with their arguing and would have loved to bash each other's heads in with their ritual batons would now be cuddled up whispering sweet nothings in front of a fire in an abandoned temple.

One can see that worldly events are indeed hard to predict. If you lived long enough, you might see any miracle.

Yan Xiaohan said, "His Majesty's intention to control military power throughout the country isn't a recent thought. Though that attempt in summer was put down by your unreasonable nitpicking and couldn't be implemented, since this matter had been brought up in morning court, it was tantamount to a public proclamation telling the armed forces throughout the country to tuck their tails between their legs and behave."

Fu Shen, dissatisfied, said, "Hey, what are you talking about? Whose unreasonable nitpicking?"

This interruption of his broke off Yan Xiaohan's line of thought. Not sure whether to laugh or cry, he said, "You won't admit it? Be reasonable. His Majesty's original intention was to send army supervisors from the central administration everywhere. He only mentioned the Feilong Guard in passing, and you snatched it up and wouldn't let go and started pointing out my flaws. You don't call that unreasonable nitpicking?"

It was fortunate that Yan Xiaohan had been somewhat adaptable that day and had gone along with him in changing to the perennial subject of "How can those dogs at the Feilong Guard be bullying a loyal and upright man again?;" that had made the matter come to nothing amid the fuss. Who would have imagined that the Marquis of Jingning would change his attitude like flipping the pages of a book and would now be stubbornly unwilling to acknowledge it!

Fu Shen nodded, outwardly fierce but inwardly cowardly. "Aiding villains in their crimes. Truly despicable."

Yan Xiaohan mockingly returned the compliment: "Doing away with a person as soon as he gets the job done. Worse than a beast."

The two of them were on the point of arguing again when a quiet whimper suddenly came from behind them. The two of them turned their heads in unison and saw the woman they had tossed aside in a corner like a ragged sack move her arms and legs slightly and slowly wake up.

CHAPTER FIFTY-SIX

THE WOMAN WOKE UP AND OPENED HER EYES. AS SOON AS SHE saw Yan Xiaohan, she immediately cried out, "You?!"

Prince Qi's party had been rare guests to Xishan Village. Almost the whole village had run over to get in on the fun that day, and Yan Xiaohan had particularly stood out among them, leaving an even deeper impression on the village men and village women. Therefore, even in her panic, the woman could still recognize him. She was scared nearly to tears. Shivering, she asked, "Have... have you come to take revenge? It was the village head and the others who wanted to hurt you, we didn't know anything!"

Fu Shen idly stoked the fire with his club and put in a word: "The way you're shivering, it doesn't look like you 'didn't know anything.'"

While Fu Shen was handsome, his manner was too overbearing. It was clear at a glance that he was a difficult person it didn't pay to offend. Yan Xiaohan's appearance, meanwhile, could fool people very well. As long as he didn't voluntarily tear through the illusion, he could put on a seamless appearance of gentleness and kindliness.

Seeing that Fu Shen had stepped in to be the bad guy, Yan

Xiaohan could only play the good guy. In a soothing tone, he said, "I fished your husband out of the river. Don't be scared. I didn't come seeking vengeance."

Only when he gave her this reminder did the woman's soul seem to return. She wiped her face with her sleeve and crawled over to hold up her husband, patting his back and clearing his nose and mouth. As she did, she remembered everything that had happened before she had been knocked out. She felt involuntary sadness welling up and burst into tears.

Neither of the two watching said anything to stop her. They listened to her mournful crying in silence.

She had cried countless times between last night and today, standing by and watching as her husband had a sudden outbreak of the vile disease and was thrown into the river by the villagers. That night, she had returned home and put a belt over a ceiling beam, ready to hang herself. Fortunately Fu Shen had been watching her every move from the shadows. At the crucial moment, he had stepped in to knock her out and take her away, not letting her succeed in her death-seeking.

Perhaps because she sensed kindness in their quiet waiting, at length, the woman's crying gradually stopped. She raised her red eyes and nervously looked the two of them over, then knelt and prostrated herself before them. "You have done me a great kindness that I am unable to repay."

She's amenable to reason, anyway, Yan Xiaohan thought. He waved a hand. "There's no need for this. It was a matter of the slightest effort. There are some things I want to ask you. All you need to do is answer with the truth."

The woman said, "I will tell you everything I know without reserve. I wouldn't dare to conceal anything from my benefactors."

Having gone through this near-death experience, the woman had no further affection for Xishan Village. She answered every question put to her, spilling all the village's secrets.

There were over a hundred households in Xishan Village,

many belonging to the Tian clan. The name of the man who had been thrown in the river was Tian Cheng. The woman's surname was Ou. She came from another village and had moved here due to her marriage.

According to Mrs. Ou, Xishan Village, surrounded by mountains and rivers, might not have been cut off from the world, but visitors from outside were still seldom seen. About a year ago, autumn night white had begun to spread in the area of Jingchu. The younger son of one of the village families was studying in the county town and was lured by a classmate to the pleasure district to "get an eye-opener." From curiosity, he had unwittingly picked up an addiction, and when he had gone home on vacation, he had shared autumn night white with his playmates of similar age. By the time his parents noticed, that younger son was already profoundly addicted; it would have been practically impossible for him to break the habit.

That family had some minor assets, and they had an exceptional partiality for this younger son. At first they didn't take autumn night white seriously. They put it about that at worst they could buy enough of the drug for him to take for the rest of his life. But as the addiction deepened, the drug taker's demand for autumn night white increased. Even in Kuangfeng County Town, autumn night white was in short supply and great demand. The average family might well be unable to afford it, let alone a family of mere farmers. So it wasn't long before that family could no longer keep their youngest son supplied. When the craving flared up, it was painful and unendurable. The younger son was so tormented that he became skin and bones. At last, he couldn't stand it. One rainy night, he ran out of the house and threw himself into the river.

Though that was what everyone said, the villagers privately all spread the rumor that the youngest son hadn't killed himself, but that his family, truly unable to bear such a burden, had drowned him, then pushed his body into the river, pretending that he had died by throwing himself in.

With this to serve as an example, apart from the kids who had come in contact with the drug at the beginning, the other villagers didn't dare to touch autumn night white, but that didn't hinder people from casting greedy eyes on autumn night white's high price; they stealthily planted some in their front and back yards.

The mishap had taken place last autumn. One day, a traveling Daoist priest came to the village. Encountering heavy rain on his way, he had nowhere to shelter, so he came to the village to stay the night. The villagers gave him a warm welcome and had him stay in an empty house in the village, and brought food and drink to entertain him.

In the middle of the night, a person in the village just happened to be having a craving flare up. The situation was very desperate and made a big stir, alerting everyone in the village. The Daoist priest was also startled awake and went out to see what was happening along with everyone else. He saw a person covered in blood rolling around on the ground in the rain, so he rushed over and pressed on some acupoints and knocked the person out, then called the villagers over to carry him home.

The Daoist knew some pharmacology. He knew at a glance that these symptoms were caused by autumn night white. But the person's family had no money to buy the drug. Though the village had planted autumn night white, it would take time to process the drug. The village had done the Daoist a kindness. He felt compassion. He went back inside and tinkered with something. When he came out, he had a paper bag containing fine brown powder. He told them to take it and use it as a temporary substitute.

The Daoist was entirely well-meaning, but since ancient times, "do not expose your wealth to others while traveling" and "a treasure will bring you to grief" have always been lessons learned in blood.

There were people in the village who could judge the quality of goods. They recognized that this was the almost impossible to purchase refined "white dew powder." At the time, "autumn white is worth its weight in gold" was already a saying in Kuangfeng County. Seeing that the Daoist had come up with an ounce of autumn night white at once, they were certain that he would have more hidden on him. These people got evil designs into their heads at the prospect of riches. When everyone had returned home and peacefully fallen asleep, they snuck into the place where the Daoist was staying and stabbed him to death.

Hearing this, Fu Shen must have remembered something. His right hand suddenly shook.

Yan Xiaohan calmly took his hand.

The villagers searched the Daoist and came up with a chunk of autumn night white the size of a woman's fist, its color pure and clear, like amber. One corner of it was stained with blood, giving it a greater peculiar beauty. The price of this chunk of autumn night white would surpass an equivalent weight in gold. The people rejoiced and hid it, then carried the Daoist's corpse out of the village under cover of night and dropped it into the river.

An itinerant Daoist priest, without family or position. No one would notice if he disappeared.

That night, in the dark, the Xishan villagers listened in silence to the sounds of knives and axes falling, blood splattering everywhere. They heard the killers shout and howl with laughter, but no one dared to speak to put a stop to it.

That night, they were all people who couldn't be woken, feigning sleep.

The river raced, carrying away the corpse of the victim of injustice. The heap of bones and the past sank together to the bottom of the deep, dark lake outside the fox immortal temple.

But true retribution had just begun.

The people who had taken the autumn night white were afraid that if they disposed of it in a hurry, it would attract suspicion. After deliberating, they determined to break it up into parts, sell the autumn night white separately in several small pieces. But before they could act, one of them suddenly came down with a strange illness. First he had a sustained high fever, coughed, rapidly lost weight, and became disoriented. Next came red spots and rashes in varying degrees, and his skin even began to fester; it was suffering worse than death.

And it wasn't over yet. Not long after, the same symptoms appeared in all the people who had taken part in the murder that night.

The villagers at last began to panic. But premeditated murder for gain was a major unpardonable crime; those who sheltered the perpetrators would be treated as guilty as well. The village head didn't dare to report this to an official. All he could do was gather the clan elders to discuss it together. An elder skilled in addressing gods and spirits performed a ritual in the memorial hall and was possessed by an ancestor of the Tian clan. The "ancestor" said that the villagers had been moved to evil designs by the sight of riches and committed murder. The soul of the unjustly dead victim was restless and had become a fierce ghost demanding lives in recompense. This was a punishment from heaven. The evildoers must atone for their crime, and their accomplices must calm the resentment.

This talk of supernatural retribution was just enough to fool the panicked villagers. The village head ordered a sacrifice to be prepared, then collected some villagers to have the killers who had fallen ill lifted onto festooned carts. Following the ancient ritual of offering sacrifices to the River God, they threw the guilty men into the water in order to calm the resentment of the murdered Daoist priest.

After this sacrifice was performed, there still fear remaining in the villagers' hearts. They gritted their teeth and tossed the inauspicious autumn night white into the river as well, thinking that this ought to calm the storm. But not long after, yet another villager developed identical symptoms!

The spirit of the murdered man at the bottom of the river had not yet let them off the hook.

One wrong step was followed by many wrong steps. In order to correct their error, the villagers had already made more unforgivable errors. They were all grasshoppers tied to the same string. No one had better think of hopping along.

This village that was like a paradise henceforth became an abyss of suffering. Every time a person developed symptoms of the illness, they would be thrown into the river by the villagers. Day after day, the river was like an enormous maw that would never be satisfied. Sooner or later, it would swallow them all, until there was almost nothing left.

Between heaven and earth, the night was boundless. Only in this abandoned temple was there a bit of precious firelight.

Fu Shen didn't speak for a long time. Yan Xiaohan remembered the bolt of heavenly lightning that had struck the divine statue. Perhaps there really was some obscure heavenly will guiding them. If not for that bolt of lightning, they would have gone directly to Jingzhou after resting at the fox immortal temple and wouldn't have lingered in this little village; they certainly wouldn't have discovered the secret that the whole village was keeping stoppered up like a bottle.

In the legend concerning the fox immortal temple, the fox had incurred the wrath of heaven by predicting a flood. So this time, could it have been the fox giving another warning, sending them to find the truth, avert the monstrous tide that was drawing near?

"There was never any fierce ghost demanding lives in recompense. It's a plague. Perhaps it was because the murderers all touched that Daoist's blood that they contracted the same illness, then infected other people in the town," Fu Shen said coldly. "This is the cycle of cause and effect. A disaster one brings onto oneself cannot be survived."

"Your husband's illness is already beyond remedy by medicine," Yan Xiaohan said to Mrs. Ou. "All that remains is for him to die. You probably have many years left to live. With such a major case in Xishan Village, when the local official comes to investigate, no one will get away. But since you have encountered the two of us, we can make an exception and permit you to seek your own means of living. What do you think about that?"

Mrs. Ou lay prostrate, weeping. "My husband and I were each other's first marriage and have lived in loving kindness for many years. How can it be broken off just like that? I hope my benefactors will be generous."

Fu Shen pitied her and was about to make a promise when he was stopped by a look from Yan Xiaohan. "His illness is infectious. However pitiful, we still can't allow him to leave alive."

He didn't keep his voice low. Mrs. Ou heard him perfectly. She was utterly devastated, but in the end she couldn't persuade the stone-hearted Feilong Guard. She was dragged out by Fu Shen and watched as Yan Xiaohan found dry wood for kindling and spread it out. Shortly, thick smoke was rising into the sky. The fox immortal temple had become a sea of flame.

Mrs. Ou knelt blankly on the ground. Her tears were already dry. The rims of her eyes were bright red, but she couldn't shed another tear.

Fu Shen gave her a fairly weighty purse and calmly said, "Your road is still long. Go somewhere else and get married again to a good man. One day you'll be able to forget him."

Having said this, he turned and walked into the boundless night with Yan Xiaohan.

Mrs. Ou clutched the purse in her hand. Her eyes reflected the golden red flames. After a long time, she whispered an answer: "I can't forget…"

How could there be a rest of her life after such calamity? In this world, it was the one who went first who wouldn't look back, and the one left behind who was most to be pitied.

CHAPTER FIFTY-SEVEN

THEY DIDN'T SPEAK AT ALL ON THE RETURN TRIP.

They returned to the inn, closed the door and lit the lamp. Fu Shen sat in a chair after bathing, staring blankly into space. Yan Xiaohan only came out when quite a while had passed and hugged him from behind, putting his chin on the wet top of his head. Quietly, he asked, "Feeling unhappy?"

Fu Shen loosely encircled his fingers, feeling so frustrated that his hair was about to start falling out. "What do you call this? I didn't do the deed, but the responsibility is still mine."

Yan Xiaohan hummed in agreement.

Fu Shen waited for him to continue, but no matter how long he waited, nothing came. He couldn't resist lifting his face slightly. "Don't you have something to say?"

"What do you think I'm going to say?" Yan Xiaohan answered languidly.

"Say that I'm softhearted," said Fu Shen, "snatching up blame, always taking everything onto myself, that kind of thing."

Yan Xiaohan laughed quietly and said, "Since you already know, why would I need to add anything? That's not what I wanted to say."

"Then what did you want to say?" said Fu Shen.

"This isn't the capital, there's no Marquis of Jingning Manor for you to draw on." Gleefully, Yan Xiaohan said, "When the Lord Marquis was being so generous, only thinking of kindness and charity, I suppose you didn't remember that that was all the money for traveling expenses you had brought along?"

Fu Shen was brought up short.

He really hadn't remembered!

"No amount of money will stand up to this kind of spending. As the proverb rightly says, 'the lack of a bit of money can take down even a hero.'" Yan Xiaohan sighed affectedly. "However, your pocket change must be worth all I have. Presumably you won't have to bend and scrape over a few dozen pounds of rice, right?"

Fu Shen narrowed his eyes, looking murderous. "Feeling fractious again?"

"Times have changed," Yan Xiaohan said unhurriedly. "Glaring at me won't work now. You'd be better off begging me. Maybe I'd be willing to lend you a bit?"

Fu Shen might be said to have lived the experience of Master Dongguo nearly being eaten by the wolf he had helped hide, and the ungrateful wolf in question was smiling like a fox demon. Yan Xiaohan drew close to his ear and gently kissed him, enticingly saying, "Or perhaps the Lord Marquis can sell his body…"

"I don't sell." Fu Shen's fingers rolled up a drooping strand of his hair. He turned his head to touch his lips. "I only take valuables by coercion."

Yan Xiaohan sighed, seeming very distressed. He bent down to pick him up and walked to the bedside. A little helplessly, he said, "Then you can take sex by coercion, too, while you're at it."

Only when the sky began to brighten did the gasps inside the bed curtains at last gradually quiet. Fu Shen was so tired he fell asleep the moment he put his head down. His last thought before he sank into the land of dreams was to suspect that he had left his brain behind in the fox immortal temple.

Taking sex by coercion? In the end, hadn't it still been Yan

Xiaohan taking advantage of him? How was this any different from selling his body?!

They had stayed up too late romping the night before. The next day, Yan Xiaohan for once slept in along with Fu Shen. When he opened his eyes, Fu Shen still hadn't woken up. Sound asleep, he looked a little more docile than usual, and his body was soft, making it impossible for idle hands to resist wanting to pinch his cheeks. Yan Xiaohan stared at him for a while, but he still didn't wake up. His vigilance had declined sharply; it was evident that he was truly exhausted.

Making allowances for how hard he had worked, Yan Xiaohan held off and didn't tease him. He quietly got up and washed, then went out. First he went to Kuangfeng County's money shop to send word to Prince Qi and arrange to meet in Jingzhou, then drew some money from the cashier and filled up another purse.

On the way back to the inn, there was a whole street selling breakfast. Yan Xiaohan went through it picking and choosing and bought some food, which was still warm when he brought it back to the inn. Fu Shen was awoken by the aroma of meat buns. Blearily, he sat up hugging the quilt. "Menggui?"

"Mhm." Yan Xiaohan ladled out a bowl of hot water and sat on the bed to wipe his face. "You're getting up late today, so eat a little something to fill your stomach, then have lunch a little later."

Fu Shen leaned dizzily against him, the warmth of the bedding still on him. Hoarsely, he said, "Did you go to the money shop?"

Yan Xiaohan's hands didn't stop moving. "Yes. How did you guess?"

Fu Shen laughed wearily. "You reek of riches."

Yan Xiaohan deliberately got up to mischief, reaching into the quilt to rub a certain unspeakable place. "What's this about? You've just woken up, and I see you haven't put your tail away yet…"

The two of them fooled around for a while. Fu Shen at last woke up from his daze, got cleaned up properly, and sat at the table to eat breakfast. In the capital, in front of all the servants, they each kept up a proper attitude of "silence at meals, quiet in bed." Now that it was only the two of them, they weren't so mired in etiquette. Fu Shen swallowed a mouthful of porridge and said, "When are you planning to go meet Prince Qi?"

Yan Xiaohan gave him a peeled salted duck egg. "Tomorrow. With the matter of Xishan Village resolved, our assignment has been halfway accomplished. The rest will depend on how the local official deals with it. What about you? Are you going with me, or returning to the capital?"

Fu Shen brought down his chopsticks and pricked the egg, coming up with clear oil. At Yan Xiaohan's words, he raised his eyebrows and asked in turn, "Lord Yan, am I a family member you're taking along on assignment outside the capital?"

"Aren't you?" Yan Xiaohan lost no opportunity to show off his status. With emphasis, he said, "You really are a 'family member.'"

This manner was a far cry from his usual one, earnest to the point of foolishness and also a little cute. Fu Shen's heart softened. "Fine, master, I've even thrown away my mask, I certainly can't go see them like this. Why don't you hide me in your purse and carry me to Jingzhou?"

As soon as Yan Xiaohan heard his mocking tone, he knew there was no chance. Grumbling, he said, "You have to see things through. My craving hasn't healed yet, and you already want to leave."

"Do I owe you anything more?" Fu Shen said. "It's already good of me to be treating it for you. Anyway, your craving is already under control, it won't get better. All you can do is pout and sulk."

While his tone was chiding, his doting and tolerance were evident at a glance. This enumeration of his wrongs made Yan Xiaohan feel wonderful. He stopped pretending to feel aggrieved. Knowing himself to be very understanding and considered, he asked, "Then where are you going next? Back to Beiyan?"

"On the day of Daoist Chunyang's execution, I said that I was planning to start my investigation in Xinan," Fu Shen said. "Since I've come all this way, I'll go have a look while I'm here."

Yan Xiaohan immediately became nervous and said categorically, "That won't do. If Xinan really is the source of autumn night white, it's too dangerous for you to charge in single-handed."

Fu Shen said, "When we talked about what happened last summer, I thought later that while His Majesty was obviously targeting the Beiyan Cavalry at the time, it was also a not inconsiderable warning for armed forces everywhere. Xinan has been a law unto itself for many years, and it has a commandery prince who doesn't belong to the royal family, who is also a former subordinate of Beiyan. In that way, it would make sense to view autumn night white as Xinan's retaliation against the court. On this point, he and I are in the same boat. He won't do anything to me. There is no need for concern."

As soon as Fu Shen made a decision, he would only give a token notice; he had no intention of discussing it with anyone. Yan Xiaohan knew his temperament and had a profound feeling of the arm being unable to persuade the leg. There was nothing else he could do. He had to agree. "As for what to do in the capital, have you already made arrangements?"

"I claimed to be convalescing and found someone to pretend to be me." Fu Shen crooked his lips calmly. "I figure His Majesty doesn't have time to attend to me now. He's ill."

The next day, the two of them packed up their dry provisions and traveling money and left the inn. They sped off in the direction of Jingzhou, riding abreast.

Fu Shen was heading to Xinan, continuing west after parting with Yan Xiaohan outside Jingzhou City, while Yan Xiaohan rode into the city alone and went straight to the official post station where Prince Qi was staying.

The two met again and benefited from each other's assistance. During his days in Kuangfeng County, Yan Xiaohan had suffered quite a bit of torment from autumn night white and lost a considerable amount of weight. As soon as Prince Qi saw his haggard look, he knew he hadn't been lying. Hearing him tell the story of Xishan Village and describe all the appalling miseries, he was involuntarily filled with righteous indignation. He banged on the table and jumped to his feet. "Living people sacrificed to ghosts... How can such daring ignorant masses exist in this empire?!"

Yan Xiaohan said, "The disastrous consequences of autumn night white are endless. It isn't only the case in Xishan Village, the shortfall of grain taxes in Jingchu is also connected to it. The local official has been aware of it and hasn't reported on it. The common people have abandoned their fields to plant this drug. Your Highness ought to use this case as an opportunity to clear the air, prohibit autumn night white."

Prince Qi and his party also hadn't been idle during their days in Jingchu. He was already aware of everything Yan Xiaohan was saying; all he had been missing was the firecracker wick of Xishan Village. As soon as this case was reported to the court and began to get settled, the officials of Jingchu were bound to be mopped up and left in disorder.

Before they had left the capital, the empress had been ordered to commit suicide, and the crown prince had fallen out of favor. And the crown princess Lady Cen's father was the military commissioner of Jingchu, Cen Hongfeng. It could be gathered that after the Jingzhou case, the crown prince being removed from his position would be a foregone conclusion.

Prince Qi immediately summoned Jingzhou's prefect to come see him. Reporting above and transmitting down, the case of Xishan Village was all wrapped up that same night. All the villagers were taken under escort to Kuangfeng County's Yamen to be interrogated. The Kuangfeng County magistrates had been lax in their jurisdiction; they might not be able to keep their own positions. For the sake of accounting for himself in front of Prince Qi, Jingzhou's prefect didn't dare to let them perform interrogations behind closed doors, so he made bold to ask Prince Qi and the group of Feilong Guards he had brought with him to cooperate with Jingzhou's officials and listen in on the hearings.

Prince Qi was just in a temper. He also wanted to personally watch the evildoers being put to death. Yan Xiaohan was concerned that there would still be sick people among the villagers and afraid something would go wrong, so he gave a few words of tactful advice. But Prince Qi had made up his mind and steeled his heart. He insisted on going in person. There was nothing Yan Xiaohan could do. He could only return to Kuangfeng County alongside him.

When they left the official post station, there had happened to be many pedestrians outside, all making a racket. While the guards fell into formation, Yan Xiaohan turned his back to the street and suddenly felt someone gently bump into him from behind.

His first thought was that this was a thief. He automatically reached back to arrest them, but came up empty. Next, a small purse fell into his hand. A low, close voice said behind him, "Your Honor, you dropped something."

Yan Xiaohan whipped his head around, nearly twisting his neck.

This person was dressed all in black, wearing a bamboo hat on his head that hid the upper half of his face, revealing only a smooth, gaunt chin and neck. Seeing Yan Xiaohan look his way, the corners of his lips rose slightly in a smile. He didn't say anything else, only discreetly withdrew back into the crowd. In the blink of an eye, he was gone without a trace.

Yan Xiaohan was taken aback.

"Your Honor." A subordinate's voice brought him back to his senses. "We can set out now."

Yan Xiaohan was distracted. He casually nodded and agreed, then leapt onto his horse. On the way, he quietly opened the little purse and had a look. Inside, the bag was full of glittering and translucent osmanthus candy.

Hadn't he gone to Xinan?!

In broad daylight, with everyone watching, the mighty Marquis of Jingning had taken part in this kind of illicit hand-off. It honestly—

It honestly… made one hardly know how best to love him.

CHAPTER FIFTY-EIGHT

ON THE PUBLIC ROAD FROM JINGZHOU TO KUIZHOU, A SKINNY horse was traveling at a steady pace. The man on the horse was wearing a bamboo hat to protect him from the sun, watching the scenery in boredom as he tossed sweet and crispy sesame pastries into his mouth.

Soon, a whole bag of sesame pastries was gone. He took a pot of water from his saddlebag and gulped down several big mouthfuls. Disdainfully, he clicked his tongue. "What the hell are these? Sickeningly sweet."

This was Fu Shen.

Two days ago, after parting ways with Yan Xiaohan outside of Jingzhou City, he had gone two li away, then deliberately turned back, just so he could tease him outside the gate of the post station. While buying the osmanthus candy, he'd happened to see sesame pastries next to them, so, his interest aroused, he had bought a bag, planning to eat them as a snack on the road.

Thinking about it now, he had no especial fondness for sweets. He might go three to five months without eating a piece of candy. He had bought the sesame pastries purely because his brain had been addled by the fragrance of the osmanthus candy.

The trip from Jingzhou to Kuizhou, which was at the center

of Xinan, wasn't long. At top speed, it would only take three days. But Fu Shen traveled for six days. It had been years since he had been so free from concerns, slowly traveling the world at liberty. Though Fu Shen was still young, he had spent close to half his lifetime being pushed beyond his capacity, busy and bustling, commanding battles and death. Never mind pretty wives and beautiful mistresses, he hadn't even come home once a year.

The Jingzhou trip had changed both him and Yan Xiaohan considerably. Perhaps it was because each had at last found somewhere to place his trust, somewhere to belong, understood that in this lengthy passage through the mundane world, he wasn't alone walking a solitary path.

Sometimes in tea shops and public houses in villages and towns along the road, Fu Shen heard some news from Jingzhou, such as that after the Xishan Village case had been discovered, the local officials had sent people to dredge the lake, and they had come up with a dozen bodies. It was said that neither insects nor fish lived in that lake, only a kind of aquatic plant that could grow wildly obtaining its nutrients from corpses. It had wrapped the bodies up tightly so they floated in the water, like a corpse forest that never saw the light of day.

There were also people who said that the imperial envoy who had come from the capital had run into heavy rain on the road and stayed the night at a fox immortal temple. Suddenly, a little fox entered his dreams and spoke in a human tongue, recounting grievances. When the imperial envoy woke, he marveled greatly and sought out Xishan Village according to what the fox had said, unearthing a major case.

Listening to this, Fu Shen laughed to himself, thinking, *"What the fox said?"* Wasn't it more like *"what the bull shat?"*

Most likely some storyteller in Jingzhou City had seen that there was a fox immortal temple beside the lake and applied a strained interpretation, casually making something up.

The "storyteller" Yan Xiaohan couldn't take being thought

about like this; he turned his head away and sneezed. The tip of his brush shook, leaving an ink blot on the snow-white paper. His halfway written memorial to the throne was completely ruined.

He tossed away the memorial and switched to a new sheet of paper. Jingzhou's prefect had moved quickly enough. In six days, he had just about finished investigating the case and presented a dossier of confessions, testimony, and material evidence to the Ministry of Justice, so they could determine the sentences. In about two days it would reach the capital. He had obscured Fu Shen's role in the memorial, only mentioning that they had nearly been struck by lightning in the fox immortal temple, and had therefore by chance ended up in Xishan Village. Yan Xiaohan had heard the legend of the fox immortal temple, so after sending off Prince Qi, he had returned to Xishan Village to investigate. Though he had been dosed with autumn night white, he had managed by good fortune to escape alive. In short, owing entirely to the protection of heaven, they had finally succeeded in discovering the truth and causing the murderers and evildoers to be put to death.

When he was finished unflappably making things up, Lord Yan ordered a subordinate to send the memorial to the capital. Prince Qi must also have had a memorial to send, but because the Imperial Investigator had the right to have his memorials come directly before the emperor, the two of them wouldn't be using the same channel, and Yan Xiaohan didn't go find out.

He went to the window and looked out at the shade of trees everywhere. He slowly let out a long breath. He felt his hands shaking again, so he took a piece of candy from the purse and pressed it beneath his tongue.

The refreshing sweetness of osmanthus flavor spread. Perhaps because of the influence of the craving, he thought that he had never missed a person so much, missed him so much that it made his heart ache.

They had only been apart for six days.

Fu Shen had once again demonstrated his surpassing foresight. Yan Xiaohan's craving had yet to completely subside. Though it wasn't serious, once Fu Shen left and he lost his support, enduring the craving when it flared up suddenly became difficult. Fortunately he still had that bag of osmanthus candy, which gave him a bit of consolation. Yan Xiaohan developed a habit of subduing the craving with candy, but for a body that had tasted true delights, this was no different from a cup of water tossed on a flaming cart. The physical suffering and spiritual suffering combined. Sometimes he wanted nothing more than to cast Prince Qi aside and go alone in pursuit to Xinan.

If only the case here in Jingzhou wrapped up soon, when he returned to the capital, he might be able to find another assignment and go to Xinan.

The thought was a nice one, but bitter reality told him: keep dreaming.

Within a couple of days, a special envoy from the capital arrived in Jingzhou with an imperial edict, first stripping the prefect, county magistrates, and all the other officials of their officials' black gauze caps, leaving them to await punishment, then ordering the chief culprits from Xishan Village to be sent under escort to the capital. Finally, there was a special edict directed to Prince Qi and Yan Xiaohan in particular.

Starting in the third month, white dew powder had turned up again and again, leading to a series of terrible disasters. First it was the capital, and then it was Jingzhou. Back during the Jinwu Guard case, Yan Xiaohan had already sent up a memorial to the throne, asking the emperor to order a strict investigation into white dew powder throughout the country in order to prevent future trouble; he hadn't expected his words to become a prophecy.

Emperor Yuantai's illness had not yet made him senile. Autumn night white had already spread unchecked to the point of impacting the grain taxes in Jingchu. East of Jingchu was the area of Huguang, Jiangnan, and Jiangxi, the granary of the empire, important locations for government revenue. If this was allowed to continue and these places suffered from this murderous scheme, instability would spread to the whole nation. Therefore, Emperor Yuantai had issued another decree, ordering Prince Qi and Yan Xiaohan not to return to the capital after completing this assignment but to follow the Yangtze River east, make an inspection tour of the area of Jiangnan, be sure to eliminate any lurking threat from autumn night white; he granted them freedom to act expediently to meet emergencies, cut first and report later.

Like a snow-bright flash of lightning in midair, the unexpected blow fell. Lord Yan's tattered wishes whirled and scattered in Jingzhou's warm spring breezes along with his tears.

Xinan, Kuizhou.

Riding his skinny horse, Fu Shen slowly entered the city. Here, Han people lived in large part together with Miao, Bai, and other such peoples; the scenery and style was very different from the Central Plains. Fu Shen had previously come up with many methods for going to see Commandery Prince Xiping, but when he got to the main gate of the prince's manor, he tossed all his previous ideas to the back of his head and boldly walked up to the porter. Putting a hand to his bamboo hat, he lowered his head slightly and said, "Please convey that I request to see Commandery Prince Xiping."

As the proverb says, the prime minister's door warden is self-important enough to be a petty official. While the Commandery Prince Manor's porter wasn't even as snobbish as a watchdog in the capital, Fu Shen had a poverty-stricken look and was hiding his face with a bamboo hat. He didn't look like he was in any position to be in contact with their master. The porter raised his eyelids indifferently and extended a hand. "Calling card," he said.

Fu Shen had seen plenty of servants like this. He tipped a

fragment of silver out of his purse and put it into the porter's coarse palm. Smiling, he said, "I have no calling card. Just say that Beiyan Army Doctor Du Leng has come to pay a visit."

The porter weighed the silver in his hand. Happiness flashed over his face. His manner was still haughty, but his tone had relaxed. "Wait here a moment, I'll go notify His Highness."

Not long after, the porter returned with a tense look. This time, he didn't dare to make a peep. Bowing and scraping, he asked Fu Shen to come inside, leading him into the main courtyard's west drawing room.

There was already someone waiting for him inside. Commandery Prince Xiping, Duan Guihong, was nearly fifty, but well preserved, his figure slender and vigorous, his visage still what it had been in the prime of life. Staring at this black-clothed man wearing a bamboo hat, his slanting brows came together slightly. Doubtfully, he said, "Who are you?"

Fu Shen took off the bamboo hat, revealing his face, and smiled politely and sincerely at him. "I have taken the liberty of disturbing you. Please do not take offense, Your Highness."

Duan Guihong was silent.

First, he froze. Then he immediately dismissed all the servants and tightly shut the doors and windows. His brows had nearly tied themselves into a fast knot. "General Fu has suddenly graced my humble abode with his presence. I wonder what valuable instruction you wish to impart?"

"No valuable instruction." Fu Shen familiarly pulled up a chair and sat down. "Don't be such a stranger, Your Highness, you're a family elder for me. You can address me by my courtesy name."

Duan Guihong's gaze traveled down, staring fixedly at his legs. "Weren't... Jingyuan, weren't you in the capital convalescing? What brings you to Xinan?"

Fu Shen picked up his hems and showed him his boots. Carelessly, he said, "The wounds are nearly healed. As for what I'm doing here, wouldn't you know that better than me?"

Duan Guihong's eyes grew cold. His whole bearing was reserved and dignified. When he clashed with Fu Shen, neither of them yielded one bit. He coldly said, "What are you saying?"

"Oh, that's not right, Your Highness probably only knows about me being in Jingzhou." Fu Shen slapped his thigh. "Would you look at this memory of mine? I only told Du Leng that I was going to Jingzhou to find Yan Xiaohan. I forgot to tell him that I was also going to stop in at Kuizhou on the way."

Smiling, he continued, "How about it? Your Highness doesn't seem very fond of me."

Duan Guihong was briefly silent. Seeming to abandon his feigned civility, he got straight to the point and asked, "When did you find out?"

The smile on Fu Shen's face did not alter, but the smile in his eyes was entirely gone. There was even an imperceptible chill in his voice. "I've found out quite a lot. What does Your Highness mean? Is it planting Du Leng beside me, or sending Daoist Chunyang to assassinate His Majesty at the Vast Longevity Feast?

"Or is it perhaps deliberately spreading autumn night white in Jingchu, planning to flip the game board, throw the whole area of Jiangnan into total chaos?"

Each and every word he spoke was like a sword leaving its sheath, ruthlessly stabbing at Duan Guihong's taciturn and tolerant bottom line.

Commandery Prince Xiping had commanded troops for many years. His disposition was resolute and serious. Though he had developed a bit of self-restraint in recent years, even that depended on whom he was facing, yet Fu Shen still seemed completely indifferent, recklessly determined to pluck the tiger's whiskers.

Gritting his back molars, Duan Guihong said, "Fu Shen, aren't you afraid… that you won't walk out this door today?"

"Would you look at that? What a coincidence. I wasn't planning on walking out this door today," Fu Shen said boldly, confident that right was on his side. "I came to Kuizhou alone with limited traveling money, and I was just worrying about having no place to stay and planning to stay some nights in your distinguished home. Would Your Highness permit it?"

Duan Guihong didn't answer.

Everything he said was choked off by Fu Shen. Though Fu Shen hadn't come as an enemy, he still felt like he was about to faint. When he had managed to even out his breathing, Duan Guihong, trying to be even-tempered and good-humored, said, "Since you know about all of that, you must also understand that I don't want to harm you."

"Naturally," said Fu Shen. "Otherwise I wouldn't be here today."

Duan Guihong's expression relaxed slightly. He sat down across from him. "Compared to everything the emperor has done to the Beiyan Cavalry, what I have done is only a drop in the ocean."

"The Beiyan commander is sitting in front of you," Fu Shen said coldly. "Though I've been lamed, I'm not dead yet. Your Highness, you want to take revenge on behalf of the Beiyan Army, but have you asked what I want?"

CHAPTER FIFTY-NINE

Fu Shen turned nasty just like that, the hit taking Duan Guihong unawares. Commandery Prince Xiping's expression, having just eased, immediately became fixed on his face. After a long time, he finally suppressed the urge to throttle Fu Shen to death on the spot and said with a snort, "When I was serving in the Beiyan Army, you were still an unweaned infant."

Fu Shen returned the compliment: "When I took over the Beiyan Army, you had already been breeding fish in Xinan for many years."

Their gazes clashed, and sparks flew in all directions. In an identical movement, they tossed their heads, inwardly spitting on the other at the same time.

Little hellion with an exaggerated opinion of himself, thought Duan Guihong.

Old fool trying to exploit his seniority, thought Fu Shen.

Only at times like these did Yan Xiaohan's worth become clear. When two foul-tempered people were steadfastly unwilling to give way, they needed a smooth-talking person to brush aside the conflict for them and let the conversation continue.

Unfortunately, Yan Xiaohan wasn't here.

Fu Shen inhaled and exhaled silently, calming his anger,

repeatedly telling himself that he had come in search of the truth. He couldn't waste time getting angry at a stubborn and bossy old geezer. Finally he turned his face back and afforded him a narrow step to get a foothold on. "Your Highness's feelings for the Beiyan Army are profound, a very rare thing to come by."

Panting with rage, Duan Guihong took advantage of this opening and said, "The Beiyan Cavalry was built by me and people like me. According to generational ranking, you ought to be calling me 'uncle.'"

Fu Shen cursed inwardly. *Old fool, trying for every scrap of ground you can get*, he thought bitterly.

Aloud, however, he dryly said, "I see. I'd heard that you were like brothers with my late father and uncle."

But Duan Guihong shook his head. "No."

"Hm?" said Fu Shen.

"The generational ranking I'm talking about starts from your grandfather, the former Duke of Ying." Duan Guigong's voice softened. "During the time of the late emperor, Duke Fu served as military commissioner of Lingnan. He received orders to pacify the rebellion of the Baiyue people of Lingnan. Later, when the court's troops had won an overwhelming victory and Duke Fu led people in cleaning up the rebel forces, he found among the disordered troops a young child. According to the court's usual practices, all Baiyue rebel soldiers were captured, the adults killed on the spot and the boys under ten castrated and sent to be slaves in the palace.

"The child that General Fu captured happened to be exactly ten years old, unusually thin and weak. General Fu pitied him, and his compassion was stirred. He couldn't bear to let the child die by the sword, so he made an exception and left him alive, releasing him to make his own way."

At this point, Fu Shen could already faintly guess what would follow.

Duan Guihong saw this and candidly acknowledged, "My birth name was Feng Yi. I was of the Baiyue people. I was rescued by Duke Fu and narrowly escaped death. At fifteen I changed my name and enlisted among General Fu's troops, waited upon him, charged the enemy lines. Duke Fu saw me as his own son and took special care to promote and educate me. In the second year of Yuantai, when the Tartars and the Zhe invaded the border, Duke Fu was transferred and became the military commissioner of Ganzhou, and I followed him there and led troops, galloped across the grasslands, and fought back the enemy with Bocun and Zhongyan."

Bocun was Fu Tingzhong's courtesy name, and Zhongyan was Fu Tingxin's.

"In the fifth year of Yuantai, when Duke Fu passed away into the West, it happened to coincide with unrest in Xinan. Before his passing, he submitted a memorial to the throne, electing me as commander-in-chief of the Western Expeditionary Army, to lead the army to pacify Xinan." With a sigh Duan Guihong said, "I did not dare to fail a deathbed request. I have stood guard in Xinan ever since, not taking a step out. Only last summer, when His Majesty conceived the design of sending military supervisors to all the troops guarding the borders, and then soon after you were ambushed in the Qingsha Gap, did I finally understand that today's court was no longer the court it had once been."

"Your Highness," Fu Shen said, interrupting him, "Du Leng entered the Beiyan Army two years ago, and moreover, my guess is that he is not your only spy in the Beiyan Army. You say that you only started getting ideas last summer—isn't that a little late?"

The general opinion of Fu Shen was mostly that he was a hero skilled in making war, decisive in felling enemies. After hearing enough of opinions like this, sometimes it would make one think that while the Marquis of Jingling might be good at fighting, he was only a plain soldier, his mind perhaps not as lively and sophisticated as those of veteran bureaucrats; even if you couldn't win against him in battle, you could take him down by strategy.

Duan Guihong hadn't had much contact with Fu Shen, had only seen him once or twice. Most of his understanding of him came from hearsay and gossip. On top of that, he was getting older and always thinking that the younger generation hadn't yet grown up. Therefore, he had always underrated him somewhat.

But he had forgotten that Fu Shen had gone into battle leading troops at eighteen. Had he not been smart enough, had he lacked finesse, how could he have quelled the old generals and subordinates made overconfident by their long service records? Never mind dealing with foreign enemies, it would have been an issue for him to gain a firm foothold among his own people.

Fu Shen had over and over again exposed the flaws in his words, not showing this "uncle" any respect. Duan Guihong was forced into a corner by his incisive questions; he had nowhere to retreat to. He had finally stopped being contemptuous of him and gradually faced him squarely as an opponent equal to himself. "You've known for some time that Du Leng was one of my people?"

Fu Shen smiled modestly. "No, it hasn't been that long. However, he poses no threat, only occasionally passes along information, and his medical skills are all right, so I've kept him around."

An important official planting a spy beside the commander-in-chief of a military force elsewhere, however you looked at it, clearly had ulterior motives. If this had happened to someone else, it certainly wouldn't have ended well, but Fu Shen understood Duan Guihong's character; the old fool was only stubborn and inflexible. Du Leng had come to the Beiyan Army primarily to help him, so Fu Shen, playing dumb, had turned a blind eye, keeping Du Leng with him up to the present.

"Your Highness's spies in the north had two hubs, one Du Leng and the other Daoist Chunyang. After the ambush in the Qingsha Gap, presumably it was because Du Leng disclosed secret information that Daoist Chunyang was able to find that broken arrow ahead of my people. However it may be, I have to thank Your Highness for this."

Duan Guihong said, "Since you know that His Majesty fears you and even didn't stint to order your assassination, why did you save his life at the Vast Longevity Feast? Righteousness doesn't command business, gentleness doesn't command troops. Soft-heartedness will kill you sooner or later."

Fu Shen said with a sigh, "When I'm useful, I'm called a 'benevolent and virtuous commander,' and when I'm not useful, I'm called 'softhearted.' Whether I'm benevolent or gentle isn't something you can decide by flapping your lips."

"You brat!" Duan Guihong was suffocated by anger. Furiously, he said, "You are unworthy of being your father's son!"

These words had absolutely no power to harm Fu Shen. He carelessly agreed, "That's right, I'm really not like him."

Duan Guihong sat in a brief sullen silence, then suddenly said, "You aren't like your father. You're more like your Second Uncle, right?"

"Perhaps?" said Fu Shen.

"Didn't you come to ask me about autumn night white?" said Duan Guihong. "Fine, I'll tell you about something that happened in the past."

"I would like to hear more," said Fu Shen.

Duan Guihong spoke of an event that had taken place in the fourth year of Yuantai, during the battle between the Beiyan Army and the Eastern Tartars.

That autumn, Fu Tingxin was carelessly injured by the poisoned arrow of a Tartar assassin. The injury was a serious one and nearly killed him. The whole army was helpless at the time, and even the imperial physician brought in from the capital was powerless to assist. Fortunately, Ganzhou wasn't far from Yizhou, where the Western Tartars lived. The two sides had always had friendly dealings, and there was a Western Tartar itinerant doctor who had a slight friendship with Duan Guihong. From the view that "anything was worth trying in a desperate situation," Duan Guihong invited him to come examine Fu Tingxin.

The Eastern and Western Tartars had once been one people and had only been forced to split into two clans because of the tumult of war. The Western Tartar itinerant doctor Duan Guihong invited did indeed recognize this poison.

There was a green scorpion on the grasslands, extremely precious and rare, the stinger of which contained powerful poison, known as the "green moon." Though the itinerant doctor couldn't find the corresponding antidote, he had once seen a medicinal plant brought by traveling merchants from Arabia, with flowers pure white as snow, whose fruit when ground produced juice like cow's milk. The Arabs had used this medicine to cure a companion of theirs who had been stung by a poisonous scorpion in the desert. Acting as a go-between for Duan Guihong, he got in contact with an Arab merchant. After word passed among many people, Duan Guihong learned of that medicinal plant's name, and under the direction of the Arabs found the plant and its seeds in the south.

This medicinal plant that had saved Fu Tingxin's life was autumn night white.

Autumn night white was very peculiar. If you only ate the juice of its fruit, it could relieve pain and cure all kinds of snake and scorpion poisons, but the chances of becoming addicted were negligible; but if it was processed and inhaled, it would become the addictive "white dew powder." Moreover, people who took autumn night white long-term would suffer internal lesions, and a small minority of people would ultimately become infected with a sickness something like plague that couldn't be cured; they could only wait to die.

Even more frightening, as soon as this medicinal plant hit the ground and put down roots, not a blade of grass would grow in its vicinity. In the south, autumn night white always grew in cracks in stones, deep in the mountains. The locals viewed it as a poisonous weed. When they saw it, they would immediately cut it down and pull up its roots, then use fire to destroy it completely; only in this way could they prevent it from spreading on a large scale.

Duan Guihong said, "In the fifth year of Yuantai, after Zhongyan recovered, the Eastern Tartars' Alma tribe was completely destroyed."

Fu Shen's heart instantly skipped. He asked, "What do you mean, Your Highness?"

"Your Second Uncle wasn't as softhearted as you imagine," Duan Guihong said directly and callously. "Do you think that in order to be a leader of troops, it's enough to learn his mercy?"

Duan Guihong told him that after Fu Tingxin recovered, he asked for all the seeds Duan Guihong had collected and sent people to sneak into the pastures of the Alma tribe and sow a large quantity. Some months later, autumn night white sprouted and grew. The Alma tribe's pastures were ruined overnight, their sheep died in large numbers. Fu Tingxin also caught a group of Eastern Tartars and made them drink water mixed with infected blood, then released them to return to their tribe. Many Alma tribespeople became infected with plague because of this, and finally they were swept clean by the regrouped Beiyan Cavalry, ending in the destruction of the tribe.

Now this truly was a debt of blood being paid in blood.

"In the legends of the Tartars, the symbol of plague is the 'inconstant plant.' That refers to autumn night white." Coldly, Duan Guihong said, "Do you know now why the Tartars hate the Fu family so deeply?"

This particular segment of history hadn't spread very widely. First, this was because it concerned confidential information. Second, it harmed the peace of heaven, so even the official historians didn't dare to record it. Fu Shen had had dealings with the Eastern Tartars for many years; he had heard of the "inconstant plant." He had thought it was only a legend, a folk tale. He hadn't thought that such a thing actually existed.

In the territory of the Alma tribe, a fire burned for several days and nights. The swaying flowers of the "inconstant plant" were swallowed by the flames, but its shadow over the grasslands remained forever.

Duan Guihong said, "When the Arabs first discovered this plant, they called it 'duaar,' the meaning of which is 'daze.' And in the local language of the south, its name is 'Sanevo,' which means—

"The God of Sleeping Death."

Chapter Sixty

Sighing with emotion, Fu Shen said, "What a sin."

A general's reputation was built upon ten thousand corpses. Behind the portrait of the hero hanging high in Qilin Palace upon Golden Terrace, flickering flames leapt, and countless souls of the dead wailed in anguish.

Duan Guihong nearly fell over in anger at Fu Shen's ill-breeding. Furiously, he said, "When two armies face each other in battle, one must die for the other to live. You pity them? Why not think of the innocent common people who died unjustly at the hands of the Tartar?! With your softheartedness, how can you possibly accomplish great things in the future?"

"Oh?" Fu Shen drawled. In an even tone, he said, "Protecting my home and my country, attacking no one unless they attack me—isn't that enough? What great things is Your Highness speaking of?"

"You!" Duan Guihong was at a loss for words. Shortly, pointing at his nose in frustration, he scolded, "You were cast aside as soon as you had served your purpose. His Majesty wanted nothing better than for you to die in the Qingsha Gap. Yet you still want to defend the border for him? Even entrenching yourself in place and making yourself king would be better than being subject to his whims, don't you understand?!"

"Entrench yourself in place and make yourself king," Fu Shen repeated thoughtfully. "Just like Your Highness."

There was no question in his words this time. He continued straightforwardly: "Xinan is far from the emperor and the capital, with people of all ethnicities living side by side, their loyalty to the central government limited. You have been operating in Xinan for many years and have put down deep roots. Even if His Majesty sent people to control you, it would be easy for you to undermine them. In Kuizhou City, among the shops and public houses along the streets, traveling traders of other nations like Annam, Zhenla[1], and so forth are common. I suppose that Xinan's income from trade with foreign nations in recent years has been more than enough to supply Xinan's troops?"

Duan Guihong's expression became slightly concerned.

"Never mind that you also had that god of whatever death in your hands, a business that lets you make big profits from a small investment." Not without sarcasm, Fu Shen said, "If you really did set up shop in Jiangnan, the money would run against the current of the Yangtze River into your honored pockets. Never mind making yourself king, when the time came, if you wanted to make yourself emperor, there would still be no one to stop you."

"A pack of nonsense," Duan Guihong said coldly.

Fu Shen seemed to be well informed, but actually he was on perilously thin ice. He knew that in his role as an elder, Duan Guihong wouldn't fight him, but the business of autumn night white made him feel that Commandery Prince Xiping was a little nefarious. Fu Shen also couldn't work out what exactly he wanted. If he wanted to stage a rebellion and would insist on dragging Fu Shen down with him, this matter would be hard to handle.

Fu Shen considered, then said, "Earlier, Your Highness told me about past events on the grasslands, said that my Second

Uncle once used that whatever god of death to destroy the whole Alma tribe. Why is it that when he was defending Yanzhou later, he didn't use the same move against the Zhe?"

This question stumped Duan Guihong. Only after a brief hesitation did he say, "When Zhongyan was in Beiyan, I was in Xinan. I am not aware."

Fu Shen nodded, understanding. "Oh, I see, because you *were in Xinan.*"

Duan Guihong sensed a kind of veiled hint in his deliberate repetition. Instantly, he had a feeling of prickles running down his back. All his muscles tensed.

"I see that Your Highness has wasted this time on me here without saying a single word of truth." Fu Shen shook his head. It was unclear whom he was mocking. "Since you won't put your cards on the table, I'll lay out the details for you.

"My late father and late uncle passed away when I was young. Before I had a chance to gain much experience following them in the army, I was pushed beyond my capabilities to go to war at the northern frontier. Your Highness says that I am an unworthy son of my father, and in fact that's true. I didn't grow up in imitation of him. Apart from a few superficial trifles I learned from my uncle, my temper and disposition came from those seven years I spent at the northern frontier."

Fu Shen stopped smiling. "So, Your Highness, don't think that listening to a story will turn me into the 'Fu family member' you're hoping for. My hands have taken down uncountable barbarians. I know what profession I'm engaged in. I've never suffered from the delusion that I would be reincarnated into bliss when I died. If I ought to go to hell, then I will, and I've always thought the same for others. When men of courage and talent have a grievance to exercise, let only their two bodies fall and the blood splash no further than five steps around. So the saying goes, and that is enough. Whoever commits the sin suffers the retribution. Why drag in those who have nothing to do with it?"

"Because of his own selfish interests," said Duan Guihong,

"he harbors a grudge against loyal and upright subjects. Even if he suffers retribution, it will still not be enough to pay back for the sin he has committed."

Fu Shen didn't respond at once. He was briefly silent, then finally said with a quiet sigh, "Your Highness... what crime have the people committed?"

Duan Guihong was also silent.

When the emperor was enraged, a million bodies would fall, the blood would splash for a thousand li around—but what wrong had those million unjustly dead done?

The soldiers who had died in the Qingsha Gap, the commoners who had died at Daoist Chunyang's hands, the innocent people who had died in Xishan Village and Kuangfeng County because of autumn night white—why did they have to die?

When God was a little unhappy, it would result in droughts, floods, plagues of locusts, years of famine; when a person of high rank was a little unhappy, it would result in bones exposed in the wilderness, not a cock crowing for a thousand li around. Mere common people, who already had a hard time feeding their families and who had layer upon layer of rule over their heads, might work hard for half a lifetime only to meet with a slight unexpected disaster that would completely destroy their whole family.

When your life was valued, your rage would lead to a million bodies falling, blood splashing for a thousand li around; when your life was cheap, you would be one of those million.

Because of his lucky birth, Fu Shen hadn't become "one of a million," but neither did he want to become "one in a million." Between killing and being killed, he wanted to walk a third path.

"Jingyuan," Duan Guihong said suddenly.

This time he wasn't angry, wasn't reproachful. He calmly called Fu Shen's name, seeming to finally put away all pretense and revealing the cold interior beneath, solid as a boulder.

"'What crime have the people committed?' Your uncle also once said these words to me."

In the fourth year of Yuantai, Fu Tingxin was injured, and Duan Guihong found an antidote for him. While treating his poisoning, Duan Guihong also learned from the shamans in the south about the frightening properties of this plant. This just happened to coincide with a stalemate in the fighting at the border. The Han forces and the Tartar cavalry were deadlocked. Duan Guihong broke the stalemate with an ingeniously planned maneuver, then went to Fu Tingxin to deliberate, planning to use that medicinal plant to destroy the pastures of the Alma; combined with the plague, once their backyard was on fire, there would be no difficulty in delivering a resounding blow to the Tartars.

Fu Tingxin thought that this method was excessively cruel and sinister. He wouldn't agree no matter what. Duan Guihong went to Fu Jian, and was once again upbraided. Just when he had thought, after suffering repeated setbacks, that there was no way through by this road, Fu Tingzhong came to him and secretly finalized this plan with him.

In spring of that year, the Alma tribe's pastures were invaded by the wildly growing autumn night white. Instances of plague were frequent. The whole tribe sank into panic and tumult. Fu Tingzhong led troops in an attack, winning a major victory over the Eastern Tartar cavalry at Mount Daqing. The Han forces even penetrated deep into the interior of the grasslands and nearly conquered the Tartars' capital.

After this battle, when Duan Guihong was complacently showing off his accomplishments to Fu Tingxin, Fu Tingxin had only said, "What crime have the people committed?"

In autumn of the same year, in Ganzhou, Fu Jian fell critically ill, never to recover. During his illness, he sent a memorial to the court, recommending Duan Guihong to become commander of the Western Expeditionary Army and head for Xinan to put down rebellion.

To this day, many people believed that this move represented Fu Jian removing an outsider; they guessed that he had wanted to leave control of the Beiyan military forces to his sons. Only Duan Guihong himself knew that that day, when Fu Jian had called him to his sickbed, he had said that he was near death and ordered him to swear an oath before the bed that he would take autumn night white with him to Xinan and keep a close guard over it, not letting a single seed end up in the Central Plains.

Blank-faced, he had listened as Fu Jian said, "Peace in the empire, a hundred years of prosperity—it can be accomplished by your hand, or destroyed by your hand. While your surname is not Fu, in your bones, you are one of our family.

"I have campaigned throughout the four corners of the world, spent half my life in the saddle. I have only one wish that is still unfulfilled. I want to see peace in the world. Now... I entrust that wish to you."

The old general had given him a final order from his deathbed. Duan Guihong, holding back tears, had kowtowed three times before his sickbed. When they had sent off Fu Jian and everything was settled, he had gone to Xinan with the court's army.

Xinan had been at peace since the sixth year of Yuantai. He had stood guard for twenty years.

During those twenty years, Fu Tingzhong was assassinated by the Tartars, Fu Tingxin died in battle, and Fu Shen was charged with leadership in a crisis, leading troops to the northern frontier. Duan Guihong was in Xinan, but not for one day did he forget the withering grasses and yellow sands of the north.

In the first years after Fu Shen went to the northern frontier, Duan Guihong watched the war gradually calm, the north become peaceful. He had thought that at the end of over a decade of twists and turns, that "peace in the world" was about to be realized.

But later, he found that he had thought wrong. The Beiyan Cavalry had passed through three generations of the Fu family. Emperor Yuantai could stand it no longer.

The members of the Fu family all died young, but Emperor

Yuantai was a long-lived Emperor. He sat by and watched as generation after generation of the Fu family accepted the seal of commander-in-chief and went into battle. The Beiyan Army became more and more powerful, and its commanders younger and younger, but he was getting older and feebler. When he turned back to look at his sons and grandsons, there wasn't a single one with a talent for rule, fit to be the master of a generation of resurgence.

If this continued, in a decade, in two decades, would the empire still belong to the Sun family?

When Emperor Yuantai ordered Fu Tingyi to take over the title and changed Fu Shen's title to Marquis of Jingning, Duan Guihong sensed His Majesty's fear and wariness toward this new young commander of the Beiyan Cavalry.

When Emperor Yuantai and Fu Jian had been a sovereign and minister on good terms, it had been because the court had been in a precarious situation, and he had needed to rely on him in matters of war; the reason he had given extremely preferential treatment to Fu Tingzhong and Fu Tingxin had been because the two brothers had each other to rely on, and there was also Prince Su sticking his oar in; but the fact that he now dared to take action against Fu Shen again and again was purely because he was taking advantage of his youth and acquiescence, and the current Duke of Ying was a good-for-nothing who might sprout wings and ascend to heaven at any moment; if anything happened, he could do nothing to help.

Just in case, Duan Guihong had sent Du Leng to Fu Shen's side. As the emperor's attempts had become more and more obvious, Duan Guihong had finally lost hope in so-called "peace in the world." He had finally understood that as long as the imperial throne was occupied, the Fu family, as well as himself, could never struggle free of "fate."

The God of Sleeping Death that had been sealed in Xinan for twenty years was awakened by its guardian and had spread east from Jingchu following the river, falling upon the landscape of Jiangnan like a ghost and putting down roots, covering the earth in its pure white flowers.

Commandery Prince Xiping finished pouring out his mind. Slowly exhaling the pent-up staleness in his chest, he said, "I have misused what was entrusted to my care, profoundly betrayed the task entrusted to me. When I come to the Nine Springs of the Underworld, I will be too ashamed to see Duke Fu."

As the foremost Commandery Prince outside the imperial family, for the sake of an entrusted task that was like a mirage, he had guarded the western frontier for twenty years. Fu Shen knew very well that he had done many things wrong, but he was in no position to condemn him.

Just as Fu Tingxin had once said "What crime have the people committed?" to Duan Guihong, now that it was Fu Shen's turn, he also could say nothing but this.

Because he knew that he himself wasn't innocent.

Of the criminal charges people were most helpless against in this world, one was a "fabricated" one, one was "attracting envy by an excess of talent," and there was yet another one that was "I didn't do the deed, but I was still responsible."

Dejectedly, Fu Shen said, "I'm also too ashamed to see the old fellow. Why don't we go hang ourselves in front of his grave together?"

Duan Guihong ignored his ridicule. "Since our talk has turned to this, I ought to make everything clear. You know that I have been in Xinan, my reach limited. It has been difficult for me to organize large-scale forces in the capital. That Daoist Chunyang was able to find a firm foothold in the capital is entirely thanks to the repeated assistance of one person."

Fu Shen's heart sank. "Who?"

---

1. Respectively, these are a former kingdom in northern Vietnam and an old term for Cambodia.

CHAPTER SIXTY-ONE

DUAN GUIHONG WASN'T IN THE HABIT OF DRUMMING UP suspense. He said bluntly: "Fu Tingyi."

It was as if a mallet had fallen out of the sky and smashed the Marquis of Jingning into the ground. Fu Shen was completely poleaxed. Forgetting his manners, he raised his voice: "Who?"

He suspected that Duan Guihong was lying to him; otherwise, he had to be hallucinating.

"The Duke of Ying, your Third Uncle." Having finally managed to shock Fu Shen, Duan Guihong was inexplicably a little pleased with himself. "I suppose you weren't expecting that?"

Fu Tingyi, renowned in the capital as the useless Third Master, a little chicken that had flown out of a phoenix's nest, a middle-aged rich wastrel obsessed with cultivating immortality, stirring out of doors even less than the young mistress of a wealthy family. That he had yet to starve to death was entirely down to his lucky birth.

Even Fu Shen had no expectations of him, and however diverse the lines of thought of others might be, they still absolutely wouldn't have connected him to a major case that had shaken the whole capital.

"He… All these years he's spent cultivating immortality and practicing Daoism, has that all been a pretense while actually he's been in contact with you all along?"

Fu Shen might have been stunned, but his brain was still working. With a hint from Duan Guihong, he could tie the sequence of events into a rough outline. Qingxu Temple had quite a name for the efficacy of its practices in the capital, and Daoist arts were Fu Tingyi's hobby. His comings and goings from Qingxu Temple naturally wouldn't arouse anyone's suspicion. And whatever Daoist Chunyang needed in terms of white dew powder and smoking paraphernalia could all first be sent to Fu Tingyi, then handed over by him to Daoist Chunyang. As a Daoist priest, if Daoist Chunyang was always in contact with Xinan, it would be easy for him to be exposed, but for the Duke of Ying, this was nothing. No wonder that at the outset Yan Xiaohan and his people hadn't been able to find the source of the drug no matter what!

"Your Third Uncle has been concealing his strengths and biding his time for many years," Duan Guihong said. "Chunyang's actions in the capital were mainly carried out thanks to him. My getting in contact with Shurang happened after you went to the northern frontier."

But Fu Shen was for once genuinely irritated. Impatiently, he interrupted him: "If he was concealing his strengths and biding his time, he ought to have stuck to cultivating his immortality. Why get mixed up in this nasty business?! Is it that he's so insulated from the outside world, or is it that he thinks the Duke of Ying Manor isn't collapsing fast enough?"

"Jingyuan," Duan Guihong said, hitting the nail on the head, "you're the same as the people in the capital. You all think that his current position is down entirely to his lucky birth, right?"

"Isn't it?!" Fu Shen said angrily. "Couldn't he have done something else? No one was stopping him from cultivating immortality! I barely managed to pluck the Duke of Ying Manor out of trouble, but he's in a rush to jump into the fiery pit. Is it an addiction of his?!"

"What are you shouting about?" Duan Guihong said, frowning. "You don't understand your Third Uncle. His mother had complications when she was pregnant with him, and he was born premature, so Shurang's health was poor from childhood. His big brother and second brother both made allowances for their little brother, afraid that if he bumped into something it would lead to more mishap. They didn't dare to let him study martial arts. I saw him a few times. As a child, he was skinny and small, didn't talk much, hid in his room all day long not coming out.

"Later Bosun and Zhongyan both went to the northern frontier, and he grew up alone in the capital. He had no particular skills in literary or martial arts, but he had two talented brothers above him. But the upshot was that the two brothers passed away one after another. Luckily, he still had a nephew to bear the weight for him.

"Jingyuan, you're used to carrying that weight. You don't think it's a burden. But for your Third Uncle, that ought to have been his responsibility. However inadequate, he's still your family elder. He didn't protect you, and he's always felt very guilty about it."

Fu Shen heard a trace of loneliness in his words and instantly understood the guilt that Duan Guihong hadn't spoken aloud, identical to Fu Tingyi's.

For a time, he was frozen.

Fu Shen had gotten where he was now without relying on anyone. He had long ago become accustomed to walking into the face of difficulties, because he knew that no one would be there to shield him from the wind and rain, and hiding would be useless. And since Fu Tingxin had died, the age at which he could pout and beg for mercy from his elders had ended forever. At his present age, even if he were to pretend, he still couldn't pretend to be a pampered junior who could easily bow and yield, act like he needed care.

"Enough, knock it off, it's no use," Fu Shen muttered somewhat uncomfortably. "So what? I don't lack for people to love me. Don't you think it's disgusting at your age to still be playing the iron-willed man with tender feelings?"

Duan Guihong didn't respond.

A wretched scoundrel, coarse and tough, spoiling all the fun. What was there about a person like this worth loving?!

"Send a message to him, tell him to knock it off." Fu Shen put a hand to his forehead, switching with difficulty to a less peremptory tone. "I have my own plans. I don't need the two of you to personally take risks. Have a heart, look at it as having some pity on your little nephew. While I'm fretting about the Beiyan Army, don't make me also have to split off my attention to worry about the two of you, all right?"

Those who had served in the Beiyan Cavalry had a peculiar frankness and sense of identity, so when Fu Shen spoke to Duan Guihong from the position of the Beiyan Army's commander-in-chief, he was direct and outspoken, standing on no ceremony, even though Commandery Prince Xiping's position was higher than his. But now that they weren't speaking of official position and Fu Shen had called himself "little nephew," Duan Guihong instantly became even more uncomfortable than him. Dryly, he said, "All right."

The two of them shared a brief awkward silence. Duan Guihong gave a dry cough. In order to cover up the awkwardness, he stiffly changed the subject and said, "Have you eaten? If you aren't leaving, then how about we drink a few cups?"

At the end of his endurance, Fu Shen nodded, then suddenly recalled something. "Your Highness, autumn night white…"

"Once the plague has spread, it's outside of human control," Duan Guihong said with a bitter laugh. "Autumn night white is the same. Even if I stop letting autumn night white flow out this very day, what has already gone out will multiply endlessly. Thinking of pinching off the source now is too late."

"After the Jingchu case," said Fu Shen, "the court will raise its assessment of autumn night white's severity. I figure it won't be long before they promulgate a decree forbidding people to privately plant autumn night white. What has already been disseminated cannot be controlled, but I suppose that the method of refining white dew powder is still in Your Highness's hands, isn't that so?"

Duan Guihong nodded. Fu Shen said, "If you stop now, I don't dare to guarantee whether there will be peace in the world. But if you do not stop, there will certainly not be peace in the world. I hope Your Highness will think carefully about what is really important here."

While white dew powder had yet to become the most highly valued of Xinan's financial resources, that outcome wasn't far off. Asking Duan Guihong to make up his mind at once to cut off his arm was unfeasible. Fu Shen didn't rush him; he left it at this. The two of them spent the night drinking. For half the night, Fu Shen had the drunk Commandery Prince Xiping tugging at him and chattering about the Beiyan Army's history. Dizzy, he pitched headfirst onto the bed in the guest room, feeling that he had overestimated the degree of Duan Guihong's steadiness.

When the sky had just begun to brighten, there was a sudden clap of thunder outside. Fu Shen had been sleeping soundly, but for some reason, the thunderclap seemed to go from his ears directly to his heart. He abruptly opened his eyes, his heart beating wildly for no reason.

The twenty-ninth day of the fourth month, night in the capital.

The imperial city was silent as death. All the palaces had their doors and windows tightly shut. A few palace maids and eunuchs were trembling as they crouched huddled in the corners of the palace. Only in front of Yangxin Hall was everything brightly lit. Prince Jin, Sun Yunchun, wearing armor, with a team composed of the Ten South Yamen Guards and Prince Jin Manor's elite troops behind him, stood facing the North Yamen Imperial Guards across a lengthy distance.

Wei Xuzhou put his hand on his sword, his furious eyes wide open. Sternly, he said, "The Emperor's quarters are sacrosanct. No one may enter without an imperial order. Your Highness Prince Jin, do you intend to rebel against the emperor?"

Sneering, Sun Yunchun said, "This watchdog dares to bark in front of me? Beat it!"

In the firelight, General Wei's features were cold and hard as iron, but a large portion of his back was soaked in cold sweat. At seven in the evening, Prince Jin had led troops straight through the Chengtian Gate, the main gate of the palace. First he had gone to the Eastern Palace to kill the crown prince, and then he had made directly for Yangxin Hall. All ten South Yamen Guards had defected in favor of Prince Jin. Wei Xuzhou had only received word when they had reached Xuanfu Gate. He had hastened along with the North Yamen Imperial Guard to protect the emperor, finally reaching Yangxin Hall ahead of Prince Jin and barring the way.

Prince Jin had a well-crafted plan. The Southern Yamen had defected to the opposite side, and the few soldiers of the North Yamen Imperial Guards couldn't hold out for long. Though Wei Xuzhou was no coward when it came to battle, looking at it objectively, even he thought that Prince Jin's rebellion was almost certain to succeed.

"Who is out there?"

The hall doors slowly opened, and an aged and dignified voice sounded amidst the firelight and the night. Emperor Yuantai's figure appeared at the door of Yangxin Palace. "Prince Jin, what are you doing?"

Sun Yunchun stepped forward and loudly said, "Father, the crown prince Sun Yunliang was plotting rebellion, harboring evil intentions. When I became aware of his plot, I feared it would cause trouble, and therefore immediately led troops into the palace to protect you. Now the traitor has been executed, and I have come to notify you, Father."

Everyone present with a discerning eye knew that the crown prince was only a wretch, and his death was unjust. Prince Jin had played the scene well, actually managing to speak those righteous and stern hollow words without batting an eye or skipping a beat.

Emperor Yuantai said, "If the traitor has been executed, then return to your manor."

Behind his back, Prince Jin made a gesture. At once, a purple-clothed official stepped forward and fell to the ground, prostrating himself. He said, "The crown prince behaved wrongfully, and he has been killed by Prince Jin. The country was unstable to begin with. The people's mood is fixed. Your Majesty, look down and behold public sentiment. Pass the throne to Prince Jin, in order to satisfy the wishes of man and heaven."

"Cui Jing." Emperor Yuantai shot him a cold glance and said, "Where are the imperial guards?"

"Father, I advise you not to rely on them." Beneath the unsteadily flickering firelight, Sun Yunchun's smile appeared unusually twisted, making one think of a viper sticking out its tongue. "All the South Yamen Guards are already taking their orders from me. Never mind that your trusted aid Yan Xiaohan is not in the capital, even if he were here, the North Yamen Imperial Guards would still have no hope in a fight."

He deliberately paused for a moment, then raised his voice and said: "The Tangzhou troops are already on the way to the capital to do all they can to serve the throne. I hope you will make your decision soon, Father!"

As Sun Yunchun finished speaking, a young eunuch ran in staggering from outside the palace gates. His hat had even fallen askew as he ran. Gasping for breath, he said, "Your Majesty! Your Majesty! A report from the envoy of the capital barracks, tens of thousands of men and horses are coming in the direction of the capital, Commander Wang has already taken the Ruifeng and Lielei Barracks ahead to forestall them."

Emperor Yuantai took a step back from the shock of this sudden news and collapsed weakly against the eunuch supporting him.

"Your Majesty!"

The thirtieth day of the fourth month, outside of Beiyan's Liangkou Pass.

A carriage from the Zhe clan's Wuluohu tribe had stood in line for a long time at the mountain pass. Spring came late in the north, and mornings were still very cold. The government soldier guarding the pass, wrapped in a thick jacket, wiped the condensed water droplets from his eyelashes and yawned. He muttered, "Pretty early this year."

The Zhe man escorting the carriage drew near, smiling brightly. He removed his hand from his sleeve and put a handful of enormous pearls into the soldier's hand.

The soldier froze. He didn't take the pearls and shoved his hand back. "Our general doesn't let us accept these. Take them back."

The Zhe clan's incursions had failed, and they had been beaten back several times by the Beiyan Cavalry. Now they paid a tribute to Great Zhou every year. The Wuluohu tribe was rich in eastern pearls. As a rule, they offered a tribute of eastern pearls to the capital every year in the fifth or sixth month. This year they had come before it was even the fifth month. While the Beiyan soldier responsible for inspecting the annual tribute thought this was a little strange, he didn't think much of it. He walked up in front of the carriage and raised the tarpaulin over a crate with the tip of his sword. He said, "Open the crate."

Several Zhe got out of the carriage, smiling. They undid the knots and opened the lid of the crate.

A whistle, which startled the birds perched in the woods into flight.

When the lid of the crate was removed, there was a dazzling display of silvery white. The crate didn't contain eastern pearls. It contained coldly gleaming weapons!

The escorting Zhe gave up their pretense and pulled swords from the crate, swarming toward the soldiers guarding the Liangkou Pass. Amid a terrifying clamor of slashing, the Beiyan soldier who had refused the pearls had a bloody wound cut into his chest. He fell face up among the rising dust.

His stiff, icy fingers moved with difficulty. He pulled a firework from his belt and shakily pulled the fuse—

A pop—a Zhe who had discovered his attempt had stabbed backward. The blade penetrated flesh and blood, piercing his heart.

At the same time, the signal representing a sneak attack rose high into the air and exploded into blood-colored fireworks in those gradually slackening pupils. The Beiyan soldier's body spasmed. His eyes faced the sky. He exhaled his last cold breath, dying discontent.

On the thirtieth day of the twenty-sixth year of Yuantai, in the morning court assembly, Emperor Yuantai Sun Xun read out an imperial decree before the court, saying that he was passing his throne to Prince Jin, Sun Yunchun.

On the same day, the Zhe clan's Wuluohu tribe, while convoying eastern pearls, launched a sneak attack on the Liangkou Pass defenses. Not long after, a large number of Zhe soldiers came south to invade. The Beiyan Cavalry urgently transferred troops to rush to the rescue.

Storm clouds were approaching. The threat to the northern frontier of seven years earlier was about to return once more.

CHAPTER SIXTY-TWO

IN OVER A CENTURY SINCE GREAT ZHOU'S FOUNDING, SUN Yunchun was the unluckiest emperor in its history, without exception.

The first day he became emperor, before he could worship at the Imperial Ancestral Temple, before a ceremony could be performed, when the civil and military officials had yet to work out what was going on, when he hadn't even sat on the throne long enough to warm it, he received urgent military intelligence sent from the northern frontier.

Soon after, the old neighbors all exploded like a swarm of bees.

The Zhe clan's Wuluohu tribe had launched a sneak attack on Liangkou Pass. The Qilie tribe joined forces with Parhae, a vassal state in the northeast of Great Zhou, and dispatched troops to assault the provinces of Pingzhou and Jizhou. The Tartars, who had been chastened only the year before, regrouped and came back stronger, invading Tongzhou and Yuzhou in turn, and were aimed straight at Beiyan's western line of defense, Yuanzhou. The Beiyan Cavalry was checked on both sides; the situation was critical.

On the third day of the fifth month, Jizhou was in crisis.

On the fifth day of the fifth month, Jizhou City fell, Pingzhou was in crisis, and in the northwest, Tongzhou and Yuzhou requested support from the Beiyan Army.

On the twelfth day of the fifth month, Pingzhou City fell, and its military commander Prince Su died in battle. The nearby provinces and counties had no strength to resist the enemy. The defending soldiers fell while keeping watch. The enemy forces were only a thousand li from the capital. And the Tangzhou troops, which ought to have resisted the enemy along the only road available to them, for the sake of aiding Sun Yunchun in forcing his father to abdicate, were still outside the capital facing off against the capital barracks.

On the thirteenth day of the fifth month, the Ningzhou forces defected, and the northwestern line of defense was broken.

The Tartars and the Zhe advanced in step, separately bearing down on the capital from the west and east. The Beiyan Cavalry was caught in between, almost isolated. There was chaos in court. Never mind mustering army provisions and making an inventory of their combat readiness, they hadn't even finished arguing about who the emperor ought to be.

On the fifteenth day of the fifth month, after galloping day and night, Fu Shen finally reached the main camp outside of Yanzhou City.

When the Beiyan soldier guarding the barracks saw him, he nearly burst into tears. Fu Shen was mentally and physically exhausted from racing here and didn't even have the strength to raise a hand to support him. He found a tent at random and sat down. Concisely and comprehensively, he said, "Pour me a cup of water, and which general is in the camp? Tell him to come see me."

The soldiers went to carry out his orders. Fu Shen used this moment of leisure to close his eyes and rest, stretching his legs out beside him. He had no more sensation from his calves down. All his bones seemed tired enough to fall apart. He was dirty and dejected, his face haggard. Casually brushing his sleeve could have dislodged a couple ounces of earth.

He had heard about Prince Jin forcing an abdication and seizing the throne while in Xinan. Before he could even feel astonished, he had shortly after received word of the attack on Liangkou Pass. This time, Fu Shen absolutely couldn't sit still. Duan Guihong had advised him to sit and wait for news; perhaps it was only a routine disturbance. But as soon as Fu Shen heard about the Wuluohu tribe using the eastern pearl conveyance as an opportunity to launch a sneak attack, he had immediately recalled the box of blood-spattered eastern pearls Yu Qiaoting had shown him when he had been married earlier this year.

There was no doubt about it. That had been a naked provocation sent by the Zhe. The barbarians refused to give up their evil designs; they had already made plans.

Seeing that he was worried, Duan Guihong couldn't resist saying, "While you are the Beiyan commander in name, you've already handed over responsibility for military affairs. When the sky falls, it's up to the tall to hold it up. Have you forgotten about the state of your legs? What's the use of returning? Are you really planning to go into battle and slay the enemy yourself?"

"Never mind that it's only my legs that were broken," Fu Shen said, expressionlessly, suppressing his anger, "even if I had only one breath remaining and had to crawl, I would still crawl back.

"Those are my comrades. Your Highness, the weight my late father and uncle have in your heart, the men of the Beiyan Army are the same to me."

Duan Guihong paused, then said, "If you want to return, of course it's up to you. But as for Great Zhou's court, I am not going to pay it the least bit of mind. Even if there is a crisis in Beiyan, Xinan still won't send troops to the rescue, Jingyuan. Think it over."

"That's exactly what I wanted." Fu Shen looked up and shot him a glance. Coolly, he said, "Look after your own turf, Your

Highness. Your little nephew had no expectations of you to begin with."

So he set off from Kuizhou that same day, with his heart in his throat, and galloped day and night, racing from Xinan back to Beiyan.

While he was going north to the Central Plains, news of the fall of Pingzhou and the death of Prince Su in battle spread. Fu Shen missed a breath and nearly fell from horseback. There was great sorrow in his heart and a sour taste in his throat. He abruptly choked out a mouthful of blood.

After Fu Tingxin had become trapped in an encirclement and, having used up his strength, died in battle, Prince Su had remained unmarried. He had requested to become the vassal prince of Pingzhou, the place closest to Beiyan's garrison and the border. In all these years, not for one day had he forgotten Fu Tingxin.

Now, after being separated for many years by heaven and earth, they could at last meet again in the underworld.

That mouthful of blood fell into his palm. Fu Shen seemed to have been stung. He closed his eyes tightly.

Prince Su's death was a jab at the guiltiest and most fearful sore spot in his heart. Throughout his headlong rush, Fu Shen hadn't dared to think of how Yan Xiaohan would react when he learned of all this. Since determining to go north instead of going to Jingchu, he had known that he had once again abandoned Yan Xiaohan.

The missed time in the past could be excused as love having yet to awaken, but now that his feelings had blossomed, could he still pretend that he had no attachments, that the only one he needed to look after was himself?

If he, like Fu Tingxin, died in battle at the northern frontier, what would Yan Xiaohan do?

"General!"

Yu Qiaoting, jingling and clanking, lifted the tent flap and swept up in front of Fu Shen like a wind. In a tearful voice, he wailed, "My dear general, what are you doing back here?"

Fu Shen wearily sat up straight. "Don't waste words, tell me concretely about the situation."

Yu Qiaoting wiped away nonexistent tears and sat down next to him. Gloomily, he said, "It's a long story…"

After hearing him recount the course of the palace coup and current situation on the battlefield, Fu Shen pinched the center of his brow and let out a long sigh.

Yu Qiaoting saw something strange about his expression and hesitantly said, "General?"

"The timing is too precise," Fu Shen said. "No sooner had Prince Jin staged his coup than the Liangkou Pass was attacked. However unlucky he might be, he couldn't be that unlucky. Most likely he fell into their trap. There must be a traitor among Prince Jin's people. First they manufactured a power struggle, then they took advantage of the opening to invade.

"Parhae has always been content with its lot. It hasn't made trouble for many years. Now that it's mustered troops and risen in revolt along with the Zhe, I'm afraid they must have been almost certain of success to be willing to step in. The matter of the Tangzhou forces is even stranger. Tangzhou's military commissioner Yang Xu had just been removed, and they were already rushing to cast aside the crown prince in favor of Prince Jin. Do you think they're headless flies bumping around at random, or were they deliberately playacting to deceive that big idiot Prince Jin?"

"That's right," Yu Qiaoting agreed, "he *is* a big idiot."

Before Fu Shen could scold him, he quickly added, "It's not just the Tangzhou forces, the Ningzhou forces simply defected. Now the defenses have fallen both in the northeast and the northwest, and we're caught in the middle. From the looks of it, the Wuluohu tribe is planning to put their whole heart into dragging the Beiyan Army to its death. If we can't extricate ourselves, the Qilie tribe and Parhae will reach the capital soon."

"Yes," Fu Shen said, "that's also the idea the Tartars have. Seven years ago they learned their lesson in blood, and they don't dare to cross swords with the Beiyan Cavalry directly. If they send only a portion of their people to stall us and go around the Beiyan Army to strike at other places, they'll have a much easier fight."

Yu Qiaoting said, "They've put us in an impracticable position between them. It's a deadlock. If we apply force on one side, they'll immediately pounce on the other side."

"Everyone knows the Beiyan Army is invincible," Fu Shen muttered. "When I first returned military authority over Ganzhou and Ningzhou to the court, His Majesty was afraid that there would be remaining ties among former subordinates, so he transferred the original generals elsewhere. Beiyan has been solid all these years, but the long line of the northern border is full of small holes…"

"It was His Majesty who wanted to isolate Beiyan. Without him, the Tartars and the Zhe wouldn't have been able to play out this strategy of defeating us one by one."

What did reaping what you sowed mean? Precisely this.

Emperor Yuantai had worried that the Beiyan Army would become too powerful, worried that the Fu family would become unruly, worried that a hundred years from now his sons and grandsons wouldn't be able to hold on to the throne, so he had pulled the Beiyan Army to pieces and turned Fu Shen into a half-cripple.

And what was the outcome?

Ningzhou's forces had defected, foreigners and barbarians were invading on a large scale, he had been kicked off the throne by his own son, and that stupid son had welcomed the wolf inside, opened the door to thieves, put the capital beneath the talons of jackals and wolves.

"Tearing down his own defenses," Yu Qiaoting said with a sigh.

"On my way from Kuizhou, I saw many people taking their

families and belongings and fleeing south. What is the situation concerning the capital now?" Fu Shen asked.

Yu Qiaoting lowered his voice and cautiously spat out two words: "Being relocated."

"I figure that's about right," Fu Shen said. "The capital is too close to the northern frontier. It would only take three to five days for the fighting to reach the gates. We can't get away, and Prince Jin has only the South Yamen Imperial Guards at his disposal. That won't even make a snack for the invaders. The capital can't be defended. Sooner or later, it has to be moved."

"What about us?" said Yu Qiaoting.

"We'll stay here to hold them up, let those in the capital catch their breaths a little," Fu Shen said. "Let's see what Prince Jin decides. We'll prepare in advance to concentrate our forces and break out of the encirclement."

Yu Qiaoting had thought that he would want to fight to the last drop of blood. He hadn't expected Fu Shen to have such an idea. He said in astonishment, "General?"

"What is Prince Jin? An idiot burning himself to death playing with fire." Fu Shen snorted. "I'm a married man. That I haven't rebelled is already giving him more respect than he deserves. Does he want me to also take the men of Beiyan to die? He can keep dreaming."

Yu Qiaoting said, "But…"

"But what? If the capital falls, Yanzhou will be completely surrounded. When they catch us like a turkey in a jar and we go with our heads held up to see our ancestors, they'll probably beat us from the underworld all the way back to the land of the living."

Yu Qiaoting exhaled slowly. "Yes, sir."

Fu Shen patted him on the shoulder. "Qingheng, while the green hill lasts, there will be wood to burn. As long as we have Beiyan's elite soldiers in our hands, we'll always have the opportunity to regroup and come back stronger."

Yu Qiaoting left with a heavy heart. Fu Shen sat in the tent, completely exhausted. He turned his head to look west, where the setting sun was like a raging flame. His upright back had at some point finally bowed.

"I can't die."

He was whispering to himself, for someone else's benefit. "... Wait for me."

Fu Shen had overestimated Sun Yunchun's luck. On the eighteenth day of the fifth month, the enemy forces reached Miyun and joined the Tangzhou forces. The capital barracks withdrew to a defensive position in Huairou. That unlucky idiot Prince Jin finally incurred the public's wrath and was killed by General Cao Fengchen of the Right Shenwu Guard. The North Yamen Imperial Guards made a clean sweep of Prince Jin's party and publicly decapitated the Zhe spy who had been working with Prince Jin. His head was hung high on top of the city wall and exhibited to the public.

Emperor Yuantai paid his respects in person at the Imperial Ancestral Temple, kowtowing bareheaded, announcing his grief before his ancestors. Then he went to court and ordered a eunuch to proclaim an edict, moving the nation's capital to Chang'an. That afternoon, imperial guards, lightly supplied and in small number, left by the Qingxiao Gate escorting Emperor Yuantai, fleeing to take refuge in Shu.

The next day, Fu Shen in Yanzhou received a secret edict that a Feilong Guard had risked his life to get to him. On it was only one sentence: "Stay or go, it is up to you."

On the nineteenth day of the fifth month, there was chaos in the capital. The officials and the people fled in a flurry. Several roads were blocked, and people trampled each other.

On the twentieth day of the fifth month, the capital barracks retreated in disorder, and the invaders entered the court.

Several days earlier, in Jiangnan's Lin'an.

"Father has already given the throne to Prince Jin..." Prince Qi was so angry his hands shook. He paced several circles around the room and cried, "Men, prepare the horses! I will be returning to the capital at once!"

"Calm your anger, Your Highness," Yan Xiaohan, standing beside him, immediately counseled. "Do not be anxious. Since Prince Jin was able to kill the crown prince and force His Majesty to abdicate in his favor, he must have backing. If you return now without any preparation, it will be no different from walking into a trap. In my humble opinion, it would be better to wait and observe the situation, then make plans."

The hot blood had gone to Prince Qi's head. When Yan Xiaohan held him back, his anger gradually abated, and he calmed down bit by bit. To the attendants who had come at his call, he said, "Go check for news from the capital and learn what changes there have been in the palace. Report to me at once."

Long after, Yan Xiaohan regretted this more than once. If the flow of time could have been reversed, he certainly would have boxed his own ears and eaten that "wait and observe the situation." What did he care whether Prince Qi lived or died? Anyone who wanted the throne could have it. The princes were welcome to go fight it out, as long as he could return to the capital, return to his general's side.

Yan Xiaohan had no idea that when he waited and observed, what came would be the ruin of the country, the loss of territory, and a lengthy separation.

CHAPTER SIXTY-THREE

IN THE SUMMER OF THE TWENTY-SIXTH YEAR OF YUANTAI, invaders captured the capital.

Emperor Yuantai traveled west in a panic. A portion of the officials with their female relatives and the common people in the capital went west to Shu with Emperor Yuantai. Another portion meanwhile took their families and fled to the area of Jingchu and Huainan.

The Beiyan Cavalry pulled back their line of defense and broke through the western lines, having a direct encounter with Ningzhou's forces along the way. The Beiyan soldiers, with their bellies full of rage, defeated the rebel force of Ningzhou. Fu Shen personally drew a bow and killed the rebel force's leader with a single arrow. On a moonless and windy night, two Beiyan soldiers climbed up the wall of Ningzhou City and hung that head from the city gate tower.

This battle established their might. The Beiyan Cavalry was as ruthless as before. Wherever they passed, no one dared to get in the way of their thrust. At the start of the seventh month, the Beiyan Army joined forces at Wuwei with the Ganzhou forces. As Fu Shen drew in the remaining soldiers from all over the north-west, reforming an army, using Ganzhou as his stronghold, he opened up land and had his troops plant in it, recuperating and waiting to make a counterattack.

With the northern defensive line broken, the Tartar, Zhe, and Parhae troops had nothing to restrain them further. They dove straight into the heart of the Central Plains. Half the nation's territory fell into the hands of foreign enemies; the court no longer existed. Under these circumstances, Huainan's military commissioner Yue Chanfeng was the first to raise an army to resist the enemy, repelling the Parhae troops in the north of the Huai River, obstructing the barbarians in their southward tread. Soon after this, Commandery Prince Xiping, Duan Guihong, claimed that "the southwest was putting its own protection first," and would only accept refugees from the north; they wouldn't send troops to come to the rescue. With these two examples before them, the other military commissioners followed suit one after another, becoming independent within the limits of their own jurisdiction, each managing their own state affairs. With the exception of resisting the foreign enemies, they arranged not to disturb each other.

The Great Zhou was on the point of splintering, and the nation's fortunes were running out. In autumn of the same year, Prince Qi Sun Yunduan established himself as emperor in Jinling and the distant Emperor Yuantai as the Retired Emperor. His dynasty was called "Zhou," the regnal title was changed to "Changzhi," long rule, and the capital fixed in Jinling. This was announced everywhere.

The day he ascended the throne, the military commissioners of Jiangnan, Jingchu, Lingnan, and Fujian, as well as the East Sea Navy, came together to deliver their congratulations and support the new emperor. The new court was composed of both the old officials who had fled from the north and the renowned worthy personages of Jiangnan. Emperor Changzhi did not establish a prime minster but imitated the old practices of the Yuantai court, opening a Yanning Hall to resolve state affairs along with key ministers.

Yan Xiaohan had followed Prince Qi from Jingchu to Jiang-nan. He had first prevented him from returning to the capital, then mediated with the various military commissioners. He poured all his ingenuity into building up the framework of the new court, single-handedly pushing Prince Qi to ascend the throne and proclaim himself Emperor. In terms of merit, this was enough to have him made a Marquis or a Prime Minister, but citing as a reason the castigation his past behavior had incurred, he preferred to hide in the background as a minister performing meritorious service. For this reason, Emperor Changzhi ordered him to lead the imperial guard and permitted him to join the Yanning Hall Assembly by special dispensation. He viewed him as his right-hand man, relying heavily on him.

Call it being pushed beyond his limits or call it making the best of a bad situation, Yan Xiaohan was forced to his ultimate achievement. He exerted boundless latent strength and at last, over a bumpy road, accomplished the magnificent feat of saving a desperate situation through enormous efforts.

Jiangnan's ministers could accept this, and the old ministers who had cursed Yan Xiaohan openly and in secret had their eyes opened. Yan Xiaohan had stood without falling through two reigns and changed overnight from a power-hungry, sycophantic minister to a minister of outstanding merit, unflappable in the face of peril, assisting his new master. This dog not only had extraordinary schemes and means, he also had rather extraordinary luck!

Regardless of what outsiders surmised, being honed during this disturbance, Yan Xiaohan's appearance had come increasingly close to a "calculating power-hungry minister." Before, whether it was sincere feelings or hypocrisy, at least there would always be a smile on his face. Even if he had to pretend, he would still put on a warm countenance; now he seemed to have completely abandoned his old self and become much more dignified and grave, imposing and introverted, his mood unreadable, and always with a faint trace of gloom that made people all the more reluctant to approach him.

The ministers of the old court bore a grudge against him, the new officials were unfamiliar with him. In this way, Yan Xiaohan seemed to have returned to the Yuantai court, once again being isolated by everyone.

Lord Yan, enjoying profound favor and trust, had absolutely no perception of the censure and sidelong glances of his colleagues; he was used to it, anyway. Their gossip was like a breeze blowing past his ears. Him racking his brain in plans and preparations for Emperor Changzhi, sparing no pains to facilitate the new reign, wasn't for the sake of wrestling achievements out of this tumultuous world. It was only that the current situation was thus, and circumstances forced one into action. If Emperor Changzhi never found a place to stand, a prince wandering destitute out in the world, he would afterward either be taken for a puppet emperor or simply killed out of hand. And his attendants, who were nothing in themselves, would naturally be even less likely to come to a good end.

Yan Xiaohan didn't want to be under others' control, and he certainly didn't want to die in Jiangnan.

During his days in Jiangnan, he sometimes started awake in the middle of the night to a cold quilt and lonely pillow, the cold rain of autumn at the window. His hand would fall on the empty bed beside him but find nothing to grasp, futilely closing on a handful of cold damp air. Each time this happened, he felt as if his drug craving were acting up again, his heart filled with an unspeakable insistent feeling, as if a worm were nibbling away at it bit by bit until there was almost nothing left, leaving behind only an empty shell of a walking corpse.

Wanting what you couldn't have was even more frightening than pure pain. Yan Xiaohan dreamed of sprouting wings and flying over the landscape by night.

But where was Fu Shen?

He knew that the capital had fallen, knew that Emperor

Yuantai had gone west, and also knew that the Beiyan Cavalry had succeeded in breaking out of encirclement, but he didn't know where Fu Shen had gone—had he stayed in the southwest? Or had he returned to Beiyan, then gone somewhere else with the Beiyan Cavalry?

There hadn't been a word. Since parting in Jingchu, they had completely lost contact.

Yan Xiaohan had asked many officials and soldiers coming south from the capital about him, and he had attempted to get information from the southwest, had even spent a huge sum of money to send people north to Shu, wanting to find traces of Fu Shen, but to this day he had received no response.

Separating them were the Central Plains, fallen to the enemy, but it seemed as if a whole world separated them.

Demanding work and frustrated emotions left him sleeping badly. Yan Xiaohan often woke in the middle of the night and couldn't get back to sleep. Usually he would keep his eyes open until daybreak, then force himself to get up to attend morning court. Luckily he was still young, and his body could sustain this exhaustion. When he was really so sad he couldn't take it, he would go to the always prepared candy box on his desk and find an osmanthus candy to eat.

In fact, this was useless. Even the psychological comfort was minuscule, because that original bag of candy was long gone, and while the newly bought candy was exquisite and sweet, its osmanthus aroma strong, the flavor was still different from the original bag.

That day outside the inn, Fu Shen had hurriedly given him a purse of osmanthus candy, and ever since, he hadn't been able to find candy as sweet as that.

Outside of Ganzhou City.

In the northwest, autumn was bright and brisk, the sky high

and vast, and beneath the blue sky were boundless fields. Fu Shen and Yu Qiaoting, each holding a piping hot bowl of lamb soup, were squatting very indecorously on an embankment between the fields, watching people harvesting wheat. Looked at from behind, they looked just like two shepherds.

Yu Qiaoting, stammering, said, "Lord Marquis, two such important generals as ourselves, it doesn't look very good for us to be squatting here, does it?"

Fu Shen sneered. "When you enter a village, you follow its customs. You're too attached to your dignity."

Yu Qiaoting said, "You've gone a little too far following them…"

Fu Shen raised his eyelids and looked askance at him. "Is the lamb soup not good?"

"It's good," said Yu Qiaoting.

"But not good enough to stop your mouth?" Fu Shen said. "Stop chattering, you're annoying me."

Yu Qiaoting instantly understood and, with a malicious smirk, asked, "Are you missing your so-and-so at home? We got news from the south, didn't we, that the new emperor has ascended the throne, and he's a minister of merit, serving as head of the imperial guard in warm and tender Jiangnan. What else do you have to worry about?"

Fu Shen had a mind to kick that scoundrel Yu Qiaoting and his pleasure at others' misery off the embankment, but there really was no one else around who he could discuss his love life with, so he just had to hold his nose and put up with it. "One in the south, one in the north, not knowing when we can see each other again—don't you think that's worth fretting over?"

Smiling, Yu Qiaoting said, "That's easy, you're planning to send out the troops next spring anyway. When you fight your way to Jinling, won't you see him then?"

"You say that as if we can get to Jinling," Fu Shen said feebly. "The barbarians have occupied the Central Plains north of the

Huai River, eighteen thousand li from Jinling. Why don't you try fighting your way there?"

Yu Qiaoting said, "As I see it, the new emperor has put together a little court in Jiangnan, and put it together very properly. I'm only afraid when we're fighting for our lives in the north, they won't be the least bit worried in the south."

Hearing this, Fu Shen was even more fretful. At Wuwei, he had once again brought the Ganzhou forces and the scattered soldiers of places throughout the northwest into the Beiyan Cavalry. He had military power in his grasp, no less than the Great Zhou court in Jiangnan had. But Fu Shen couldn't use their soldiers to set himself up as an independent power. The Beiyan Army had vowed loyalty and devotion to the nation for many years; naturally they saw retaking the Central Plains as a matter of course.

But that they thought so didn't mean that the various independent military commissioners and the Jiangnan court would also think so.

The capital had possessed three lines of defense—the Beiyan Cavalry, the capital barracks, and the imperial guards—and it had still been toppled by the foreigners. Relying solely on the strength of the Beiyan Army, how many years would it take to wrest the Central Plains back from the hands of the enemy? And even if they took it back, how would north and south once again combine into one? Who would have legitimacy? And what position would the Beiyan Army find itself in then?

Long-term considerations and present worries weighed down on his heart in layer upon layer. Fu Shen's breast could contain only so many feelings. For a time, he felt so weighed down he couldn't draw breath. He gave a long sigh and raised his head to look at the sky. By chance, he happened to see a wedge of wild geese flying by in formation.

Fu Shen narrowed his eyes, figured the distance, and shoved his empty bowl into Yu Qiaoting's hands while he himself stood and took the longbow off his back. He backed up a few steps, reached back to take an arrow to put on the string, then drew the bow and took aim.

The arrow flew away with a whistle. A few breaths later, a wail came from midair. A wild goose at the end of the formation fell straight down out of the sky and landed not far from them.

Before Fu Shen could go pick it up himself, a farmer over there had already brought it over for him. The wounded wild goose was still alive, one of its wings pierced by the arrow. It flapped constantly in Fu Shen's grasp. Yu Qiaoting looked up and praised him: "Not bad. Very fat."

"I didn't shoot it down so you could eat it." Fu Shen held his bow in one hand and the goose in the other. He turned and walked back. "Have Du Leng come by my place and bring ointment to treat wounds."

"Huh?" Yu Qiaoting was all at sea. "What for?"

Without so much as a look back, Fu Shen said, "So Du Leng can treat its injury. Isn't that goose going to fly south? Well, it can help me out while it's at it."

"What?" said Yu Qiaoting.

"Haven't you heard the legends of fish and wild geese acting as messengers? Unfortunately, I lack the extreme beauty to make fish sink and birds alight. All I can use are my martial skills." Having said this, Fu Shen pondered and thought it was a little inexcusable that, having something to ask of the goose, he had injured it, so he raised the goose he was holding and earnestly said to it, "Brother Goose, I'm very sorry."

The wild goose was speechless.

Yu Qiaoting, left behind still holding two bowls, was also speechless.

Had the Marquis of Jingning fallen prey to his obsession and finally gone mad?

Winter Solstice, Jinling.

After getting off duty late, Yan Xiaohan left the palace at dusk. It was Winter Solstice today. After the Yanning Hall Assembly was held, His Majesty, according to the custom of the capital, had given very particular instructions to the imperial kitchen to make lamb dumpling soup and serve it to all the ministers. Some old ministers from the north had burst into tears on the spot as they held their bowls. Emperor Changzhi, recalling old memories, also couldn't resist weeping. With sovereign and subjects holding hands and wailing, the four officials from Jiangnan delivered some hypocritical words of consolation from the sidelines. Only when Emperor Changzhi had stopped his tears did everyone disperse.

Yan Xiaohan seemed to have had his lungs burned by a mouthful of hot soup. Walking through the cold and wet long street, he felt pierced by pain and cold. He didn't want to go home and strolled idly through the streets. After a long while of walking in bewilderment, he somehow ended up at a market that had yet to be taken down. Someone suddenly bumped into his shoulder.

A person ran past him, crying out loudly, "I want to see! Let me see!"

A group of people was gathered not far up ahead, surrounding a market stall and observing some fun. Yan Xiaohan's ears were sharp. He heard the man with the loudest voice in the crowd say gruffly, "... I brought this wild goose down outside the city, I never expected there would be a strip of silk with writing on it tied to its leg. It's like in the old saying, the fish and geese act as messengers!"

A chord was plucked in Yan Xiaohan's mind. He suddenly became a little curious and couldn't help coming up to get a closer look. He was tall, and even from outside the crowd could see a dead wild goose lying on the chopping block. The man held a strip of silk folded in quarters and was showing it off to everybody. "Everyone knows that a northern goose flies south. Now that communications have broken down between north and south, maybe someone in the north has used it to send a message?"

Someone heckled him: "What does it say? Open it up and let everyone get a look!"

The man said, "No! No! This is a rare item…"

"How much for that goose?" Yan Xiaohan said suddenly. "Including that strip of silk. I'll buy them together."

The crowd watching the fun immediately made way for him. The man, seeing that he was luxuriously attired and had an uncommon bearing, knew that he had encountered a rich fool. He said, "Five taels of silver!"

Yan Xiaohan casually took out his purse and, without so much as looking, tossed it right to him. The man weighed it in his hand and found that it was quite heavy. He was so glad he burst into smiles and repeatedly gave thanks, respectfully offering up the strip of silk with both hands. Yan Xiaohan took it, but he didn't open it to read it. Instead, he put it into his sleeve. The spectators saw that he had no intention of displaying it and were very disappointed. Smacking their lips, they dispersed. Yan Xiaohan turned and left the stall. Behind him, his attendant stepped up to carry the goose away.

With a breath caught in his chest, Yan Xiaohan reached a place without any people, then repeatedly took up the strip of silk and let it go. His palm was full of cold sweat. He warned himself again and again not to harbor delusions. It was only a coincidence that "northern goose" happened to be homophonous with "Beiyan," and letters delivered by geese were an old story that had grown trite with use. He had to be crazy to have impulsively bought a completely meaningless thing like this.

But he was in too much need of some old thing from previous haunts to sustain his longing, even if it was only a false image.

After calming his breath for a long time, his heartbeat gradually slowed. Yan Xiaohan hesitated again and yet again. Opting to make the best of his mistake, he gritted his teeth and closed his eyes, and finally, trembling, pulled the piece of white silk from his sleeve and carefully opened it along the folds.

That wild goose had flown a long way from north to south. The white silk tied to its leg was dirty, and the writing had gotten wet, soaking the silk with now-dried ink splotches.

Though it was blurry, he could still clearly distinguish the not very tidy writing, because the note contained only four words—

"Is my wife well?"

Chapter Sixty-Four

He had lived for over two decades, and only now was he learning that there really was such a thing as a sentence, a handful of words, that could break your heart.

Yan Xiaohan was petrified. In a panic, he thought, "Was this written for me?"

He was like a person nearly frozen to death in an icy wasteland, on the point of losing all hope, suddenly seeing a gleam of light. It didn't matter whether it was an illusion or phosphorescence, it would still be as if he had grasped a last thread of lifesaving gossamer.

The original shapes of the characters were blurry. There were no distinctive traits to speak of. But Yan Xiaohan still kept his eyes fixed on those four words, his gaze scorching, as if trying to burn a hole in the white silk. Had Fu Shen been present, he would have recognized that this bewitchment was simply identical to the symptoms of the drug craving breaking out in Kuangfeng Town at the very outset.

The craving for autumn night white was long gone, but the craving of the heart fostered by Fu Shen grew stronger by the day.

The cold wind pierced him to the bone. Gradually, his roiling

161

emotions calmed beneath the blowing wind. Yan Xiaohan let out a long breath. His tense shoulders suddenly relaxed. The outcome was that his figure shook, and his legs nearly collapsed out from under him, sending him to the ground. He quickly put a hand on the wall and steadied his footing, and only then noticed with surprise than on such a cold day, his back was covered in sweat.

He carefully folded up the white silk and put it away. It was as if he had absorbed a bit of warmth and strength from it. He slowly walked in the direction of his mansion.

In the blink of an eye, it was the New Year.

Because in the previous year there had been war everywhere, the political situation unstable, the nation in jeopardy, all the celebrations and ceremonies in the palace were simple this year. Emperor Changzhi made offerings and prayed, and promulgated edicts relieving Jiangnan's grain taxes for the year and granting general amnesty. On the sixth day of the first month, it became apparent that Lady Xue was pregnant. This was the first child to be welcomed to the palace by the new court in the new year, a very auspicious omen. Emperor Changzhi was very pleased and promoted Lady Xue to Pure Consort, and richly rewarded her father, brothers, and other family members.

When Yan Xiaohan heard this news, he felt somewhat uneasy, so he went in private to question a eunuch who attended on the empress. At present he was nominally the head of the Imperial Guards, but in reality, because the emperor had no one else to employ, there was no head eunuch overseeing the department of eunuchs, so in internal affairs they would obey Yan Xiaohan. He was like the head steward of the emperor's backyard, tasked with minding the manservants, and the serving women and children. He was very unwilling, but there was no other choice.

When the capital had fallen, Princess Qi Fu Ling, taking a baby still in her swaddling clothes, had fled to Jiangnan under the protection of servants from the prince's manor and guards from the Duke of Ying Manor, with alarms but no injury. When Emperor Changzhi had first ascended the throne, Fu Ling had been conferred the title of empress. Husband and wife had previously been very close, but the new court had just been established, and in order to win over the important families of Jiangnan, Emperor Changzhi had accepted a number of highborn women as concubines. The previously desolate harem had swiftly become a battlefield without the flash of swords. The empress's temperament was outwardly soft but inwardly firm. She was not skilled in fighting for attention and was spurned several times. Emperor and empress gradually began to grow somewhat apart.

At first, Yan Xiaohan hadn't taken notice of the intrigues in the harem, but at the end of the past year, the empress's child, Princess Gaoyang, had suddenly broken out in pustules and run a fever. The symptoms were dangerous, and she almost didn't make it. The empress had suffered a serious illness on this account. After hearing about this, Yan Xiaohan had kept an eye out, ordering people to investigate in private, and had actually ferreted out a palace maid who was secretly passing information to a concubine in another palace. Under torture, the palace maid had admitted that she had used a handkerchief brought in from outside the palace to wipe the princess's hands. Her testimony was later presented to the emperor for inspection. Emperor Changzhi was enraged, but in the end he had let it go easily, ending the matter by simply sending that concubine into the cold palace.

It was only starting then that Yan Xiaohan knew what kind of life the empress was leading in the palace. Though the Duke of Ying Fu Tingyi had also escaped to Jiangnan, he had always abstained from the material world and only counted as "better than nothing." Fu Ling didn't have a sufficiently strong family backing, and she was the mistress of the harem. Naturally she became the target all the concubines were falling over each other to provoke.

Not long after, that concubine hanged herself out of nowhere in the cold palace. After this, Yan Xiaohan devoted a bit of time every month to going and asking what the empress's situation was. He didn't deliberately avoid others in doing this, and didn't even object to others coming to ask about it. He and Fu Shen were legitimately married; naturally it was a matter of course for him to prop up Fu Shen's little sister.

No more needs to be said. Relying solely on this movement, Fu Ling's days in the harem immediately improved.

Lady Xue's father was one of the four Jiangnan officials taking part in the Yanning Hall Assembly, and she was the most favored of the consorts and concubines in the harem. The empress had yet to give birth to a son. Now that Lady Xue was pregnant, it would be all right if it turned out to be a girl, but if she gave birth to the emperor's eldest son, it certainly wouldn't be good news for the old ministers of the Yuantai court. Yan Xiaohan had questioned the eunuchs and heard that the empress was only melancholy; she had no other plans. He put an end to the notion of taking preventative measures on her behalf, only had servants take extra care to keep others from plotting against her.

But, after all, worldly events are hard to predict. On the twelfth day of the second month, the Flower Festival, there was suddenly a stir in the palace. It was said that someone had rammed into Lady Xue in the garden, and she had unfortunately miscarried. The child died.

The person who had bumped into Pure Consort Xue was a palace maid who did the sweeping in the empress's palace. When she was brought up for questioning, she didn't say a word. She prostrated herself before the empress, then ran headfirst into a pillar in the hall, dying on the spot.

In this instance, anything the empress said would make it worse. Even if she was in the right, she couldn't have explained herself. Emperor Changzhi was furious. Keeping in mind the mutual affection between husband and wife, he at any rate didn't punish her severely, only ordered the empress to be confined to her quarters for a month, shut up her palace and examine her conscience. Matters in the harem would temporarily be overseen by the Quiet Consort.

The Quiet Consort was a pushover. Her background wasn't illustrious. She had long ago thrown in with Pure Consort Xue.

Emperor Changzhi wasn't necessarily unaware that the empress had very likely been framed, but he didn't need the truth. Behind Lady Xue were Jiangnan's influential families, half the support of the new court; Emperor Changzhi could still rely on these people to serve him. But behind the empress, the Fu family was only an empty shell. Comparing the two of them, weighing up the priorities, the outcome was clear at a glance. For the sake of the bigger picture, he had to choose to sacrifice the empress.

But he had forgotten that there was still a "Fu family member" at court whose surname wasn't Fu.

On the fourteenth day of the second month, the second day of the empress's confinement to quarters, Pure Consort Xue, who was still recovering, was dragged from her sleeping quarters to the cold palace. Here the courtyard was old and shabby, and few people came by. Gagged with a handkerchief, her hair falling loose, she whimpered and struggled as she was tossed by two sturdy eunuchs into an empty room.

This was where the concubine who had tried to harm the princess had lived. After her death, the palace maids and eunuchs had felt that the place was unlucky and didn't readily step in. With no one to sweep it for months, it was covered in spiderwebs, and the moss was growing in the courtyard. Pure Consort Xue was thrown on the icy, filthy ground, her unsullied beauty immediately picking up a layer of grime. She was in a wretched state.

She was a precious daughter who had grown up pampered by her family. When had she ever been treated like this? She was shocked and afraid, with no one to turn to for help. Involuntarily, she began to cry.

In her hazy vision, someone seemed to block the light from outside. Light, steady footsteps approached. Shortly, a pair of black boots stopped in front of her. From above her head came a young, intimate male voice: "Her?"

The eunuch holding her had a ferocious look, but he was unusually polite to this person. "Your Honor, this is Lady Xue."

The man gave a quiet "mhm" and went around her, going forward. A table and chair in the hall had already been wiped clean for him. An edge of his dark red brocade robe was raised. He pulled up a wooden armchair and sat down in front of Lady Xue, then instructed, "Hold her up, remove the gag."

The handkerchief in Lady Xue's mouth was removed. She cried so hard she kept gasping for breath. Enduring the pain she felt, she got up, but when she got a clear look at the person sitting upright in front of her, she was stunned in spite of herself.

Though the number of men she had seen was limited, each and every one had been young and refined, with remarkable looks, but this man could be called the loveliest she had seen in her life.

His features were serene, with a gentleness and softness even when he wasn't smiling. Seeing Lady Xue lost in thought as she looked at him, the corners of his eyes curved slightly. He asked, "Do you know who I am?"

With a sudden start, Lady Xue realized she had forgotten her manners. She quickly bowed her head and stammered, "N-no."

"My surname is Yan. I have been tasked with leading the Imperial Guards. I am on somewhat friendly terms with your father, Minister Xue."

The words "Yan" and "Imperial Guards" were like a bucket of cold water splashed right into her face. Lady Xue's heart instantly turned to ice. Only two words remained in her mind: *It's over.*

Since the princess had nearly died last year, the concubines and consorts in the harem had for the most part restrained themselves, and they had gained some additional reverence for the empress—it wasn't that they respected the empress, but that they feared the person backing her, the one who had arranged for the death of the concubine who had schemed against the princess.

The emperor's trusted aid and courtier, the commander of the Imperial Guards, one of the members of the Yanning Hall Assembly—Yan Xiaohan.

During Emperor Yuantai's reign, the Feilong Guard had run wild, its power overwhelming the court and the commons, the sound of their name making people turn pale. This man was the boss of the Feilong Guard, said to be eccentric in conduct, ruthless in his methods. He had brought harm upon countless loyal and upright people, but his position had always been unshakeable; Emperor Changzhi even continued to set great store by him in the new court.

The shock of his beauty passed, and only alarm remained. Lady Xue backed away hastily. Trembling, she said, "What are you going to do to me?"

"Your Ladyship the Pure Consort," he carelessly asked in turn, "do you not know what I am about?"

"I don't know!" Lady Xue forced herself to calm down. Blustering, she said mulishly, "A minister intruding on the palace precincts is a crime punishable by death. You dare to raise a hand against me? Aren't you afraid that His Majesty will find out?"

"My orders are to guard the palace precincts," said Yan Xiaohan. "Naturally I can't sit by and watch all of you poisonous women dupe your sovereign. This business is within the scope of my responsibilities, and I have a duty. From the looks of it, I think Your Ladyship has heard of me. Since you know who I am, then you ought to understand that, never mind you, even if your father were here, I would still carry on with what I was doing."

In a shaking voice, Lady Xue said, "You... I am His

Majesty's consort. You have no right to punish me... I want to see His Majesty!"

As if he had heard a joke, Yan Xiaohan laughed. "I called you 'Your Ladyship,' so you really think you have the status?"

Though he was smiling, the desire for murder in his eyes was plain to see. Coldly, he said, "Framing the empress, conspiring against the life of the emperor's offspring—do you think you're going to walk out of these palace gates alive today?"

"You're the empress's man. Why are you helping her?" Lady Xue was finally scared to tears. Incoherently, she cried out, "Whatever she gave you, I can give you that, too! You—"

"Because her surname is Fu," Yan Xiaohan interrupted her lightly. "When you framed the empress on the Flower Festival, you took it upon yourself to violate my taboo. You were courting death."

The Flower Festival? What did it have to do with the Flower Festival?

Lady Xue was completely bewildered, but of the eunuchs standing by in attendance, one had come from the north. As he thought of the Flower Festival, he immediately understood: Huh, wasn't that precisely the date on which Officer Yan had married the Marquis of Jingning last year?

Marquis Fu's whereabouts were unknown, and the empress was his only full-blood little sister. No wonder Lord Yan was so angry. Lady Xue truly was unlucky to have offended him.

Since coming to Jiangnan, Yan Xiaohan had rarely sent people into the West, but when he occasionally struck, he seemed increasingly perverse and vicious. This form of venting his feelings was in fact completely useless. It was only that when his sore spot had been poked, he would be in pain, so the wrongdoer had also better not think of getting away easy.

The eunuch stepped forward with a strip of white silk in both his hands. Softly, he said, "Your Ladyship, please go ahead."

Lady Xue looked at Yan Xiaohan in disbelief, her eyes nearly popping out of their sockets, but he didn't look at her. He was staring out the window at a cluster of white flowers, thinking about something unknown.

Seeing her hesitate, the eunuch said inscrutably, "If Your Ladyship is unwilling to take it upon yourself, then I will have no choice but to send you on your way."

Now Yan Xiaohan turned his head toward them and flatly said, "I've heard that you are high-born, well read in the classics since childhood, and skilled at singing and dancing. A fortuneteller once asserted that your fate was elevated, that you were certain to marry well." At this point, he couldn't resist a snort. "That is the rumor throughout all of Jinling City, and I'm sure Your Ladyship believed it as well and thought you were going to be the next Wei Zifu[1].

"This strip of white silk is already affording you enough dignity." Leaning against the arms of the chair, Yan Xiaohan stood and looked down on her from on high. Darkly, he said, "I recommend that you take some initiative, Your Ladyship. If you continue not to know what's good for you, I'll turn you into a Madam Qi."

Lady Xue reacted as if a viper had caught her in its sights. Her blood ran cold. She knew something of poetry and literature and had studied history. She immediately understood Yan Xiaohan's threat and knew that there was no way for her to escape her fate. She was sure to die.

Madam Qi, favorite concubine of Emperor Gaozu of the Han dynasty, whose son Liu Ruyi, owing to the great favor she received from the emperor, several times nearly replaced the crown prince Liu Ying. After Gaozu's passing, Liu Ruyi was called to the palace by Empress Lü and poisoned to death, while his mother Madam Qi had her limbs cut off, her eyes removed, and her ears cut off; she was forced to drink a toxin that made her mute, made to live in a latrine, and called a "Human Swine."

Between the Pure Consort and the empress, it wasn't only a harem power struggle. It was also a struggle over the future crown prince, a silent clash between the old ministers of the north and the new nobility of Jiangnan.

Yan Xiaohan departed with a flick of his sleeves.

In the first year of Changzhi, on the fourteenth day of the second month, Pure Consort Xue suffered postpartum frenzy. Her mind became deranged, and she hanged herself in the cold palace.

That night, stars were scattered in the sky like snow. The Changqiu Palace hurriedly asked an imperial physician to come and take the empress's pulse. Upon examination, Empress Fu turned out to be pregnant. Among the court and the commons, everyone took this as a propitious sign.

---

1. An empress consort during the Han dynasty, who had the second-longest term as empress in Chinese history.

CHAPTER SIXTY-FIVE

No sooner had Yan Xiaohan gotten through taking care of Lady Xue than Emperor Changzhi received word of it. He flew into a rage and ordered him to be called to the palace, planning to mete out a severe punishment.

A minister outside the palace, he had killed the emperor's favored consort right under his nose, and that favored consort's father was a colleague of his, serving as an official in the same court. However you looked at it, Yan Xiaohan had completely bungled it this time. But he wasn't afraid in the slightest. He walked calmly and steadily into the palace and said, "Long live Your Majesty," giving Emperor Changzhi a faultlessly proper bow.

Emperor Changzhi was angry. He didn't permit him to sit at once as he usually would have, deliberately leaving him standing in the middle of the hall. Coldly, he said, "Yan Xiaohan, an official entering the harem without authorization, compelling a consort to her death—you're very bold!"

Yan Xiaohan simply knelt. "I am guilty. Your Majesty, please relieve me of my post of commander of the Imperial Guards and reduce me to an ordinary citizen."

"You!" Emperor Changzhi's heart stuttered. He had been planning to give Yan Xiaohan a dressing down, make him stop acting without the slightest scruple, without consideration for the emperor, then let this matter go at that, delivering a minor punishment to prevent greater future wrongs, just as he had always dealt with things. But what he hadn't expected was that Yan Xiaohan would be so resolute, coming in ready to give up his position in disgust and go home.

Though Yan Xiaohan had a variety of shortcomings, he had exerted all his efforts on Emperor Changzhi's behalf when the latter had been at his most destitute, single-handedly placing him on the throne. When the new court was first established, the loyalty of the various military commissioners had also been won by Yan Xiaohan. He was only the commander of the Imperial Guards in name; in reality, he was the "ninth minister" of the Yanning Hall Assembly. Yan Xiaohan was independent of both sides; from start to finish, he had kept a balance between the old ministers of the north and the new nobles of Jiangnan on the emperor's behalf, letting the court carry on operating smoothly and steadily. Now that he wanted to leave his post and return home, Emperor Changzhi was the first to object.

After being stifled for a long time, Emperor Changzhi sighed heavily and helplessly said, "Minister Yan, you... Forget it, We won't speak of you leaving your post again. Servants, bring him a seat."

Yan Xiaohan was outwardly unmoved, but in the depths of his heart, he sneered to himself.

An unworthy son of his father.

Emperor Yuantai had been too strong, suppressing his sons so much that they had become either rebellious or weak. The crown prince had been opportunistic, that idiot Prince Jin went without saying, and Emperor Changzhi appeared strong but was actually weak. He seemed sagacious, but in reality he was cowardly. He had no definite thoughts of his own, and he was often indecisive and given to throwing aside the old in favor of the new.

This sort of person was a typical case of changing under the influence of poverty, riches, and authority. Before, he'd had his powerful father and brothers around him and could quietly, without making trouble, act out the role of a prince content with his lot. But when he had been asked to shoulder a burden on his own, His Majesty's spine had immediately gone soft.

With an emperor of this temperament, it was almost a given that the court would trend toward a weak ruler presiding over strong ministers. Therefore, though Lady Xue had been a favored consort, Yan Xiaohan had dared all the same to present her with a length of white silk. Before acting, he had already foreseen this outcome: since Emperor Changzhi could wrong the empress for Lady Xue's sake, naturally he would also be willing to let Lady Xue's death go easily in order to keep an important minister like Yan Xiaohan.

"We are aware that the empress has been inconvenienced," Emperor Changzhi said, moaning and groaning, sounding care-laden, "but We have done nothing to her, only confined her to quarters. In the future she will receive greater consolation. But you simply forced Lady Xue to kill herself. When Minister Xue asks about it in the future, what answer would you have Us make to him?"

Lord Yan, a henpecked husband who would have preferred to inconvenience himself for the sake of his wife, absolutely couldn't understand His Majesty's line of thought. "Confined to quarters" was only a nice way of putting it. He had reduced the empress's dignity to nothing for the sake of a favored consort; didn't he think that was "doing something to her?" Had the empress really arranged for the death of Lady Xue's child, what would he have done?

Yan Xiaohan sat on his stool and silently recited a couple of lines of scripture, calming his anger. As mildly as possible, he said, "Your Majesty, you sit upon the imperial throne and hold power over everyone's lives and property. You have no need to account for your actions to anyone."

Emperor Changzhi was briefly quiet, then hesitantly said, "But Lady Xue…"

"Your Majesty, Lord Xue sent his daughter into the palace and secretly arranged for people to publicize Lady Xue's elevated fate. Haven't you realized yet what he is attempting?" Yan Xiaohan said gravely. "It isn't untrue that you rely heavily on Jiangnan's wealthy families, but Minister Xue wants to change the court into Jiangnan's court. Your Majesty must be sure not to look only at what is before your eyes. Great Zhou embraces the four corners of the landscape. It isn't only comprised of Jiangnan. In the future, you will recover the Central Plains and return to the capital, live up to the ardent hopes of the people, not let down your ancestors and the country."

As expected, Emperor Changzhi's expression wavered. He had already forgotten Yan Xiaohan's offense of overstepping his authority. His thoughts had been entirely carried away by Yan Xiaohan. "Of course We wish to go on an expedition north, but the new court is not yet firmly established. Men, provisions, funds —We lack everything We need. What will We use for an expedition north?"

"That isn't a big problem, actually. At the outset, several military commissioners promised that if the court wanted to retake the Central Plains, they would of course send troops in aid," Yan Xiaohan said. "However, the court still has to raise a presentable army. We can't rely on the military commissioners alone. Furthermore…"

"Furthermore what?" Emperor Changzhi pursued.

Yan Xiaohan hesitated, then at last said quietly, "Your Majesty, the military commissioners place themselves in positions of importance by amassing troops. There is practically no difference between them and vassal princes who have seceded from the empire. Supposing we do take back the Central Plains in the future, the court will still require sufficient troops to overawe the various military commissioners."

He came to a halt, unexpectedly remembering the Beiyan Cavalry, as well as their commander-in-chief.

Emperor Changzhi took his point. He nodded and said, "That is well said. This matter ought to be handled earlier rather than later. Have you made any plans? If so, present a memorial to the throne discussing them."

Yan Xiaohan stood and agreed. It seemed that Emperor Changzhi's thoughts had gone in the same direction as his. With a sigh, he said, "If We had an elite force like the Beiyan Cavalry in Our hands, what need would there be to worry about retaking the Central Plains?! What a pity that the Marquis of Jingning…"

He shook his head and stopped regretfully.

Since entering the palace, Yan Xiaohan hadn't ceased to sneer inwardly. This time, he really couldn't resist interjecting: "If the Marquis of Jingning were here, however bold Lady Xue might have been, she still wouldn't have dared to provoke the empress."

Emperor Changzhi looked sheepish and said in displeasure, "Enough. We wouldn't have thought that your relationship with the Marquis of Jingning was good enough to merit you speaking on the empress's behalf time and again."

Yan Xiaohan considered briefly and thought that he and Fu Shen couldn't pretend forever that they didn't get along. Sooner or later, the two of them would openly be going everywhere together. Being frank with Emperor Changzhi now would be better than being guilty of "lying to one's sovereign" later.

Cupping his hands, he said, "Permit me to explain, Your Majesty. When the Retired Emperor arranged this marriage for me, there were unmentionable secrets involved."

As expected, Emperor Changzhi's curiosity was provoked. "Let Us hear of them."

Pushing the blame onto the late crown prince and slightly glorifying the true reason behind Emperor Yuantai arranging their marriage, Yan Xiaohan explained everything in detail. Emperor Changzhi listened, entranced. He said in astonishment,

"So Father... From what you say, you and the Marquis of Jingning aren't truly husband and wife in fact, and you have only been taking care of him for the sake of Beiyan's military power?"

Unflappably, Yan Xiaohan hinted, "Your Majesty, the wounds to the Marquis of Jingning's legs will not heal fully for the rest of his life. He can't continue leading troops. But the Beiyan Cavalry will always be under his control. The empress is his only full-blood little sister. If you treat the empress well, you will no longer need to use any crafty maneuvers. The Beiyan Cavalry will naturally be a major aid to the court."

Emperor Changzhi, not letting him off, pursued, "So what is actually going on between you and Fu Shen?"

"..." Yan Xiaohan hadn't thought that His Majesty would ignore proper business in favor of being extraordinarily interested in his domestic life. He could only say, "Your Majesty, I was born a cut-sleeve and will never have offspring. The Marquis of Jingning is young and soldierly. I want the military power that he holds. Being married to him while I am about it poses no conflict."

Though he loved him, love had its limits. Power was more important than love. But leaving aside this point, overall, he still loved him.

The way he described himself was practically like a reproduction of Emperor Changzhi. Emperor Changzhi felt sympathy for someone in a similar position to himself, and he had understood the implicit promise of "never have offspring." He was satisfied with Yan Xiaohan's good sense, and some of his wariness had vanished. He magnanimously waved a hand and said, "All is well. You may withdraw."

Yan Xiaohan bowed and left with a sneer in his heart.

As if to bear out what Yan Xiaohan had said, not long after, news came from the north that the Beiyan Cavalry, entrenched in Ganzhou, had sent troops to Ningzhou. The wretched Ningzhou rebel troops once again got things going and were pounded to scrap iron by the Beiyan soldiers, who were like tigers released from a cage. Five days later, the Beiyan Army had retaken all of Ningzhou.

Along with battlefield reports sent to all the military commissioners and the new court in the south, there was also a letter personally written by the Beiyan commander, the Marquis of Jingning Fu Shen.

At morning court, Yan Xiaohan hid his hands, trembling like chaff being sifted, in his wide sleeves, but no one took note of his unusual condition, and no one cared what was written in that letter.

Amid extreme shock, everyone was digesting the same fact: Fu Shen was back.

Just looking at that handwriting with its knife-edge strokes, you seemed to be looking at General Fu himself, eternally striving against the current, capable of turning the tide. Since the catastrophe, he was the first person to raise a banner in support of the throne, the first to retake Ningzhou, the first to send word to all points, to ask the various military commissioners to send aid to join him in expelling the foreign enemy and retaking the Central Plains.

Of all the soldiers in the country, only the Beiyan Cavalry had followed through on the words "defend our homes and our nation."

Not even the court of Jiangnan, which considered itself to be legitimate, necessarily had as strong a power to rally support as he did. Before half a month had passed, all the military commissioners had answered one after another. Huainan and Xiangzhou were the first to dispatch troops, pushing the defensive line of the Tartar and Zhe army back to the north of the Han River. The Beiyan Cavalry had Fu Shen to oversee it. They went through the opposing forces as if splitting bamboo, rapidly retaking the provinces and counties west of Chang'an.

In the fourth month, Jiangnan's court dispatched troops that went north by two routes. On one route, they assaulted Xuzhou with the Huainan forces; on the other route, they encircled Chang'an with the Xiangzhou forces and the Beiyan Army.

The sixteenth day of the fifth month, in Tangli Town at the foot of Mount Jiming.

There had only been a small portion of the Tartar and Zhe army here. The Beiyan Cavalry had swept them away cleanly without exerting much effort. There was a very deep river near Tangli Town, called the Ziyang River, which converged with the Han River to the east. Fu Shen led a team of cavalry in an inspection beside the river and determined that there were no remaining enemy forces there to ambush them. Looking into the distance, he saw human figures flickering in the forest across the river. There seemed to be hoofbeats coming to the riverside. So he beckoned and called over a young soldier. "Go around to the other side and scout around, see who those people are."

The young soldier was just about to obey orders when it seemed that the other side could wait no longer; someone rushed out of the forest, urging on his horse. Fu Shen, hearing movement, turned his head and was just about to take up his bow when, unexpectedly, he happened to meet the eyes of the person on the opposite bank.

His mind roared.

On the other side, Yan Xiaohan froze into a wooden post on the spot. Unconsciously, he tugged his horse's reins. The warhorse neighed and nearly threw him off.

It was as if his soul had been yanked out and he was walking in a dream. He blankly opened his mouth, but he didn't make a sound.

Fu Shen, relying entirely on a scrap of reason, gripped his horse's belly loosely with his thighs and approached the river. He was just about to give a shout to confirm his identity when he saw Yan Xiaohan across the river, like a wandering spirit, urge his horse up to the bank and take a few steps into the water. Then the horse, afraid of the depth, didn't dare to go on, and he simply jumped off, quickly removed all the heavy things on him, and dove right into the racing river.

There was no need to confirm. Apart from the one he had at home, you wouldn't find a second person in the world who was that stupid.

Fu Shen lost his mind on the spot. "Yan Menggui! Are you trying to get yourself killed?"

He dismounted and charged to the riverside and called loudly to a soldier next to him: "Go get rope!"

Fortunately it wasn't yet summer, and the river hadn't risen. Yan Xiaohan was a decent swimmer. When he reached the middle of the river, he caught the rope thrown by Fu Shen and was dragged up onto the bank. His strength was exhausted, his chest heaving. Never mind speaking, even breathing posed difficulties. But, as if possessed, he stared fixedly at Fu Shen, his eyes bloodshot, so red that blood seemed about to pour from them.

Before Fu Shen could feel happy, he was frightened by his condition. He had never seen such an original means of recklessness. Scolding words had already come to his throat, but as soon as he moved, Yan Xiaohan suddenly threw himself at him. As if afraid that he would run away, dripping wet as he was, he hugged him tightly.

The towering flames of rage instantly burned out into a stream of powerless smoke.

"…"

Fu Shen squeezed his eyes shut. His mind was a blank. After a long moment, he put his arms around his faintly trembling back and clutched tight.

He heard that his own voice was shaking, too.

"I've been longing day and night… and finally I really see you."

CHAPTER SIXTY-SIX

THERE WERE THOUSANDS OF WORDS IN YAN XIAOHAN'S HEAD, but it was as if his throat were stuffed with cotton. His grip was so strong he was practically about to squeeze the breath out of the man in his arms. His soul had flown away somewhere, and he was numb all over. After a long time, sensation at last returned bit by bit. He felt Fu Shen gently patting his back.

Following the tempo of the patting, his heartbeat slowed gradually. A voice broke through from the bottom of his heart. This time Yan Xiaohan followed his desire, naturally speaking the thought aloud.

"I've missed you so much."

The wad of cotton loosened at last, and Yan Xiaohan regained control of his throat, but perhaps he hadn't yet had enough practice. His voice was extremely hoarse. "Since we parted in Kuizhou City, it's been a whole year…"

"I know." Fu Shen's heart was aching, the rims of his eyes burning. He had a premonition that he was going to humiliate himself today. "… I've been counting the days."

"We hadn't even been married half a year." Yan Xiaohan softly let out a breath, not daring to exert himself. He seemed to be acting with the fearful utmost caution of having at last struggled free of a nightmare, escaped pain. "This year has been so long, almost longer than my whole life.

"I couldn't wait for you to retake the capital and pacify the nation, so I came to find you. Even if I can only be your foot soldier—"

He gritted his teeth, as if swallowing at once all the agony of long nights spent tossing and turning. Emphasizing each word, he said, "I will never take another half a step away from you."

Fu Shen's face was pressed against his neck. He laughed quietly, then very tolerantly said, "All right. You won't move an inch from me. Whenever I go out to fight, you have my permission to sit in my lap and watch the battle. How does that sound?"

Yan Xiaohan still had tears in his eyes. This statement brought him up short.

Couldn't he let him fully indulge in some sentiment?!

That he could speak and hold a conversation proved that he had passed the most agitated period and had returned to being an ordinary person in his right mind. Fu Shen loosened his grip slightly and looked into his face. He wiped the beads of water from his eyelashes, then suddenly said with a laugh, "After hugging me for so long, how come you haven't said my name?"

Yan Xiaohan froze.

He didn't dare.

He was afraid that all of this would be like countless dreams, boundlessly tender, but if he spoke, he would suddenly start awake and be left with only a quiet and deserted room, all on his own.

"Hm?" said Fu Shen, smiling.

The one in front of him was his real beloved, warm and living, who could fight and scold.

Yan Xiaohan closed his eyes. A water droplet suddenly rolled down from the tip of his eyebrow. That sound seemed to drain away all his courage.

"Jingyuan."

Fu Shen took his hand and pinched the acupoint between his thumb and forefinger while firmly agreeing, "Yes."

That "yes" accompanied by the sharp sting on his hand went straight to the top of his skull, clearing his mind. Yan Xiaohan gave a start at the pinch and suddenly opened his eyes wide.

The dream was over.

He was still here.

Fu Shen drew back his hand as if nothing were the matter and carelessly said, "Better? Then let's go. Are your people on the opposite bank? We'll go—"

Yan Xiaohan deftly pulled him to a stop and lowered his voice. "Lord Marquis, could you have your people withdraw?"

"Why?" said Fu Shen.

"I want to kiss you," said Yan Xiaohan, "right now. I can't wait."

Fu Shen said, "… Open your eyes and take a look around. Is this the time?"

"You said it yourself," Yan Xiaohan said calmly, "you'd give me whatever I wanted. I want to kiss you."

The irresistible display of feeling just now was already over-stepping the bounds. The soldiers accompanying him all wished they could stretch their necks and grow rabbit ears. If he let him kiss him now, Fu Shen's dignity would fall to rock bottom. He gave a dry cough but softened his grandeur somewhat in spite of himself. "I'll have to owe you for now. You're so sensible, don't take advantage of being favored to demand unreasonable indulgences."

Hearing this, Yan Xiaohan's eyes curved. Instantly, it seemed that all the radiance of spring in the world was contained in that smile. Even Fu Shen's heart, sturdy as steel, wavered. "You… Forget it, how many people are there on the other side? Who's leading the troops?"

"I went ahead to scout out the way with a dozen people. The main force is behind us." Yan Xiaohan upended all his resources and laid them out on display without hesitation. "General Zhao Xicheng is leading the troops."

"General Zhao. That's easy enough to handle, then." Fu Shen suddenly remembered something. "Hey, how did you end up coming with them?"

Yan Xiaohan rubbed his nose and awkwardly said, "I'm not skilled in military affairs. I had to shamelessly beg His Majesty to get a position as military supervisor."

Fu Shen very disrespectfully laughed aloud. "Fate can't be avoided. We must resign ourselves to it."

Yan Xiaohan watched him helplessly and indulgently. Fu Shen beckoned over a soldier and handed him his token. "Go to the opposite shore and take this to General Zhao. Tell him that the Beiyan Cavalry is garrisoned in Tangli Town. I'm holding his military supervisor so he can have a few days of peace."

Yan Xiaohan said, "Jingyuan…"

"Oh, you heard me." Without evasion, Fu Shen took his hand and turned to say to the dumbfounded soldier, "General Zhao is welcome to come here and visit whenever he has time. We'll discuss how to attack Chang'an."

He and Yan Xiaohan rode on a single horse and raced back to Tangli Town as swift as the wind. On returning to the house where the Beiyan Cavalry was temporarily garrisoned, Fu Shen kicked open a door and pushed Yan Xiaohan inside. He ordered the bodyguard behind him, "Bring a pail of hot water."

This was Fu Shen's residence. It was unusually simple and crude, with only an adobe kang bed-stove and a damaged table. There was a messy pile of writing materials on the desk, and a wooden wheelchair in a corner.

When Yan Xiaohan saw that wheelchair, his pupils contracted slightly, but he didn't say anything. Just then, Fu Shen walked in and turned up a cloth bundle from the kang. "Take off your wet clothes, don't catch cold. Make do with mine for now…"

Before he could finish, he was suddenly embraced tightly

from behind. Yan Xiaohan said heavily into his ear, "Lord Marquis, can I kiss you now?"

Fu Shen performed a clever maneuver, quickly pressing him onto the kang. He stroked his chin maliciously. "Are you so impatient?"

There was a bang as the door of the room opened wide. Yu Qiaoting charged in anxiously and yelled in a great voice: "General, I heard you fished up a beauty from the river…"

Fu Shen was pointedly silent.

The two of them were in a very indecent posture. General Yu nearly went blind. The "beauty" being pressed against the bed by the Marquis of Jingning with no power to resist narrowed his eyes. His gaze was like a knife, murderous energy spreading everywhere. Fu Shen straightened up slightly and asked softly, "Qingheng, what did you just say?"

Not for nothing had General Yu seen his share of the world and its mores. He answered with a grave mien: "General, I heard that you fished a wife out of the river. Carry on, I will make myself scarce."

Having said this, as if his ass were on fire, he left with his tail between his legs.

"That scoundrel…" Fu Shen shook his head and laughed. Suddenly, his collar tightened. When he came back to himself, he was forced to bend. "What is it?"

Like an enraged pufferfish, Yan Xiaohan asked with his hackles raised, "Why didn't he knock before coming into your room?"

Fu Shen didn't answer.

Before he could protest against this injustice, his mouth was firmly stopped by Yan Xiaohan.

His lips were chilled from being dunked in the river, very soft, but soon they became savage, with something of the force of wishing to devour. Fu Shen retreated again and again, but the small of his back and the back of his head were irresistibly held. Finally, his arms cramped from the awkward posture of propping himself up with his hands beside Yan Xiaohan's ears. He staggered and fell against Yan Xiaohan's chest, his lips and teeth finally forced apart. Then, holding him, Yan Xiaohan rolled in a half-circle at the bedside, turning to hold him down. His lips again came pressing close.

Enveloped by familiar breathing, Fu Shen was giddy from being kissed. HIs breathing was rapid. Indistinctly, he said, "How jealous can you get…"

Yan Xiaohan produced a quiet laugh from his throat, then indeed eased off, no longer dominating, only affectionately pecking his lips. He was just about to speak when a knocking came at the door. The bodyguard said from outside, "General, the hot water is here!"

Fu Shen sat up, looked at the mess the vinegar jar fished out of the water had made, and pointed menacingly at him. He himself stood up and went to open the door and take a big pail of hot water. Yan Xiaohan conscientiously went over with a small wooden bench. Fu Shen rolled up his sleeve and tested the water temperature, then said, "Fine, come here and wash. I'll watch the door for you."

Yan Xiaohan silently undid his belt and removed his wet clothes, revealing the edge of a white bandage on his shoulder. Fu Shen glimpsed it from the corner of his eye and immediately reached out to hold him back. "How did you get that? How far does the wound go?"

"It's nothing, I was careless and got some skin scraped off. It's probably scabbed over by now," Yan Xiaohan said. "The army doctor got worked up over nothing and insisted on bandaging it."

Fu Shen was still concerned. "Turn around, let me see."

Yan Xiaohan obediently sat on the short bench with his back to him and his upper body uncovered, using a damp towel to wipe the traces of water from his body. Fu Shen carefully removed the bandage on his shoulder and saw that a bright red wound, over four inches long, made by a sharp blade, lay across the smooth skin and muscle. Though it was already closing up and healing, the scab was only a thin layer that seemed as if it might break at any time.

Fu Shen's military campaigns had covered the four points of the compass. He had seen far too many injuries more serious than this. If he had received such a wound, he probably wouldn't even have frowned. But now, with this wound spanning Yan Xiaohan's shoulder, the pain he felt was a little unbearable.

After a brief silence, he lightly touched the still puffy swelling at the edges of the wound with the dry pads of his fingers. "Does it hurt?"

Yan Xiaohan laughed. "If I say it hurts, will there be candy for me?"

Fu Shen murmured indecipherably and suddenly lowered his head. Yan Xiaohan felt a soft, warm sensation lingering briefly over his wound. The newly grown tender flesh was extremely sensitive. A slight tickle was like a spark hitting hot oil and dry kindling. Warmth swept through his whole body with a crash. His limbs and muscles hovered on the edge of a shudder. His voice instantly became disgracefully hoarse. In a trembling voice, he said, "Jingyuan... what are you doing?"

"Keep washing." Fu Shen straightened up and gently slapped his bare back, then rebuked him as if nothing were the matter: "Even wounded, you dared to jump into the river. What if it gets infected? You'll be crying about it later."

Yan Xiaohan, at the end of his endurance, was about to throw the towel into the pail when Fu Shen yanked it out of his hands, soaked it in the hot water, and slowly wiped along the back of his neck. Quietly, he said, "Don't move."

If he hadn't come to find him, with Yan Xiaohan's position in the little court in Jiangnan, an arduous task like going to the front line would never have fallen to him no matter what.

He had been wounded for Fu Shen's sake.

"Is your heart aching for me?" At first Yan Xiaohan had been bewildered. Then he gradually understood. Had he had a tail, it would have been sticking up to the sky now. "If I can get a kiss from you in exchange for a little wound like this, then…"

Fu Shen said, "Do you dare to finish that sentence?"

"No, I don't dare." Yan Xiaohan turned and looked at him with a smile in his eyes. "Since I know that the Lord Marquis's heart aches for me, I will be sure to be more careful in the future."

Fu Shen looked at him suspiciously, suspecting that he had something to add.

As expected, Yan Xiaohan nimbly grabbed his wrist and lowered his head to kiss the back of his hand. He raised his head and warmly said, "I couldn't bear to make your heart ache."

CHAPTER SIXTY-SEVEN

TEASING AND FOOLING AROUND, DOTING AND CLINGING, IT TOOK the two of them over an hour to finish bathing. Fu Shen was the target of Yan Xiaohan's deliberate mischief, getting splashed all over with water. There was really nothing else he could do. He also had to change. By the time they were all cleaned up and went out, they once again ran into Yu Qiaoting, who was passing by.

General Yu's gaze revolved between the two of them. He acutely picked something up at once and said with a smirk, "Congratulations to the general on your great happiness!"

Fu Shen, bewildered, said, "What is there to be happy about?"

Chuckling, Yu Qiaoting said, "A reunion after an absence is sweeter than being newlyweds. Doesn't that in itself merit congratulations?"

Fu Shen's head began to hurt from the injustice. He was just about to snap back when Yan Xiaohan suddenly said unhurriedly from behind him, "You're joking, General Yu. With the war still in an unsteady state, the Central Plains not yet stabilized, as a minister, naturally I am taxing my thoughts and ingenuity to the utmost to ease the tribulations of the nation. How could I indulge in matters of romance, forget my duty to be faithful to my sovereign and love my country?"

Yu Qiaoting simply didn't dare to believe that these resonating words had come out of Yan Xiaohan's mouth. He looked at Fu Shen, completely bewildered, but saw their general looking at Yan Xiaohan, his expression natural and serene, tenderness and doting ready to drip from the corners of his eyes and brows.

Yu Qiaoting was in awe.

So the reason the two of you were shut up in that room so long behind everyone's backs was to discuss how to retake old territory and rescue the lives of the people? Pardon his lack of manners, truly.

In addition to lying through his teeth, Yan Xiaohan, after speaking, also shot Yu Qiaoting a sideways look holding the suspicion that he was a beast, then unblushingly stalked off with awe-inspiring righteousness.

Yu Qiaoting inexplicably shrank four inches beneath his gaze. Fu Shen, spectating from the sidelines with pleasure at his misfortune, said, "Got your idle hand scratched, did you? You deserve it."

Not for nothing was this the number one crafty sycophant of both the Yuantai and Changzhi courts. He'd been here less than half a day, and already Fu Shen's relations with his comrades were tottering on the brink of disaster!

In the evening, Yan Xiaohan ate along with the Beiyan Army's high-ranking officers. Through a mutual tacit understanding, everyone ignored his position as the new court's army supervisor and only treated him as Fu Shen's family member. The meal was marvelously harmonious. After the simple and crude reception feast was eaten, Fu Shen prepared to go inspect the campsite as usual. A deputy general ought to have accompanied him in this, but tonight all the Beiyan Army's officers seemed to be practicing the art of silence. Seeing this, Yan Xiaohan knew that it was everyone showing respect for his feelings, so he conscientiously consented. "In that case, I can accompany the general."

"How perceptive of you," Fu Shen said with a false smile.

Yu Qiaoting had accompanied Yan Xiaohan and Fu Shen when they had gone up Golden Terrace together; naturally he was well aware of how matters stood between them. The other officers, even if they hadn't known originally, having heard what had happened by the river today, also ought to have understood that a ruse had turned into reality for these two as they developed feelings for each other. Fu Shen hadn't brought this out into the open directly, but by bringing Yan Xiaohan back to the Beiyan Army's garrison, he had as good as tacitly acknowledged that Yan Xiaohan was on their side.

That being the case, no one was going to be so tactless as to want to stick himself between the two of them. With unprecedented unity, the Beiyan Army made time for intimacy without anyone to disturb them for this pair of ill-fated lovebirds at last reunited.

Immediately outside of Tangli Town, there were lofty mountains and a torrential river. The night breeze carried a delicate scent of flowers. The starry sea above their heads was radiant. The two of them strolled abreast on horseback beneath the vast heavens. This past year's separation and the racing around, the pain of longing, all flowed into the distance like the river, leaving behind only the huge unmoved rock of the heart after the waves had washed the sand away.

There wasn't much worth telling about Fu Shen's activities in Ganzhou. It had been nothing but storing provisions and drilling soldiers. Yan Xiaohan, meanwhile, carefully explained the situation of the new court to him, especially Emperor Changzhi's attitude and the struggle between the factions of north and south, old and new. When he mentioned this, it was unavoidable to touch upon the several wrongs experienced by the empress in the harem. Yan Xiaohan considered it repeatedly and decided that he couldn't conceal this from him, so he gave a detailed account of the facts.

Fu Ling marrying into Prince Qi Manor had been a marriage Fu Shen had undertaken to choose for her. He had thought that Prince Qi was mild-mannered and sincere, that this would be a perfectly satisfactory marriage. Who could have expected worldly events to be so inconstant? The country had been broken up, and now it seemed instead that he had personally pushed his little sister into the fire.

Of all the things he had promised Fu Ling, he hadn't accomplished a single one.

Fu Shen was expressionless, his profile in the night like a stern, solid stone statue, but Yan Xiaohan kept thinking that he seemed peculiarly frail. He was just about to say something to console him when Fu Shen spoke ahead of him, shoving his consolations back into his belly. "Thank you for looking after her.

"Even if I had been there myself, I may not have been as attentive and thorough as you." He gave a sad, self-mocking laugh. "Moreover, I couldn't have offended the leading light of the Jiangnan party for her sake and run the risk of being banished."

Though Yan Xiaohan hadn't explained it in detail, Fu Shen had waded through the mire of officialdom. Putting that together with what he knew of Lady Xue, of course he guessed that what Yan Xiaohan had called "begging the emperor to be assigned army supervisor" had been an excuse made up for the sake of putting him at ease. Xue Sheng was the head of one of the six ministries, a high minister taking part in the Yanning Hall Assembly, and his daughter with the best future prospects had died out of nowhere at Yan Xiaohan's hands. However biased His Majesty might be in Yan Xiaohan's favor, he still had to appear to be impartial.

He hadn't asked to come with the army at all... he had been kicked out of the central administration for committing an error.

For a moment, guilt and frustration were like waves billowing to the sky, pressing down on him as though he were drowning. Fu Shen knew very well that whatever road he had chosen, he could only continue to walk it; there was no chance of retreat. But right now, unprecedented doubts rose in his heart, like a gale blowing, like a mountain shaking.

Had he really taken the right path?

He was a useless brother. He hadn't given his sister, alone in the palace, any support, instead allowing her to become a thorn in everyone's flesh. He was also a useless husband. When war had first erupted, he had chosen to go north, leaving Yan Xiaohan to hold up the situation in Jiangnan by himself, after which he had still needed Yan Xiaohan to clean up his mess for him, leading to him being forced to leave the central authority and come to the dangerous front lines.

Protecting one's family and one's nation was the vocation of the Beiyan Cavalry, but he had nearly ruined his family.

Yan Xiaohan gave a tug, reining in his horse. He stopped where he was. Seeming somewhat displeased, he flatly said, "We haven't seen each other for so long that you seem to have grown distant from me."

He didn't call Fu Shen by his name, and he didn't teasingly say "Lord Marquis" or "General," making this statement seem unusually cold and harsh. Fu Shen's heart instantly tightened. Uncertainly, he thought, *What does he mean? Is he angry?*

As soon as a person gets caught in a dilemma, his judgment will plummet as steeply as a cliff face, and his intellect will be gone forever with it. If this were in ordinary times, Fu Shen would have had countless words, countless means of answering Yan Xiaohan's statement. He would even have been able to pass over the surface concerns and understand what Yan Xiaohan actually meant.

But now he could only force himself to control his frantic heartbeat and, feigning calm, say, "No, I haven't, what are you talking about?"

Even under cover of night, Yan Xiaohan still noticed the

unnatural stiffness of his whole body. He sighed silently, unable to keep up even this slight false front of coldness. He inwardly admonished himself that in front of him was a club impervious to reason. He couldn't get fretful. He had to pull his reasoning to pieces and crush it up, slowly explain it to him.

He jumped off his horse and moved aside, then reached out his arms toward Fu Shen. "Here, come down."

Fu Shen certainly didn't need him to catch him. He automatically jumped down on his own. Yan Xiaohan helplessly walked over and took him by the hand. He found a big, smooth stone beside the river and made him sit on it.

The level area on top of the stone was limited. Two grown men sitting shoulder to shoulder were unavoidably squashed together. Fu Shen put an arm around Yan Xiaohan, making sure he didn't fall off. Frowning, he said, "The wind is cold at night. We'll only stay a little while. Don't catch cold."

Unexpectedly, Yan Xiaohan said, "Jingyuan, in your heart, don't you think that only you are a great hero able to support heaven and earth, and others are all three-year-old children?"

Fu Shen gave a dry cough and awkwardly said, "What great truths are you babbling about?"

"… Settle down," Yan Xiaohan said, "I'm being serious."

"How could I?" Fu Shen couldn't help laughing. "Isn't it obvious?"

Yan Xiaohan said, "Since you know that others aren't three-year-old children, then why are you always striving to be everyone's mother and father, shield them from the wind and rain?"

Fu Shen's arm involuntarily tightened around him.

"General, you must admit, you don't have three heads and six arms, and you aren't a god. There will always be matters you can't attend to." Yan Xiaohan gently poked his temple. "If you could solve all the world's problems on your own, what would the rest of us fatheads be doing here?"

Fu Shen said, "I…"

"No one in the world owes anyone else," Yan Xiaohan said.

"Even though you and I are husband and wife, even though you and the empress are brother and sister, we still can't use that to hijack you, sit there crying and waiting for you to rescue us whenever anything goes wrong."

Fu Shen understood what he meant, and at the same time his description jabbed his sense of humor just right. It truly became a matter of not knowing whether to laugh or cry. "If you're going to be reasonable, then do it right. Don't sulk."

Yan Xiaohan threw open his arms and pulled him into his embrace. Right into his ear, he softly said, "The empress has a tenacious temperament, and if she's inconvenienced, she has nowhere to go to complain about it. Not taking care of her properly really was wrong of you. But me leaving Jiangnan to come here, while I did use the impetus of my discord with Xue Sheng, don't you understand yet what the true reason was?"

The tip of Fu Shen's ear was trembling from his warm breath. That tremor followed his blood and went to the deepest and safest place at the bottom of his heart.

"No one forced me. I wanted to come find you. I had already waited seven years. I didn't want to wait any longer for anyone's care." Yan Xiaohan bent his head and kissed the hair on his temple. "Jingyuan, I'm your husband, not your burden, so don't grow distant from me. If it happens again, I'll really be angry."

There was nothing in the night but endless silence.

After a long silence, Fu Shen took his hand and pressed it to his chest. Gruffly, he said, "But, Menggui, if I can't even take care of my own family, how could I have the face to pose as a 'loyal subject,' speak rashly of retaking territory, protecting my home and my nation? Wouldn't it all be a joke?"

Yan Xiaohan closed his eyes in vexation, took a deep breath, and thought to himself that they couldn't get past this tonight.

Fu Shen's sense of obligation was too heavy. Since he had gone north, this shadow had begun to lie over his heart. And a year's separation was like poison. With the extra ingredient of the empress, the multi-faceted reaction had at last fermented this guilt into an obsession.

"Enough. If you insist on making yourself unhappy, I'll help you out."

Yan Xiaohan straightforwardly said, "As an older brother, you have failed to take proper care of your little sister; you ought to be punished. I am two years older than you, and you called me 'gege' yourself. This past year, I've been busy building up the new court and didn't go north to seek you. That being the case, as your gege, shouldn't I also be punished?"

CHAPTER SIXTY-EIGHT

YAN XIAOHAN'S ANGLE OF QUESTIONING WAS TRULY CUNNING. No
matter what answer Fu Shen gave, it would amount to acknowledging him as "gege;" if he didn't answer, it would still be taken
by Yan Xiaohan as tacit acknowledgment. This way, he had the
advantage. He spoke of being "punished," but in the end it
would most likely come to another of his numerous tricks for
offending public decency.

But with this interruption from him, the guilt that was like a
lead weight in Fu Shen's chest seemed to have lightened; it was
no longer heavily burning. Yan Xiaohan was very skilled at
sorting him out. Probably it was because Fu Shen had taken in
what he had said, and those words were gradually planting a suitable sense of security in Fu Shen's heart. While it hadn't reached
the level of "reliance" yet, at least when he ran into trouble, Fu
Shen was willing to talk it over with him instead of concealing
everything and preferring to bear it alone to the death.

"You ought to be punished." Fu Shen turned his hand over
and rubbed it against his cheek. "Then I sentence you to perform
physical labor and carry me back to town on your back, all
right?"

"Fine," Yan Xiaohan readily agreed.

Having said this, not yet satisfied, he egged him on: "This is an opportunity not to be missed. You don't want to give me some other punishment?"

Fu Shen hooked his chin with one finger and laughed. "My lady, what you're thinking of isn't called 'punishment.' It's called 'be wary of strangers bearing gifts.'"

"What a dirty mind you have to see such filth everywhere," Yan Xiaohan said virtuously. "We're at the front lines, of course I'm not thinking of doing anything to you—*I'm* not a beast."

General Fu, having inexplicably turned into a "beast," was speechless.

With his arms around Fu Shen's shoulders, Yan Xiaohan pulled him up in front of him. Fu Shen had been leaning crookedly against Yan Xiaohan to begin with. Now he simply lay down with his head pillowed on Yan Xiaohan's lap. Yan Xiaohan bent down and kissed the center of his brow. "Don't be impatient. It won't be long before I'll have a chance to satisfy you."

Fu Shen wasn't in the mood to try demonstrating his innocence. Hearing this, he lazily said, "I advise you not to speak with such satisfaction. When we've taken Chang'an, are you really not going to return to court? Or are you planning to change occupations and come along with the Beiyan Cavalry as army supervisor?"

"Can I sit in the Lord Marquis's lap as army supervisor?" Yan Xiaohan quietly asked in turn.

Fu Shen imagined this scene and laughed uncontrollably, nearly rolling out of Yan Xiaohan's lap. Yan Xiaohan quickly reached out to hold him in place and said, "I'm not planning to return."

Fu Shen looked up and asked, "Why not?"

"Jiangnan is too cold," said Yan Xiaohan. "I don't like it there."

"Nonsense," said Fu Shen, laughing. "It's already the fifth month."

"Lord Marquis, do you know the meaning of cold bedding

and a deserted pillow, wandering great distances in your sleep?" Yan Xiaohan sighed, seeming very depressed. "Whether I come with you or continue to follow the army, it's all right as long as I stay in the north and don't go too far away from you. It was so hard to find you. If you make me go back to the taste of tossing and turning in bed, how could I not be cold?"

These words accurately hit Fu Shen right in his weak spot. He was briefly speechless, then said with difficulty, "Have you been taking classes behind my back? You've started reciting poetry."

Yan Xiaohan held back laughter. "Now that you mention it, I've remembered something. Do you know, while I was in Jinling, I ran into a hunter who was selling a wild goose he had brought down." Somewhat sheepishly, he said, "I was a little out of my mind then. I grabbed onto that thing from the north and wouldn't let go. I kept thinking, what if it was you…?"

"Ahem, well," Fu Shen interrupted him. Uncomfortably he said, "There's no 'what if' about it, it was me."

Yan Xiaohan was bewildered. The point of his throat bobbed. Hoarsely, he asked, "You… what?"

"There was a piece of white silk tied to the goose's leg, and on it was written 'Is my wife well?', right?" Fu Shen took his hand and frankly said, "That was me. When I was in Ganzhou, I really missed you unbearably, so I thought of this method."

Who would have thought that a bit of sweetness could still be extracted from those bitter days? It was as if Yan Xiaohan had fallen into a dream. His chest heaved. After a long moment, he said in a daze, "It's over ten thousand li from north to south. That such a coincidence should happen to us…"

With an awkward laugh, Fu Shen said, "Yes, truly a coincidence."

Yan Xiaohan heard something wrong in his tone and looked down at him suspiciously. Fu Shen recalled the foolish things he had done and felt rare embarrassment. He felt the urgent need to squeeze into a hole. "I didn't do much else, it's only that I thought that it was a single wild goose—how much of a coincidence would it take for it to fly to Jinling City? So I got the soldiers in the city to help me, well... take down another dozen or so. I thought that this way, maybe one of them would end up in your hands."

"A dozen or so?" Yan Xiaohan repeated.

"About that many?" Fu Shen considered for a while and uncertainly said, "Anyway, there was one or two every day when we drilled, probably? I don't remember precisely."

"You..." Yan Xiaohan simply didn't know what to say to him. "You're really..."

"I nearly turned Du Leng into a vet," Fu Shen replied calmly. "I missed you, too. You think that because Jiangnan is cold, Ganzhou isn't cold?"

When in all his dreams he had wished to fly across vast stretches of mountains and rivers, how could the person beyond those mountains and rivers not think of him? Only after the reunion, a mixture of sorrow and happiness, did they find that each of them had been as obsessed as the other, each as solitary.

They looked at each other without words, rendered speechless. Only a deep kiss and a close embrace could slightly soothe the pain at heart.

In this moment, the universe was quiet. Stillness reigned supreme, the world seeming to have come to a standstill. Only the river raced endlessly onward, always forward, flowing toward the horizon.

The next day, before daybreak, Fu Shen woke in Yan Xiaohan's arms and sat up slowly with the weariness of inadequate sleep. The hand on his waist slipped down. Yan Xiaohan, coming up empty, quickly woke up as well. Hoarsely, he asked, "Are you getting up?"

"Kept you up last night, did I?" Fu Shen gently patted him on the back. Probably because he had just woken up, his voice and movements were unbelievably gentle. "There's nothing to do today, you can lie down for a while."

He never slept deeply, and with the vast fluctuation of emotions last night, he had gone in and out of sleep during the night. As soon as he moved, Yan Xiaohan would sleepily pull him into his arms, say some soothing words, and fall fast asleep again holding him.

"I'm all right." With difficulty, Yan Xiaohan struggled free of the warm bedding and threw himself forward, hanging himself entirely from Fu Shen's back. Drowsily, he said, "Don't wear those boots today, use the wheelchair, I'll help you get cleaned up."

Though the boots made by the Beiyan Army's armaments department could let him walk as normal, they weren't his real legs, after all. The means of exerting force wasn't the same, and wearing them long-term put an especially great strain on the midsection. Therefore, while traveling with the army, Fu Shen also had to bring along a wheelchair and use it instead when he wasn't so busy.

Yan Xiaohan had noticed it when he had come in the day before, he just hadn't said anything. Only now did he bring it up, pretending as if it were normal. Fu Shen understood his quiet consideration and nodded to give permission. "All right."

On his way back from fetching water, Yan Xiaohan forgot to close the door. Yu Qiaoting, who had gotten up early, unluckily happened to be passing by the room again and couldn't hold back his exuberant curiosity. Through the half-ajar door, he snuck a peek inside and was nearly startled into dropping the dough cake in his hand.

The Marquis of Jingning, who killed without batting an eyelash and whose name alone struck terror into the hearts of barbarians, was sitting obediently on the edge of the kang while Yan Xiaohan wiped his face and hands with a towel, skillful and solicitous as an old maidservant. When Yan Xiaohan had cleaned him up entirely, Fu Shen lazily reached out his arms and said something. Yan Xiaohan bent down and picked him up, then placed him in the wheelchair.

From this scene, you wouldn't have thought he had broken his legs. You would have thought instead that he had fallen and hit his head.

General Yu, still a bachelor to this day, simply couldn't understand it no matter what: what had happened to the Beiyan Commander, with civil accomplishments enough to calm the nation and military accomplishments enough to pacify the universe, to turn him into a husband who cared for nothing but his wife?

Soon, this question came to be shared among all the Beiyan Army officers garrisoned in Tangli Town.

They hadn't seen Fu Shen while he had been convalescing at Yan Manor; that was truly what was known as needing only to extend your hand for clothing and needing only to open your mouth for food. Now, out in the hinterlands, while Yan Xiaohan wanted to look after him, he could only display his prowess within limits.

In fact, anything improper was done behind closed doors. Outside in front of others, especially in front of a crowd of subordinates, while Fu Shen wasn't particular about the dignity of a commander, Yan Xiaohan still had to keep a grasp on propriety to keep from being denounced. But the more conscientious he was, the more small actions like pouring tea and even whispering into his ear seemed restrained but tender.

It wasn't long before everyone had run off groaning in the face of their clinginess.

Fu Shen picked up his tea and drank a mouthful. Puzzled, he said, "What's going on today? Each and every one of them is acting like a lovesick maiden."

Yan Xiaohan smiled a small, discreet smile. "Who knows?"

No long after, a bodyguard came to report that General Zhao

Xicheng had already crossed the Ziyang River and was just outside the garrison requesting an audience. Without prearrangement, Yan Xiaohan and Fu Shen looked at each other. Fu Shen instructed: "Ask him in." Then, taking advantage of the interval, he turned and said with a smile to Yan Xiaohan, "General Zhao could hardly wait to come. Clearly you have some weight as an army supervisor."

"Just a few pounds and a few ounces, nothing worth mentioning," Yan Xiaohan said generously. "If the Lord Marquis is willing to take me, you can have me for free."

Fu Shen laughed heartily. "Why would I want you for? So I can keep you to cook and eat at the New Year?"

Pretending to be well behaved and docile, Yan Xiaohan said, "Actually, you can also keep me around to entertain you, and go to sleep hugging me."

Fu Shen really did like everything about him. He hadn't felt so pleased and happy since leaving Xinan last year. The smile had yet to fade from his eyes when Zhao Xicheng came in. General Zhao was stunned by the sight. *The Marquis of Jingning looks as though spring has come*, he thought. *Could it be that Chang'an City is on the verge of being taken?*

Zhao Xicheng had previously been an officer in Fenzhou's forces. When the Tartar and Zhe invaded, Fenzhou's commander had died in battle. After Emperor Yuantai had gone west, Zhao Xicheng had been unwilling to defect, so he had led the remnants of Fenzhou's forces to Jingchu. When the new court had been established, he had joined the others in submitting to Jinling's authority.

He was one of the few military officers from the north available to Yan Xiaohan. Fu Shen had fought the Tartars alongside Fenzhou's forces before, and he still had some memory of Zhao Xicheng. He only remembered that he had a frank temper and was a little stubborn. He had always been kept down by Fenzhou's commander. He'd never thought that after the commander's death, Zhao Xicheng would step forth to uphold the standard of the Fenzhou forces, experience his fill of miseries, and finally fight his way back to the Central Plains.

General Zhao was over forty, but he was still extremely respectful toward Fu Shen. The two of them politely deliberated how to attack Chang'an. Seeing that he was in a good mood, Zhao Xicheng said tentatively, "Might I ask, Lord Marquis, how confident are you of success in Chang'an?"

"Hm?" Fu Shen smiled slightly. "Thirty to forty percent, I think. Chang'an is easy to defend but hard to attack. It will be a bitter battle."

Then what are you smiling about?!

Yan Xiaohan sat with them, not saying a word as he listened to their voluble talk, pretending to be a pretty ornament. Every now and then, he glanced at Fu Shen, as if he couldn't see enough of him.

When the discussion of military affairs came to a temporary close, Zhao Xicheng hesitated time and again, then finally stammered out his other goal in coming here: "Lord Marquis, since we will be opening hostilities in a few days, why not have Lord Yan return with me? The army work…"

Fu Shen interrupted before he could finish. "What, you can't fight if you're missing an army supervisor?"

"Well…" General Zhao was brought up short, then said, frowning, "Lord Yan is an army supervisor specially dispatched by His Majesty. I'm afraid it would be against the rules for him to remain with the Beiyan Army."

"Get with the times," Fu Shen said, his smile dimming. "General Zhao, do you want to nitpick about the rules of your new court with me when you're in Beiyan Army territory?"

The two sides weren't one family now. Fu Shen held many territories in the northwest and could all but stand shoulder to shoulder with the new court. Sweat appeared on Zhao Xicheng's forehead. He quickly stood and apologized, repeatedly saying, "Sorry to have given offense."

"When the Retired Emperor issued an edict arranging a

marriage for me, his words held weight. Everyone in the country was aware." Fu Shen put aside his teacup and coolly said, "It is true that Lord Yan is in service to the court, but he is mine. Even the new court's emperor has to obey by first come, first served. If I want him to stay here, then not one hair off his head will leave by this door. General Zhao, do you understand me?"

CHAPTER SIXTY-NINE

QUIETLY SERVING AS THE SOURCE OF CALAMITY, YAN XIAOHAN pretended not to have understood the undercurrents running between Fu Shen and Zhao Xicheng.

The conflicted relationship between the Beiyan Army and the new court would sooner or later be brought to the forefront. It was true that Fu Shen wanted to rebuild the country, but it couldn't be a matter of him fighting up ahead while the new court plugged leaks in the back, ending up empty-handed with only a reputation for being "loyal and obedient."

Emperor Yuantai's assessment of Fu Shen was that he was "loyal to the nation rather than to the sovereign." While he imagined Fu Shen to be excessively rich in ambition, this statement was quite accurate. That Fu Shen had been willing to bow to Emperor Yuantai had been in memory of former affection, but with Sun Yunduan, it was different. Never mind former affection; just in view of the new emperor's treatment of Fu Ling, Fu Shen couldn't let him off.

Moreover, Emperor Yuantai was doing just fine in Shu. Fu Shen hadn't previously intervened to dethrone an emperor, but that didn't mean that he wouldn't step in in the future to determine who sat on the throne.

Fu Shen's words had caused cold sweat to stream from Zhao Xicheng. He felt that he oughtn't to have been loose-tongued. What had he brought up Yan Xiaohan for? Wouldn't it have been nice if everyone could have happily talked over how to take Chang'an?

General Zhao didn't have a deep understanding of Yan Xiaohan and Fu Shen and didn't know what their relationship actually was. More than that, he couldn't work out Fu Shen's intention in keeping Yan Xiaohan with him. It was just that the rumors of "the court's dog injuring a loyal and upright man" had entered people's hearts too deeply. Because of this, looking on as an outside observer, he felt that the greatest likelihood was that Yan Xiaohan had committed too many sins in the past, and now he was suffering retribution.

"I will bear the Lord Marquis's thoughts in mind," Zhao Xicheng said with sincerity all over his face. "Since Lord Yan is also not opposed, then we will follow the Lord Marquis's arrangements in all things."

A soft laugh suddenly sounded in the silent room. Yan Xiaohan slowly raised his head and met the gazes of the other two as they came his way. With a false smile, he said, "Very well. Then that's what we'll do."

When Zhao Xicheng had bid farewell and left, Fu Shen abandoned his gravity and shook his head, smiling. "Lord Yan, it seems that you really are unpopular. He threw you away just like that, without a bit of hesitation."

Yan Xiaohan also shook his head. "I truly had no idea that I would one day be taken by force."

"What are you talking about?" Fu Shen said. "Don't blacken my name. I legally married you, obviously."

Yan Xiaohan couldn't maintain a serious expression. He laughed, his heart softening into a pool of water. Clinging, he drew near to demand a kiss. Fu Shen kissed the corner of his lips. The upshot was that Yan Xiaohan bit back. Holding him down in the wheelchair, he kissed him firmly to win back his losses.

Some days later, all the armed forces assembled outside the city, and the battle of Chang'an formally began.

Chang'an was also called Xijing, the western capital. It was the old capital of the previous dynasty, located at the center of the Central Plains. The population of Chang'an was numerous, and its prosperity no less than the capital's. After the Tartars had come south and invaded, they had treated it as a major strategic location. They had looted the city for several days, causing great suffering to the people, leading to them missing the rule of the Zhou dynasty. When the Beiyan Army had stamped out resistance in the surrounding towns and villages, a lot of people had secretly run from the city to furnish them with secret information. It was said that inside Chang'an there were many roving braves and righteous men who often took advantage of cover of night to assassinate the Tartar officers, and the common people every now and again set fires at the city gates, causing smoke and dust to spread everywhere, creating a false impression that the army was attacking.

They were well provisioned and had inside and outside working together. It was a good time to attack the city.

On the thirtieth day of the fifth month, all forces mobilized. Zhao Xicheng formed the vanguard, the Beiyan Cavalry were the main guard, and Xiangzhou's forces were the rear guard. The Tartar and Zhe massed forty thousand troops outside of Chang'an. The soldiers of the new court were for the most part border troops who had escaped south to Jiangnan after the war was lost. At the outset they were somewhat timid in battle. The Tartar high general Zhehu spied out a flaw in their defenses, and, relying on brute force, charged through wielding his sword and actually cut a swath through the vanguard. The Tartar cavalry surged forward in a body, and the vanguard's formation was dispersed. The bodyguards around Zhao Xicheng were cut down from their horses in rapid succession, and he was also wounded in action. The army was in disorder. That Tartar high general became increasingly savage. Around him, a small empty space no one dared to enter formed.

At the critical moment, Yan Xiaohan arrived, leading a team of Beiyan soldiers, and extricated the besieged General Zhao. "Everyone remain calm!" he cried. "Shield bearers forward, the rest form a sword formation. Don't panic!"

Before Zhao Xicheng could catch his breath, he saw Yan Xiaohan spur his horse onward. Holding an anti-cavalry sword, like a gale sweeping by, he cut down several men in the blink of an eye. Covered in fresh, sinister blood, he tore through the enemy's encirclement, and, riding at the head, charged up in front of Zhehu.

On a battlefield, it was easy for the blood to go to your head. Yan Xiaohan was killing people like flies, but he was well aware that the main guard's eastern flank had just encountered a sneak attack from the barbarians' hidden forces. Fu Shen couldn't spare himself to come look after the vanguard now. If the vanguard was dispersed and the main guard was caught between two enemy forces, they could give up any thought of returning today.

To take down a man, you first took down his horse. To capture thieves, you first captured their king. The first priority was to kill this fierce-looking Tartar blockhead.

Yan Xiaohan came from the Feilong Guard. He was decent at directing a small band in a brawl, but he had no experience leading troops. Therefore, he didn't fight over command with Zhao Xicheng, but single-handedly cut a path to cross swords with Zhehu. That was where his strong point lay.

On horseback, Zhehu was a head taller than even Yan Xiaohan. He held a wrought iron broadsword. When he wielded it, the force was fit to split mountains and part seas. Even the gust of its passing could sting your face. Yan Xiaohan wouldn't meet him directly in a match of strength. Instead, he took a deft and peculiar approach, his angle cunning and ruthless, each attack jabbing at a vital target. He had made up his mind to hound him to death.

He had made a crude appraisal of the situation earlier and knew that this Tartar was the backbone of the barbarian army. If he could drag him down, when Zhao Xicheng caught his breath, he would naturally be able to regroup and enter battle with the enemy again.

The two of them fought inextricably. The sounds of their swords clashing came as closely as a strong rain pattering down. Zhehu had probably never encountered an opponent on the battlefield who came from the imperial palace. He was dazzled by his lively and elegant swordplay. He couldn't keep up right away and exposed a flaw in his defense. Yan Xiaohan's eyes chilled. Without hesitation, he dealt a backhanded stroke. His thin blade slipped into a crack in Zhehu's armor like a viper, and using the momentum of that stroke, it twisted, cutting off Zhehu's arm like slicing through tofu—

Then there came a sudden sound of something whistling through the air. He split off his attention to look from his peripheral vision and saw a chilly blade chopping slantwise at his back. This was Zhehu's subordinate officer who, having noticed things were going badly, had rushed to the rescue.

On the momentum of his earlier strike, Yan Xiaohan's second strike had already come near Zhehu's neck. Giving up now would have been a failure right on the point of success. Not looking sideways, he didn't shield himself. There was nothing in his eyes but the vigorously pulsing artery under the flesh of that man's neck. He was actually planning to take the blow—as long as he could take down Zhehu's head!

A splash of blood. The dull sensation of the blade cutting through bone still lingered at his fingertips. A glaring, wide-eyed head fell beneath the horses' hooves, but the anticipated pain from his back didn't come on schedule.

"Getting distracted? Haven't you killed anyone before?!"

Yan Xiaohan turned his head in confusion and found that Fu Shen had at some point arrived behind him. A headless corpse had fallen at his feet. He had his reins in one hand and a sword in the other. The point of the sword was still dripping blood. Beneath his helmet, his visage was handsome, cold, and stern. His features seemed frosted over. His scrutinizing gaze was like an icicle, stabbing right into Yan Xiaohan's eyes.

His bodyguards immediately encircled them, tightly protecting the two of them.

Fu Shen seemed to want to scold but narrowly held himself back. He only coldly said, "Come here, follow me, don't run around. If there's a next time, it won't go so well."

Lord Yan, who had just killed a Tartar high general in two strikes, was more well trained than a Pekinese; without daring to delay for an instant, he spurred his horse on and leapt toward him.

Grim-faced, Fu Shen issued commands, ordering the vanguard to raise their swords, form a wall and move forward. The Beiyan Cavalry had already cleaned up the ambush, and the general Zhehu had been killed. The rest of the Tartar cavalry had lost the initiative and become timid. Their speed of attack had slowed. Now the Xiangzhou forces came up from behind in a pincer movement with the Beiyan Army. The posture of the battle took a sudden turn.

The battle took a full eight hours to fight. The Han forces beheaded many thousands and at last wiped out the main strength of the Tartar cavalry. The survivors of the defeated army abandoned the city and fled.

At seven o'clock in the evening, Fu Shen sent a team of soldiers to pursue and attack the stragglers. The three armies lined up and entered the city. The people crowded the streets, cheering and weeping, all offering food and drink to congratulate the officers and men. At this point, Chang'an had been retaken.

Making a count of the dead and wounded, arranging for city patrols, dealing with officials of all stripes... Fu Shen was busy all night, so Yan Xiaohan also stayed up all night. Only when it was full daylight and the Beiyan soldiers who had been sent in pursuit of the stragglers returned to the city and shut the Tartar officers they had captured in the prefecture office's prison was a rest called to the rush and muddle. Everyone was unbearably weary and each went to their rest.

Fu Shen and the other officers were staying in an official's mansion, a vast improvement on the run-down house in Tangli Town. Yan Xiaohan was struck by a rare attack of obsessive cleanliness and washed himself several times before the smell of blood was gone from his body. When he returned to the bedroom, Fu Shen, who had finished washing up before him, was already asleep, leaning against the head of the bed.

Only now did he feel his own heartbeat, throb after throb, full of rhythm, almost like some poetic meter, not urgent in the least. In a moment, the clamorous battle cries at last receded, and the small noises of his surroundings came to his ears, as if he were returning from hell to the land of the living, coming back to life.

He stood there blankly for a long time, until Fu Shen's slow breathing paused. With his eyes closed, he lazily asked, "What, standing as punishment?"

"Hm?" Yan Xiaohan abruptly came back to himself. He walked up to the bed and moved him to its inner side, then lay down beside him. "Why are you awake?"

"With you standing there staring like you've lost your mind, how could I not wake up?" Fu Shen covered his mouth and yawned. He rolled over and put his arms around Yan Xiaohan's shoulders, touching the wound there. "Today... no, it was yester-day, you were a little too careless. I'm not going to scold you for it this time. You can learn from it yourself."

"I was impatient," Yan Xiaohan willingly admitted his error. Through a thin inner robe, he embraced his gaunt back and softly asked, "But how did you find out? There was so much distance between us."

But Fu Shen didn't answer directly. Carelessly, he said, "If you were stabbed right under my nose, I'd have no more use for my life. I'm tired. Let's sleep."

Yan Xiaohan didn't ask further. He considered it carefully for a while and thought that he had inadvertently found a drop of the tender feelings hidden deep beneath General Fu's armor.

He had grown up in the capital. He had never been on a battlefield before. His experience facing the enemy amounted to nothing. Though an army supervisor had no need to go into battle, Fu Shen had still been uneasy, which was why he had insisted on keeping him close to him, so he could keep a constant eye on him and avoid him being mistakenly injured in the heat of battle.

On the battlefield, in order to rescue Zhao Xicheng, he'd had to brace himself and meet the enemy. If Fu Shen hadn't constantly been keeping part of his attention on him, how could he have been in time to block that attack?

"How can you be so good?" Watching Fu Shen's sleeping countenance, Yan Xiaohan thought that he faintly tasted the sweetness of osmanthus candy. Restlessly, he thought, *I can hardly help myself any longer.*

When everything in Chang'an had been settled, Yan Xiaohan found a reason to take Fu Shen out of the city. The two of them slowly went along a mountain path, looking at the blooming mountain flowers all around. When they had come midway up the mountain, a white marble memorial arch with relief carvings appeared at the end of the shady mountain road.

From a distance, Fu Shen narrowed his eyes and looked that way. "Azure Lotus Pool? What is this place?"

Yan Xiaohan smiled without answering. Taking his hand, he went forward. Not long after, the whole picture appeared. Inside was a villa built against the mountain, with pavilions and kiosks in picturesque disarray, trees and flowers coming in and out of view, and a gurgling stream surrounding it. At a rough glance, its area had to be close to two hundred acres. Only a wealthy and extravagant person could have lived in such style.

"This mountain is called Mount Shuangbai. There are many hot springs on the mountain." Yan Xiaohan took Fu Shen through a covered corridor around the main building, and they came to a pool behind, wreathed in curling white steam. "This manor was my adopted father's personal property, which came to me when he went into the West. Hot springs activate energy flow and ease pain. I've always wanted to bring you, but there was never any time. Fortunately my wish has at last been fulfilled. Take a look, Lord Marquis. Are you satisfied?"

"The differences between people truly are exasperating," Fu Shen said, sighing. "Look at your father, who left you a villa with hot springs, and then look at my father, who left me a band of big, strapping men."

Yan Xiaohan hugged him from behind and smilingly said, "It doesn't matter. The villa and I are both yours."

Fu Shen raised his eyebrows. "Can such a thing be?"

Yan Xiaohan's unruly hands had begun to undo his belt. Hearing him, he kissed Fu Shen's face and unblushingly said, "You said last time that you had legally married me, so… why don't we do some things that you can only do once you're married?"

CHAPTER SEVENTY

ALL THAT TALK OF HOT SPRINGS STIMULATING CIRCULATION AND relaxing muscles were total nonsense. After taking a soak, not only did Fu Shen's legs not improve, his waist was nearly useless. Worn out, he retreated all the way to the opposite end of the pool. Pointing to the self-satisfied chief culprit, he said, "Stay away from me. Don't come near."

With sincere innocence, Yan Xiaohan said, "Why don't I massage your waist for you? I won't do anything else."

"No need," said Fu Shen. "Scram."

So Yan Xiaohan said nothing else. Fu Shen rested his eyes briefly, heard that there was no movement from him, and couldn't help feeling a little uncertain. He wondered whether he had spoken too strongly. He felt as if he had kicked a person out of bed right after sleeping with him, rather lacking in gentleness and consideration. So he silently exhaled and decided to smooth his ruffled feathers.

When he opened his eyes, he found that Yan Xiaohan had at some point "floated" from directly across from him to at one side from him. If he had kept hesitating, his sneak attack may well have succeeded.

Yan Xiaohan gave a dry laugh. "Why don't you close your eyes and go back to sleep?"

Fu Shen was pointedly silent.

"You're too badly behaved," he said helplessly. "Keep you around for entertainment? I'd be better off cooking you and having you for dinner."

Yan Xiaohan silently gave him a winning smile.

The crystalline ripples in the water sparkled. There were water droplets on his face, making the outlines of his features more distinct than ever. His pitch-black hair floated beside him. On his shoulders, neck, and collarbones revealed out of the water were a string of dotted red love bites. That smile was even more luminously moving. Even the green mountain and clear water faded beside it. It made Fu Shen look down and knit his brows, feeling that if this went on, he wouldn't be able to resist lighting the beacons of war[1].

Yan Xiaohan had grown up eating the ordinary foods of the mortal world like everyone else and hadn't absorbed any particular magic from the universe. How could he look like this?

Seeing Fu Shen close his eyes like a monk bewitched by a demon, putting him out of sight and out of mind, Yan Xiaohan knew that this was tacit consent, so he drew near, all smiles, and carefully pulled him into his arms. "Jingyuan."

Fu Shen gave a "hmph."

"It's nothing, I just wanted to say your name," Yan Xiaohan said. "I'm so happy that I keep being scared I'm dreaming."

Maybe it was pain that had left him frightened. Now, when he thought of it, he still felt his heart palpitate. Though in his arms he held the greatest satisfaction of his life, he still anxiously recalled the feeling of trying to sleep alone.

His agitation wasn't groundless. Never mind for the moment that the will of heaven was inconstant—now that Chang'an had been retaken, Zhao Xicheng would remain here to await the court's orders, while the Beiyan Cavalry would continue to advance east. The threat of separation had nearly burned up to their eyebrows. To say goodbye now would be no different from gouging out a hunk of Yan Xiaohan's flesh.

Fu Shen took his hands out of the water to toy with them. Suddenly, he said, "I wonder what our house is like now."

"Hm?"

"While this is a good place, it still isn't my home," Fu Shen said idly. "Put aside your 'happiness' for now. There will be time for sighing when we've retaken the capital."

Unable to help laughing, Yan Xiaohan bent to his ear and said in a low voice, "You mean that after we return to the capital, in the pool in our house, we can also… ow!"

Fu Shen had given him a jab with his elbow, making a splash. "Impressive."

Yan Xiaohan wrapped him up with arms and legs together. During this harassment, he said hypocritically, "All right, don't fool around, let's be serious. When everything here has calmed down, I'm planning a trip to Shu."

Fu Shen frowned. "Planning to see the Retired Emperor?"

"Yes," said Yan Xiaohan. "After the incidents in the capital, the Feilong Guard and a large portion of the imperial guards, as well as a minority of the capital barracks, went west with the Retired Emperor. You've seen it yourself. While I can manage to put a word in the new court, my influence is too shallow compared to the deep-rooted Jiangnan families, and there are too few people at my disposal. Things can't continue like this."

"So you want to get your old subordinates back from the Retired Emperor?" Fu Shen asked. "Why would he agree?"

But Yan Xiaohan was unwilling to explain. Leaving him in suspense, he said, "I have my ways."

"Fine." Fu Shen knew he wouldn't ask recklessly and wasn't planning on meddling. He only said, "You know what you're doing. Do you need my help doing anything?"

Yan Xiaohan said the first thing that came into his head: "Make sure I've eaten my fill before I go?"

Fu Shen pushed his big head underwater.

The two of them fooled around in the manor. Yan Xiaohan made it known that he wanted to collect on a whole year's debt, but time truly was limited. Reasoning by every possible method, ceding territory and paying indemnity, making a whole heap of ridiculous promises, he at last managed to talk him into canceling out half a year's debt and leaving the rest to be discussed when they returned to the capital.

Two days later, the two of them left the mountain and returned to the city. Yuan Huan, one of the Beiyan officers Fu Shen had sent out from Ganzhou, was left to guard Xijing, while Yu Qiaoting continued leading their forces east, making preparations to capture Luoyang. With the Beiyan Army to serve as an example, Xiangzhou's military commissioner followed suit, stationing a trusted officer in Chang'an. Zhao Xicheng had thought that once Chang'an was taken, it would belong to the new court, but he had taken his eyes off things for a moment, and it had turned into shared property among three parties. He was all right when it came to leading troops and doing battle, but he wasn't skilled at intriguing, and he had offered up Yan Xiaohan to the Beiyan Army camp. Now, finally realizing that things weren't going well, he went to ask for Yan Xiaohan and also sent a messenger to ride at top speed back to Jinling and request orders from the emperor.

Sadly, he didn't even get to see Yan Xiaohan's face this time. Fu Shen, with a cold expression of *And just who do you think you are?* that couldn't be hidden by politeness, asked him to leave the Beiyan Army camp in exactly the same manner as before.

Not long after, the Jiangnan court issued a decree, ordering Zhao Xicheng to continue leading the army north, joining the Beiyan Cavalry in an effort to take back Luoyang and leaving Chang'an temporarily ruled by the three parties. But not a single word mentioned Yan Xiaohan.

In the eighth month, Luoyang was retaken.

At the end of the eighth month, news got out that Yan Xiaohan had entered Shu and paid his respects to the Retired Emperor, then restructured the imperial guards and the old capital barracks into the Tianfu Army. Jinling's court was in an uproar.

Only Emperor Changzhi seemed to have predicted this. He issued a decree conferring upon Yan Xiaohan the title of representative of the Tianfu Army and made the Tianfu Army part of the emperor's personal guards, then ordered Yan Xiaohan not to return to court but to continue going north to join Zhao Xicheng and retake the capital.

Only now did the Jiangnan party in court realize that Yan Xiaohan offending the emperor and being expelled from the central authority had from the outset been a show acted out by sovereign and minister together for their benefit.

With Jiangnan's families to obstruct it, the northern campaign had taken a long time to get settled. Had Yan Xiaohan not dealt almost provocatively with Pure Consort Xue, Xue Sheng, head of the four Jiangnan ministers, wouldn't have decided he would rather concede on the northern campaign if it meant kicking him out and agreed to the court dispatching troops to join the Beiyan Cavalry in encircling Chang'an.

They had miscalculated. Emperor Changzhi had little talent but great designs. While he frequently had no ideas of his own, he certainly wasn't without wild ambition. He had known prosperity and was in the end unwilling to be content with sovereignty over only the corner of Jiangnan. In his bones was a yearning to retake the Central Plains and unify the entire empire.

At the outset, when Yan Xiaohan had received orders to form an army for the court independent of the military commissioners, he had pointed out two paths to Emperor Changzhi. One was open—reorganize the surviving soldiers of the defeated forces and recruit new soldiers; this was the army that Zhao Xicheng was commander-in-chief of. The composition of Jiangnan's army was uneven, their fighting ability low. They were purely a motley crew cobbled together at the last moment, but they were enough to put up a front. The other path was hidden —and his most important mission on leaving Jinling.

Those who had gone west with Emperor Yuantai were all the elite forces of the North Yamen Imperial Guards and the capital barracks. The imperial guards were Yan Xiaohan's followers, and the capital barracks were the imperial family's followers. The Tianfu Army composed of these two groups would be an army that Emperor Changzhi and future emperors could truly rely on.

Carrying out action in the open to conceal the hidden plot— when Xue Sheng thought he was eating sand on the front lines, Yan Xiaohan was already in Shu, having finished restructuring the Tianfu Army. When Minister Xue at last understood that he had once again been made a fool of by Yan Xiaohan, Yan Xiaohan was already rushing with this elite force onto the battlefield to join the Beiyan Cavalry, which had just seized Luoyang.

At this point, Jiangnan's families had completely lost the advantage. Retaking the Central Plains and uniting north and south was imperative. Even if they pulled Emperor Changzhi off the throne now, they would have no way to hold back the local armies sending out troops one after another like bamboo shoots sprouting up after the rain, and they certainly couldn't stop the iron heel of the Beiyan Army and the Tianfu Army as they flagrantly marched north.

At the end of the year, news of victory was pouring in from all over. Everything from the lower reaches of the Yellow River and south had been retaken. The Beiyan Cavalry and the Tianfu Army had successively taken Qingling, Luzhou, and three other locations, closing in on the major target of Yuanzhou, where the Tartars and Zhe had their main forces stationed. At the turn of the year, the Jiangnan Court sent a delivery of provisions and armaments, richly favoring the Tianfu Army. There was also a secret letter in the emperor's own hand sending his regards to the Marquis of Jingning.

When Fu Shen returned to his camp in the evening, the sky was as dark and heavy as though it were about to snow. He was so frozen that his hands were numb. He lifted the tent flap, but a warm fragrance came right at him. The commander's tent, which ought to have been dark and deserted, was brightly lit. The turtledove that had occupied the magpie's nest was sitting at the head of the bed reading army dispatches. Hearing movement, he looked over, all smiles. He put down the letters and extended his arms toward Fu Shen.

With such a person here, the simple and crude tent seemed to have become an immortal palace.

His dry, icy hands were held between warm palms. Fu Shen bent down and deliberately pressed his icy cheek to Yan Xiaohan's face. "What are you doing here again?"

Yan Xiaohan said unblushingly, "It's almost the New Year, how could I leave you alone? I came to warm the Lord Marquis's bed."

Fu Shen shook his head and laughed. With a helplessly indulgent *I can't do anything with you* written all over his face, his chin was caught and he was kissed.

It was a funny thing to say—in the Tianfu Army, from the commander to the ordinary soldiers, practically everyone had made up their minds to cling tightly to the Beiyan Cavalry's leg. Since joining up at Luoyang, the Tianfu Army had turned into the Beiyan Army's little tail. For one thing, this was because the two commanders had a close relationship. For another thing, it was because the Tianfu Army for the most part came from the capital and its environs and had a kind of natural sense of closeness to the Beiyan Army.

Besides, Yan Xiaohan's experience in leading troops was still limited, and he regularly needed to have Fu Shen looking out for him. Therefore, when no one would notice, Yan Xiaohan went almost every evening to the Beiyan Army's camp to "consult" with Fu Shen. Fu Shen had long ago instructed his bodyguards to let him through. Over time, everyone became accustomed to this. Even Yu Qiaoting, bumping into Yan Xiaohan coming out of Fu Shen's tent in the morning, could greet him with a normal expression and tell him to eat before he left.

"What are you reading?" With his help, Fu Shen removed his armor and changed into casual house clothes and went to wash his hands in a bronze pan full of hot water. As he dried them, he listened to Yan Xiaohan say, "News from court. The Zhe and Parhae have sent envoys to Jinling. They want to negotiate peace."

Fu Shen sat at the edge of the bed and undid each clasp on his boots in turn. "That's about what I would figure. What do they say?"

"With a border running from Qingzhou to Luzhou, they want to return everything south of it to the court and have everything north governed by the three clans. North and south would leave each other alone and open trade routes. Jiangnan would give the Tartars, Zhe, and Parhae several thousands in an annual gift." At this point, Yan Xiaohan gave a soft laugh. "And their emperor wishes to become His Majesty's sworn brother."

Fu Shen soaked his feet in hot water and idly sneered. "Ha! Coming on strong. The soldiers are already at their gates. Do they think they've come to attend a market?"

Yan Xiaohan said, "His Majesty won't waver for now, but there are many in court advocating in favor of the peace negotiations. Especially the Jiangnan group. They won't want to impoverish the south in support of the north. I'm afraid there will be arguments about this."

"Let them argue," Fu Shen said with a cold laugh. "Truly strange that it isn't the people of the north who get to decide whether the peace talks go forward, and it isn't the soldiers campaigning at the front lines. Instead, it's those lords holding steady at the rear who get to give up half the Central Plains by flapping their lips—this goes beyond daydreaming."

---

1. A reference to King You of Western Zhou, who lit the war beacons to make his concubine, Bao Si, smile, ultimately leading to the downfall of Western Zhou.

CHAPTER SEVENTY-ONE

THEIR BEAUTIFUL COUNTRY HAD FALLEN INTO THE HANDS OF THE foreign enemy.

The barbarians viewed the Han people of the Central Plains as dogs and trash, wantonly pillaging and burning. For the past two years, natural and manmade disasters in the north had come in an endless stream. As the army traveled, they often saw villages that had been wrecked by the flames of war, nine out of ten houses empty, skeletons exposed to the elements by the road.

If they were still going to negotiate a peace under these circumstances, what did the soldiers who had shed blood at the front lines and the common people who had looked south to the royal army until their deaths amount to?

Yan Xiaohan walked up to the table and raised his brush to write a few characters of his report. In an even tone, he said, "Indeed. The arrow is already on the string. Even if the arguments in Jinling rise to the heavens, they still can't recall the army pressing on the border. The initiative is in our hands now. The southern court has no say in it. There's no need to heed them."

At present, surrounding Yuanzhou alone were the Beiyan, Tianfu, Jiangnan, and Xiangzhou armies. Heading east, there were the troops massed in their own provinces by the military commissioners of Huainan, Jingchu, and Suizhou. Apart from the Jiangnan Army and the Tianfu Army, which nominally took their orders from the Jiangnan court, the rest of the military commissioners and local officers had each taken up self-reliance and self-defense before the new court had been established. It was up to the heroes to determine events now; whoever's fist was the hardest would be the one to speak. However clamorous the cries of the lords of Jiangnan, they wouldn't be as effective as a single order from Fu Shen.

"Pedants endangering the realm," Fu Shen lamented insincerely. He stretched out his neck to look at the tabletop. "What are you writing so late at night?"

Yan Xiaohan dropped his brush and turned to pick up a cloth nearby to cover Fu Shen's feet. He picked up the wooden pail and went outside to pour out the water. He casually answered, "Writing a report to the court. It's nothing. Hurry up and lie down, don't freeze."

When he raised the tent flap, a breeze blew in, turning over the pages. Fu Shen hadn't meant to pry, but he couldn't help how good his eyesight was. At a glance, he caught a line of precise regular script on the page.

The moment he saw it clearly, his heart inexplicably missed a beat. He was agitated, but not confused. Rather, he had a feeling of enlightenment, as if a vista had broadened and cleared.

There were only a few words in the report—"Better fight to the death than negotiate peace."

Back when Fu Shen had returned to the capital, Yan Xiaohan had constantly been calling himself "crafty and fawning," and he had been denounced in speech and writing by all the nation's scholars as the court's dog. But times had changed. When storms had passed it was easy for moral integrity to alter and loyalty to break. But he was one of a small number of people who had remained standing upright.

Now, who would still dare to say that he was a sycophant who only knew how to curry favor and harm loyal subjects?

There were some sounds, and Yan Xiaohan returned from outside. Fu Shen was wrapped in a quilt that had been warmed by body heat. He sighed comfortably and called out, "Menggui."

"Hm?" Yan Xiaohan was just washing his hands. He turned his head and asked, "What do you want?"

"I want you," said Fu Shen.

At this unexpected hit to the chest, Yan Xiaohan froze. Then he laughed. He dried his hands, loosened his clothes, and got into bed to lie down next to Fu Shen. "What for?"

Fu Shen drew near and kissed the tip of his nose. With justice on his side, he said, "Nothing. I want to show my wife some affection. Can't I?"

Yan Xiaohan pulled him firmly into his arms and bent his head to find his warm, dry lips and mock-threateningly bumped him with his head. "Provoking me again. I think you don't want to sleep."

Before Fu Shen could put all the honeyed words in his belly to good use, they were held back and turned into indistinct little moans. In the cold winter night, the two of them became increasingly heated as they rolled around, until Yan Xiaohan felt that if they kept grinding against each other like this, he wouldn't be able to hold himself back and managed to release him. There was sweat on Fu Shen's forehead. Panting, he gave a laugh. "Don't take it from me, my wife, but your vitality is a little excessively firm…"

"Whose fault is that?" Yan Xiaohan pulled his hand into the quilt and said with a sigh, "My Lord Marquis, can't you hurry up and retake the capital, let me come home and do as I please? If you keep killing without burying the bodies like this, I really won't be able to hold myself back from injuring a loyal subject."

Fu Shen let out a low groan and said, gritting his teeth, "Right now… you don't call this doing as you please? Do you want to ascend to heaven?"

The long winter night in the last month of the year flew by as quickly as a night in spring.

It had snowed in the middle of the night. When Fu Shen woke early in the morning, it was still dark outside, with heaven and earth all clothed in silver and white. Yan Xiaohan must have gotten up not long ago; there was still lingering warmth on the other side of the bed. Fu Shen propped himself up, slowly clearing his head of sleepiness. Out of the corner of his eye, he saw that the marten coat that had been hanging there was gone. He figured that he had gone back to the Tianfu Army's camp, so he draped on his clothes and got out of bed, ready to go to the canteen to get something to eat and patrol the camp while he was at it.

Before his feet hit the ground, he heard footsteps at the door. Yan Xiaohan ducked inside and put the big steaming bowl in his hands on the table. With his scalded-red fingers, he pinched Fu Shen's earlobe and said, "You really woke up early. I was planning to wake you when I got back."

Fu Shen belatedly worked out what was happening. He sat up at the head of the bed and tilted his head back to look at him. "What were you doing first thing in the morning? You didn't return to your camp?"

"Why would I?" Yan Xiaohan leaned down and kissed the center of his brow. Warmly, he said, "Have you forgotten what today is? Happy birthday, Lord Marquis, may you have good fortune and long life."

Only then did Fu Shen remember that today was indeed his birthday. It was just that he was normally so busy with military affairs, and it wasn't a full decade birthday, so he had tossed this fact to the back of his head. Besides, it was a time of emergency. No one was in the mood to celebrate birthdays. It was only Yan Xiaohan who would remember it for him.

"Thank you…" Fu Shen's throat felt blocked. Perhaps because he had just woken up, he seemed a little baffled. His diction also seemed distant and stiff. "You've gone to quite some trouble."

Looking at his expression that spoke of never having celebrated his birthday, Yan Xiaohan felt both amused and sad. He couldn't resist the itch to stroke his head. "The year before last, you were in Beiyan, and last year we were apart, one north and one south. This year we've finally managed to be in the same place. I have nothing to give you now, so I prepared a bowl of longevity noodles for you. My handiwork is subpar. Would the Lord Marquis honor me by tasting it?"

Fu Shen nodded, his eyes fixed on that tall, slender figure as it went to bring him the noodles, silently thinking to himself, *I don't want anything at all. Having you is enough.*

Yan Xiaohan wasn't being modest. He had said his handiwork was subpar, and indeed the flavor of the noodles was only average. But never mind that it was only "subpar," even if Yan Xiaohan had brought him a bowl of arsenic, Fu Shen would have swallowed it without batting an eyelash.

Today, the Beiyan Cavalry officers joining Fu Shen on patrol felt an unprecedented pressure. The Marquis of Jingning, who for the last few days had threatened to "wait until the enemy was exhausted" and "sit still while the enemy moved" suddenly seemed to have been provoked by something. While analyzing the situation, he got off track, changing the subject from how to deploy forces in Yuanzhou to how to take the capital as soon as possible. He seemed ready to make their heads roll if they couldn't retake the whole nation within three months.

Xiao Xun poked Yu Qiaoting with his elbow and quietly asked, "Has the general been possessed?"

Yu Qiaoting's expression was grave. "As I see it, that Yan has probably fed him another bowl of bewitching potion."

Fu Shen shot the two of them a cold look. "We received word from Jiangnan last night. The Tartars and Zhe have sent envoys to Jinling, bringing up peace negotiations. They want to split control of north and south with the line between Qingzhou and Luzhou as border, and they want to ally with our nation. I think that among those present, none of you is willing to give those wolf cubs money every New Year?"

All the officers immediately restrained their playfulness. Their expressions turned grim.

"As soon as we've celebrated the New Year, we move. If we can seize Yuanzhou and Xiangzhou, the capital will have no protection. Taking back the Central Plains within three months isn't an idle boast." Fu Shen put down a map and sternly said, "Gentlemen, the disgrace of the capital's defeat and the northern frontier falling to the hands of the enemy ought now to be wiped out by the Beiyan Cavalry in person."

New Year's Eve came once a year. Though the world had fallen on hard times and there was desolation throughout the north, sporadic firecrackers still went up at times in the cities. For the majority of the Han people, however badly off they were, they still had to celebrate the New Year.

Outside the cities, however, beneath the pitch-black canopy of heaven, were arrayed a multitude of stern, warlike cavalrymen.

One wondered what splendor and magnificence there were in Jiangnan on this night.

The officers of the four armies gathered in the empty space in front of their camps to make final deployments ahead of the battle. When they were finished, Yan Xiaohan called over a bodyguard and gave each person a bowl of hot wine. He raised his head and said, "This wine is a send-off for you gentlemen. May heaven bless our armies and grant us victory in this battle."

The officers raised their bowls, making crisp clinking noises in midair. Together they said, "To a speedy victory!"

The strong liquor went down their throats and set all the blood in their bodies boiling. The others returned to their respective armies. Only Yan Xiaohan hung back. Fu Shen seemed to have worked out his plans. Raising his eyebrows, he said with a laugh, "Do you want to say something to me in private?"

There was a faint redness at the corners of his eyes from the alcohol. Smiling, his features didn't seem as cold and hard as usual, instead bearing a trace of tipsy affection. Yan Xiaohan knew very well that the time wasn't right and the setting wasn't right, but his heartstrings still trembled involuntarily.

He hated to see Fu Shen go into battle, but there was no denying that in fact this was the look of his he most admired.

"It's New Year's Eve, I ought to say something auspicious." Through the blustering north wind, Yan Xiaohan distantly raised his cup to him. "I hope our country will have stability, prosperity, and peace."

Fu Shen was slightly startled. Then he lowered his eyelids. He seemed to be sighing, and also to be laughing.

He raised his cup to return the salute. His voice wasn't loud, but through the wind, Yan Xiaohan heard each word clearly.

"I hope to be with you for many years and grow old together."

Having said this, he drank the dregs of wine in his cup in one gulp and urged his horse into the boundless night.

CHAPTER SEVENTY-TWO

IN THE SECOND YEAR OF CHANGZHI, AT THE START OF THE NEW year, Han forces attacked Yuanzhou by night, scoring a major victory against the barbarian forces, beheading many thousands and capturing over thirty Tartar and Zhe military officers, government officials, and nobles.

In the second month, Huainan's three armies retook Xiangzhou.

At the end of the third month, the seven armies joined into a crushing force in Zhuozhou, which was at the extreme south of the capital's environs. Not long after, with Fu Shen taking the lead, the seven armies' officers gathered in one place to discuss the division of forces for the campaign north and the retaking of the capital.

Over the course of these events, all the military commissioners had openly or covertly probed Fu Shen's intentions. The battle of the capital was right in front of them, but after that battle, what would they do, and where would they do it? Would they continue as separatist forces, or return military power and submit to the court, become idle nobles by merit? Though all the military commissioners silently acknowledged that they were fighting on behalf of the court, no one wanted to be working for nothing, and they certainly didn't want to be the bridge destroyed after it was crossed, the donkey killed as soon as it left the millstone.

There had been too many object lessons in the year before last. Their faith in the court was limited. At present, it was Fu Shen, the first to raise troops in support of the emperor, who had the greater power to rally supporters.

In the middle of the fourth month, the army's deployments were fixed. The Tartar, Zhe, and Parhae envoys went around the Jinling court and went straight outside the city to request to see the Beiyan commander. Once again, they brought up peace negotiations.

The envoys promised that the three clans would withdraw their troops from the capital and retreat outside the pass. The two sides would use the Great Wall as a border and not attack each other. They also requested that Great Zhou give increased annual payments to the three clans, and permit them to enter the passes every winter and spring to herd horses.

On the fifteenth of the fourth month, a few days before meeting with the foreign envoys, Fu Shen and Yan Xiaohan found some leisure amid their busy affairs to go to Golden Terrace in the capital's outskirts.

When the capital had been breached by the allied armies, the Tartar and Zhe soldiers, to vent their feelings, and to humiliate Great Zhou's imperial family, had burned this place to barren land. The towering halls had been reduced to rubble. The splendor of previous days had turned into a scene of devastation as far as the eye could see. Though Fu Shen had been prepared, when they truly came near, he was still stunned when he saw this scene.

In a daze, he leapt from horseback. When he landed, his legs were a little weak, and he didn't find his footing. He was pulled into the arms of Yan Xiaohan, who charged up from behind. "Jingyuan?"

"It's fine." Fu Shen patted his hand and jaggedly said, "I...
ahem, I'll go in and have a look."

This place had a very particular meaning for Fu Shen. If not,
he wouldn't have brought Yan Xiaohan here to make their bows
to the parents. According to his memories of the past, Fu Shen
found where Qilin Palace had been, made a few circles, and with
difficulty determined the locations of his father and grandfather's
portraits. He raised the hems of his robes and slowly knelt amid
the smashed tiles and charred wood all over the ground.

Yan Xiaohan followed him in silence and also knelt.

Fu Shen faced emptiness and lowered himself, firmly and
loudly kowtowing three times, but he said nothing.

A century of glory utterly destroyed in a fire like this. Of the
yellowing portraits, not a single one remained, just like the brave
souls who had passed away. They had lingered reluctantly, but in
the end they had floated away in all directions with the winds.

Were they still protecting Great Zhou, protecting the Beiyan
Cavalry?

Yan Xiaohan saw the corners of Fu Shen's eyes redden. In
those long and narrow beautiful eyes, there was wavering and
perplexity that he had rarely seen. Yan Xiaohan pondered
briefly, then stood and walked a few steps forward, then went
down on one knee beside him. Softly, he said, "General, is there
a weight on your mind? Would you like me to ease it for you?"

Fu Shen looked up. There was still a glimmer of unshed tears
in his eyes. "How did you know?"

"While you haven't said it, I am your closest kin, general.
Naturally I could tell." Yan Xiaohan gently wiped the corners of
his eyes and his temples. "It's all written in your eyes."

Fu Shen lowered his eyelids. He seemed to be laughing, but
also appeared to be sighing. He said, "It isn't a weight on my
mind. It's a deranged thing, a revolt against orthodoxy, which will
be universally condemned."

"Oh?" Yan Xiaohan raised his eyebrows. "What a coincidence. Isn't one of the foremost rebels against orthodoxy and expert in being universally condemned right in front of you?"

When he had brought this up, there was nothing more Fu Shen could say about it. He simply found a clean place to sit and got into position to have a long talk sitting knee-to-knee. "Now that you ask me, I don't even know where to start. Do you still remember Ceng Guang?"

Yan Xiaohan pursed his lips like a child and said, "Isn't that the Gu Shanlü's teacher? He made a request of you, and you made me intercede on behalf of that Ceng Guang."

Fu Shen was speechless. "Truly amazing, Lord Yan. Have you been ruminating on this old jealousy all this time?"

"See what you've said there, Lord Marquis." Yan Xiaohan's eyes curved slyly. He drew near and said mysteriously, "Wouldn't you know best of all how amazing I am, Lord Marquis?"

Fu Shen didn't answer.

"Don't disturb me." Not knowing whether to laugh or cry, he pinched Yan Xiaohan's cheek. Then, composing himself, he said, "To business. After the attack in Qingsha Gap, I made my peace with certain things, but there were still some things I was unwilling to accept.

"The Beiyan Cavalry's position is too difficult. We spend our lives fighting on behalf of Great Zhou, but in the end, we become a splinter in the eye, a thorn in the flesh, pricking the emperor so much that he spends all day considering how he can kill me, kill us. I fretted every day then. This generation's sovereign doesn't trust us, and the next generation's wouldn't trust me, either. Since time immemorial, how long has it taken to produce a wise and capable ruler? My lifetime won't amount to a hundred years. How long will it take? What if I die before it happens?"

Yan Xiaohan nodded. "Indeed, it's better to believe in yourself than in others. Then there are only two paths. Either make yourself king, or command the emperor and his nobles."

Fu Shen laughed in spite of himself. "I have no hankering to be Emperor, and I don't have the makings of it."

Yan Xiaohan knew that he wasn't joking. Had Fu Shen truly had that thought, he could have formed his own faction when he was in Ganzhou, or even earlier, during the Yuantai court; the imperial decree arranging their marriage would have been a ready-made reason.

But he hadn't.

When a gentleman conducts himself in society, there are actions he must take, and actions he must not take. When Fu Shen said something, he would put it into practice up to the hilt.

"Later, during the Kuangshan Academy case, I happened to come upon Ceng Guang's *Essays from the Xuemei Temple*. I thought they were quite a revelation," Fu Shen said. "'The nation belongs to all, and is not the private property of a single family.' To say it is to offend the whole of society, but thinking closely, it's not without sense."

Fu Shen had read Ceng Guang's essay and felt that while this old gentleman was advanced in age, his heart was wild, carrying a beautiful dream to eat enough in one bite to grow fat. The Kuangshan Academy's teachings had seemed like pure fantasy at the time, and even now, they still seemed very strong. But through the writing, some of the old gentleman's hopes hidden inside it had happened to subtly accord with Fu Shen's ideas.

This was the so-called "third path" he had been looking for.

Yan Xiaohan felt that he had dimly groped his way to the edges, but he still couldn't seize the main point. "You mean…"

Fu Shen considered repeatedly, then, with utmost caution, gave a two-word answer.

"Shared rule."

The generals who guarded the borders, the military commissioners who held troops all over the nation, the senior administrators who enlightened and governed, the ministers who gave frank criticism and aided in ruling the nation… These people ought to have been crying out and busying themselves for the sake of the common people, but instead they were bound by the emperor's power, bowing their heads and submitting to a single most revered family.

Fu Shen's hopes for a sagacious ruler had long since been discouraged, and he had never had the thought of taking that place for himself. Obscurely, there seemed to be some commandment binding generation after generation of heroes and men of ambition. Prosperity and decline, rise and fall, all seemed to have their fixed terms. Fu Shen vaguely perceived this "heavenly law," but he had no way to express it—until he had inadvertently leafed through *Essays from the Xuemei Temple*, and the sentence "The nation belongs to all those who live in the nation" had laid bare his perplexity, and the hazy thought in his mind had finally broken through the earth and grown into a new shoot.

What was shared rule?

All citizens within the nation's borders taking part in state power; important affairs of state, enumerated in full and put to public opinion to be resolved.

But he wasn't absolutely certain. He didn't know whether this was fine timber or a poisonous weed.

After hearing him out, Yan Xiaohan did not speak for a long time. His attitude wasn't actually all that important, or rather, it wasn't more important than anyone else's. But Fu Shen, knowing very well that disapproval and incomprehension were normal responses, still felt perturbed in spite of himself because of his silence.

"So…" Yan Xiaohan said confusedly, "the reason you made me help you rescue Ceng Guang really wasn't because you were testing me, but because… because of this?"

Fu Shen didn't answer.

Sometimes he really wanted to open up Yan Xiaohan's head and have a look at what the hell was actually in there.

Seeing him speechless, Yan Xiaohan laughed heartlessly. "You're not nervous, are you, Lord Marquis?" he ridiculed.

"What will you do if I say you're indulging in wild fantasies? What will you do if I say you're a heretic?"

Of course Fu Shen wouldn't do anything to him. If Yan Xiaohan didn't like it, then at worst, after taking the capital, he would resign his post on account of illness, abandon all his outstanding achievements, and retire into seclusion with Yan Xiaohan, putting affairs of state out of sight and out of mind, letting them all mess around however they liked.

There was nothing in this world that Fu Shen wouldn't part with, apart from Yan Xiaohan.

"Nothing," Fu Shen said expressionlessly, poking his face. "Do you think I could cast you off because of a thing like this?"

Yan Xiaohan fell onto him, laughing. Fu Shen, hugging his heavy wife, didn't know what he had to be so pleased about. He was just about to remind him to have some dignity when he heard Yan Xiaohan say, "I think it's great."

"What?" said Fu Shen.

"The Retired Emperor said that you were a subject loyal to the nation, not to the ruler." Yan Xiaohan stopped smiling and earnestly said, "It isn't the least bit surprising to me that you would say such a thing, because you are Fu Jingyuan. You've never changed.

"No matter what your plans, go ahead and carry them out to the full. Even if you fail, I'll still be with you. Husband and wife are one, sharing in glory and disgrace. In future ages, your name and mine will always be written together. I think that's great. There's nothing better."

Fu Shen's mind was shaken. His countenance showed visible emotion.

He silently hugged Yan Xiaohan, squeezing very hard, as if afraid he would run away. He understood that he would never have the luck to meet a better person than him.

After a long time, Yan Xiaohan suddenly struggled free slightly and indicated for him to turn his head. "Look."

Fu Shen looked in the direction he was pointing and saw beneath a blackened and decaying pillar, in a crack in a brick, there was a tiny wildflower swaying in the wind, petals extended, leaves jade green; amid the disorder, it seemed incredibly frail and likely to wither, but it was also the only thriving bit of life amid all the burnt-out cinders.

The two of them looked at each other and smiled. By tacit agreement, they said nothing, only pressed their foreheads against each other and gently touched their lips together.

The most thorough conflagration was waiting for the next year's spring breezes.

On the eighteenth of the fourth month, the officers of the seven armies met with the three clans' envoys beneath Golden Terrace.

This innovative location had been selected by Fu Shen, and it got excellent results. The officers of all the armies, on seeing the envoys come for peace negotiations, didn't show them a trace of good will. A trace of a not very natural expression flashed over the Zhe envoy's face, but after all, they were the ones who had come to sue for peace. They had to pretend they didn't notice. They forced themselves to sit.

The three clans had each sent a lead envoy and an assistant envoy. Yan Xiaohan sat at Fu Shen's right hand, looking on. He found that the Tartar envoy seemed to be carrying himself with arrogance, the Zhe envoy was the slickest, but the Parhae envoy spoke very little; even when he spoke, it was to echo the words of the Zhe envoy.

It was evident at a glance how relations stood between the clans.

The Zhe and Parhae were wild dogs; they only wanted to tear enough flesh from Great Zhou. The Tartars were wolves; they had an implacable hatred for Great Zhou. Even if this time they temporarily endured humiliation and bent their heads, they would still stage a comeback in the future.

Bottomless greed and the wild ambitions of a wolf cub—rather than saying they were here for peace negotiations, it would be better to say they were in their death struggles. They must have taken an accurate read of the Jiangnan court's attitude and had come here to carry out a daylight robbery.

Fu Shen had nothing to say to the Tartar envoy. Afraid he wouldn't be able to suppress his anger, he had Yu Qiaoting deal with him in his place. When it came to the Zhe envoy, he suddenly recalled something and said to the short envoy, "I forgot to ask. Since your Yintu Khan wishes to sue for peace, how does he intend to demonstrate it?"

The Zhe envoy froze, unsure where he was going with this.

Yan Xiaohan put in a timely word: "Why would you ask that, Lord Marquis?"

"I have heard that Yintu Khan has always been courteous and hospitable," Fu Shen said. "When I was married, he went out of his way to send an anonymous wedding gift."

"What?" said Yan Xiaohan.

"A box of bloody eastern pearls." Fu Shen narrowed his eyes, murderous intent glinting within them. "I so appreciate him taking the trouble—"

The Zhe envoy was locked in place by his gaze. He instantly began to tremble incessantly. His heart was about to jump out of his throat. Quickly, he said, "A misunderstanding, it must have been a misunderstanding…"

But Fu Shen suddenly laughed. "Come."

At his laugh, everyone's gazes converged on him. From an attendant behind him, Fu Shen took a bowl of uncooked rice and brought it up in front of him. In front of all the envoys and officers, he slowly overturned and emptied it. "Let us be upfront with each other. If Yintu wishes to sue for peace, then he can make a show of good faith. A head for each grain of rice. He can start the count with his own family. Once he has enough, I will immediately withdraw our troops. If he can't make up the number, I will bring this bowl of rice to his grave myself next year."

The snow-white rice spilled, making a shushing sound.

There was dead silence inside the tent.

The Zhe envoy was nearly angry enough to attack him on the spot. "This is a scandal! You… That's impossible! You go too far!"

Yan Xiaohan darkly said, "You haven't even tried. How do you know it's impossible? Why not go and try it first."

The other two clans' envoys treated this as nothing to do with them and didn't make a sound. The Zhe envoy hopelessly realized that he was no longer faced with the Jiangnan ministers, playing up their own positions and putting on an act of kindliness. Here there was only a crowd of generals who had trampled through mountains of corpses and seas of blood and had killed their way to the capital. When they had sat down, the blood on the tips of their swords had yet to dry.

"Now you remember that you ought to reason with me? Too late," Fu Shen said coldly. "Go back and tell Yintu that starting from when he provoked me and launched a sneak attack on Liangkou Pass, our fate as enemies was sealed. A hatred on behalf of my nation, a heavy debt of blood. Unless he dies, this will not end."

"You bastard!"

The Zhe envoy jumped to his feet and was just about to attack when the sounds of several swords being drawn from their sheaths abruptly came from behind him. Snow-bright sword glare dazzled the eyes. There was a chill at his neck.

On Yan Xiaohan's face appeared a false smile very familiar to the envoy, which he had seen on the faces of the Jiangnan officials.

"Since the talks have failed, we will see each other on the battlefield. Gentlemen, show them the door."

This meeting had always been heading for a collapse of talks.

The only outcome Fu Shen could accept was the three clans going back where they had come from. The further they went, the better. With hundreds of thousands of the army's troops in Zhuozhou and victory assured, the military commissioners would have had to go insane to agree to the Tartar envoy's terms, which seemed to be yielding but were in fact an attempt to use a small advantage to gain a greater one.

The three clans' envoys left in a hurry with their tails between their legs. Soon, only their own people remained in the tent. Xiangzhou's military commissioner Wang Shiqi, seeing that there was nothing here to deal with, was about to stand and leave the table when suddenly Fu Shen, at the head of the table, said, "Not so fast, gentlemen. I have something else to say—"

The first song had been sung. This fine opera had just begun.

CHAPTER SEVENTY-THREE

THE EIGHTEENTH DAY OF THE FOURTH MONTH IN THE SECOND year of Changzhi was a day certain to remain forever in the history books.

With the Beiyan Cavalry's command-in-chief Fu Shen initiating, the Tianfu Army's representative Yan Xiaohan holding the brush, and the joint signatures of Huainan's military commissioner Yue Changfeng, Xiangzhou's military commissioner Wang Shiqi, Jingchu's military commissioner Cen Hongfang, Suizhou's military commissioner Fang Gao, and the commander of the new Jiangnan Army Zhao Xicheng, all the generals raised a memorial to the throne entitled *Request to Establish New Laws Expanding the Yanning Hall Assembly*.

This memorial was also known as the "Golden Terrace Memorial." Put together from the collective views of the seven armies' officers, it contained twelve articles.

1. Expel the barbarians, retake the capital, and restore the Zhou dynasty.

2. Give up no territory, pay no tribute, make no political marriages.

3. After north and south are united, all armies will fall under central administration; all military commissioners will retain their rights to self-defense.

4. We request an expansion of the seats in the Yanning Hall Assembly, permitting each area to select and send a military and civil official to enter the assembly and the border defense forces to send two military officials to enter the assembly, to participate in handling state affairs.

5. We request that trade routes in the north be opened with specialized forces to guard them.

...

12. We request that these new laws be promulgated and issued for enforcement throughout the empire, commanding those inside and out to comply, to be administered as a benefit, setting an example for posterity.

This memorial to the throne made huge waves in the Jiangnan court, enraging nearly all civil officials. The denouncements to the memorial were unending. "Assembling a personal army as a challenge to the government" and "abusing power to the detriment of the nation" were the lighter accusations, and many old ministers lined up at the palace doors prepared to expostulate with their deaths, afraid that once His Majesty agreed, the nation would fall apart, and the world would never again know a day of peace.

But some wicked imp copied out the contents of this earth-shaking memorial to the throne and leaked it to the public. Now, the common people also fell into turmoil. The military commissioners who nominally supported the Jiangnan court began to communicate privately; evidently, they were moved by the contents of the memorial.

In comparison to the fiercely opposed ministers, the common people's views on this were not entirely censorious. Since the capital had fallen in battle, people who wished to retake the Central Plains and unify north and south had not been in the minority. Tribulations brought on introspection. When the beautiful dream of a wealthy and powerful dynasty had been ground beneath the iron heel of foreign invaders, the imperial family had built a little court in the south amid the storm but had been unable to gather an army for a northern campaign. Only because Fu Shen had made a public appeal and the various military commissioners had deployed troops was there hope for the nation's revitalization. Many people, while they didn't say it out loud, began involuntarily in their hearts to have doubts about the "court" and the "emperor."

When the empire shook, it was often a time of contention among new ideas and new schools of thought. Though there was no lack of heresies among them, sometimes there would be voices so loud that even the deaf would hear. It was precisely on this rejuvenating east wind that the Kuangshan Academy emerged as a new force; the wise gentleman Ceng Guang's idea that "everyone has a say in the nation" was especially in vogue.

"The nation belongs to all, and is not the private property of a single family. The rule and disorder of the nation do not mark the rise and fall of a single clan, but are the anxieties and joys of all the nation's people."

The calamity of the smashing of the nation's territory had overturned a dynasty. But amid the ashes of desolation, the stars were still burning in the sky.

All the necessary conditions were present. The point of transformation was finally at hand.

Just as the army in the north hung back and Jinling's ministers argued until their heads spun, with no one willing to yield or compromise and the situation fallen into a deadlock, the military commissioners of Jiangnan, Lingnan, and Fujian suddenly presented a joint memorial to the court, asking Emperor Changzhi to approve the memorial presented by the seven northern armies. The commander of the East Sea Navy followed suit soon after, also submitting a memorial. Soon after that, Jiangnan's military commissioner also sent the Retired Emperor's decree, pronouncing that Emperor Changzhi could "canvas public sentiment, decide at your own discretion."

Fu Shen hadn't expected that Jiangnan's three military commissioners would stand up to speak in their favor so soon. He had planned on exerting pressure on Jinling with the retaking of the capital; if he dragged it out for a month, he was convinced that His Majesty would agree. This was better. The overall situation was already decided; even the Retired Emperor had spoken in support. It was only a matter of time before Emperor Changzhi gave the nod.

"Truly strange." He looked at Yan Xiaohan in total confusion and asked, "What kind of potion did you feed them in the first year of Changzhi that it hasn't worn off yet?"

In this aspect, Yan Xiaohan actually understood things better than him. "This memorial has only advantages for the military commissioners, and no disadvantages. Besides, they aren't the only ones facilitating this. There are also the wealthy merchants behind them.

"You spend all your time in the north and know little about the circumstances in Jiangnan. Jiangnan's business is prosperous. Jiangnan and Huainan are the wealthiest places in the empire, Fujian and Lingnan have a flourishing sea trade. Especially after His Majesty succeeded to the throne, with only half the nation left to him, in order to expand its financial resources and increase revenue, the court not only didn't beat down merchants, it gave them extra encouragement, expanded trade routes. And the military commissioners, in order to keep soldiers, have to treat the merchants still better.

"In this way, the wealthy merchants have become the court's greatest support. They also want to climb to the next level, but there is only a single path to becoming an official. If in the future the military commissioners can select and send military and civil ministers to Yanning Hall, the major merchants will have representation in the central administration. Their own interests are heavily bound up in this. Of course they are willing to support it."

All the small and quiet changes assembled and at last became a huge wave that could carry boats or capsize them.

On the fourth day of the fifth month, Emperor Changzhi sent an edict to Zhuozhou, permitting their memorial.

In the seventh month, the capital was retaken. The remaining Tartar and Zhe forces were beaten back to Miyun. The Beiyan Cavalry continued north to eliminate the remaining enemy troops. In the ninth month, Beiyan's Three Passes came back into the hands of the Beiyan Cavalry. The line of the northern frontier was reestablished. That same year, there was internal strife in Parhae. The insurrectionist army compelled their original ruler to capitulate. They were willing to pledge allegiance to Great Zhou, submit to its rule and pay tribute, forever be a vassal state.

In the twelfth month, Emperor Changzhi arrived in the capital. On New Year's Day the next year, he received the good wishes of all the ministers in Taiji Hall, rewarded all the generals, conferred upon Sun Hui, the son of the empress in the central palace, the title of crown prince, and promulgated a set of Assembly Laws.

In the spring of the third year of Changzhi, Fu Shen was promoted Duke of Jing and conferred the additional title of General, Pillar of the Nation. While he was the initiator of the new system, he had no attachment to power and position. As soon as he received his titles, pleading a relapse of his leg problems, he submitted a memorial requesting to resign his post as Beiyan commander.

Back when the Beiyan Army had retaken the Three Passes in the ninth month of the previous year, it had been restructured by Fu Shen. The army was separated into four parts, to defend the four provinces of Jizhou, Pingzhou, Beiyan, and Yuanzhou, commanded respectively by the four high generals of Beiyan. Fu Shen no longer led troops and devolved the bulk of his military authority to Yu Qiaoting.

When the memorial to the throne had first been submitted, the Beiyan Cavalry had been considered as a single army unit. Now, after being split up, according to the new laws, the four generals each amounted to the military commissioner of a province. Emperor Changzhi's head simply ached. Fu Shen hadn't stopped at asking to resign; he had expanded Beiyan's assembly members from two to eight.

Ruler and minister went back and forth for half the day and ultimately hammered it out: each army of the four Beiyan provinces would send one person to the assembly; apart from that, while Fu Shen wouldn't be commanding troops, he would still join the assembly as the Beiyan Army Commander-in-Chief.

The Tianfu Army joined the imperial guards, and Yan Xiaohan joined the assembly as representative of the Tianfu Army.

At this point, the eight provinces at the northern border, the five provinces of the Central Plains, the five provinces of the south, one province of Xinan, the East Sea Navy, the Tianfu Army, and the original old ministers from Jinling, forty-eight assembly ministers in all, became the central authority of Great Zhou's new court.

The fledgling form of the new system was emerging, quietly getting onto the right track. Everything seemed to be developing in the best direction that could be expected.

—Apart from Xinan.

Commandery Prince Xiping Duan Guihong had been the first to bring up "self-defense," and he had suited action to word. Since then, he had had no further contact of any sort with the Central Plains. When everyone had been busy with battles and power struggles, with hardly even the time to look after themselves, no one had had the time to attend to what his intentions actually were. Now the emperor had restored the dynasty, the new system had just been put into effect, and an era of peace and prosperity was about to be ushered in, but there had still been no activity or word from Xinan.

Emperor Changzhi had sent an envoy to negotiate with Xinan, but he hadn't even seen Duan Guihong. Little by little, Xinan's attitude became self-evident. Commandery Prince

Xiping had turned against them; he was planning to oppose the court to the bitter end.

With the nation's territory missing this corner, in the eyes of Emperor Changzhi, whose vanity had been fostered by uniting north and south, it became a fishbone caught in his throat.

In late spring and early summer, three rainstorms fell in the capital in succession. Fu Shen's old complaints acted up, and he asked for leave to recuperate at home. Yan Xiaohan followed suit. He insisted on saying that his old affliction from Jingchu was also acting up; he also asked for leave.

Fu Shen of course knew that his so-called "old affliction" wasn't any proper ailment, but the two of them had spent nearly two years racing around without pause. Now that things had finally calmed down, they ought to be making up for the debt of affection and embrace. Considered like this, he figured Yan Xiaohan could do as he liked.

On a certain day in the sixth month, the two of them woke from a midday nap. In the coolness coming from a bucket of ice, they were fooling around and splitting fruits on a daybed. The butler walked in quietly and, standing outside, reported through the screen: "Master, there's someone here from court. His Majesty has summoned the Duke of Jing for an audience."

Yan Xiaohan's expression immediately turned unhappy. "It's such a hot day. What if you get heatstroke? Don't go."

"Do you think everyone is as finicky as you?" Fu Shen plucked a grape and stopped his mouth with it. He rolled over, got out of bed, and put on his shoes. "Stop groaning, I'm going."

However vigorously Yan Xiaohan cried out, he still couldn't cling to his waist and not let him go. He gloomily bit down and got a mouthful of icy grape juice.

Unexpectedly, the next moment, the person who had said he was leaving suddenly leaned down and drew near. The tip of his tongue swiftly drew a circle on his lips, flirtatiously and dissolutely stealing a taste. With a smile, he said, "So sweet."

Yan Xiaohan said, "You…"

Fu Shen raised his eyebrows. Not without mockery, he said, "Lord, I've already paid your illegal toll fee. Can you let me go now?"

The old palace in the capital already had centuries of history. Though it had been renovated several times, it hadn't changed overall. The old buildings had a natural quiet to them. Even if it was the hottest part of summer outside, it would still be very tranquil and cool in the depths of the palace.

But the coolness now seemed to seep into the cracks in your bones. With the accompaniment of Emperor Changzhi's stormy face, Fu Shen's rheumatic legs dimly began to ache.

"Your Majesty, the north has been freshly calmed, the people urgently need to recuperate and rebuild. The court's new system has only just begun to be put in practice. Forgive me for being blunt, but this is not a good time to deploy troops. The problem of Xinan can be put aside for the time being. It will not be too late to discuss it when the court has replenished its strength."

Emperor Changzhi snorted. His expression was grim. He clearly hadn't taken his words to heart.

Fu Shen had been completely unprepared for the current situation. He knew that Emperor Changzhi had sent an envoy to Xinan, but he didn't know that Duan Guihong had angered His Majesty to this degree. He had come in under the scorching sun, and before the sweat had evaporated from his brow, Emperor Changzhi's words hit him right in the face: "Commandery Prince Xiping is going to revolt one of these days. Minister Fu, I wish to hand you the banner of raising the troops to deal with this rebel."

Fu Shen had to listen carefully to work out what had happened. According to the old system, the fifth and sixth months were when the various vassal states paid their tributes. For the past couple of years, the court had been busy with battle and hadn't had time to attend to this, but this time the legitimate court had been restored. On New Year's Day, the envoys of several foreign nations had come to pay their respects at court, and in recent days, some tributes to the court had straggled into the capital. This ought to have been cause for celebration, but Emperor Changzhi had been hung up on Xinan lately, and he had deliberately examined the list of gifts submitted by the Ministry of Rites.

He wouldn't have known without looking, but once he looked, he found that the three vassal states bordering on Xinan —Annan, Zhenla, and Linyi—seemed to have arranged it between themselves: they hadn't come in person on New Year's Day, and their tributes hadn't come either!

Emperor Changzhi was very upset. He ordered the Ministry of Rites' officials to closely investigate what had happened. But before the Ministry of Rites' special envoy could set out, an envoy from the three nations had belatedly arrived with a diplomatic note from their governments.

The diplomatic note was written with majesty and grandeur, but it contained only one thought: the three nations wished to rescind their vassal relationships with Great Zhou and stand on an even footing, no longer submit to Great Zhou or pay tribute to it.

These three blows stabbed Emperor Changzhi directly in his sore spot. He had already been displeased with the business of Commandery Prince Xiping. Now that the three nations had come up with this, if one said that Duan Guihong hadn't been egging them on, who would believe it? To Emperor Changzhi, all of these things seemed to be connected.

Fu Shen hadn't previously thought that Emperor Changzhi was an obstinate person. Perhaps this was a mistaken impression Yan Xiaohan had given him. Because of this, he still held out hope that he could move him with reason and sentiment. "Permit me to report, Your Majesty. Annan and the other nations taking this move is indeed unthinkable, but it is not necessarily directly connected to Xinan. It has been some years since the court has had dealings with the other nations. There is no knowing yet whether there are other secrets involved. If we rashly open hostilities without verifying the situation, it will be a loss to the humane and just air of this court. I hope that Your Majesty will reconsider and postpone this action."

"Minister Fu," Emperor Changzhi suddenly said coldly, "do you think that We have not been sufficiently lenient and forbearing toward Commandery Prince Xiping?"

Fu Shen quickly replied, "I would not dare to think such a thing."

"When the military commissioners wanted military power, wanted to defend themselves, wanted to join the assembly, We agreed to it all," Emperor Changzhi said. "If Xinan returns to the Central Plains, it will receive the same treatment. Why is he unwilling?"

Fu Shen snuck a glance at Emperor Changzhi, his face like deep water, and sighed inwardly. He had a premonition that another storm was about to break out.

While Duan Guihong couldn't be said to have an implacable hatred for the imperial family, probably he wouldn't bow his head and submit again to anyone with the family name Sun for the rest of his life. It was only that Fu Shen knew the secrets behind this, while others didn't know. From the deadlock between the two sides now, it did indeed appear that Commandery Prince Xiping was unwilling to be controlled by the emperor and was preparing to set himself up as king and revolt.

"Duan Guihong has been managing Xinan for many years. He calls himself the 'Prince of Xinan.' When there was chaos in the Central Plains, he calmly kept on playing local despot in Xinan. We could tolerate all of this." As Emperor Changzhi spoke, he finally broke out into true anger. Banging on a table, he said, "We have sent envoys to Xinan over and over, afforded him ample dignity. But what about him? He has put Our dignity beneath his heel and ground it into the earth!"

Fu Shen had no answer to give. He could only say, "Calm your anger, Your Majesty."

With a sneer, Emperor Changzhi said, "We have it worked

out now. Duan Guihong holds the little favors of the court in contempt. He has meant to rebel for a long time. Guarding Xinan, gathering his strength, then allying with the three nations. When the time came, he would be able to set himself up as king, dominate the region, stand on an equal footing with Great Zhou.

"Nurturing a tiger invites calamity," he muttered quietly to himself. "Truly this is what it means to nurture a tiger and invite calamity."

"Your Majesty." After a brief silence and repeated consideration, Fu Shen at last spoke to urge him. "Commandery Prince Xiping..."

"There is no need for you to continue, Minister Fu," Emperor Changzhi said heavily. "We are aware that he once served under the previous generation's Duke of Ying and is a former subordinate of your Beiyan Army. Think carefully, Minister Fu. Do not harm the loyalty and righteousness of the Beiyan Army for the sake of a traitor and usurper."

Fu Shen's face instantly stiffened, then quickly recovered an expressionless look. He bowed and said, "I will closely abide by Your Majesty's instructions. I will take my leave now."

The sunlight outside was all-consuming. Fu Shen walked out with a chill in his heart and was hit by a wave of heat. His temples instantly began to ache as though pricked with needles. The walls of the palace were dazzlingly red. After a few steps, he ran into a red-robed official even more garish than the walls. When their gazes met, both of them froze.

This was the Minister of the Ministry of Appointments, Xue Sheng, Lord Xue, who, despite never having crossed swords with him directly, had accumulated quite deep rancor against Fu Shen for all kinds of reasons.

In fact, Xue Sheng wasn't especially old, and he didn't seem elderly. It was only that contrasted with the elegant and handsome General Fu, there was a bit of unspeakable haggardness about him. Neither of them spoke, leaving only awkwardness between them. Finally, Xue Sheng saluted him, and Fu Shen returned the civility with a nod of his head. The two of them coldly brushed past each other.

When he exited the palace gates, the carriage from home that had come to pick him up was waiting outside. Before Fu Shen could get near it, a page cooling in the shade beneath a nearby tree suddenly ran up in front of him and said with a nimble bow, "Greetings, Lord Duke."

The carriage driver, seeing him waylaid, jumped down and was about to go over but was stopped at a distance by a gesture from Fu Shen. He lowered his head and asked the page, "What is it?"

"My master ordered me to wait here for you and invite you to come to the Jinghe Building for a drink this evening." The page respectfully presented a name card with both hands. "This is my master's name card. He said that you would understand when you saw it."

Fu Shen took a glance and immediately saw the words "Kuangshan Academy;" he immediately understood. He put the name card away in his sleeve unflappably and, nodding agreement, said, "Understood. Return and tell your master that it would be impolite of me to decline such a courteous invitation."

CHAPTER SEVENTY-FOUR

THE JINGHE BUILDING HAD A LONG-STANDING REPUTATION, and its Yanzhou cuisine was the finest in the capital. When Fu Shen came in, there was already someone waiting in the private room. Gu Shanlü was dressed in casual clothing. He stood to welcome him. "Here you are, general. Please come in."

Last time, during the send-off outside the city, Gu Shanlü had still been a minor censor with little manpower or resources. Following the turmoil of war, he had been put into quite an important position by Emperor Changzhi in Jiangnan, promoted to senior official of the Court of the Censorate, ranking as one of the nine high ministers in Yanning Hall. After returning to the capital, he had remained in control of the Court of the Censorate, controlling impeachment of officials and maintaining order, able to learn of the contents of memorials to the throne.

This person's position was very delicate. He came from Jiangnan, but he was no high-born aristocrat. In his youth, he had enrolled in the Kuangshan Academy and studied under Ceng Guang. Later he had passed the imperial examinations and, as was to be expected, joined the Court of the Censorate to accumulate experience. Prior to this, Gu Shanlü had always been a nobody. The first time he had stuck his neck out was during the

Eastern Tartar diplomatic mission case, and the upshot was that the case had come to nothing, and his teacher had been sent to prison. He had spent a miserable half a year, and finally it had been Fu Shen who had asked Yan Xiaohan to get his teacher out.

Because of this, while at court in Jinling, Gu Shanlü had always stood with the old ministers from the north, but Jiangnan's new nobles had treated him differently from the rest. On returning to the capital, they had further expressed goodwill and attempted to win him over many times, trying to win Jiangnan a helping hand in Yanning Hall.

Though imperial censors did not inspire joy in courtiers, they were indeed an excellent weapon when it came to dealing with one's political opponents.

But Gu Shanlü's attitude had always been ambiguous. He seemed cultured and refined, no less shrewd than the old foxes. Since returning to the capital, he'd had almost no contact with people like Fu Shen and Yan Xiaohan. The average person wouldn't have thought that he had an old friendship with the two of them.

Gu Shanlü said, "As an imperial censor, it is inappropriate for me to communicate openly with you, general. I hope you will see fit to forgive me for having to resort to this move. I have taken the liberty of asking you to come here today because of the matter that has recently caused His Majesty concern."

Fu Shen twirled a wine cup in his fingers. He wasn't the least surprised at his direct opening. Calmly, he said, "Has he spoken to you as well?"

"That's right." Gu Shanlü refilled his wine cup. "His Majesty wishes to launch an attack against Xinan, so he must first obtain the approval of Yanning Hall. At present, the forty-eight assembly members seem scattered, but in fact there are only a few leaders. If he sounds them out in turn, he will be able to understand Yanning Hall's attitude."

"His Majesty wants me to lead the troops," Fu Shen said. "I spent ages trying to talk him out of it, but I couldn't move him."

With a bitter laugh, Gu Shanlü said, "When I went to the palace in the morning, His Majesty was just raging about the matter of Annan and the two other nations. He suggested that the Court of the Censorate censure Commandery Prince Xiping, which would give him just cause. Furthermore, I am not certain that Yanning Hall will oppose this matter."

"I would like to hear more," said Fu Shen.

Gu Shanlü said, "Xinan becoming independent has a hundred disadvantages and no advantages for the court. For one thing, it's too close to Jingchu and Lingnan. If Commandery Prince Xiping wishes to expand his sphere of influence, those two places will be among the first to come to grief. Second, Xinan is in communication with Annan and Zhenla. If Xinan allies with these small nations, not only will it be difficult for the court to communicate on land with the nations of the southeast, it will also impact sea trade.

"And since the army took back the capital, the court and the commons have all been beside themselves with complacency. I hear that they praise you up to the skies, say that the Beiyan Cavalry is made up of divine soldiers and divine generals, all-conquering. So if it were someone else leading the troops, perhaps they would think it over, but if it is you leading the troops, then they will not have so many misgivings."

Fu Shen had no answer to give. He could only respond with a sneer. "They truly have a good opinion of me, it seems."

"There is one other thing," Gu Shanlü said seriously. "Commandery Prince Xiping is a former subordinate of the Beiyan Army, profoundly connected to you and to the Duke of Ying Manor. Perhaps you have already noticed it, general—there are many eyes at court fixed on you, and the one above them is no exception. If anything should go wrong in the western expedition… the circumstances would be suspicious. It is hard to say what would happen."

"Is there any need for so much scheming?" Fu Shen picked up his wine cup and drank. Self-mockingly, he said, "If I had wanted to do a bit of something, would I have needed to wait this long?"

"It is precisely the fact that you haven't done a bit of something that is making some people uneasy," Gu Shanlü said. "With your power and influence now and your reputation at its prime, by the time you truly plan to do something, who would be able to bar the way?"

He sighed gently. "As the proverb says, 'You must prepare for all eventualities.'"

Fu Shen didn't know whether Gu Shanlü had invited him to eat or come here deliberately to annoy him. At any rate, when he finally left the restaurant, smelling of alcohol and with a bellyful of fury, he was seized and forced into a carriage by a certain highway bandit who had been lying in wait for ages.

"All right," Yan Xiaohan said darkly, grinding his teeth, "you told me to stay home and wait for you, then ran off drinking with someone else."

Fu Shen silently threw his arms open and pressed down, hugging him heavily.

The tail end of Yan Xiaohan's threat instantly changed tune. With a dry cough, he said, "What are you doing, don't think you can get out of this by being cute... What's wrong, has drinking made you depressed?"

"Menggui," he whispered.

Before the last wave could fall, the next one arose. They had switched emperors twice, but the current one was still as suspicious and paranoid as the others. The words "Great achievements disturb the master" were like dark clouds forever looming. As long as Fu Shen lived, he would never be able to leave this haze.

His voice made Yan Xiaohan's heart instantly feel as if a cat had scratched it. He stopped smirking and stopped being moody.

He carefully pushed him up a little higher. "All right, I'm here. What's wrong? Tell me, what happened?"

Fu Shen didn't want to talk. He suddenly felt a little sad, so he hugged Yan Xiaohan tighter.

Seeing him not speaking, only snuggling into his arms seeming deeply aggrieved, Yan Xiaohan couldn't resist a quiet laugh. In the helpless tone of one too indulgent to be capable of doing anything, he said, "All right, if you don't want to tell me, you don't have to. Are you sleepy? Go to sleep for now."

The carriage was jolting, the embrace was warm, and the wine had gone to his head. Amid a daze of disappointment, Fu Shen fell asleep.

When he woke in the middle of the night, he found himself lying calmly in bed, clean and fresh, with no smell of alcohol. From the other side of the pillow came another person's long, even breaths. Yan Xiaohan was turned toward him with a hand lying on his waist through the quilt. By the obscured weak light coming in through the bed curtains, Fu Shen could see his peaceful and quiet sleeping countenance.

He was awake, and he had sobered up. Fu Shen lengthened his breaths slowly calmed down in the tranquil night. Now when he remembered Emperor Changzhi's notification in the afternoon and Gu Shanlü's warnings, his feelings weren't so acute.

He even felt a little ridiculous. Before, Emperor Yuantai had first tried to assassinate him and then arranged a marriage for him, bringing all kinds of means to bear in turn, one bolt out of the blue after another, and hadn't he gotten through it all just fine? Why, after so many things had changed, when he stood even higher, he was worse than before, worried enough to sulk at Yan Xiaohan over a trifle like this?

It was all Yan Xiaohan's fault!

Only now did Fu Shen learn that he was truly at ease beside Yan Xiaohan. It was a powerful sense of security that he had never derived from another person before. Never mind the rest—if this had been before, with someone next to him, Fu Shen definitely wouldn't have been able to put his head down and sleep after drinking, and he certainly wouldn't have been moved this way and that, washed and undressed, and still not have woken up after all that.

The emperor had only just had this thought. To put it into practice would require going through one barrier after another. It might take ages until they really opened hostilities. Even if Yanning Hall gave the nod and permitted it, and he really had to take troops out on an expedition, he could still take his time and discuss it with Duan Guihong when he got to Xinan. At worst he could drag it out for a year or two.

What was there worth worrying about?

Sometimes, "coming to the end of the road" didn't mean there truly was no line of retreat, but that your bottom line was too high. Facing Emperor Yuantai, Fu Shen had had some scruples; but if Emperor Changzhi one day pushed him into a situation like that, for the sake of the empire, Fu Shen naturally wouldn't object to installing a new emperor in the depths of the imperial palace, to rule over the vast territory.

He became lost in thought and accidentally rolled over. The outcome was that at this slight movement, Yan Xiaohan actually woke up and murkily asked, "Jingyuan?"

"It's nothing, go back to sleep." Fu Shen was wide awake. He pulled the thin quilt higher over him. Yan Xiaohan made a soft sound of agreement and seemed to sink back into dreams. But not long after, he opened his eyes again and looked at him with a clear gaze. "Are you sober?"

"Yes." Fu Shen picked up a lock of hair from beside the pillow and wound it around his finger. "Don't worry about me. Go back to sleep."

"When you're awake, why would I sleep?" Yan Xiaohan draped a robe over himself and got out of bed. He poured two cups of tea and carried them back. The two of them silently moistened their throats. Yan Xiaohan lit a lamp, then lay back down in bed. "Can you tell me now?"

"What?" said Fu Shen.

"When the emperor summoned you to the palace this after-noon, did he talk about Xinan?" Yan Xiaohan hugged him loosely. "And did Gu Shanlü invite you in the evening to talk about the same thing? Look how upset they've made our Lord Duke."

It had been many years since Fu Shen had had an opportunity to experience the skills of this boss of the Feilong Guard. He was disbelieving. "How do you know? Did I put you in my purse when I went out?"

"Nothing to it," Yan Xiaohan said, laughing. "It's only my old profession."

The familiar ability to get into everything. What exactly had Emperor Yuantai raised? Not even his own son could escape being deceived.

While the Feilong Guard had been dissolved, the old staff remained, and what was more, since returning to the capital, the imperial guards had been controlled entirely by Yan Xiaohan. He had long ago arranged countless spies, both in the open and in the shadows. After the affair of the Golden Terrace gathering, Emperor Changzhi had become suspicious of him, and there was Xue Sheng and other such people stirring up trouble every day; he didn't trust him as extensively as he had before. But the people at the emperor's disposal truly were limited. Apart from Yan Xiaohan, he could find no one else capable of directing the imperial guards, so he had to hold his nose and continue to use him.

The consequence of this was more or less equivalent to leading the wolf into your house and placing your throat at its sharp teeth; it was too late to close the door.

Moreover, there was Yan Xiaohan himself, taught by instruction and example from a young age by the foremost eunuch in the Yuantai court, Duan Linglong. He had joined the North Yamen Imperial Guards as a teenager and served as a guard before the emperor. Later he became the Imperial Investigator of the Feilong Guard, running rampant throughout the court and commons. Politics and intrigue had become like breathing, instinctive in nature.

Noticing a change in Emperor Changzhi's attitude, he had put some slight effort into "playing up to the emperor," and as expected, Emperor Changzhi was once again pleasant and amiable toward him, relying heavily on him.

Fu Shen was forced to acknowledge that where cheating and swindling were concerned, Yan Xiaohan was far superior to him. This was a talent that couldn't be learned. If it had been Yan Xiaohan who had gone to the palace for an audience with the emperor this afternoon, perhaps he could have coaxed Emperor Changzhi into changing his mind.

"His Majesty is very persistent about this. I'm afraid he won't easily let it go."

Having heard out Fu Shen's account, Yan Xiaohan rejected the idea that he would have been able to convince Emperor Changzhi. "You must have worked out what His Majesty's temperament is, too. He can't bear upsets, and he aims higher than he can reach. Before ascending to the throne, at least he knew to be afraid and understood when to hold back. But as soon as the empire was his to command, he became completely self-centered and excessively stubborn."

A mediocrity wasn't frightening—a person with lofty aims and underhanded means was frightening; a fool wasn't frightening—a person who tried to be clever was frightening.

"He doesn't have the Retired Emperor's strength, but he wants to imitate the Retired Emperor's methods. Before, in Jiangnan, he put the old ministers from the north into positions of power, but now, for the sake of equilibrium, he wishes to raise the Jiangnan families," Yan Xiaohan said. "Apart from this, there is also the problem of national prestige, the problem of Jiangnan's safety… On the subject of the western expedition, His Majesty's position is identical to that of the Jiangnan families, so he can't be convinced, and too many attempts to convince him will make him angry at you."

Fu Shen frowned. "So there's nothing else we can do? We have to let him have it his way?"

"Unless there is an earthquake on Mount Tai or unusual celestial phenomena, this situation will be difficult to save." Through a layer of clothing, Yan Xiaohan massaged his shoulder. "Gu Shanlü's warnings make sense. You're a thorn in the flesh for many people now. Whether this ultimately succeeds or not, they're all going to be thinking of ways to find fault with you, and even seize the opportunity to drag in the empress and the crown prince. You have to be careful."

"I know," Fu Shen said with a sigh. "It seems that not even Yanning Hall can get in the way of him seeking death."

"You have to eat your food mouthful by mouthful, and the new system has to advance step by step. Don't be impatient." Yan Xiaohan pressed down on the center of his brow. "Come on, don't frown. Smile."

"It's the middle of the night, what are you raving about now?" Fu Shen said expressionlessly. "I won't smile. Why don't you give me a smile?"

"Be good, smile," Yan Xiaohan said enticingly. "You made me wait all afternoon today. Shouldn't you make it up to me somehow?"

Vexed and plagued like this, Fu Shen's colossal fretfulness dispersed. He had meant to hold on to his stern expression for a while longer, but the outcome was that he couldn't resist laughing. He poked at a small patch of exposed skin on Yan Xiaohan's chest. "Rascal."

Yan Xiaohan said with justice on his side, "A good man doesn't find a good wife, a rascal finds himself a beautiful branch."

The "beautiful branch" shook until he had nearly turned into a beggar's club.

When Fu Shen at last managed to even out his breathing,

Yan Xiaohan pulled him into his arms along with the quilt and fiercely proclaimed, "I'm going to wreck you."

"Hahaha…"

Events proceeded as they had foreseen. Not long after, Emperor Changzhi introduced the subject of the punitive expedition against Xinan in Yanning Hall, and apart from the northern frontier armies, which still stood on Fu Shen's side, the other forty-some assembly members, including Yan Xiaohan, agreed to His Majesty's proposal.

After this event, there was an extra layer of meaning in the gazes people leveled at them. During the northern campaign, the Beiyan Army and the Tianfu Army had still presentably marched together, but hardly any time had passed, and now the undercurrent of disagreement between the two of them had been brought to the forefront.

The nation was easily changed, but character was hard to alter. A sycophant was always unreliable.

In spring of the following year, the Duke of Jing Fu Shen led an army of a hundred thousand south, under orders to carry out a punitive expedition against Commandery Prince Xiping Duan Guihong.

This time, it wasn't his former subordinates in the Beiyan Cavalry who went on campaign with him, but a strengthened army of the court. Its main force was composed of the Jiangnan Army that Zhao Xicheng had led while retaking the Central Plains.

Once again they were upon Golden Terrace in the capital's outskirts, banners flapping, war horses neighing.

Emperor Changzhi in person left the city to see off the army, just as Emperor Yuantai had once led the civil and military officials to send off the teenage general on his way north to resist the enemy. They seemed full of magnificent sentiments and lofty aspirations, but in reality they were only coldly looking on.

Yan Xiaohan stood not far from Emperor Changzhi. His eyes

swept over the various high ministers and at last settled on Emperor Changzhi's slightly plump figure.

Yan Xiaohan had no expression, his face looking cold and indifferent, but this instead made him seem more real than the ruler and his ministers with their faces full of feigned emotion.

From a distance, Fu Shen looked up and sent a glance his way. Their eyes met in midair. Yan Xiaohan nodded gently.

He dimly felt that under his hard helmet, that person seemed to be smiling.

The night before his departure, Yan Xiaohan had said to Fu Shen, "All you need to worry about is going south. I'm here to guard the rear for you. There's nothing for you to worry about."

Fu Shen hadn't said anything at the time, only smiled, and lifted his chin to kiss him. He seemed completely ignorant, yet also to see the truth clearly.

A spring breeze swept over the countryside. Yan Xiaohan watched the commander's flag gradually recede into the distance. In his mind, he silently completed the words he had left unfinished the night before.

When you come back, I will give you back a clean court.

CHAPTER SEVENTY-FIVE

THE HEIGHT OF SUMMER WAS PASSING, THE SWELTERING HEAT gradually dissipating. To make ready for Emperor Changzhi's trip to Jiangnan in the ninth month, Yan Xiaohan was dispatched to go on ahead to Jinling and make all the arrangements for the temporary imperial residence, its guards, and so on.

The day before leaving, when he had finished handing over assignments to Wei Xuzhou and other such people, had returned home and was walking down the corridor watching the servants rushing in and out to pack up his luggage, empty-handed and utterly bored, he toyed with a snow-white hydrangea next to him. The setting sun on the horizon was spilling golden light all over the ground. Lord Yan sighed into the wind. He thought that if he went on like this, he would start spouting lines of poetry like "the setting sun shines with longing on the river's flow."

It was already two months and more since Fu Shen had gone on campaign to Xinan. Yan Xiaohan wasn't concerned about his safety, he only missed him to distraction. Separation was long, yearning was a torment. He had already tasted enough of it in Jinling, and now he had to taste it anew. It was only because his patience was good and his reason still present that he could still have a thought for Emperor Changzhi. Otherwise he would long ago have thrown it all over and gone in search of his husband.

"Master!" The butler trotted over from the other end of the courtyard holding a thin letter, which he offered up with both hands. He said, "Master, an army messenger just came to deliver a letter, he says it's the Lord Duke's personal letter brought back from Xinan."

Yan Xiaohan's hands gave a fierce shake. A portion of the hydrangea was immediately plucked bald. White blossoms fell over the ground. His ears were filled with his own pulse. He forced a calm expression onto his face and said, "Let me see it."

The envelope was very thin and tightly sealed. There was only one transparently thin piece of writing paper inside. When Yan Xiaohan pulled it out, he was afraid of using too much force and tearing it.

Why was it only one sheet? That four-word note reading "Is my wife well?" was still branded heavily on his heart. During this separation of vast distances, what would he have written?

When he had unfolded the letter paper that had been folded twice, Yan Xiaohan went completely rigid in the posture of holding up the letter.

What the hell was this?

There were no words, only an illegible scrawl of a pitch-black inkblot. Yan Xiaohan stared at it for ages before finally, exercising his impoverished imagination, he caught up with Fu Shen's bold and unrestrained style.

The black was back, the white was belly, sticking out in front was a mouth, stuck up behind was a paw, and the strokes on top escaping at a slant were... wings?

No, that was wrong, what creature had four wings?

Fu Shen was, at any rate, a son of nobility. While his drawing and calligraphy skills weren't fit to be handed down through the ages, at least it was always clear what he was drawing. What was going on with this scribble that could have been stuck up as an exorcism talisman?!

Yan Xiaohan hadn't realized at all that his own appearance, caught between laughter and tears, gritting his teeth, might be even more frightening in the eyes of others than the drawing. He was like a small child whose attention had been caught by a new toy, all his mind bent on seeking an answer. He hadn't remotely considered the possibility that this drawing had just been casually scrawled, without any meaning.

Of course, Fu Shen wouldn't have sent a letter all this way to make fun of him, but this drawing was truly exhausting his efforts.

Yan Xiaohan spent ages trying to decipher it. He looked at it right-side-up and upside-down. Finally he realized that his earlier judgment had been wrong. Sticking out at the front wasn't a mouth, it was two birds' heads, and what was stuck out behind wasn't a paw, it was a tail. The four lines of ink were two pairs of wings. Adding in the black backs and white bellies, the answer at last began to come clear.

The drawing on the paper was a pair of wild geese.

The moment he understood, the look in his eyes abruptly softened, as if something had launched a sudden attack on his heart. The corners of his lips turned slightly upward, but there seemed to be tears welling up in his eyes.

The letter had been sent back along with the military reports. Because there was a danger of its being opened by someone else, Fu Shen couldn't express his feelings straight out, so he had used this means to send him a "goose letter."

The meaning of the "goose" was a tacit understanding that would make sense only to the two of them.

The goose was a loyal bird. It mated for life and flew to the ends of the earth with its partner.

That night, while Yan Xiaohan couldn't sleep from the agitation of that letter home and was kept up tossing and turning, at the other end of the capital, in Minister Xue's manor, there were also people who couldn't sleep.

Recently the Court of the Censorate had impeached two officials of the six ministries. His Majesty, after reading the memorials to the throne, had according to convention permitted the two of them to temporarily leave office to shut their doors and reflect on their conduct while their case was handed over for investigation to the Imperial Court of Judicial Review. This was all in the ordinary course of business to begin with, and the so-called "impeachment" only concerned insignificant little problems. No one had taken it seriously. What no one had expected in a million years was that the shovel of the Imperial Court of Judicial Review would reach down all the way into the past—it really did dig up evidence of these two people perverting justice in exchange for bribes!

Once the gap opened, there was no stopping it. The Imperial Court of Judicial Reviews' Minister Zhu Can was renowned at court for being upright and above flattery, unmoved by force or persuasion. Though he knew that both of these individuals belonged to the Jiangnan party, he still had no intention to letting them off easy. It wasn't long before the Imperial Court of Judicial Reviews' memorial came before the throne. Emperor Changzhi was enraged and permitted the Ministry of Justice to keep those two people jailed in expectation of beheading, to be executed after the autumn trials.

Xue Sheng lost two capable people in one go, instantly turning his position delicate. Emperor Changzhi's attitude had also been slightly cold lately. This evening Xue Sheng had a guest at home, Zheng Duanweng, the Ministry of Rites' Assistant Minister of the Right and Imperial Instructor, who like him came from Jiangnan. He had brought him a piece of news that may have been good or bad.

"This afternoon, a messenger brought a military report from Xinan. The army has already been stationed outside the city in excess of a month, yet the two sides have yet to cross swords and test each other. The Duke of Jing writes in his report that Duan Guihong has sent envoys many times to the camp to ask to see the commander-in-chief. He plans in a few days to meet face-to-face with Commandery Prince Xiping and induce him to capitulate.

"When His Majesty had read the report, his expression simply wasn't to be beheld. He was so angry he shook. He asked me, 'We sent people over and over to Xinan, and he pleaded illness and wouldn't see them, so how come as soon as Fu Shen gets there, he's in a hurry to explain himself? What unrighted wrong is there that We are unable to redress, one that he can only lay out before Fu Shen and no one else?'"

Xue Sheng had been the first to approve Emperor Changzhi's punitive expedition to Xinan, so every time some matter came up in the military situation in Xinan, Emperor Changzhi would call him to the palace to discuss it. But now that he had been splattered with mud, he had missed his opportunity, allowing Zheng Duanwen to appear in front of His Majesty. It sounded as if Emperor Changzhi placed quite a bit of trust in him.

The matter had profound implications, and Zheng Duanwen was uncertain. He cautiously asked: "Yunping-xiong, listen, do you think this means His Majesty is dissatisfied with Commandery Prince Xiping, or does he have some... notions about that gentleman?"

The Jiangnan party had always seen the Duke of Jing Fu Shen as a major enemy. Not to speak of the large number of troops at his disposal, his ploy on Golden Terrace had nearly swept the Jiangnan families out of court, such that Xue Sheng and the others periodically gave counsel before Emperor Changzhi along the lines of subjects of great merit causing trouble for their master and assembling a personal army being a potential challenge to the throne. Emperor Changzhi pulling a long face as soon as Fu Shen was mentioned now was in large part owing to the efforts of these people.

Xue Sheng smiled a cold inward smile and gathered up his many revolving thoughts. He wasn't in a hurry to answer. Instead, he asked in turn, "How did you handle it, Fangde?"

"Well…" Zheng Duanwen said hesitantly, "I only said that Duan Guihong was a traitor, and even if he were offered amnesty and submitted, he might decide to rebel again later. This move on the Duke of Jing's part is rather inappropriate."

Xue Sheng raised a hand to smooth his mustache. He said meaningfully, "Fangde, do you still recall when the Tartars and Zhe sent an embassy to Jinling to engage in peace negotiations with the court? At the time, Yan Xiaohan and Fu Shen were both at the front lines. The memorial to the throne they sent back then contained only a few words: 'Better fight to the death than negotiate peace.' Why now, facing a mere commandery prince, has he become overcautious?"

"You mean that…"

"It's true that Duan Guihong is a former subordinate of Beiyan, but that is a friendship from his father's generation, a story that's grown long in the tooth. How could Fu Shen have an old camaraderie with him? It is only an excuse," Xue Sheng said. "No matter what the reason, Fu Shen is unwilling to meet Duan Guihong in battle. This is a truth no one can erase. With our court using such a person to face our enemy, what if he should coordinate an offensive with Duan Guihong? Wouldn't that cause great commotion?"

Weren't you the one who single-handedly egged on his majesty to send him to the front lines in Xinan?

Zheng Duanwen picked up a murderous edge in his even words, and a chill went up his back in spite of himself. "Yunping-xiong, you mean that Fu Shen is colluding with Duan Guihong and intends to revolt? That is a major crime that people lose their heads for! Why would he do such a thing?"

"It isn't 'why would *he* do such a thing,' it's 'why would *we* do such a thing,'" Xue Sheng said calmly. "There are evidently people at court scheming against us. If we do not act now, the next ones to lose their official's caps will be you and me. It isn't important whether Fu Shen is planning to revolt. We only need His Majesty to believe that he is going to revolt.

"If we can knock him down, the alliance of the northerners will naturally crumble. Without us needing to step in, they will become mired in internal strife. That will be when our chance to act freely comes."

The heat of the summer night was stifling, but a drop of cold sweat slid down Zheng Duanwen's temple all the same.

He really was on Xue Sheng's side, but he had also heard the praises of the Beiyan Cavalry for quelling foreign enemies and defending the frontier for many years. Forming a faction was one thing, but how had it suddenly come to the point of making a false charge against a distinguished minister, finding happiness in Fu Shen's death?

"It's enough for His Majesty to believe that he is going to revolt"—wasn't that... a trumped-up charge?

With his mind in a daze, Zheng Duanwen bid farewell to Xue Sheng. With the butler leading him, he passed through the courtyard and came to the front gate.

It was deep into the night, but there were still voices outside. When the two of them left through the gate, they found a young man of unremarkable height standing on the steps outside. He was watching with a squinting gaze, uttering filthy curses. The porter had a club in his hands. Expression fierce, he yelled, "Hurry up and leave! If you dare to make trouble again, I'll report you and have you arrested and sent to prison!"

Zheng Duanwen came back from his thoughts at this yell. Putting on an official's severity, he slowly said, "Whence comes this hubbub late at night?"

Xue Manor's butler frowned imperceptibly, then said to Zheng Duanwen with an obsequious smile, "The servants are insolent. I will be certain to discipline them sternly. Please be magnanimous, Your Honor."

Just then, the young man suddenly looked at Zheng Duanwen and rudely asked, "Did you come from in there? Do you know Xue Sheng? I want to see him, hurry up and tell him.

Don't waste words, you'll hold up great affairs. Don't say I didn't warn you later."

Zheng Duanwen, a mighty minister of the Ministry of Rites, bossed around like a servant, became angry at once. But he had just stepped forward, ready to castigate the young man, when his gaze fell on his clothes and personal adornments. He changed what he was going to say at the last moment, asking, "Who are you? What business do you have with Lord Xue?"

Impatience all over his face, the young man said, "Let me in, and I'll naturally tell you."

The butler could take no more of this and was planning to call over a servant to chase the brat away, but Zheng Duanwen abruptly raised a hand to stop him. He said, "Go in and notify Lord Xue." Then, to the young man, he said, "Come with me."

The butler was all at sea, but he couldn't talk him out of it. He had to go inside and report to Xue Sheng. Before long, Zheng Duanwen led the young man inside and said a few words into Xue Sheng's ear.

Xue Sheng's expression was astonished. Shortly, he turned to the young man and with reasonable politeness asked, "The servants have been rude. Please don't take offense, sir. What business brings you here so late at night?"

"Have your servants withdraw," the young man said coldly. "Leave only you and me." Then he pointed to Zheng Duanwen. "He stays, too."

CHAPTER SEVENTY-SIX

IT HAD BEEN PITCH-BLACK OUTSIDE JUST NOW, SO ZHENG
Duanwen hadn't noticed while leading him inside—now that he
was standing under the lights inside, he realized that one of the
young man's legs was lame.

Xue Sheng dismissed the servants and invited the young man
to sit down and speak.

"Might I inquire what the gentleman's name is?"

"Fu Ya." A mocking expression appeared on the young man's
face. With a crook of the lips, he said, "I suppose Your Honor
hasn't heard of me. But I have an older brother, named Fu Shen,
whom you must know of."

Zheng Duanwen had seen outside that his clothing was all of
rare quality and that while there was only a purse hanging from
his belt, it was also exquisitely made. He didn't look like a ruffian
or a vagabond, and he had been unwilling to say his name. It was
because of this that he had thought there was something fishy
and brought him in. He'd had absolutely no idea that he had
"casually" brought back their archrival's little brother!

But to tell the truth, while they had been in the capital for
some time, they had indeed heard nothing of this brother of Fu
Shen's.

When the Duke of Jing had still been the Marquis of Jingning, he had already moved out of the Duke of Ying Manor to live elsewhere. All these years, he'd had little contact with his original residence, and they had hardly visited each other. After the turmoil of war, though the Duke of Ying Manor was in a daily decline while his power and influence were at their prime, he still hadn't once stepped in to aid the Fu family.

The disagreement between north and south was something that individuals outside of court couldn't experience, but as the son of nobility, Fu Ya ought to have an understanding of the situation at court. For him to come see Xue Sheng at a time like this meant that he and his brother were not merely "not close;" they were "at odds."

"When I was in the south, I heard that Lord Xue's beloved daughter killed herself with a grievance on account of the empress," Fu Ya said. "While Your Honor has not expressed it, I suppose you must harbor resentment to this day."

With his scar suddenly prodded, Xue Sheng's expression chilled slightly. Gravely, he said, "Since you know my hatred for those with the surname Fu, how can you still dare to come to my door?"

"Because I am the same as you. I also hate people with the surname Fu." Fu Ya laughed feverishly, and the tip of his tongue unconsciously licked his canine tooth. "Especially that one."

In his manner was an undisguised, almost artless malice. When he laughed, his eyes narrowed, emitting a light like a viper's eyes, chilling the two old men to the bone. A bit of sweat appeared in Xue Sheng's palms. Forcing himself to be calm, he asked, "So what you're saying is, you want me to help you deal with him?"

"No." Fu Ya shook his head and took something rolled up from his sleeve. He shook it at the two of them. As if flaunting, he said, "*I* am the one who has come to help *you* deal with him."

Xue Sheng didn't rush to ask for the item. He sat upright,

unmoving. "Then what do you want from me, Young Master Fu?"

Fu Ya's eyes turned. He made a gesture at him. "This number, in silver-backed banknotes."

This was a gesture commonly used by traders. Xue Sheng didn't understand it and turned his head to shoot a glance at Zheng Duanwen. Zheng Duanwen quickly said into his ear, "Six thousand taels."

Xue Sheng nodded and said, "Will you allow me to see it first?"

Fu Ya tossed the roll of papers to Xu Sheng, and Zheng Duanwen drew near to look as well. After skimming through it quickly, he gasped. Cold sweat streamed down from him. He couldn't even manage to speak smoothly. "This… this is…"

"Letters written between my own uncle and Xinan's traitor Duan Guihong. The assassination attempt at the Vast Longevity Feast that once caused a sensation in the capital is inextricably linked to him." Fu Ya crossed one leg over the other and asked in self-satisfaction, "How about it—didn't expect that, did you?"

There were two letters in the roll, and some present lists and documents. On them was clearly stated in writing how many "specialty products" Xinan would send to the Duke of Ying Manor every year, and that Fu Tingyi would transfer these gifts of local products to the Qingxu Temple.

Xue Sheng's hand trembled slightly as he held the pages. The veins on the back of his hand broke out one by one. He had never thought that Fu Ya would dare to use this in exchange for money. "Do you know what this is?"

"I know, how could I not? I'm not an idiot." With a manic laugh, Fu Ya said, "Who would have thought it? The capital's renowned useless Third Master turns out not to be useless, and, under so many people's noses, he's been sending you all on a merry chase! Hahaha!"

His laughter ceased abruptly, as if he had suddenly fallen into some kind of chaotic frenzy. Furiously, he said, "These bullshit

dukes and generals, they're all fucking beasts! With their sancti-
monious human skins, their mouths filled with false benevolence
and righteousness—who'd even think of what's actually in their
hearts?! He deserves to be married off to a man, have his bloodline cut off, die and go to hell..."

Fu Ya's speech was full of filth, bringing loathing to the faces
of Xue Sheng and Zheng Duanwen, both highly cultured civil
officials. They didn't know how a perfectly good young master of
good family could have been raised into this. He seemed to be
demented in his fury, a deranged lunatic.

Zheng Duanwen gave a dry cough and said, "Young Master
Fu, do you know what a great catastrophe these things will incur
for the Duke of Ying Manor? Fu Tingyi is your elder. If he and
Fu Shen have truly committed heinous crimes, even if you have
the merit of reporting it, as a rule, you will also be punished.
You... you must think it over."

Xue Sheng glanced at him, seeming not to have expected
him of having this streak of benevolence.

Fu Ya had sunk entirely into his own feelings and couldn't
take in anything being said to him. He laughed so hard he rocked
back and forth, until he was hoarse. It seemed as if blood were
about to burst from his throat. "Hahaha... Let me die, let us all
die! Leave no one behind! Then there's that dog... The boss of
the Feilong Guard, Yan Xiaohan. He must be executed by being
hacked to pieces!

"What a wonderful family of high-ranking officials, each and
every one loyal and upright! At the end, everyone will be
punished without distinction, be swept clean away!"

"Yunping-xiong," Zheng Duanwen said quietly to Xue
Sheng, "from his appearance, he seems to be exhibiting symptoms of taking autumn night white. He's delirious. The credi-
bility of his words must be investigated before we act upon
them."

"I know." Xue Sheng carefully rolled up the pages and, not
batting an eyelash, gave his guest notice to leave. "It is already

late. Fangde, return home. I'll see about having someone make arrangements for little Young Master Fu. What we spoke of tonight must not reach the ears of another."

Zheng Duanwen's heart went cold. He bowed deeply to Xue Sheng. "Then I will leave it to you, Yunping-xiong."

The dim candlelight cast deep shadows beneath Xue Sheng's sunken eyes and nostrils. His face was like a sharply cut statue, all expression concealed beneath indifference. Out of nowhere, he seemed aged and strangely grim.

He nodded lightly to Zheng Duanwen and said, "Go on."

The moment he stepped out of Xue Manor, the gates shut gently behind Zheng Duanwen. He let out a long breath and unexpectedly had the impression that he had narrowly escaped death. There was a chill in the late-night air that raised all the hairs on the back of Zheng Duanwen's neck. His whole body was soaked, his clothing sticking to his back. But he had no thought to spare for his condition now. He hastily got into his carriage and ordered the driver to take him home.

The next day, Zheng Duanwen pleaded illness and asked for leave to remain at home. He never went to court again.

It was said that he was elderly and had picked up a chill on his way home at night. The next day, the servants found him lying in bed, half his body paralyzed, the corners of his mouth crooked. They quickly brought in an imperial physician to treat him, who pronounced that he had had an attack of apoplexy. Because he had not been treated in time, it was impossible for him to recover to his previous condition. He had to stay in bed and convalesce, take medicine and recover over time.

When Xue Sheng heard this, he didn't seem surprised, and he wasn't at all regretful. He ordered his butler to send medicinal ingredients to the Zheng family, rounding off this shallow friendship between colleagues.

Within two days, the Duke of Ying Manor's little young master suddenly disappeared. His family came weeping to report it to the officials in Shuntian Prefecture. Sadly, the present was unlike the past. The chaos of war had sent the Duke of Ying Manor, which had already been slipping, completely into decline. No one was even willing to pay attention to a superficial matter like this report to the authorities. The petty official who received the case impatiently went through the motions, then tossed the dossier aside to collect dust.

The tail-end of high summer still remained, and autumn had yet to arrive, but there were already omens speaking of "the autumn of all things."

Xue Sheng sat upright at his writing desk, listening carefully to a subordinate reporting on what he had investigated concerning Fu Ya's life. After hearing it, he smiled coldly. "Inadequate son of a mighty father. If Fu Tingzhong knew what a fine son he had fathered, would he sit up from his coffin?"

Some years ago, Yan Xiaohan had twice punished Fu Ya, openly and in secret. Once had been cutting off his line of descent, and another had been having him dragged out of the wedding banquet and beaten. That ruthless beating had given Fu Ya pause for a time, but before he could think of how to get his revenge, the chaos of war had broken out, the capital had been breached by foreigners, and Fu Tingyi had taken his whole family to flee to Jiangnan.

The journey had been a jolting one, and survival had been critical. No one had had time to spare to look after him carefully. Sickly Fu Ya had held out until Jinling. Then Jiangnan's winter was extremely damp and cold, and the wound to his leg hadn't entirely healed. It had left behind lameness.

Ironically, his big brother, with both legs crippled, was galloping on the battlefield, while Fu Ya, perfectly healthy, had in the end become lame.

With a lame leg and no offspring, Fu Ya was unable to settle his mind, and on coming to a dizzyingly luxurious place of drunken dreams like Jinling, he had begun to loiter in brothels, living a life of debauchery, spending without restraint. And Fu Tingyi was an unworldly being with one foot nearly in the immortal realms. He was unwilling to spare attention to discipline him, which had let him fritter his time away until now.

He had picked up autumn night white in the brothels of Jiangnan, and after returning to the capital had still needed to keep taking the drug. His allowance had been insufficient, so he had bit by bit begun to steal things from home to pawn them.

In the capital, white dew powder was contraband goods, prohibited by an explicit order from the local authorities. It could only be bought off the black market, and the price was exorbitant. Fu Ya not only sold off his own things, he even stole his mother's dowry and sold it. When he was discovered by Madam Qin, there was a storm of crying and cursing, ruining the household's peace, throwing it into total disarray. The Duke of Ying Fu Tingyi couldn't stand noise in the house and simply packed his bags and went to live in a Daoist temple, putting it and him out of sight and out of mind.

Fu Ya had been upbraided by his mother and didn't dare to extend his hand toward her room. He was truly hard up, so he snuck by night into Fu Tingyi's room and turned it upside down, yet he didn't find anything worth money. He had become bold, and he was in urgent need of money. He suspected that Fu Tingyi, disdaining them, had secretly taken the family property to the temple. So Fu Ya hired a marketplace thief and ordered him to steal some things from Fu Tingyi's lodgings. The outcome was that the thief went in circles around the plain room for ages and finally turned up a locked wooden box in the depths of the wardrobe.

He believed with all his heart that there would be silver-backed banknotes hidden inside and had gladly and diligently brought it to Fu Ya. While the lock was ingenious and hard to open, Fu Ya had been desperate and simply cut a hole in one side of the box. When he finally got it open and looked, he found that inside was a stack of correspondence with Xinan.

However stupid Fu Ya might be, he still knew how serious these things were. He was at once shocked by Fu Tingyi's hidden depths and realized with clarity that this might be a heaven-sent opportunity.

With these things in his hands, he could bring the whole Fu family to ruin in no time. He could also drag Fu Shen down from the sacred altar, so that he would never be able to get back up.

While the overmastering pleasure and desire for destruction surged through his body, Fu Ya could still free up half of his thoughts to consider calmly. He couldn't simply take this evidence and make a report, because next to Fu Shen there was still the cunning Yan Xiaohan. If he delivered himself up, it would be no different from walking into a trap.

His resources and manpower were limited. He needed to find a person who could contend against Yan Xiaohan and Fu Shen, use that person's hand to accomplish this business.

After repeated deliberation and discreet inquiries, he had gone to Xue Sheng's gate with his "proof of allegiance."

In the study, Xue Sheng's subordinate finished his report, then added, "Your Honor, with such important letters, why would Fu Tingyi not have burned them after he had read them but kept them with him? Could it be a trap the whole family has put together?"

Xue Sheng shook his head. "This matter concerns Xinan. However bold Fu Tingyi might be, he still wouldn't dare to test me with a thing like this. The reason he has kept these things is none other than fear of asking a tiger for its skin. He kept evidence in case he got into a tiff with Duan Guihong one day. But it's hard to protect against traitors from within—" Half sighing with emotion and half sneering, he said to himself, "Duke of Jing, this is the will of heaven. Don't blame me for helping you on your way."

The next day, Xue Sheng went to the palace to have an audience with the emperor. He dismissed everyone and presented the private correspondence between the Duke of Ying Fu Tingyi and Xinan to Emperor Changzhi.

"Commandery Prince Xiping, the Duke of Jing, the Duke of

Ying..." Emperor Changzhi said "fine" three times in a row. He seemed unable to control the directions his facial muscles moved in, making him seem exceptionally savage. Holding up those letters, he trembled for ages, then suddenly stood. With a wave of his sleeve he swept the writing brush and inkstone and the teacups from the desk. Clenching his teeth, he shouted angrily, "Traitors and rebels! They have hoodwinked Us grievously!"

When the eunuch outside the door heard this, he opened the hall door a crack in trepidation. He just happened to be glimpsed by Emperor Changzhi, who picked up a white jade brush washing bowl and hurled it at the door. Wrathfully, he said, "Get the hell out!"

After a crash, the room fell into silence. Xue Sheng stood amid the mass, deeply pleased with himself, and perfunctorily counseled, "Your Majesty, calm yourself."

After standing rigid for a moment, Emperor Changzhi fell straight into his chair.

His countenance was purplish, his chest heaving violently. He panted unceasingly and mumbled, "Two dukes in one family... Ha, a high position with handsome pay, yet it's turned out a bunch of heartless and ungrateful curs..."

Seeing him in a violent rage, Xue Sheng finally stepped forward and deferentially said, "Your Majesty, I have a request to make of the throne."

Emperor Changzhi broke off a small portion of his attention from his daze and said, "Go on."

Xue Sheng raised the hems of his robes and knelt in the center of the big hall, kowtowing. "The Duke of Ying Fu Tingyi has colluded with Xinan's traitorous vassal Duan Guihong, attempted to assassinate the Retired Emperor, and endangered the state. The Duke of Jing knew of this and failed to report it, instead shielding him and concealing these matters on his behalf. He also has a deep friendship with Duan Guihong. These three are thorough traitors. If they are not eradicated, they will one day revolt.

"With matters as they now stand, I would make so bold as to request Your Majesty to act on behalf of future generations, be decisive when the time to make a decision comes—wipe out the Fu family and their rebel faction to avoid future trouble!"

After the shock he had given him, Emperor Changzhi recovered with difficulty, and wearily said, "Dear Minister Xue, what decision do you suggest I make?"

"Permit me to reply, Your Majesty. Fu Shen is in Xinan, and he is able to coordinate at a distance with the troops at the northern frontier. If the Imperial Court of the Censorate takes part in the case and the three judicial chief ministers conduct a joint trial, it will be bound to incur discussion, which will gravely thwart the proceedings. If he is forced to an impasse, Fu Shen will join with Duan Guihong and revolt then and there, and there will be absolutely nothing the court can do about him," Xue Sheng said. "It is my belief that the only plan possible now is to strike in secret, first kill the head of the conspiracy, then mop up the remnants. In this way, future trouble can be prevented without being likely to lead to instability at the northern frontier."

Emperor Changzhi's heart instantly lurched. While his anger had gone to his head, he knew that when it came to punishing an important minister like Fu Shen, one had to give him a chance to defend himself. He hadn't expected Xue Sheng to come out with a fatal stroke at once. In spite of himself, he said, "He... After all, Fu Shen has performed great service for the nation. How could We use methods like this against him?"

"Your Majesty is generous, but a traitor and rebel will not appreciate your care," Xue Sheng said softly. "Your Majesty, have you forgotten how Fu Shen compelled you back when the army surrounded the capital?

"Fu Shen has great popularity at court and many adherents to his faction. If not for that, he would not have the boldness to dupe his sovereign." Lying prostrate with his forehead touching the ground, he wailed, "If this traitor is not eliminated, the land

and the state will be in great danger. Please reconsider, Your Majesty!"

Emperor Changzhi was silent.

On the surface, Xue Sheng was all awe-inspiring sorrow, but inwardly he was calmly waiting for Emperor Changzhi to think carefully. He knew that the thorn planted in His Majesty's heart in former days would ultimately sprout before this ironclad evidence, turn into poisonous vines, seize his mind and reason.

Fu Shen must die.

No matter how loyal and upright he normally was, even if he had retaken the territory of the north for Emperor Changzhi, none of that trust was reliable. A person wouldn't necessarily remember all the good that another person did, but he would certainly remember all offense and injury.

If a white jade annulus had the smallest nick, it wouldn't be far from cracking.

Indeed, after a lengthy silence, Emperor Changzhi spoke roughly. His voice was even somewhat hoarse and trembling. "Dear Minister... what strategy do you offer?"

Xue Sheng counted his own breaths, waited until the deafening pulse in his ears had slowly receded, then at last with an altered countenance bowed once more and said, "I am dull-witted. I am willing to aid Your Majesty in these difficulties, serve you faithfully."

Outside of Yangxin Hall, the eunuch keeping watch at the door could only hear the dialogue inside in intermittent snatches through the crack. A few words and phrases were enough to make him quake with terror. The hands hidden in his sleeves were full of sweat.

After a long while, the vermilion doors creaked as they were pushed open from within.

Xue Sheng stepped out of the hall and paused at the steps. He narrowed his eyes with his head raised to the overwhelming sunlight. The eunuch stole a glance at him and inexplicably thought that while there was no expression on Minister Xue's face, there was clearly a smile spilling extremely slowly from the corners of his eyes.

It was the cold smile of having a well-laid plan and being certain of success, a smile that hid knives and poison.

"Yuan Zhen."

Emperor Changzhi called from the hall. The eunuch named Yuan Zhen quickly averted his gaze and trotted in. In a mincing voice, he said, "At your service."

"Have the hall cleaned up," Emperor Changzhi said. "Go make Us a cup of tea. Take this decree to have a seal affixed, and have it sent at once to Xinan."

Yuan Zhen bent his head and received the imperial decree with both hands, then went to carry out his orders.

That night, an army messenger carrying the imperial decree set out from the capital at top speed, racing toward Xinan.

That same night, Wei Xuzhou received Yuan Zhen's notice and immediately sent a trusted aid to travel through the night to Jinling to pass the information to Yan Xiaohan.

The imperial guards left to watch the capital sent the information as quickly as was in their power, but after all they were no match for Xue Sheng, who had been prepared in advance. By the time Yan Xiaohan received the letter from the capital and set off in a hurry for Xinan, he was a step too late.

On the fifth day of the seventh month in the fourth year of Changzhi, the Duke of Jing Fu Shen suffered an assassination attempt during a face-to-face meeting with Xinan's rebel general Duan Guihong. He vomited blood and fainted on the spot. In the chaotic fighting, Fu Shen was carried off by Xinan's rebel army, his condition and his whereabouts unknown.

CHAPTER SEVENTY-SEVEN

ON THE SEVENTH DAY OF THE SEVENTH MONTH, YAN XIAOHAN traveled through the night and, carrying wind and frost, charged brazenly into Xinan's military camp.

He was seen in with a sword at his throat. Duan Guihong was at loose ends dealing with everything he had to attend to. Hearing that this court lackey had burst into his camp, he simply flew into a rage. Stamping with fury, he said, "How can you have the face to come!"

"Jingyuan is here with you, right?" Yan Xiaohan seemed not to feel the sword at his throat. He strode toward Duan Guihong. "Where is he?"

A bodyguard was afraid he would harm Duan Guihong. He quickly brandished his sword and said, "Stop!"

"I asked you, where is he?!"

As Yan Xiaohan bellowed, the sharp blade sliced through his neck, and fresh blood came zigzagging down, instantly staining a large portion of his collar red. Red-eyed, Yan Xiaohan looked at Duan Guihong. In a hurry, he removed his sword and dagger and threw them to the ground. He was burning with impatience, his words almost beseeching. "You can kill me or cut me to pieces, as you like, but let me see him, Your Highness."

Duan Guihong froze, saying to himself that Yan Xiaohan shouldn't be so frantic, should he? Didn't the two of them only get on in public? Had the arranged marriage really turned into genuine feeling?

Frowning, he asked, "Who sent you? The emperor?"

"Xue Sheng advised His Majesty to kill Jingyuan in secret, and I wasn't in the capital, I rushed over here from Jinling after receiving word from my spies in the capital."

His travel-stained appearance and the exhaustion on his face couldn't be faked. From east to west, it was a distance of a thousand li, and Yan Xiaohan had covered it in less than two days. He hadn't once closed his eyes. If not even this could be taken for sincerity, then he had no choice but to die on the spot so Duan Guihong could see it.

"Your Highness, it was the Feilong Guard that took the lead in investigating the assassination attempt at the Vast Longevity Feast, I know that Chunyang was your man, and I know that white dew powder spread from Xinan. Jingyuan never concealed the friendship between the two of you from me." Urgently, Yan Xiaohan said, "Otherwise, I wouldn't have come here directly to see you. You couldn't have hurt him, it must have been a plant of His Majesty's at his side."

"It was that damned emperor who put them up to it?" At first Duan Guihong had only had a faint suspicion. Now, with Yan Xiaohan's verification, his fury instantly soared. He shouted out his inner feelings: "Fine, the father gets through harming him, then the son wants to harm him, too. Did Fu Shen kill the whole Sun family in a past life that he should deserve to be tormented by them like this in this lifetime?!"

A decorated war hero covered in scars, yet that was still worth less than a few words before the emperor from a favored minister. Fu Shen had spent his life fighting for Great Zhou, and in the end he had come to this sorry fate.

Like feels for like—thinking about this, what did his two decades amount to?

His loyal and righteous heart had been taken and trampled on, his profound kindness and friendship had been used to let him down.

When Duan Guihong finished roaring, his anger dispersed, and boundless cold and grief surged up in his heart. He stood there blankly for a moment, like a lion who has finally noticed that he has grown old. When he spoke again, his tone was lower. "Go ahead and leave, there's no need for you to see him again. Just treat him as dead.

"In the future... don't burden him with the nation again."

Yan Xiaohan was still in the midst of a pain like having all his organs rupture. He wasn't really all that lucid. All his mental energy was hanging from that thread of pain. He had done his utmost to be polite to Duan Guihong, to be tactful. But when he spoke these last words, Yan Xiaohan truly couldn't hold back.

"Your Highness, don't you have the slightest idea whose burdens have brought him to this state?

"What right have you to feel aggrieved on his account?" He finally tore through the appearance of goodwill and glared coldly at Duan Guihong. The words he spoke were more aggressive than a sharp sword. "The reason he came to the front lines at Xinan, the reason His Majesty wanted to kill him... isn't it all because of you, Commandery Prince Xiping?

"If not for you scorning the emperor over and over, how could the court and Xinan have reached the point of open fighting? If not for the sake of keeping you safe, what need would there have been for Jingyuan to drag this out for three months, unwilling to open hostilities, such that the emperor began to doubt him?!" There was rare sternness on his face. Aggressively, he asked, "If Your Highness's heart aches so much for Jingyuan, then why haven't you considered any of this? When everything was going fine, why would His Majesty suddenly decide he wanted him dead?!"

His repeated questions struck Duan Guihong into blankness. Before, he had only seen Yan Xiaohan once at a distance and had thought he was only a useless decorative pillow. He'd had no idea that when he deployed his imposing manner to its fullest extent, it would be in no way inferior to what people like him, who had come off the battlefield, could manage. When his seemingly frosted-over eyes swept over him, Duan Guihong even had a slight impulse to retreat.

Yan Xiaohan said, "You colluded in private with the Duke of Ying, used his hand to sell autumn night white at a high price in the capital. You thought the plan was seamless, that no one would ever be the wiser, but now it's all been exposed, and it's Jingyuan who's ended up bearing the blame for the two of you. Before, he preferred to accept the arranged marriage rather than revolt, and now, because of your little dirty dealings with the Duke of Ying, the heart's blood he's spilled over half a lifetime has all gone for nothing. You still have the face to complain of injustice against him? Your Highness, forgive me for being blunt, but if you really want to let him live some years longer, then mind your own hands, don't do what you shouldn't do, and don't hatch any plans you shouldn't hatch!"

Yan Xiaohan was also mad with anger, without any sensibility left. His interrogation had practically run up against Duan Guihong's dignity, but Duan Guihong wasn't at leisure to take note of the offense. He mumbled, "… It's because of me?"

"You have committed the sin, but he is the one being struck by lightning," Yan Xiaohan said. "Your Highness, I'm the one who ought to beg you. I'll kneel and beg you to let Jingyuan off, not burden him again, all right?"

This blow was steady, accurate, and relentless. When it fell, Duan Guihong was rendered entirely speechless.

"Stop arguing!" Du Leng, busy with rescue work in the inner room, could at last listen to this no longer. Loudly, he called, "Lord Yan, come in and lend a hand!"

This time, no one stopped him. Yan Xiaohan strode in.

At a single look, he felt that his soul had been yanked out. In his aching lungs was the belated fear of having narrowly escaped disaster. Floating, like a wandering ghost, he silently came to the side of the sickbed.

Fu Shen was lying in bed with his eyes closed, his face as white as paper, his lips blueish, acupuncture needles stuck into half his body. If not for the slight undulation of his chest, there would hardly have been any difference between him and a corpse.

Du Leng was so busy that his head was streaming with sweat. He was Duan Guihong's man, and he was also an army doctor. When Fu Shen had been attacked, he had snuck over and defected to the enemy to snatch him back from the hands of the Kings of the Underworld. He hadn't shut his eyes for a day and a night. His voice was hoarse, so his words were unusually terse and cold: "If the general struggles, I won't be able to hold him down. Help me."

But Yan Xiaohan had yet to recover his senses. He stood still by the bedside, rigid from his fingertips to the ends of his hair.

Du Leng clicked his tongue. He backhandedly pulled out an acupuncture needle and held it between his fingers. With a cold flash, he took aim at an acupoint on Yan Xiaohan's back and stabbed. Yan Xiaohan shook all over as if having convulsions, then suddenly turned his head again and abruptly coughed up a mouthful of blood.

"Acute anxiety. Your vital energy and blood were running backward," Du Leng said flatly. "Don't just stand there, and don't be in a hurry to cry. I'm going to pull out the needles. You hold him down for me. If he can make it through the night, he'll be all right when he wakes. Sit."

Yan Xiaohan coughed twice. Thanks to Du Leng's needle, his mind had cleared from its maddened chaos. He quickly wiped clean the bloodstains on his hand and sat at the bedside. He reached out to hold down Fu Shen's shoulders.

Fu Shen was also as cold as death. His temperature made Yan Xiaohan's heart give a violent shake. An ominous thought suddenly arose. In his terror, he thought irrelevantly: if Fu Shen really did die, what would he do?

As Du Leng removed the needles, Fu Shen's body gradually warmed. Faint tremors began to appear in his arms and legs. When only the needles in the major acupoints on his torso remained, he furrowed his brow in his unconsciousness. His right hand came up slightly and made a grab in midair.

Yan Xiaohan quickly reached out, and his wrist was immediately grasped by Fu Shen.

"Careful." Du Leng shot him a glance and warned, "Hold him down."

The next moment, with both hands working in unison, he swiftly pulled out the remaining acupuncture needles. Fu Shen's body gave a violent spasm. Then he began to struggle as if he had lost his mind. Yan Xiaohan was nearly elbowed off the bed. Sharp pain exploded in his right wrist. "Jingyuan!"

"Don't let go!" said Du Leng.

In a moment of emergency, Yan Xiaohan threw himself forward and hugged the incessantly struggling man, allowing the gaunt, hard bones and joints to collide against his chest. It caused a series of dull thumps, but he didn't groan from start to finish.

He wouldn't let go, not even in death.

The two of them were locked in a stalemate for a long time. Fu Shen's struggles gradually weakened. At this, Yan Xiaohan panicked a little. He was just about to ask Du Leng what was wrong when he heard a faint sound come from the throat of the person in his arms. Then a mouthful of blood sprayed out.

Half of Yan Xiaohan's heart instantly went cold.

But Du Leng heaved a large sigh of relief. His legs went weak, and he collapsed into a chair. "It's done. Let him spit up all the blood."

Yan Xiaohan said nothing. He didn't dare to feel relieved. As long as he lived, he wouldn't forget tonight's scene: Fu Shen in his arms coughing up mouthful after mouthful of blood, him watching the blood turn gradually from purplish black to dark red. At last, the whole room reeked of blood. The fronts of both their clothes were covered in blood, as if they had sat down in a pool of it.

Then, suddenly, he could no longer feel pain or worry. Instead, he seemed unusually calm. Holding this person who was on his last gasp, there was only one thought in his mind: if Fu Shen died, he would go to the capital and rip off the emperor's rotten head, then stab himself and go down to keep him company. Everyone would become ashes together. No one would be spared.

Duan Guihong had entered the inner room at some point. Fu Shen had stopped coughing up blood and had sunk into a stupor. He stood waiting a while at a slight distance, saw that Yan Xiaohan didn't react, then gave a slightly awkward cough. "Well… Listen, why don't you go change, have Du Leng bandage up your wound, then come watch over him."

Yan Xiaohan tilted his head slightly. He had clearly under-stood. Supporting the back of Fu Shen's head, he carefully and gently laid him back onto the pillow. Then he stood, his back perfectly straight. Cold-faced but without discourtesy, he nodded to Duan Guihong. "Will you please have a tub of hot water brought in, Your Highness? I will bathe once I have wiped the blood off him."

"Oh." Duan Guihong hadn't expected him to be so polite. He froze momentarily. "All right."

The man from before, his words like knives, aggressive but red-eyed with anxiety, seemed to have swapped souls. He was enveloped in a chill that kept people a thousand li away. He had turned indifferent and self-possessed, urbanely polite.

Had Fu Shen been awake, perhaps he would have recognized this as his most familiar aspect, that of the Imperial Investigator of the Feilong Guard.

This was the crafty sycophant who brought destruction onto the empire, stopping at nothing, wicked and merciless.

Yan Xiaohan cleaned Fu Shen and put him into clean clothes

and went to an outer room himself to wash off the dust of the road. When he returned, he sat idle all night at Fu Shen's bedside by the light of a not very bright little lamp. Neither Duan Guihong nor Du Leng tactlessly came forward to disturb him.

In the still, long night, he held Fu Shen's hand, which refused to warm up, and pressed a kiss as light as a dragonfly skimming the water onto his dry lips.

His heart was full of roaring flames, hatred rising to the skies, but that kiss was soft and restrained, as if he couldn't stand to shatter a beautiful dream.

Yan Xiaohan whispered into his ear: "I'm going to kill him."

CHAPTER SEVENTY-EIGHT

THE WORLD WAS COLD, HARD GRAY-WHITE, AND HE SEEMED TO BE locked into an iron-gray cage, unable to distinguish night from day, unable to feel the passage of time. Only his consciousness was still feebly active, interminably asking him: Who am I? Where am I?

The gray world gradually lit up, and he raised his hand to feel rough stone grooves. This sensation touched certain memories, and he remembered—this was the wall of Yanzhou City.

When he was eight, his Second Uncle had taken him to the grasslands, to the Beiyan Army's sternly guarded garrison, and up onto the city gate arch of Yanzhou City.

He had been a little sprout then, not even as tall at the wall's battlements. He had tensed his little arms to cling to the cracks in the wall, and then Fu Tingxin had picked him up and put him on his shoulders.

In that moment, the world became vast, the mountains and rivers remote.

Outside the city were boundless mountains and grasslands; inside the city sat orderly and clean houses and streets. Outside the city were sentry posts and warhorses idly eating grass; inside the city were crowds of people coming and going, tall steamers selling steamed buns, which let out a big cloud of steam when the lid was raised.

Fu Tingxin had still looked very young, the skin of his face blown somewhat coarse by the winds of the border, his beard scraggly, but that didn't cover up his height and his handsomeness. When he smiled, there was an unexpected little dimple in his left cheek.

"Let's go back, hm?" Holding him on his shoulders, Fu Tingyi turned and descended the city wall. "The sky is getting dark. It's going to rain soon."

He reached out his hand in confusion. Indeed, from the vast slate-gray dome of heaven, a few little rain drops pattered down.

The scene suddenly shifted.

This time, he was standing at the top of Yanzhou's city wall, already grown tall, become an adult, like a cold steel sword facing into the wind. Outside was a dense and dark Zhe army.

He no longer needed to sit on anyone's shoulders to overlook this patch of earth.

"General." A black-armored, kindly-faced lieutenant general walked over to him. "The Beiyan Cavalry is all assembled. We can join battle at once."

"Fine." He reached out his hand and caught a raindrop that suddenly fell. Apropos of nothing, he softly said, "It's raining."

The scene changed again.

He was kneeling amidst heavy rain, cold to the marrow as it poured over him. His deep red hem was like a maple leaf floating on the water, unwilling to drift away. At the end of the tiled floor were the tightly shut vermilion palace gates.

Icy rain hit his face nonstop. His mind was a blank. He only dimly thought that something was missing. In confusion, he asked himself: Who am I waiting for?

Countless scenes flashed before his eyes like a revolving lantern. He saw many faces, some familiar and some that had blurred in his memory. Yet that certain person who ought to have appeared at the depths of his memory wasn't there.

But he clearly had no memories of that person.

The scene suddenly fixed on a certain image. It was still raining heavily, but the rain was kept out by the building. There was only the endless sound of the rain. He was leaning on a club with one leg crossed over the other, his gaze wandering and unfocused, falling absently onto the profile of the man who had sat down by the fire.

That person seemed very indifferent toward him, hardly attending. When he stared at him, he wouldn't turn his head his way.

He thought: Have I offended him?

Thinking it over carefully, he seemed to have said something just now, seemingly something not very pleasant, and that person had at once turned hostile.

The memories accompanied by the dimly heard sound of the rain surged together into his mind. Icy drops of water struck his face. He finally realized that this wasn't rain.

"If I left him to drift through the world all alone, I wouldn't be able to close my eyes even in death."

Why won't he speak?

Is it because... he doesn't trust me?

As soon as he recalled these words, it was like a beam of light passing through the sky, illuminating the chaotic universe. All the vague, disorderly memories gradually took on their original colors once again. Through his tightly shut eyelids, he sensed for the first time the daylight of the outside world.

Fu Shen's fingers, curled up in Yan Xiaohan's hand, twitched slightly. Just this tiny, almost imperceptibly slight movement succeeded in nailing a living man in place.

"Du... *ahem*." When Yan Xiaohan spoke, his voice was hoarse, and the tail ends of his words shook. "Army Doctor Du, I think he moved just now..."

"Really?" Du Leng suspected that he was being oversensitive and walked over. "Let me see."

Yan Xiaohan stood up from the bedside, planning to make

room for him. He was just about to let go and he suddenly felt a tightness at his fingertips as he was held fast.

"Don't go…"

Those tightly closed eyes were now open.

The rims of Yan Xiaohan's eyes instantly reddened. From fingertips to arm, he stiffened into a club. He shoved out a few sounds practically from the depths of his throat. Not daring to believe and softer than soft, he asked, "Jingyuan?"

Like a cruel and heartless queen mother breaking up love-birds, Du Leng pushed apart their clasped hands and charged forward to take Fu Shen's pulse. He said, "Make way… General, how do you feel now? Does anything hurt?"

Fu Shen wanted to shake his head, but he had been in bed so long that he was powerfully dizzy. He had to lie unmoving. In a weak voice, he said, "It doesn't hurt, just dizzy. I just had a dream, I dreamed of kumquats falling from the sky. They knocked me awake. Just feel if you don't believe me. My face… is it wet?"

Yan Xiaohan was pointedly silent.

Du Leng, his expression holding volumes, turned his head and looked at Yan Xiaohan with his still-reddened eyes.

What kind of tears could knock a person awake from a deep stupor? He must have been weeping the fucking elixir of life.

Fu Shen's eyes never left Yan Xiaohan. Du Leng, enduring the atmosphere of the room, which was very unfriendly toward him, devotedly and conscientiously examined Fu Shen and finally said, "The poison has been cured. Though your internal organs were injured, there was no great harm. I'll prescribe you two medicines, and after a period of recovery you'll be leaping and frisking around."

"Thank you," Fu Shen said feebly. "You've taken a lot of trouble."

Du Leng waved a hand. He didn't want to exchange civilities with him. He gave Yan Xiaohan some instructions concerning prohibited food and drink, then very tactfully took his leave.

When his steps had faded outside the door, Fu Shen reached out toward Yan Xiaohan, standing rigid at the foot of the bed, and said, "… Come here."

"What for?" Yan Xiaohan immediately fell out of that completely non-responsive state and abruptly realized that he had forgotten himself. He walked over quickly and leaned down to ask, "What's wrong?"

Fu Shen grabbed his hand, brought it to his lips, and lightly rubbed them against it.

"Nothing," he said softly, "I just wanted to kiss you. Stop crying."

With utmost restraint, Yan Xiaohan drew in a lengthy gasp. It was as if someone had tapped one of his acupoints. His whole body went rigid, and he even forgot how to blink. A big drop of water fell right onto the back of Fu Shen's hand.

"Gave you a scare, huh?" Fu Shen pulled up the corners of his mouth and laughed very softly. "It's fine. I'm awake, aren't I?"

Yan Xiaohan slowly leaned down. Not daring to use force but still as tightly as possible, he hugged him and buried his face in the hollow of his neck, an ear pressed to the pulse beating there.

There were countless things he wanted to tell him, but he couldn't manage a single word. He could only call out to him in a trembling voice: "Jingyuan."

"Yes, don't be scared," Fu Shen said. "I told you before. If I left you alone in the world, I wouldn't close my eyes even in death."

This isn't a joking matter to make a casual promise about.

Therefore, you have to trust me.

"Enough talk about dying and living. You're just running at the mouth." When Yan Xiaohan raised his head again, there were no more visible signs of crying. He carefully kissed the corner of Fu Shen's mouth and, gentle as water, said, "Sit up, drink some water, all right?"

Fu Shen nodded. His eyes curved as he regarded him. There was inexpressible tenderness and affection in his gaze.

Yan Xiaohan built him a thick nest from the pillow and quilt, then stood to pour water.

Those few sentences just now having used up all his strength, Fu Shen half closed his eyes in exhaustion and leaned against the head of the bed, but his mind was very clear. He remembered how a few days earlier, the army dispatch sent back from the capital had given official written acquiescence to him engaging in peace talks with Xinan's rebel army, so Fu Shen had had a crude tent set up between the two armies and arranged a face-to-face meeting with Duan Guihong. The day things went wrong, for the sake of appearances, he and Duan Guihong had both left their guards outside, and each one of them had only brought a lieutenant general into the tent. The outcome was that before they had said a couple of sentences, when he went to pick up his teacup, the world had suddenly spun before his eyes, sweetness had surged up in his throat, his vision had gone dark, and he had fallen.

With his awareness on the point of dissipating, Fu Shen had heard his own lieutenant general shout, "An ambush! It's a trap!"

His own last thought at the time had also been that it was a trap. Duan Guihong couldn't have poisoned him. That lieutenant general was lying through his teeth. It had to be him.

"Here, rinse your mouth first."

Yan Xiaohan put an arm around him from behind and brought a small teacup to his lips. A few years down the line, his skills in caretaking didn't seem unpracticed. As instructed, Fu Shen rinsed his mouth, then drank a few mouthfuls out of his hand. Only then did he feel that he had thoroughly come back to life.

"How did you get that?" Fu Shen asked, eyes fixed on the bandage on his neck. He had spat up blood several times, and his body was weak. He didn't dare to exert himself when he spoke. All his words were very soft. "Your neck."

Yan Xiaohan split off his attention to look down and indifferently said, "Had a little disagreement with His Highness and got a little scrape, nothing major. More water?"

Fu Shen shook his head to indicate that he didn't want more and leaned limply against his shoulder. "In my condition now, I can't help you get back at him. You'll have to arrange a duel with him yourself another day... He'd even beat up his nephew's wife. Disgraceful."

Duan Guihong, having heard that Fu Shen was awake, was just getting ready to walk in to pay him a visit. He was rendered speechless.

What the hell was this?! An ingrate who forgot his mother as soon as he had a wife!

Yan Xiaohan finally couldn't resist laughing quietly. Hugging him, he said in a faintly grousing tone, "You're sick, why do you still have idle chat in you? His Highness went to all that trouble to rescue you, and you just want to beat him up."

Outside the room, Duan Guihong, who had taken a step forward, took it back, dithered briefly, then left with complicated emotions.

Inside the room, Fu Shen secretly breathed a sigh of relief and said to himself, "Oh, god, he's finally laughing."

He knew that he had given Yan Xiaohan a scare. That he could dream meant that his subconscious had already recovered its sense of the outside world, he just hadn't woken up yet himself. So the rain he had constantly felt dripping on his hand in his dreams probably hadn't been an illusion.

A weeping beauty was of course also a lovely sight, but in his current condition, he couldn't hug him or cheer him up, so it would be better to get past it.

"That lieutenant general of mine..."

As soon as Fu Shen spoke, he was uncompromisingly shut up by Yan Xiaohan. "You don't need to worry about any of that, leave it to me. You just need to get better, and I won't be worried about anything."

Fu Shen didn't fight him over it. He buried his face against his chest. "My wife has the final word."

Fu Shen's energy was failing. Soon he was drowsy. Yan Xiaohan personally fed him his medicine, then appropriately tucked him into his bedding. When he was about to leave, Fu Shen suddenly opened his eyes and pulled on his sleeve. "Where are you going?"

"Going to say a few words to His Highness. I'll be back very soon," Yan Xiaohan said gently. "Sleep."

"You're not allowed to go." Fu Shen dragged him toward the bed. "Come lie down with me for a while. How long since you slept?"

Yan Xiaohan froze. All his exhaustion seemed to have been called up by these words. It finally surged up and launched a counterattack against him.

He didn't refuse Fu Shen's consideration. He removed his outer robe and got into bed. Fu Shen shifted inward, making room for him. The two of them lay shoulder to shoulder in the not especially wide little bed. While it was crowded, the touch of limb to limb was more effective than any consolation. Yan Xiaohan, with his arms around Fu Shen's waist, quickly fell into a heavy sleep, as if he had been clubbed over the head.

Two hours later, Du Leng came into the tent to check on Fu Shen's injuries, but he saw the two of them nestled together on the narrow bed, like a pair of mandarin ducks. He found it funny in spite of himself.

He had understood that for General Fu, Yan Xiaohan was more useful than any medicine.

Du Leng didn't want to disturb the two of them, so he dropped the curtain and was about to retreat, but it was just then that Fu Shen awoke. Their gazes met. Fu Shen looked down at the sound asleep Yan Xiaohan and made a silent gesture at him, then beckoned him over.

Du Leng was confused. Fu Shen propped up half his body,

freed one hand, gently rolled up Yan Xiaohan's sleeve, and indicated the bruise on his wrist. He mouthed, "Salve."

He hadn't expected him to notice even this. Du Leng was a little incredulous, but he quickly took his meaning and took a bottle of salve for treating bruises from his medicine chest. Fu Shen took the bottle and silently said to him, "Thank you."

Their gazes met lightly in midair. Fu Shen was thanking him for this bottle of salve, and also thanking him for saving his life.

Du Leng had heard from Duan Guihong that Fu Shen had learned of his identity long ago but hadn't exposed him. Now, his face heated involuntarily. He quickly waved a hand and tiptoed out.

By the time Yan Xiaohan woke up, it was early morning of the next day. He had slept too deeply and couldn't open his eyes at once. Blearily, he felt someone fiddling with his wrist. The salve was slightly chilly, the hand was warm. It gave him an instant sense of being cherished.

"Awake?" Injured as he was, Fu Shen was a little more alert than him. He had at some point switched to the outer side of the bed and was holding his wrist, applying salve. "You've slept for a whole day. Does the wrist still hurt?"

If he hadn't mentioned it, Yan Xiaohan wouldn't even have remembered that his wrist was injured. He rolled over and, impervious to reason, bundled Fu Shen entirely into his arms. "No. As long as you're all right, I'm impervious to all injury and poison."

Fu Shen's heart ached, but he also wanted to laugh. "Well, aren't you a marvel! When you get up, remember to change the dressing on your neck. Xinan is damp and warm, you can't be careless. Take care that it doesn't get infected."

He didn't need to do anything. Just sitting there, he could give you a sense of infinite consolation. The bone-chilling murderous urge in Yan Xiaohan's heart was smoothed by him, sinking beneath the water. He nodded meekly and said, "All right." The two of them lay in bed for a while longer. Only when Fu Shen's medicine had been prepared and was brought in did they get up, wash up, and have breakfast.

Fu Shen still needed to recover, and Yan Xiaohan didn't want to make him go to any trouble. He bent down, asked for a kiss, then went out to see Duan Guihong and Du Leng.

Today was the eighth day of the seventh month. Four days had passed since Fu Shen had been poisoned. The court's army was in chaos. News of Fu Shen's death had raised clouds up to the sky. The two armies stood opposed at a distance, a battle on the brink of breaking out between them.

Events had been too sudden that day. When Fu Shen had spat up blood and fallen, Duan Guihong had been startled. Before he could work out what was happening, he saw the lieutenant general who had entered the tent along with Fu Shen draw his sword and shout, "An ambush! It's a trap!"

This cry had shaken heaven and earth. The guards outside the tent had burst in at once in answer. Xinan's people were in the dark, but they couldn't stand there and watch Duan Guihong get surrounded, so they had also charged into the tent. The two sides had immediately become embroiled in a chaotic fight. Duan Guihong had only frozen for a moment, then immediately understood that he had been framed. But the circumstances at the time were in fact unaccountable. Duan Guihong didn't have time to grab that lieutenant general. He ordered his people to pick up Fu Shen and withdraw. On returning to his main camp, he summoned an army doctor to examine him, who confirmed that he showed symptoms of poisoning but couldn't discover what the poison had been.

Credit was due to Du Leng for being willing to run the risk of fleeing through the night. He was more reliable than the army doctor in Duan Guihong's camp. He determined that Fu Shen had been poisoned with a kind of scorpion venom. This kind of scorpion frequently appeared in the deep mountains of Guangnan. The venom was transparent and colorless, its smell sweet and mellow, like wine, so the locals called it the "drunken scorpion." When a living scorpion was soaked in wine and its venom forced out, that made a kind of poison called "daylight drunkenness."

The most distinctive characteristic of this poison was that symptoms wouldn't appear immediately after it was taken. It would only take effect at midday the next day. Since the poison tasted no different from watered-down wine and its effects were delayed, the poisoning victim wouldn't notice it, and treatment would have nowhere to start. The victim would die as soon as the poison took effect.

Xinan had been damp and rainy during this period, and Fu Shen's legs sometimes ached. Du Leng had advised that he drink a bit of wine every evening to chase away the damp. It was at this point that the weak spot had emerged, giving Xue Sheng's man an opening to exploit.

A lucky break amid this misfortune was that Fu Shen had been brought back to Xinan's camp by Duan Guihong, rather than being snatched back by the court's army. Autumn night white was especially effective in overcoming snake and scorpion venom. Duan Guihong might not have anything else, but he certainly had autumn night white. That medicinal plant had once saved Fu Tingxin's life on the grasslands of the northern frontier, and now it had also saved Fu Shen's.

"By carrying Jingyuan off, Your Highness, you perfectly substantiated the rumors about the 'ambush and assassination,'" Yan Xiaohan said pensively, knocking on the table. "But that isn't the worst outcome for us."

Duan Guihong's impression of this "nephew's wife" was very confused. The night before, Yan Xiaohan had ruthlessly scolded him, so he had thought he was a really fucking difficult character, but when he had heard a few words outside the door last night, he had thought that compared to that scoundrel Fu Shen, Yan Xiaohan at least had some conscience.

"What are you planning to do?"

Yan Xiaohan said, "His Majesty respects and fears Jingyuan.

While Xue Sheng holds evidence of the Duke of Ying's illicit dealings with Xinan, he doesn't dare to produce it. Instead, he has used this means of secret assassination, and tried to put the blame on Your Highness. That shows that he's afraid that once this business gets out, there will be trouble at the northern frontier. They wouldn't be able to stay on top of the situation.

"To judge from the current circumstances, if Jingyuan really did die while in your hands, the Beiyan Cavalry and its former subordinates would put it down on Xinan's account. And without Jingyuan, the northern frontier's monolithic faction will naturally come apart, and the court will no longer be coerced by a 'strong army.' It would be killing two birds with one stone. They would have their goal," Yan Xiaohan said. "Given His Majesty's temperament, he would treat death as the end of everything. Most likely he wouldn't continue to pursue the Fu family's wrongs, and Jingyuan's heroic name would remain."

Duan Guihong asked, "And if he doesn't die?"

"Then his relationship with Xinan would be hard to explain," Yan Xiaohan said. "In that case, when they brought out the Duke of Ying's letters again, a mostly made up story would turn into the absolute truth. What would happen to him is hard to say, but his reputation would certainly be destroyed."

Duan Guihong picked up on his implication and said peevishly, "So what do you mean? Do you want him to die and have it over with, change his name and go live in the wilderness, while you would be free to look for all the pretty wives and beautiful concubines you could want, enjoy your wealth and rank in peace, right?"

Yan Xiaohan didn't take offense. He shook his head and said, "Your Highness overestimates me.

"Never mind living apart from the world, even if he went to the blue heavens or the yellow springs of the underworld, I would follow him," he said. "It isn't Jingyuan who can't live without me. It's I who can't live without him."

CHAPTER SEVENTY-NINE

ON THE EIGHTH DAY OF THE SEVENTH MONTH OF THE FOURTH year of Changzhi, according to information sent back from the Xinan front lines, the commander-in-chief of the western expeditionary army, the Duke of Jing Fu Shen, was attacked by the rebel army and unfortunately passed away.

On the tenth of the seventh month, the Tianfu Army's representative Yan Xiaohan detoured from Jinling to Xinan and unsuccessfully demanded Fu Shen's remains from the rebel army. Before the troops, Duan Guihong angrily rebuked Yan Xiaohan, calling him the court's sycophant, who had formed a clique for personal benefit, injured a meritorious minister, deceived the ears of the emperor, and caused Fu Shen to die harboring resentment. The Xinan army took an oath to rid the emperor of his "evil" minister and punish the sycophant for the sake of Fu Shen's deceased soul.

Fu Shen was convalescing in the Xinan camp. After hearing Du Leng retell Prince Duan's speech before the troops, he nearly choked himself laughing. "He didn't come up with that himself, did he?"

If Duan Guihong had had such skills in calling black white

and lying through his teeth, he couldn't have ended up coming to such an impasse with the emperor.

"Who else could it be?" Duan Guihong said cuttingly as he walked in, out of breath. "Of course it was that 'nephew's wife' of mine of the dazzling wits who told me what to say."

Fu Shen didn't see this as a disgrace but rather as glory. "You're overpraising him. It's just a bit of cleverness, nothing to be proud of."

Duan Guihong didn't respond.

Being violently rebuked in front of the troops seemed to have embarrassed Yan Xiaohan greatly. When he returned among the army, he strictly ordered all the soldiers not to let this matter leak out. But Fu Shen's death was already a subject of great suspicion. The stricter the order, the more it would make people think that what Duan Guihong had said was the truth, and the rumors only spread wider and wider. There were even people who said that Emperor Changzhi, fearing that Fu Shen held too much military power, had sent his trusted aid to assassinate Fu Shen, then stuck Duan Guihong with the blame after the fact.

Notice of his death and the gossip and rumors reached the capital together, shaking the whole court. The troops at the northern frontier nearly mutinied on the spot. The four high generals sent several memorials to the throne in a row, asking the court to perform a thorough investigation. Emperor Changzhi couldn't stop the slanderous gossip from spreading throughout the court. Bowing to public pressure, he was forced to reconvene the Yanning Hall Assembly to discuss conferring posthumous honors upon Fu Shen and filling the vacancy he had left behind.

On the thirteenth of the seventh month, when the Yanning Hall Assembly met, Yan Xiaohan returned to the capital with Fu Shen's armor and seal of command and went straight to the palace. All the assembly members were silent. He didn't say a single extraneous sentence, only tossed the armor heavily onto the table. There was a crash, which shook the teacup in front of Xue Sheng to pieces.

The armor was dotted with bloodstains that had yet to be washed off.

The assembly members of the northern frontier's four provinces cried themselves hoarse on the spot. The others either cast down their eyes and became lost in thought or remained silent. Xue Sheng's face was as grim as deep water. Emperor Changzhi was apprehensive. Involuntarily, some conciliation appeared in his tone. "Thank you for your hard work, dear Minister Yan. Sit down... Come, bring tea."

The favored Eunuch Yuan Zhen, who had pride of place at the emperor's side, hurriedly came forward and poured tea for Yan Xiaohan. "Here, Your Honor," he said deferentially.

Yan Xiaohan, his face like winter frost, swept him with a look. Yuan Zhen hunched his shoulders, not daring to breathe loudly, and hurriedly slipped back to the emperor's side with his tail between this legs.

"The Duke of Jing has served the nation in battle for many years and has performed many meritorious deeds in support of the ruler in governing. Based on his merit, he is qualified to leave his portrait in Qilin Hall." Chen Zhi, the new minister of the Ministry of Rites who had replaced the former minister Zheng Duanwen in the assembly, brought up the subject in trepidation. "Only Golden Terrace is still undergoing repairs, so this matter will take some time. According to His Majesty's decree, the Ministry of Rites has drawn up some posthumous titles. A ceremony to confer the titles and the funeral are currently being arranged.

"Also, the Duke of Jing's honors ought to have passed to his descendants, but the two lords... are without issue, though I recall that the Duke of Jing also has a brother..."

"That is unsuitable," someone said. "The Duke of Jing's brother is the heir of the Duke of Ying Manor. Even if he is to inherit a title, it will be the title of the Duke of Ying. He has no male offspring, and his older brother has no son for him to adopt.

That being the case, the Duke of Jing's title ought to be retaken by the court."

Yan Xiaohan suddenly spoke up. "I heard that little Young Master Fu went missing the other day. Has he been found, Lord Xue?"

Perhaps Xue Sheng hadn't been sleeping well lately. He had heavy bags under his eyes, and his eyelids drooped, making his gaze seem inexplicably treacherous. "How would I know about the Fu family's business? You are asking the wrong person, Lord Yan."

Yan Xiaohan said coldly, "Lord Xue would know better than me whether I am asking the wrong person."

These words were ambiguous, but the hint was very clear. Everyone's ears pricked up. They felt that they were about to hear some terrific and shocking inside story.

Xue Sheng said in displeasure, "The situation is chaotic, and affairs are many and complicated, yet Lord Yan insists on pestering me here. I wonder what your intentions are?"

Yan Xiaohan said, "Do you know that the situation cannot be controlled now? When this happened, I was not in the capital, so I would like to ask for your guidance. Just who was it who pushed the court into the heart of the wind and waves?"

"Since you have just returned from the front lines, you ought to be aware that the Duke of Jing was killed by the rebel general Duan Guihong," Xue Sheng said, gritting his teeth. "As for that traitor calling black white and raving accusations, is Lord Yan actually planning on using that to find fault with me? Look carefully, this is Yanning Hall, not your Feilong Guard!"

"Enough! Everybody be quiet!" Emperor Changzhi shouted sternly. "Fighting like this in public! What a disgrace!"

Yan Xiaohan and Xue Sheng ceased hostilities. Each rose to apologize. Emperor Changzhi had an immense headache. Helplessly, he said, "The deceased is gone. The Duke of Jing's merit persists. His family ought to receive generous consolation and compensation. On the matter of Xinan, we must once again deliberate…"

Before he could finish, there was a sudden bout of pain in his chest. He couldn't hold himself up and fell headfirst toward his table. Yuan Zhen quickly raced forward to support him and burst out, "His Majesty! Imperial physicians! Hurry, summon the imperial physicians!"

Yanning Hall instantly descended into chaos.

Emperor Changzhi's face was ghastly pale, except for two circles of unnatural bright red on his cheeks. He leaned against Yuan Zhen, unceasingly gasping for breath, one hand pressed tightly against his chest. A bit of pale red froth leaked out beside his lips. After the imperial physicians arrived, they immediately applied acupuncture needles to Emperor Changzhi as emergency aid, then ordered medicines brought and decocted. There was trampling and turmoil all the way until afternoon, when Emperor Changzhi's symptoms lessened sightly. Only then was he removed to Yangxin Hall.

His Majesty's illness was a matter of great importance. After all the assembly members dispersed, some got together in groups and sent messages. From the looks of it, His Majesty had heart disease, which might suddenly become a heart attack at any given moment. The crown prince was young, and the emperor had no other male offspring, but he had several brothers who were still young and vigorous. When it came time for the throne to change hands, there would unavoidably be another crisis.

These assembly members belonged to the central administration, but in reality they each had their own way of managing affairs. Selfish little calculations were clacking away in their minds. For a time, the atmosphere at court became immeasurably peculiar.

In the evening, Emperor Changzhi woke once. The empress and all the concubines and consorts were waiting at his sickbed. He moved his fingers and let out a faint sound. The imperial physicians swarmed up around him. Emperor Changzhi, in a daze, let them fiddle around. He feebly beckoned over Yuan Zhen, who was standing ready to serve by the bed.

Yuan Zhen immediately drew near. "Your Majesty?"

"What... time is it?"

"Your Majesty," said Yuan Zhen, "it is seven in the evening."

"Cancel tomorrow's court session..." Emperor Changzhi's breaths were weak. Each word and sentence was spoken slowly. "We have encountered a difficulty... A full assembly of Yanning Hall must be convened. Where is Yan Xiaohan?"

"Your Majesty," Yuan Zhen said cautiously, "Lord Yan has... has returned home to observe mourning..."

Emperor Changzhi found it hard to breathe for a time. An imperial physician quickly said, "You must not become agitated, Your Majesty."

"Tell him to come back." Emperor Changzhi closed his eyes wearily. "It's a time of emergency, there is no need to stand on ceremony. Have him preside over the Yanning Hall Assembly."

At this point, he recalled something and glanced down at Empress Fu, who was silent, her head hanging down. She was dressed in mourning garb, without any jewelry or hair ornaments. He sighed softly and instructed, "There is no need to attend at the sickbed. Yuan Zhen will remain to provide service. Everyone else withdraw."

There was sorrow on Fu Ling's brow. She was spare and delicate. She daintily prostrated herself before the imperial bed, like a white flower dimly seen through rain and mist, and quietly said, "I will take my leave."

That night, Yan Xiaohan received a message from a court eunuch ordering him not to shut himself up to observe mourning but to return to court to preside over the Yanning Hall Assembly. In spite of himself, he sneered. "That's what they call no sooner gone than forgotten. The funeral hasn't even been held, and already he thinks nothing of him?"

Yuan Zhen's expression didn't alter. He minded his own business, pretending that he hadn't heard a thing.

"Return, I understand," Yan Xiaohan said. "It's only a few months. I can wait."

From then on, there was no improvement in Emperor Changzhi's condition, and the planned trip to Jiangnan in the ninth month could not be carried out. When winter began, his condition became graver and graver by the day. At first, Emperor Changzhi could still occasionally put in an appearance at court. After the tenth month, he was entirely confined to his bed. The imperial physicians in the palace held their tongues. They told only glad tidings, not ill ones. Despite this, some well-connected people still learned from various indirect sources that the emperor was unlikely to survive and began to prepare in secret.

On the fifth day of the eleventh month of the fourth year of Changzhi, the first snow since the start of winter fell on the capital.

Late at night, the imperial city was all somber whiteness. A man of average height, wrapped in a cloak and wearing a hood, holding a storm lantern, knocked on the side door of Yan Manor and said quietly to the butler, who had come to open the door, "Message from Eunuch Yuan. Hurry and ask your master to go to the palace at once."

No long after, a small carriage stopped outside the Zhangxuan Gate. A man in white mourning garb got out of the carriage. Yuan Zhen had been waiting inside and quickly called a young eunuch over to hold an umbrella for him. He couldn't resist chattering on. "Your Honor, you're finally here. Quick, if you come any later, we won't be able to stop…"

"What are you panicking about?" A snowflake fluttered and fell on his eyelashes and turned into a small water droplet. Yan Xiaohan walked evenly toward the palace and casually said, "Does it matter who kills him? It's bound to happen sooner or later."

Inside Yangxin Hall, the candlelight flickered.

Emperor Changzhi had been tormented for several months and was now so thin he was only a handful of bones. Lying in bed, his body hardly raised the covers lying over him. His face was as white as paper, but his lips were blackened. His breathing was almost inaudible. His eyes were deeply sunken in. Not a trace remained of his former genteel and refined, handsome appearance.

Fu Ling was wiping his face with a damp towel, perfectly meticulous. There was no one in the large hall, only the flickering candlelight, which cast her gaunt shadow against the bed curtains, twisted and slanted. Looked at dimly, it was like a creeper that had climbed out of the gloom.

Her eyes lingered on Emperor Changzhi's forehead and nose, counting his shallow breaths, her fingers constantly tightening on the towel, as if keeping suppressed some dangerous thought trying to get out.

He seemed ready to die at any moment, his throat so fragile that it would snap as soon as it was clutched.

Fu Ling's wrist trembled. She seemed almost unable to keep hold of that towel. But obscurely, there was some invisible cord guiding her hand, making her fearfully but persistently bring that damp towel to Emperor Changzhi's nose and mouth.

This man had once been her support and her resting place in this life, but it was also he who had personally forfeited many years of affection between husband and wife, even sent her only older brother to his death.

For the imperial family, there were no fathers and sons, no brothers, and naturally, there were also... no husbands and wives.

Creak. The door opened wide, and a northerly wind blew into the warm hall. Fu Ling's expression froze. She yanked her hand back as if scalded and quickly dropped the towel into a pail of water. She stood and sternly said, "Who is outside?"

CHAPTER EIGHTY

"Do not be afraid, Your Ladyship."

Yan Xiaohan walked through the door and bowed to her. He had Yuan Zhen close the door, then sat before the imperial bed and bent his head to inspect Emperor Changzhi's condition.

Fu Ling hardly recognized Yan Xiaohan. Her impressions of this person were very complicated. She knew that he had once helped her, but she also hated him bitterly for sullying her brother. On top of that, she currently had a guilty conscience. Therefore, when she spoke, her tone was slightly harsh and alarmed. "What did you come here for?"

"I came to help you," Yan Xiaohan said calmly. "You are the crown prince's mother. It would be better if you weren't tainted by regicide."

Fu Ling said in astonishment, "You…"

"Has Your Ladyship forgotten? You have my people at your side." Yan Xiaohan raised the lid of the beast-shaped incense burner and sprinkled in a handful of new incense. Then he evenly explained: "Even if you do nothing, His Majesty's end is still near at hand. When it comes to a matter that will have one's name to go down in history as a byword for infamy, just allow me to do it. Do not dirty your hands."

In his tone and manner as he spoke was a dependability that made one involuntarily believe him. Fu Ling stared blankly at the mourning garb he wore, incredulity and revelation simultaneously surging up in her heart. She whispered, "His Majesty's illness… was engineered by you? Was it for… him?"

The chilly smell of the incense spread as the beast's mouth spat smoke, diluting the decaying smell of medicines and the warm incense fragrance in the room. It seemed as if they had instantly been transported into a world of ice and snow.

On the bed, Emperor Changzhi's limbs began to convulse. His breathing became rapid. Phlegmy gasps came from his throat.

"It was for him, though it wasn't entirely because of this incident," Yan Xiaohan said with a smile. "Has Your Ladyship noticed that, since returning to the capital, His Majesty has had no more offspring?"

Since the affair of Pure Consort Xue, Yan Xiaohan had been aware that Emperor Changzhi was an unreliable, fickle man. In his hands, the positions of the empress and the crown prince were in imminent danger. So after Emperor Changzhi had returned to the capital, he had begun secretly ordering Yuan Zhen to put a drug in the emperor's tea.

Drinking tea was a prevailing custom among the people of the times, and Emperor Changzhi in particular liked tea. It was precisely because of his skills at making tea that Yuan Zhen had ended up in the emperor's good graces. What Yan Xiaohan had given him was an herbal medicine extremely similar in form to tea, with a scent that was also similar. It was toxic and damaged the ability to have offspring. Emperor Changzhi had been drinking this "no children tea" for years, and indeed he had not planted a single dragon's seed.

This drug had the effect of strengthening the heart. In combination with the tulip incense Yan Xiaohan had just lit, it could easily make a person exhibit symptoms similar to heart disease. The imperial physicians couldn't tell that he had been poisoned and continued to give Emperor Changzhi medicines that strengthened the heart. It was just like piling frost on top of snow, pouring oil on fire. Over time, his illness had become increasingly severe with treatment, and at this point, he was beyond saving. He was only suffering through his remaining days.

Yan Xiaohan had planned to move slowly, wait until the crown prince was a little older to let Emperor Changzhi suffer heart disease and die. But he had underestimated Xue Sheng and Emperor Changzhi's ambitions, and he certainly hadn't expected Fu Ya to jump in and thrust his oar in, making the situation immediately irretrievable.

Luckily Fu Shen was all right. While his plan had had to be moved up, it had still succeeded.

"The night is still long. I'll keep watch here. Your Ladyship should rest. There will be things to do tomorrow." Yan Xiaohan turned his head and said to the silent eunuch by the door, "Yuan Zhen, take the empress to a side chamber."

It was still snowing. The darkest part of night had come. Soon, day would be breaking, the snow clearing and the sky brightening.

Fu Ling was uncompromisingly "invited" into a side chamber. She lay in bed with her clothes on, hundreds of thousands of thoughts tumbling in her mind into a tangled skein that couldn't be unknotted. Only near dawn did she fall into a muddled sleep.

In a daze, the sounds of a somber bell seemed to come from the distance. She missed a step in her dreams. Her heart lurched, and she suddenly woke up.

There was silence all around. It was still gloomy outside. Fu Ling sat up in bed, her breathing flurried, feeling her heart still pounding uncontrollably. Just then, someone gently knocked on the door. Yuan Zhen's voice came through the door: "My lady, are you awake? Lord Yan has dispatched me to ask whether you wish to see His Majesty one last time?"

It was as if Fu Ling had been struck dead by lightning. Without forewarning, two tears rolled from her eyes.

Her throat strung. Holding back sobs, she said, "Wait a moment, eunuch. I'm coming."

When Fu Ling had cleaned herself up and reached the main hall, Emperor Changzhi was already in a stupor. There were many people around the imperial bed—eunuchs, court historians, imperial physicians—only Yan Xiaohan was standing aside at a distance, his expression bland, as if this had nothing to do with him. At this critical moment, he was lost in thought, like an outsider.

After everyone had bowed, they made way. Fu Ling knelt beside the imperial bed. Tearfully, she called, "Your Majesty…"

Emperor Changzhi's eyelids twitched faintly, as if reacting to her voice, but he didn't open his eyes. Fu Ling clutched his emaciated hand and, sobbing, said, "Do not worry, Your Majesty, I will be sure to teach Hui'er well and not disappoint Your Majesty's ardent hopes."

Emperor Changzhi's fingers twitched a few times in her hand. His breathing was as weak as a dying candle in the wind. It was said that before death, everyone would have a moment of recovered glory, but while the imperial physicians waited with bated breath, Emperor Changzhi ultimately didn't wake again, and under the gazes of the crowd, his breathing slowly came to a stop.

"May you restrain your grief, Your Ladyship."

After a while, Yan Xiaohan stepped forward and said softly behind Fu Ling, "His Majesty has passed."

As soon as these words were spoken, everyone in Yangxin Hall knelt in unison. Yan Xiaohan saw Fu Ling still in a daze and had to prompt her: "Your Ladyship?"

Fu Ling was like a wooden dummy. She blinked leadenly, shaking the very last teardrop from the corner of her eye. She extended a hand toward Yuan Zhen at her side.

Yuan Zhen quickly gave her his arm. Yan Xiaohan retreated, swept aside his robes, and knelt.

"His Majesty… has passed."

Fu Ling faced the spacious hall, her red lips slightly parted, her voice hoarse and trembling. There was a sob in her words, but she gritted her teeth and persevered in saying her piece. "Send messengers to notify the public, the officials, the princes, and the concubines immediately. Shut the palace gates and the city gates. Impose martial law throughout the city. Ask the—"

Before the words "new master" could be spoken, a loud cry suddenly came from outside. "His Majesty has passed. Why was I not summoned to the palace to hear his posthumous edict?!"

Someone must have leaked the information. Outside Yangxin Hall, with Xue Sheng in the lead, dozens of assembly members congregated at the foot of the steps, and there was a place as well for Emperor Changzhi's brother by another mother, Prince Zhao. Leaning on Yuan Zhen's arm, Fu Ling walked to the front of the hall, her gaze coldly sweeping over one face after another, young or old. Sternly, she said, "The imperial physicians will bear witness that His Majesty did not wake from his stupor. There was no posthumous edict."

"Perhaps there was," Xue Sheng said meaningfully, "but Your Ladyship does not know of it."

Fu Ling said, "My son was invested with the rank of crown prince by the emperor himself. He is the heir apparent. Regardless of whether there was a posthumous edict, he is still the new master of the empire. What objection does Lord Xue have?"

Xue Sheng gave a cold laugh and opened a wooden box he was carrying. From it he removed a bright yellow imperial edict and raised it high. "This is a posthumous edict written in His Majesty's own hand, which he entrusted to me when his illness became grave, to be proclaimed throughout the empire upon his demise!"

There was a moment of silence outside the hall, followed by an explosion.

The empress said there was no posthumous edict, and a favored minister said the posthumous edict was in his hands. What did this mean? It meant that it was likely that the successor named in the posthumous edict in Xue Sheng's hands wasn't the crown prince!

Yan Xiaohan's eyes narrowed slightly. His hand, concealed by his sleeve, gripped a knife. He began to give earnest consideration to how he could wrap things up afterward if he stabbed Xue Sheng here and now.

That Xue Sheng dared to bring forth this imperial edict, regardless of whether it was real or fake, made it clear that the successor to the throne he had set his heart on was not the crown prince, but Prince Zhao, hidden among the crowd. But given Emperor Changzhi's disposition, would he really have cast aside his own son in favor of handing over the nation to a half-brother he wasn't familiar with?

Before he could reach a conclusion, urgent hoofbeats suddenly sounded in the distance. Two black steeds trod over the snow, speeding from outside the palace.

A voice long unheard came from afar, falling upon everyone's ears like a thunderclap—

"The Retired Emperor's decree has come! Ministers, attend to the decree!"

Yan Xiaohan turned his head in astonishment. Wild wind struck him in the face. At the end of the night and the snowstorm, a tall and upright figure gradually came clear in his vision along with the pale light of dawn in the east.

A red martial robe, a black marten coat, a sword at his waist—dashing and spirited, like a martial god descended to earth, the star of command incarnate.

"Fu Shen!"

"General!"

A haze of snow splashed. The Duke of Jing Fu Shen reined in his horse before the hall and came to a halt. He greeted the crowd from on high. "Gentlemen, it has been a long time since we met." Then he focused his greeting on Xue Sheng: "Lord Xue, I hope you have been well?"

On seeing this ghost, Xue Sheng felt as if a pail of ice water had been poured over his head. An enormous chill and panic seized his heart. His eyes nearly burst from their sockets. His countenance was hideous, half afraid, half a cornered beast ready to fight. With difficulty, he squeezed out from between his teeth: "It's you…"

"Heaven has not granted your desires. I did not die. I am sorry." With a smile, Fu Shen said, "Lord Xue becomes ever more impressive. After this long separation, I look upon you with new eyes. Before you restrained yourself to poisoning. I did not think that now you would even falsify an imperial edict."

"Slander and calumny!" Xue Sheng shot out like gunfire. "You colluded in secret with Duan Guihong with the intention of rebelling. Your plot was discovered by His Majesty, causing him to order your death! The Fu family has committed the great crime of treason, and the empress is your close kin. It is because of this that His Majesty wrote this posthumous edict in his own hand and entrusted it to me, intending to pass on his throne to Prince Zhao! You traitor, how dare you show yourself here to upset the situation?!"

Fu Shen was not angered. He only clicked his tongue and said, "Listen, don't you feel guilty saying such a thing, Lord Xue?

"If I had truly plotted rebellion," he said with emphasis, gaze sweeping over the ministers outside Yangxin Hall with a false smile, "would you be standing here today raising a hue and cry against me? Never mind the capital, you would have died stranded in Jinling.

"The western expeditionary army's Lieutenant General Li Xiaodong has made a full confession. You ordered him to poison me during my peace talks with Xinan, and to frame Duan Guihong. I have brought him before the Imperial Court of Justice for you. The handprint on his confession is still fresh. Lord Xue, why don't you run along with the 'imperial decree' and go keep him company?"

Word after word shook the earth and the heavens. Fu Shen had swiftly spilled the whole truth. The assembly members from the northern frontier were the first to react. They were mad enough to burst their lungs. Glowering, they said, "Old oaf! You dare to dupe your sovereign in this way?!"

Yan Xiaohan made a gesture at the imperial guards not far away. Xue Sheng cried out sternly, "I am still an appointed official of the court! Without cause or evidence, who dares to arrest me?!"

"I dare," Fu Shen said coldly. "Where are the imperial guards?"

Not for nothing was he a commander-in-chief who regularly commanded troops. This sentence was dignified and awesome, with a clang as of metal striking metal. To either side, imperial guards responded in unison, voices soaring up to the clouds. "Here!"

"All officers and men, attend. Arrest the traitor who sought to rebel and throw court discipline into chaos, and escort him to be locked up in the imperial prison to await trial." There was murder in Fu Shen's voice. Grimly, he said, "I have been in the army for a decade. My sword has drunk the blood of countless men. Do you think it cannot carry out a punishment for usurpation upon a traitor like you?!"

The imperial guards were their people to begin with. Hearing these words, they were at once like tigers and wolves released from a cage. They swarmed forward to hold Xue Sheng down and bind him, then dragged him away.

From Xue Sheng standing forth to his capture, there had been several reverses, and it had all happened in a flash. It was thanks to Fu Shen's uncompromising, direct methods that he had in a single brief stroke cut through and eradicated this palace coup. The average person was unlikely to experience such a scene even once their whole lifetime. The ministers were all struck dumb with astonishment. For a long time, they could not recover their senses. No one had ever expected that such a bizarre shift could take place. But carefully considering it, in their hearts they felt a sense of matters coming to rest in spite of themselves.

The situation was settled. Though the Retired Emperor's decree had yet to be read, there was no suspense as to the outcome.

Fu Shen had returned. Throughout the empire, who could now rise above the crown prince?

Yan Xiaohan composedly put away his knife and walked up to Fu Shen's horse. He offered his hand and, in the calm tone of ordinary spouses talking about domestic trivialities, he asked, "Didn't I tell you to stay put and look after your health? Why did you sneak back?"

This time, General Fu finally stopped playing dumb. Without any attempt at concealment, he jumped from the saddle holding his hand and said, "Was I supposed to let that old thief Xue Sheng bully my widowed little sister and her child?"

He turned his head to give Fu Ling a look. At the top of the steps, the empress's tears instantly became unstoppable.

Fu Shen sighed and gravely said, "Restrain your grief."

There was still a bright yellow imperial decree in his hand, but Yan Xiaohan held on, unwilling to let go. Fu Shen glanced down and with a quiet, feeling sigh said, "Listen, my wife, your grip is a little too strong."

Yan Xiaohan said nothing.

Fu Shen laughed and didn't struggle free. He raised his hand and tossed the imperial decree to a eunuch who had come with him. Pithily, he said, "Read it."

Hearing news of Emperor Changzhi's grave illness, Fu Shen had worried that Yan Xiaohan would be unable to handle it alone, so without him knowing, he had snuck away from Xinan to hurry back to the capital. The Beiyan Army had its own connections in the palace. He had entered the palace with the aid of the eunuch Cheng Fengjun. On the way, he had heard that news had leaked out and Xue Sheng and the others were heading for the palace. Just in case, he had gone out of his way to see the Retired Emperor and request a decree. He hadn't expected this ultimately to turn into such a farcical performance.

"By the grace of heaven, the Retired Emperor decrees: *We restore to Ourselves the authority of emperor…*"

Emperor Yuantai had abdicated the throne due to irresistible pressure. If it came down to it, his hand and eye were countless times stronger than Emperor Changzhi's. Fu Shen preferred to rely on him rather than trust an idiot like Emperor Changzhi.

According to the Retired Emperor's edict, Sun Hui, son of the empress, would inherit the throne. But the new master was young, so affairs of state would continue to be resolved by the Yanning Hall Assembly, with the empress dowager to preside from behind a screen.

In addition, five ministers would aid in rule: the Tianfu Army's representative Yan Xiaohan, the Duke of Jing Fu Shen, Dongji Hall's Official Gu Shanlü, Guanhai Hall's Official Li Huayue, and Jianning Pavilion's Official Xiao Tong.

When the decree had been read, the only two people on the scene who were holding hands, as if soaring upon clouds and riding the mists, had suddenly been raised to the highest position of authority in the empire.

Those who knew the inside story could not avoid being surprised. Emperor Yuantai had once exercised the dirtiest tactics against Fu Shen, wanting nothing better than to kill him, but on the brink of a new age, he seemed to have set aside all misgivings and firmly offered up the greatest authority to Fu Shen with both hands.

An emperor's heart was a needle in the sea. What enlightenment had come to him was perhaps known only to Emperor Yuantai himself.

"Has it been read? My turn now." Fu Shen turned to Yan Xiaohan. There was a subtle smile at the corners of his mouth. Raising his voice slightly, he said, "Oral instructions from the Retired Emperor. Yan Xiaohan, attend."

Yan Xiaohan was slightly surprised. He let go of his hand and took a step back, swept aside his robes and knelt.

Fu Shen said, "If the new master can be aided, do your utmost as his trusted aide. If he is incompetent, you may take his place."

There was dead silence in the snow.

Everyone apart from Fu Shen, including Yan Xiaohan and the empress, were all poleaxed.

Yan Xiaohan? Why Yan Xiaohan?

His ears were full of the rush of clamoring blood. These words were like a club over the head, striking Yan Xiaohan so hard he lost all sense of time. It was as if he had been thrown into the midst of a vast field of snow. He felt no happiness. There was only out-and-out bewilderment.

What did this mean?

He raised his eyes in a daze to look at Fu Shen. Their gazes met in midair. The corners of Fu Shen's eyes curved slyly. Then there was a sudden darkness before Yan Xiaohan's eyes as a thick, dark shadow swept over his head, carrying Fu Shen's body heat and a trace of medicinal odor, and solidly settled over his shoulders.

Fu Shen had removed his marten coat and draped it over him.

Yan Xiaohan was dressed all in plain mourning garb, almost invisible as he knelt in the snow. But when he was enveloped in this pitch-black marten coat, the red walls and yellow roof tiles, the gray bricks and white snow, and the two men in the snow, one kneeling and one standing… for some reason, the whole scene suddenly turned vivid and detailed.

Fu Shen bowed slightly and reached out a hand for him. Softly, he prompted him, "Lord Yan, will you obey the decree?"

His movement seemed to have some ritual significance. The assembly members of the northern border were the first to kneel. Closely following them, the dozen or so assembly members from other places also knelt in unison.

"We solemnly obey the Retired Emperor's edict."

Yan Xiaohan's attention was focused on Fu Shen, who was looking back at him.

"I... solemnly obey the imperial edict. As proper, I will spare no effort in carrying it out and be worthy of the responsibility given to me."

Dawn had passed, and day was here. The wind and snow had ended. The sun rose slowly from the distant horizon. Clear light shone upon the thin coating of snow on the glazed roof tiles, glistening brightly, almost splendid enough to dazzle. But none of it surpassed the figure standing before him with his back to the light. It seemed as if his slightest movement could spread gentle waves of light as far as the eye could see.

Sorrow and joy and parting and reunion, life and death and calamity and trial, wild laughter and tearful songs, twelve years gone by like the course of a long river—all of it flowed gently past in the instant their eyes met.

In that look was his vast territory, the safety of his home and nation, and there was also his promise to grow old together, unchangingly faithful til death.

End.

Extra 1 – Menggui

The Zhou dynasty had lasted in excess of a century, and during that century and more, the woman generally acknowledged to be the most beautiful in the empire was born in Jiangnan's Qiantang during Emperor Hongjing's reign.

Emperor Hongjing was a sovereign who inherited a peaceful nation and built on the successes of his predecessors. While he could not have been said to have worked hard and conscientiously day and night during his reign, he had still governed diligently. Apart from this, he was a wise lord who was willing to take advice. During this twenty-nine years on the throne, many able ministers and competent officials emerged who took their places in history.

He was a "wise ruler" all his life, the sole condemnation future generations had to make against him being that this emperor had excessively indulged in feminine charms. He possessed a magnificent harem. Even when he was fifty-three, the year before his passing, he sent representatives from the palace out into the world to select women of good family to be brought into the palace.

So in the twenty-eighth year of Hongjing, the daughter of Qiantang's Qu family was chosen by Duan Linglong, who had been sent as courier on the Jiangnan Road. She waved goodbye to her parents and family members and raced with the convoy to the vastly distant capital.

Her beauty was natural, an undiluted and unparalleled glamor of the mortal world. She was talented in singing and dancing, had an understanding of music, and was also talented in drawing and calligraphy. As soon as she entered the palace, she caught Emperor Hongjing's eye. She obtained the title of Noble Consort, most favored in the imperial harem.

But Noble Consort Qu had been born in Jiangnan. Her health was delicate. On first coming to the capital, the climate of the north did not suit her. As soon as winter came, she became listless and sick, like a pampered canary that was difficult to keep alive. To please her, at the start of winter in the thirtieth year of Hongjing, the emperor went out of his way to take her to a temporary imperial residence to avoid the cold.

One evening, Emperor Hongjing suddenly took ill. Noble Consort Qu urgently summoned imperial physicians, but rescue efforts were unsuccessful, and the emperor ultimately died of his illness.

Duan Linglong and Noble Consort Qu had attended on Emperor Hongjing to the very last moment before he died. When the imperial physicians confirmed the emperor's passing, Noble Consort Qu came out and handed his posthumous edict to the Imperial Instructor Yang Gong to read out. Prince Zhou, the son most favored by Emperor Hongjing, had not accompanied him on this trip. The only ones who had come with the emperor were the eldest prince Sun Zhang and the second prince Sun Xun. But, contrary to everyone's expectations, Emperor Hongjing had not passed on his throne to Prince Zhou, but had instead chosen the second prince, who would later become Emperor Yuantai.

The suspicion of later generations that Emperor Yuantai had not come by the throne honestly proceeded from this. There were those who said that the Imperial Instructor Yang Gong had pretended to be reading the imperial decree, and those who said that Duan Ling-long and Noble Consort Qu had together forged the imperial decree.

When Emperor Hongjing passed away, the position of empress had been empty for many years. Emperor Yuantai had originally thought of giving Noble Consort Qu the title of Consort Dowager, but she requested to retreat to the Wanxiang Temple and become a nun. The beauty of a generation, like a flower that had bloomed too early. Her loveliness had been on display for only two years before she so resolutely cut the ties of affection and turned to withdraw into Buddhism.

In another year, in the third winter after her coming to the capital, Lady Qu died of illness in the Wanxiang Temple.

Great Zhou's peerless beauty of the century was like a gorgeous but dimly seen outline in the history books, descriptions scant and stories handed down even fewer. After a few strokes, she suddenly vanished without a trace.

But that was far from the whole truth.

Only a small portion of the imperial family's affairs could be brought out in public with grandeur. The history books were after all limited and could not be exhaustive—at least, so it was with Noble Consort Qu.

She hid far more secrets than anyone knew.

For example, that the reason she was unwilling to stay in the palace as Consort Dowager was that while Emperor Hongjing's coffin was being sheltered in the temporary imperial residence, the new emperor repeatedly graced the hall she resided in with his presence late at night. After returning to the capital, because Imperial Instructor Yang Gong had aided Emperor Yuantai in ascending the throne, his daughter, the second prince's first wife, at last became Empress, as was only to be expected.

For another example, when she left the imperial palace for Wanxiang Temple, Noble Consort Qu was in fact already pregnant.

Presiding over the Wanxiang Temple was a kindhearted,

merciful old nun, and there was the powerful minister Duan Linglong to put things in order for her, cover up and make arrangements, so in the end, it was successfully hidden from everyone when in the last month of the second year of Yuantai, she gave birth to a male infant.

On the night of the birth, Noble Consort Qu's forces had been nearly spent holding out until the baby was born. Duan Linglong brought the baby to her bedside. The rims of his eyes faintly reddened, he softly said, "Your Ladyship, choose a name for him."

Inside the gauze drapes, Noble Consort Qu tilted her head slightly. Suddenly, in a thin voice, she asked, "Outside... has the snow stopped?"

"Yes," said Duan Linglong. "As soon as the little lord was born, the snow outside stopped."

"*At the ends of the earth... the frost and snow clear on a freezing night,*" Noble Consort Qu said haltingly in a voice as thin as gossamer. "So call him 'Hanxiao,' for the freezing night. My name is 'Yan,' so give him 'Yan' for a surname..."[1]

Duan Linglong thought to himself that this name was overly mournful, but seeing how hard it was for Noble Consort Qu to speak, he didn't dare to interrupt her, only nodded.

Noble Consort Qu rested briefly, gathering strength, then continued: "Do not let him acknowledge his parentage... The imperial family is ruthless. I wish my son to live a peaceful and happy life, to be free, not be trapped in an inescapable cage like his mother."

"Your Ladyship..." said Duan Linglong.

"Duan-da-ge," she said, extending an emaciated hand with difficulty and tightly clutching Duan Linglong's robes, "I want to ask something of you..."

There was no strength in her hand. Duan Linglong could in fact have thrown her off with the slightest struggle, getting rid of great trouble in the future. But for some reason, he was frozen for a long time, then finally sighed as if reaching a compromise, conceding. "Name it, Your Ladyship."

"I want to ask you... to take him as your adopted son, look after him for me, protect him as he grows up, not let others bully him... In the future, he can take care of you in your old age and bury you... I have no way to repay you in the present life. I will requite your kindness in the next life..."

Suddenly, Duan Linglong covered the back of her hand, stopping her from finishing what she was saying.

"When I brought you to the palace, I never expected that there would come a day like today," he said quietly. "I am the one who did you harm. There is no need to speak of repayment. We will just say that I owe you."

Watching him, Noble Consort Qu's eyes gradually filled with tears, but the corners of her mouth slowly turned up, forming an extremely small arc.

She had been reduced to skin and bones by the torments of illness, but this smile made Duan Linglong recall in a daze how, when he had brought her to the palace two years earlier, she had mounted the carriage step by step supported by a servant girl, tears plainly standing in her eyes, but when he had looked her way, she hadn't forgotten to give him a shallow smile.

A dewy peony, so bright and beautiful it scorched the eye. That was the true peerless beauty of a nation.

Who could have thought that after a bout of wind and rain, before the flower's youth had passed away, before the rosy cheeks had faded with age, that beauty would be gone forever.

"I won't live to see him grow up." Her voice grew ever more quiet. "Duan-da-ge, you are his adopted father, choose a courtesy name for him..."

Duan Linglong thought about it for a while, then finally said, "*A sojourner in a foreign land, returning in dreams on freezing nights.*[2] Let his courtesy name be 'Menggui' for returning in dreams. If—"

He turned his head and suddenly stopped speaking.

On the crude, simple bed, Noble Consort Qu's eyes were

tightly shut, her countenance serene. There were no more signs of undulation in her chest. In that moment of time, she had already passed.

Returning in dreams on freezing nights—but she would never again return to Qiantang.

The child in his arms suddenly began to bawl, breaking Duan Linglong out of his abstraction. He said a few words to calm him, then stood up holding the child, replaced Noble Consort Qu's hand, which lay outside the quilt, and pulled the quilt over her, covering her pale and emaciated countenance.

Passing through the room full of silence and the soul of the departed, still near, he promised, "So it shall be."

Later, Duan Linglong, thinking that the name "Yan Hanxiao" as she had chosen it was too desolate, and in order to avoid observant persons linking him with Noble Consort Qu, changed it to "Yan Xiaohan," with a different character for "Yan." He kept this child with him and educated him with great care.

Only Yan Xiaohan was truly too similar to Noble Consort Qu in appearance and manner. The first time he had an audience with the emperor, Emperor Yuantai, at first sight of him, couldn't hold back. He summoned Duan Linglong and asked him what was going on.

At the time of Noble Consort Qu's death, Duan Linglong had already begun to plan and prepare for this day. He had thought of sending Yan Xiaohan away to have him raised by someone else, but who knew what would become of him elsewhere? Besides which, given the state of the world, if he didn't enter the court, had no wealth or influence, spent his whole life as a commoner with even his next meal in doubt, how could he be called "free?"

And he was a son born of the clandestine affair between Emperor Yuantai, who was in mourning, and the late emperor's consort. His identity could never be revealed to the light of day. Even his existence was a lurking threat to Emperor Yuantai.

Luckily, Duan Linglong had made ample preparations. He

gave Emperor Yuantai an honest account of Noble Consort Qu giving birth shortly before her death, stressing the wish she had expressed: she did not want this child to acknowledge his parentage, only asked that he could live a peaceful life.

Finally, he took out his trump card—a portrait that "reportedly" had been drawn by the Noble Consort in her own hand to give to Emperor Yuantai as a keepsake.

At the time, Emperor Yuantai had only been attracted to Noble Consort Qu's beauty. He had been rather regretful on hearing of her early demise, but he had only said to himself that since ancient times, beauties had had troubled fates. He hadn't thought that such secrets would be hidden in this story. That portrait suddenly pulled up many memories for him. The sight of it made him miss its owner, putting him in no mood to pursue and punish Duan Linglong's concealment of this.

Not only that—as he had aged, in his heart, Noble Consort Qu, like Lady Li for the Martial Emperor, became harder to forget, and so the mistier her memory became. Sometimes, looking at Yan Xiaohan, Emperor Yuantai thought that he was very pitiable, and he couldn't resist thinking: if Yan Xiaohan were a legitimate prince, wouldn't he be a better credit to him than all his present sons?

Under the subtle influence of these imaginings, Emperor Yuantai tacitly acquiesced to Duan Linglong's fostering of Yan Xiaohan, took him into the Feilong Guard, and even, after Duan Linglong's death, made an exception to promote Yan Xiaohan to the position of Imperial Investigator of the Feilong Guard.

As for Yan Xiaohan's parentage, Emperor Yuantai and Yan Xiaohan were both well aware of the truth, and each knew that the other was perfectly clear on this subject. Over time, this had become a tacit understanding that did not need to be spoken.

As long as Yan Xiaohan scrupulously carried out his role as an official, Emperor Yuantai would give him power and position to the greatest extent possible without granting him the identity of prince.

For years, Yan Xiaohan had always "strictly abided by the rules." The only time he had almost directly come out and asked something of Emperor Yuantai had been while retaking the Central Plains, when he had personally gone to Shu to borrow troops from the Retired Emperor.

With the nation's territory ripped apart, when a prince whom he had abandoned, who could never be a prince in name, came to him to ask for troops, it was for the sake of restoring Great Zhou's empire.

It was also then that Emperor Yuantai had at last belatedly picked up a trace of something not quite right about Yan Xiaohan and Fu Shen's relationship.

The late emperor was in his coffin in the palace, the new master was young and unable to take charge. The empress instructed the ministers-regent to assist in preparing the funeral. The palace maids and eunuchs busied themselves laying things out, the officials wept before the hall, and the palace was in exceptional disorder, not calming until evening.

The sun set early in winter in the north. It had snowed during the day, coinciding with a day of national mourning. The imperial city was cloaked in white, unspeakably bleak. Yan Xiaohan, draped in the black marten coat, walked up in front of a palace through snow that had yet to be swept. Without waiting to be announced, he quietly opened the door himself and entered.

The room was dimly lit, with the remnants of incense hovering in the air. A tall figure sat at a table, dozing with his head propped on his hand. He might have been sleeping for a long time.

Yan Xiaohan unconsciously pursed his lips, not knowing why he was nervous.

He quietly walked up in front of Fu Shen and looked at his slumbering countenance by the weak daylight. His gaze was like a carving knife, bit by bit carving out the high nose bridge, the distinct lines, and the slightly curved... corners of the mouth.

"Peeping at me, hm?" he said laughing with his eyes closed. "You can't look for free, you know."

Yan Xiaohan's slightly knitted brow relaxed. He reached out to stroke Fu Shen's face. "Why did you fall asleep sitting? Aren't you cold?"

Fu Shen took his hand, opened his eyes, and indolently said, "It's all right, I was just dozing. I was slacking on the job anyway. Has everything been settled with empress dowager?"

"Yes."

Worried that Fu Shen's serious injuries had yet to heal, as well as about the longstanding complaint in his legs, Yan Xiaohan had been unwilling to let him keep kneeling outside. Following a few not very important procedural matters, he had found him a room in the palace where he could slack off. Anyway, martial law had been imposed throughout the palace. No one would dare to say anything to his face.

"You…"

The two of them spoke simultaneously. Their eyes met, and they shut their mouths in unison. It was Fu Shen who was the first to speak: "You've been standing there wanting to say something but holding back for ages. You go first."

Yan Xiaohan didn't know how he had discerned that he was "wanting to say something but holding back," but he did indeed have something to say. "Do you know?"

These words were a non sequitur, but Fu Shen immediately understood him.

"I said before that you look something like the late emperor," Fu Shen said. "Last night in the Retired Emperor's quarters, I saw a portrait of a beauty and nearly thought that my spouse and constant companion had changed clothes and was standing there in front of me. Is there anything left for me to guess?"

"Indecent," Yan Xiaohan said, laughing at his words. "I'm an illegitimate son who can't see the light of day. The Retired Emperor coming up with this move has made me a little uneasy. I'm afraid he's guessed at our relationship and wants to use this imperial decree to drive us apart. What will you do if I wrest away your nephew's empire one day?"

"Listen to you. You have too many things on your mind." Fu Shen sighed. "What else could I do? Feed my body to the tiger, beg you to be merciful... prince regent."

Yan Xiaohan quickly put a hand over his mouth. "My ancestor, please shut up. I'm terrified of you. How can you just say that?"

Fu Shen heartlessly laughed into his palm. "Impressive. You have the will but not the guts."

Yan Xiaohan was unamused.

He was at the end of his endurance. He could only bend down and lower his head, planning to shove his ridicule back down his throat.

"Hey." Fu Shen put a hand up to block his face as it drew near. Sternly, he said, "It's a day of national mourning. How can you be so undignified?"

Yan Xiaohan remained fixed in that posture, looking at him through the gaps between his fingers. His gaze was calm and profound, but it had an inexplicable trace of abject piteousness.

There was nothing Fu Shen could do when he looked at him like this. He could only turn and put a hand to his face, draw near in resignation to his fate and peck his lips.

"Forget it... The court won't permit conjugal activities, but would they forbid us a kiss?"

---

1. The opening quote is from Tang Dynasty poet Du Fu's 阁夜 ("Night in the Watchtower"); the original line is 天涯霜雪霁寒宵, the last two characters being the characters of Yan Xiaohan's given name reversed. The overall mood of the poem is desolation. For the rest, Noble Consort Qu's given name 颜 is a different character from Yan Xiaohan's surname (严), though pronounced the same.

2. Quote from Tang Dynasty poet Yu Wuling's 客中 ("Sojourn"); the original lines are: 异国久为客，寒宵频梦归, the latter half including the characters for both Yan Xiaohan's given name and courtesy name.

Extra 2 - Empire

As the most powerful favored minister outside the imperial family in Great Zhou's history, Yan Xiaohan was heavily swaddled in rumor; all kinds of things were said of him. To the outsider's imagination, he had forty-eight hours in a day, and each one was spent attempting to usurp the new master and make himself emperor, and he only held back, not daring to act, because of the deterrence of the Duke of Jing Fu Shen.

There was another well-known "insider story" that went around the palace, which said that the new master, Emperor Chengming, was young and relied heavily on his maternal uncle the Duke of Jing, frequently clinging to his leg unwilling to let go. And Yan Xiaohan was like a weasel squatting outside a chicken coop, harboring ill intent toward the whole family. If your attention wavered briefly, his claws would reach out for the little emperor, and he would again and again say something to sow discord between His Majesty and the Duke of Jing.

One day, near dusk, Fu Shen ought to have bid farewell and left the palace, but the little emperor clung to him fiercely, stubbornly preventing him from leaving. Yan Xiaohan, seeing this, said in jest: "The Duke of Jing is a member of my family. If Your

Majesty is bent on keeping him here, what will you give me in exchange?"

Though all the little emperor did at present was eat, sleep, and play, he lived up to his imperial bloodline. From childhood, he displayed surpassing courage and insight. He said: "Bestow the empire upon you."

Hearing this, Empress Dowager Fu was alarmed and lost her grip on her bowl of tea, dropping it onto her skirt.

Yan Xiaohan's loose-tongued moment was fully recorded by the imperial historian. The next day, countless memorials of impeachment flew onto His Majesty's desk like snowflakes, bitterly berating Yan Xiaohan for disregarding ethics, taking advantage of a young ruler, having no respect for social rank, intending to plot rebellion; if such a usurper were permitted to hold state power, the empire would one day be destroyed at his hands.

The ministers once again raised a cry in their death throes: If this person were not eliminated, he would sooner or later become a grave peril!

As another high minister raised by the dying emperor's will, Gu Shanlü was compelled by his colleagues to the point of developing a headache. Privately, he went to Fu Shen to spill his grievances: "Lord Duke, please keep him under control. The Court of the Censorate won't be held back for much longer, they've even written their suicide notes, just waiting to remonstrate with their deaths at the assembly tomorrow. As a mercy on me, tell Lord Yan to keep still for a couple of months, stay out of the center of attention, all right?"

Fu Shen clicked his tongue. "All this fuss over nothing. They're ready to die as martyrs, just like that? Not for nothing, but at their age, how can the gentlemen of the Court of the Censorate be so hasty?"

Gu Shanlü knew he was defending Yan Xiaohan despite the right and wrong of the situation. He grabbed his hand and entreated in an anguished and solemn tone: "General, this matter concerns the order of the court, the stability of the empire. It all depends on you!"

"… Well, then," said Fu Shen, "let go of me. Things will get complicated if he sees this."

As if avoiding a thief, he withdrew a yard away from Gu Shanlü and nearly jumped up among the rafters. With lingering fear, he said, "Say whatever you have to say, don't touch me."

Gu Shanlü had learned to be crafty over the last couple of years. He pretended not to have heard the remarkable words Fu Shen had blurted out, only smiled without speaking, only cupped his hands toward him in an *I'll leave it to you* gesture.

Fu Shen's scalp went numb at the false smile in his eyes. He thought that Gu Shanlü had misunderstood something.

The two of them were locked in a brief stalemate, looking at each other in dismay. Then Fu Shen, acknowledging his fate, waved a hand and irritably yielded. "I understand, I'll leave in a few days, I won't stick around at court to offend your eyes. Satisfied? If you're satisfied, then hurry up and get out."

With a *better you than me* attitude, Scholar Gu, having bloodlessly cut through a thorny difficulty, without needing to be seen off by Fu Shen, left by himself in satisfaction.

After his guest had left, Fu Shen strolled back to the rear courtyard in leisurely fashion. Yan Xiaohan, hearing his footsteps, was just about to turn his head when he felt a sudden chill on his temple. A clear, sweet floral scent faintly wafted by, and an enormous pink-edged white rose brushed by his face as it was brought up before his eyes.

With feigned unwillingness, he turned around and pulled a long face. "What?"

"See how good this flower is."

The white rose, coquettishly clinging to his cheek, slid down all the way to his lower jaw and gently caught on his chin. The person holding the flower, however, was full of uprightness and sincerity. "Accompanied by a beauty, it's even better."

Yan Xiaohan immediately sucked in a breath.

All smiles, Fu Shen said, "Does my wife not like it?"

"No," said "his wife," icily.

Soft flower petals tapped rudely against his lips, as if punishing him for saying the opposite of what he felt.

Fu Shen calmly withdrew the flower, bent his head to sniff, his lips briefly touching the petals, seemingly inadvertent. "No? Then forget about it, I'll find a place to stick it…"

Before he could finish, he was caught in an embrace along with the flower.

"I like it, I adore it, all right?" Yan Xiaohan said irritably. "Come back, stop ruining my flowers."

"Louder," said Fu Shen, "say it again. What exactly do you like?"

"I like you." Yan Xiaohan bent his head and plucked the flower out of his hand. Expression unwavering, he said, "I adore you."

Many people didn't know that the heretical dialogue that had reached the court had had an aftermath.

After the little emperor had said "Bestow the empire upon you," it wasn't only the empress dowager who had bristled; Yan Xiaohan had also bristled.

Even more of a rascal than the emperor, he had seized Fu Shen's hand. Suing his victim before he could be prosecuted, he repeatedly rebuked: "Look at this! For the sake of his own amusement, His Majesty is even willing to offer up his empire. Isn't it awful? What are all the imperial instructors doing to earn their keep? What are they teaching His Majesty? And then there's you, you're always too yielding to His Majesty…"

Fu Shen couldn't stand to hear any more. He furtively pinched his waist, and in a low voice said, "Bullshit, you dare to say I'm yielding to him? Aren't you ashamed?"

There was no answer.

Expression unwavering, Yan Xiaohan said, "In sum, the sovereign of a nation whose word is absolute must not speak so triflingly. It's all our fault as ministers for serving our sovereign inadequately. It is our negligence that has led to His Majesty saying such things. I make so bold as to ask the empress dowager to issue an imperial decree that, starting tomorrow, the Duke of Jing will no longer come to the palace every day to spend time with His Majesty, and instead Scholars Gu, Li, and Yang will take turns each day obeying the decree to lecture to His Majesty on ancient and current wisdom and the way of the monarch."

The empress dowager's skirt was still dripping. She was stunned by his thorough and loyal advice. Stalling, she said, "Well…"

She looked at her older brother as if soliciting his advice, but she saw him with his hand pressed to his forehead, with *this is outside my control* written all over his face, without any further desire to speak.

Helplessly, Empress Dowager Fu answered, "Then that's what we'll do."

Having obtained the empress dowager's decree, before Yan Xiaohan could have time to celebrate, a sonorous wail suddenly erupted in the hall. The emperor, clinging to Fu Shen's leg, bawled, "Want Uncle!"

How could Fu Shen stand to let him cry like this? He was about to bend down to pick him up on the spot. But as soon as he moved, he felt Yan Xiaohan hold him back. He stepped forward himself, half knelt before the little emperor, and gently but irresistibly pried his delicate little fingers off Fu Shen, one by one.

He quietly said something to the incessantly wailing little emperor, and the deafening crying first paused, then suddenly rose in pitch, nearly bringing down the hall's ceiling beams.

Fu Shen had only vaguely heard a few words. He didn't know how this ancestor had offended that little ancestor now. Angrily, he said, "Don't tease him…"

Yan Xiaohan suddenly turned his head and gave him a profound look.

His eyes were very cold, without a trace of a smile, but there was an indescribable firmness that inexplicably put one in mind of icy metal and frozen-over lakes.

Fu Shen seemed to be held fast by his gaze. He froze in spite of himself.

Before he could work out the meaning of this gaze, Yan Xiaohan had stood, bowed to the empress dowager, and took him away, bidding farewell.

The outcome was that after this, he was in a temper with him for fully the next four days.

Lord Yan was unwilling to admit that he had been jealous of a child, but Fu Shen had already seen through him. Moreover, Yan Xiaohan belonged to that difficult to appease, childish category. His style of getting revenge was very unique. It was to hide Fu Shen's boots and wheelchair, leaving him without aid and unable to provide for himself, obliged to submit to tyrannical abuse, permitting this sycophant and lackey to make no end of trouble for him, do whatever he pleased.

Today he had finally managed to cheer him up. While he was at it, Fu Shen mentioned the outcome of his discussion with Gu Shanlü earlier. "… And I think the court presently has no use for us, so why don't we find an excuse to leave the capital and rest for a while? How does that sound? Do you want to go south or north?"

"Jingyuan." Yan Xiaohan didn't answer him but instead suddenly said out of nowhere, "I've never wanted you to be too close to the emperor. While he is your nephew, in another ten or twenty years, when he holds power, can he continue to treat you as he has always treated you? Will he be like his father and grandfather, full of fear of you?"

"I know that," said Fu Shen, confused. "What's wrong? That has nothing to do with anything. What are you talking about?"

Yan Xiaohan gripped his shoulder and lowered his upper body slightly. Staring into his eyes, he said earnestly, "These worries are all idle thoughts and may not necessarily come true in the future. Even if they do come true, I'll still take care of them for you. I don't need you to choose between me and the emperor, and I don't insist on you leaving the capital and staying aloof from the palace. So... let's defer the discussion of leaving the capital until later. Think carefully, don't give yourself grief on my account, all right?"

Fu Shen opened his mouth, but he didn't know what he ought to say. He was briefly silent, then gave a faint sigh that encapsulated many things. "Oh, you."

He said, "Ever since I joined the army, I have held firmly to the notion of dedicating my life to the country, being buried on the battlefield. I didn't expect luck to toy with me—"

Yan Xiaohan's fingers curled. Unconsciously, he felt that what followed might be nothing good. Unexpectedly, Fu Shen glanced at him, and the weighty regret at the tip of his tongue changed course and became a light jab: "I didn't succeed in giving my life for my country. You got the best of it."

A cord in his heart seemed to give a crisp twang, leaving lingering echoes trembling after it.

"Over the years, all these things, while I am a stubborn person, perhaps I've resigned myself." Fu Shen took his hand and laced their fingers together. "The cycle alternates. It has its fixed course. I can leave the empire for others to worry about. I am no Buddha come to earth. Can I spend my whole life worrying about the world? Worrying about you is enough."

The rest of his words were drowned in peppered kisses and the clear, sweet fragrance of white roses.

In the summer of the fourth year of Chengming, Fu Shen and Yan Xiaohan obeyed orders to perform an inspection tour of Jiangnan, leaving the capital to go south in the sixth month.

The little emperor struggled to read and practice calligraphy with the imperial instructors, and sometimes he had a palace servant write a letter to his uncle for him, to ask when he would come back; he wanted to take him to see the new lotuses in the imperial garden.

Though he never asked a single word about Yan Xiaohan, he

never forgot that petty aunt of his who, while he treated him all right, made himself unlikeable.

Later, when Emperor Chengming had grown up and become the ruler of the nation, with the wealth of the four seas, he still firmly remembered what Yan Xiaohan had said to him in the palace that day.

"He's mine. Take back your empire, I'm not trading."

EXTRA 3 - HUADIAN

"DAMN IT, HOW FAR IS THE DIPLOMATIC MARRIAGE MISSION FROM Yuanzhou?"

The tent flap was lifted aside, and the young general strode out. Beneath the bright moonlight at the frontier pass, he wore armor, with a sword hanging at his waist. His features were clear and handsome, holding anger and violence, like a solemn jade carving of a god of war. In a stern voice, he said to the bodyguard outside the tent: "Chongshan, go put together a team to ready their things and accompany me at once!"

The murderous aura about him chilled the hearts of the soldiers passing by the commander's tent on patrol. The officer responsible for the patrol, Yu Qiaoting, seeing the situation, reined in his horse and came to a halt. He called a greeting: "General, are you going out so late? What's happened?"

The soldiers were assembled in an instant. Fu Shen took his war horse's reins, hopped on, then raced out of the camp riding abreast with Yu Qiaoting. On the way, he said, "It's a long story. The Western Tartars were driven out of the grasslands by the Eastern Tartars and have lived along the western border for many years. They are inclined to associate with our nation. That the tumult the year before last was resolved was in large part owed to them sending troops in aid, and at the end of last year, His Majesty sent a diplomatic mission to give thanks, and the two sides used that opportunity to arrange a marriage between their children. The khan is sending his daughter to the capital for a diplomatic marriage. The team accompanying her is already on its way."

"Isn't that a good thing?" said Yu Qiaoting.

"Good, my ass," said Fu Shen. "As a show of good faith, the Western Tartars' khan threw a white jade divine statue into the princess's dowry. That thing is the national treasure of the ancient state of Woyan. After Woyan broke apart, the divine statue was taken into the west by the Western Tartars. The Eastern Tartars have used up all the means at their disposal to get this national treasure. The two clans break into fighting on sight and go at it like fighting cocks."

Yu Qiaoting was a smart person. He understood the hint. "Oh, the princess hasn't had a restful trip."

Fu Shen said, "The Western Tartars must also be afraid of it turning into something major. They got in touch with the court in advance, and in addition to the princess' escort, His Majesty also sent his own trusted bodyguards to receive her."

"So you..."

"From west to east, the area that includes Tongzhou and Yuanzhou is the closest to the Eastern Tartars, the hardest to travel." Sneering, Fu Shen said, "That bunch of good-for-nothings can't hold out, so they've sent someone to Yuanzhou to request aid."

"Oh, I see." Yu Qiaoting nodded, then asked, "Does this merit you going in person? You could have just sent people to meet them."

Fu Shen waved a hand. As they spoke, the two of them had reached the exit of the camp. He didn't speak further but led the team of horses and men speeding into the distance, sending dust flying.

Yu Qiaoting watched them recede into the distance and

suddenly realized that something was off. "Huh? Who was it that tipped him off and told him to receive the Western Tartars' diplomatic marriage mission?"

Had it been a decree from the court, Fu Shen wouldn't have left so urgently. From his manner, he clearly hadn't been informed ahead of time and had received a sudden request for emergency aid.

Since when had the Western Tartars been so friendly with Fu Shen?

The Beiyan soldiers traveled quickly over dark mountain roads and thickets, racing for the area around Yuanzhou's border with Tongzhou. There was wilderness all around here, without a village ahead or an inn behind—an ideal place for murder and looting. Fu Shen had keen instincts. Amid the whistling wind, he caught a trace of unusual movement and gestured at once at the soldiers behind him. He slowed and turned to Xiao Xun. "What is the place in front of this slope?"

Xiao Xun said, "Go around this slope, and you come to the public road."

Fu Shen nodded. "Don't say a word," he said, "and move quietly. Follow me."

The further ahead they went, the clearer the sounds became. Having climbed halfway up the slope, they could already hear the clash of cold steel from the other side, accompanied by shouts and cries. It seemed exceptionally horrifying in the pitch-black night. Fu Shen thought to himself that this wasn't good. He shook his horse's reins and charged up the slope. By moonlight, he took a rough look and saw a few scattered bonfires burning brightly in the wilderness like stars, human forms flickering in the camp, the glitter of weapons, two groups of men locked in struggle. When the battle was at its most deadlocked, there was a figure being surrounded by many people. That person had a sword in hand that turned like the wind but still seemed incapable of meeting the demand, ability falling short of ambition. The person nearly had an arm cut off at the shoulder and trampled into a bonfire.

Fu Shen narrowed his eyes and doubtfully muttered, "Is the Western Tartar princess… so skilled in combat?"

"What?" Xiao Xun, following him, was all at sea. But before he could finish his question, Fu Shen had already charged ahead down the slope. Where the snow-bright edge of his sword passed it was as if he were chopping melons. Heads instantly fell. He broke through the encirclement alone and scooped the princess with her long hair flying onto his horse. Gravely, he said, "The Beiyan Army is here. Princess, do not be afraid…"

The black-haired, white-skinned, brightly dressed and adorned "foreign princess" heard this and abruptly looked up to stare at him, with a sword still grimly dripping blood in hand.

A slightly hoarse male voice said into his ear: "Thank you, general. I'm not afraid."

Fu Shen was dumbfounded.

He had been so far away earlier, and it was so dark. He had only seen the flying long hair and brightly colored dress, and automatically thought that this would be the only woman in the diplomatic mission. Instead he had snatched up a fake—what kind of performance was this tall and stalwart scoundrel playing?!

"You…" The corners of Fu Shen's mouth twitched, and the veins on his temples jumped wildly. After a lengthy silence, he finally got out, gritting his teeth, "I had no notion that Lord Yan had this sort of interest."

"I had no choice." Yan Xiaohan awkwardly cast down his eyelids. His deliberately embellished eyebrows were unusually delicate, but unexpectedly they didn't look out of place on the man's face. Instead, there was something a little alluringly coquettish about them that made you want to look again. "I'll explain a little later. The enemy is in front of us, let's focus on our lives…"

Before he could finish, he suddenly put an arm around Fu

Shen and pressed him down hard, turning to avoid a little arrow shot from behind. With his other hand, he raised his sword and parried a blade slicing toward the two of them. Fu Shen unexpectedly bumped against the hollow of his shoulder and nearly broke the high bridge of his nose. He straightened and, with tears welling in his eyes, pulled the reins. Pained and angry, he said, "Sit properly, don't get in the way! Whoa!"

The warhorse gave a long whinny and raced away, carrying the two of them on its back. The attackers' encirclement was once again dispersed, and bodyguards immediately scrambled forward to guard the two of them. The original escort had been struggling to resist, but once the Beiyan Army joined the fray, the situation took a rapid turn. With their numerical advantage, they rolled over the other side almost overwhelmingly. Seeing that the battle was as good as lost, the other side was well aware that this was no time for zealous fighting. They called a few loud phrases in the Eastern Tartar language, and the remaining assassins immediately broke off, scattering in all directions, swiftly disappearing in the boundless night.

Xiao Xun was about to go in pursuit but was stopped by Fu Shen. "You won't catch up to them, don't waste time. They can find any random gully to squat in, and we'll be looking for them until the end of time."

"Yes, general." Aloud, Xiao Xun gave an affirmative, but his line of sight was uncontrollably drifting to the "princess" in front of Fu Shen. This person was slim, with a slender neck, with black hair hanging down and covering half the face. Perhaps the hair's coils had been loosened in the fighting just now. Now the gold hairpins were aslant, a string of carnelian tassels tangled in the hair flashing in and out of view. Apart from the huadian remaining at the center of the forehead[1], all the other ornaments had been left behind somewhere. The person sat like this on the horse, back to the crowd, yet still with a dainty charm.

But what was going on with their general's expression, face twitching as if he had eaten sour grapes, looking as if he wanted

to laugh but was holding back? And also, why did that princess…
seem to be a little taller than even General Fu?

"What do we do next?" Fu Shen gave a dry cough, masking
the irresistible smile in his voice. Quietly, he asked Yan Xiaohan,
"Are your people going to stay here, or go to Yuanzhou to rest
and regroup?"

As if he couldn't stand his mocking look, Yan Xiaohan
turned his head away uncomfortably. Struggling to keep his
expression serious, he said, "After being taught a lesson, the
Eastern Tartars probably won't try again. Thank you for your
assistance tonight, general."

"So you ought to be thanking me." Fu Shen reached up to
adjust his disheveled hair, tangled up in hairpins. "If not for me,
Lord Yan's corpse would be going cold here, hm?"

Yan Xiaohan didn't respond.

"All right, that's enough." Fu Shen turned his horse's head
and disparagingly said, "Let's go and wash your colorful makeup
off. It really is an offense to the eye."

Having said this, he didn't make him dismount, just slowly
returned to the camp carrying him. The Beiyan Cavalry was well
practiced, following him at a middle distance. Only when Yan
Xiaohan had gone into the tent to change and wash up and the
people of the diplomatic marriage mission stepped forward to
thank him did Fu Shen turn his head, look loftily down, and
haughtily said, "Your nation is sending its princess to my country
for a diplomatic marriage, and you've only brought a few people.
Did you really think the Eastern Tartars were nothing, or were
you prepared not to return?"

The Western Tartar diplomatic envoy thought he was only
concerned for the princess's safety. Smiling obsequiously, he said,
"Thank you, thank you, general. But there is no need for you to
worry. The princess is not here. She has already been escorted
away by the troops of your honored nation."

With a slight effort of thought, Fu Shen understood the tricks
involved in this. He was caught between anger and amusement.

At last, he dismounted with a snort and instructed Xiao Xun: "We will be stationed here for the night. Increase the defenses, in case there is another attack from the Eastern tartars. Remember to send someone with a report for Yu Qiaoting."

Xiao Xun gave an affirmative and went to make arrangements. Fu Shen ignored the fearfully trembling Western Tartar envoy. He went straight into the princess's tent, making a loud noise with the flap. Yan Xiaohan was just struggling to remove his makeup. Hearing the sound, he turned to look at him. Fu Shen irritably slammed his sword on the table and derisively said, "How quickly you've advanced in my absence. It's been half a year since I saw you, Lord Yan, and you've even learned to sacrifice yourself for the sake of another. I truly never would have thought it."

Yan Xiaohan sighed and said, "There was nothing else I could do, you'll have to excuse me."

Fu Shen stared as he rubbed the rouge and powder off his face and clumsily undid the ornaments in his hair. All of a sudden, he said, "The Feilong Guard acted under orders to receive the Western Tartar diplomatic marriage mission. Due to concerns of an Eastern Tartar attack, they split their forces. One force went ahead to escort the princess, while the remaining people continued along the previously fixed route to act as bait and attract the notice of the Eastern Tartars. This way, the Eastern Tartar assassins would attack the diplomatic mission, while the real princess and the divine statue would have a chance to clear the pass safely right under their noses. Such a clever plan. Who came up with it?"

Yan Xiaohan's movements paused. After a brief silence, he said with a bitter laugh, "Thank you for the compliment."

"Since you're so clever, how did you dare to act as bait yourself?" Fu Shen said softly. "With your wits, Lord Yan, it would be impossible for you not to have anticipated tonight's circumstances."

"Well, didn't you get there in time?" Yan Xiaohan said. "I got through it without any mishaps."

Fu Shen strode up to him and seized Yan Xiaohan by the collar, nearly lifting him from his chair. "Lord Yan, do you understand the position or not? Are you capable of speaking a single word of truth? How could you be certain that your letter requesting aid would come to my hand? How could you dare to guarantee that I would be able to bring people in time?

"If I had been a step too late, were you planning on making me bury you? Huh?!"

This question came crashing down and even shook the legs of the table slightly. Inside and outside the tent, there was a moment of absolute silence.

"All right, all right, don't get mad." Yan Xiaohan regarded him helplessly, squeezing Fu Shen's wrist gently with one hand. He explained good-naturedly, "I was the one who ran the risk here, but if I hadn't, the diplomatic marriage mission would still have met the Eastern Tartar assassins, and if anything had happened to the princess and the divine statue, the Feilong Guard couldn't have escaped censure."

"A slip-up by the Feilong Guard wouldn't be yours to take the blame for as a minor captain," Fu Shen followed up. "What were you fretting about?"

Yan Xiaohan didn't speak, only crooked his lips in a very forced smile.

Fu Shen's thoughts moved lightning fast. Instantly, he had a realization.

He quickly let go of Yan Xiaohan's collar and said dazedly, "Your adopted father…"

"Isn't doing so well," Yan Xiaohan said quietly. "My adopted father is getting on in age, and he is grievously troubled by rheumatism. He has already sent in a memorial retiring on account of old age. His Majesty has permitted him to return home to convalesce."

Without needing to be told in detail, Fu Shen already understood what he meant. Duan Linglong was Yan Xiaohan's greatest support in the Feilong Guard. Now that he was on the point of death and a new office holder had yet to be settled upon, Yan Xiaohan's position in the Feilong Guard had instantly turned delicate. No wonder he had been pushed out to dress up as the princess, take the most dangerous role of bait. Presumably this was the outcome of internal strife among the Feilong Guard. If he hadn't risked his life in combat, Yan Xiaohan would have borne the brunt of any minor issue during the course of the Feilong Guard's escort.

"You…"

"Don't worry. It's not like I'm a real princess. Keeping myself alive at the hands of the Eastern Tartars isn't a problem." Yan Xiaohan seemed to know what he wanted to say and instead said consolingly, "Anyway, I arranged a backup plan. Thank you for being able to come."

He was unwilling to say it outright, but both of them were well aware: henceforth, there would be no one to block the wind and rain for him. If Yan Xiaohan wanted to continue to go upward, he would have to rely on his own feet to climb one step at a time, losing teeth and swallowing blood, struggling to find a path to survival amongst the mud.

But—

In the mirror, Yan Xiaohan snuck a glance at Fu Shen, standing not far from him with his forehead tightly furrowed. All of a sudden, he said, "Strange, I can't seem to get this huadian off…"

"Hm?" Fu Shen came back to himself, his attention distracted. He bent down and considered the dark red mark at the center of his brow and said, "Let me see, is this thing glued on? Wow, there's gold leaf, too. Can you just pick it off with your fingers?"

"… I don't think so," said Yan Xiaohan.

Fu Shen laughed heartily for a spell, then said, "I'll have them bring some hot water and dab it on for you, see if we can get it off. Besides which, I never thought Lord Yan wouldn't only be a beautiful man—put on some women's finery, you still make quite the stunning lovely lady, hahaha…"

He casually stroked Yan Xiaohan's pitch-black crow's wing hair and turned to go out and find water. From his peripheral vision, Yan Xiaohan watched his figure until it had vanished from sight, then at last averted his face, cast down his eyelids, and smiled a slight smile that seemed both self-mocking and satisfied.

The road ahead was hard, but he still had a person he wanted to protect—a person who had ridden the moonlight in the dead of night to come rescue him.

With such a goal at heart, one could drink blood as though it were sweet syrup.

---

1. 1. A huadian is a type of facial ornament that can be either painted or stuck on between the eyebrows.

Extra 4 - Tryst

THE SEVENTH DAY OF THE SEVENTH MONTH IN THE FOURTH YEAR of Chengming.

The Jiangnan Road, Taizhou Prefecture.

Jiangnan had always been a rich and prosperous area. Despite the chaos of war everywhere a few years back, because of the various military commissioners' self-defense strategies, the south had been able to think only of itself. Adding in Emperor Changzhi ascending the throne in Jinling and entrenching himself in in the southeast, Jiangnan had not only avoided being touched by the conflagration; because of the exceptional preferential treatment it had received from the new court and new policies, it was even more flourishing than in the past.

Near noon, the Baiyuan Tea Shop was mostly full. There were those stopping to rest during their travels, and those having tea and listening to stories. The storyteller stood at the southeast corner of the main hall, colorfully telling a story:

"We had come to the point where the wind and rain had broken out. Everyone was resting in the fox immortal temple. But there came a rumble, and a bolt of lightning came out of the sky, shattering the clay divine statue. The late emperor was greatly astonished. At that time, the Feilong Guard representative Yan

Xiaohan was on the scene to attend him. He raised his sword and stepped forward. In a mighty voice, he called, 'What manner of creature disturbs us in the dead of night!'

"Then from behind the shrine came a gorgeous woman with light makeup, wearing plain clothes. She prostrated herself daintily before the late emperor and introduced herself: 'I was once a wild fox in the mountains…'"

A customer sitting alone by the window, having listened up to this point, unfortunately choked on half a mouthful of water and immediately began to cough violently, covering his mouth. Nearby, people heard and looked his way. They saw the man's gaunt figure, dressed in a dull gray robe without visible ornaments. From head to toe, everything about him said "short on money" in large writing.

The customer in the gray robe hurriedly finished drinking the dregs of tea in his cup and called someone over so he could settle his bill. The waiter saw that this person had ordered only two cheap side dishes, and the tea was also the most ordinary green tea, and knew at once that this was a pauper with straitened finances. So he languidly asked, "Would you like to settle your bill, sir? Three parts silver."

But the gray-robed man said, "Half a pound of shaoxing wine, a layer box with eight kinds of food, and pick out four pastries that aren't greasy. No almonds. Wrap it up and bring it to me."

The waiter's eyes opened wide. His thoughts turned a circle, and he said at once with a fawning smile, "Wait a moment, sir, I'll go prepare it. But with our small scale of business, we can't extend credit. Would it be possible…"

The man naturally understood his implication and didn't quibble over this minor offense. Unhurriedly, he took a shriveled purse from his sleeve. Under the waiter's doubtful gaze, he tipped a gold ingot out of it.

"Enough?" he asked.

The waiter was stunned. He repeatedly said, "Enough." The

gray-robed man, as easy as before, mildly instructed, "Be diligent about it."

The waiter ran off like the wind. The gray-robed man leaned carelessly against the table, listening to the storyteller's exultant recitation, but his gaze passed through the half-open window to keep an eye on the bustling street in the distance. Shortly, the waiter respectfully brought over a food box. He accepted it, avoided the curious gazes of the watching tea shop customers, and headed outward, his back slightly stooped.

Bang!

A teapot suddenly fell from the second floor. Shards flew everywhere, and tea gushed. The customers in the main hall were startled. In the silence of the hall, the gray-robed man, without making a sound, stepped aside and raised his head to look at the second floor.

The shopkeeper's first response was to rush forward to make a formal apology. "My dear customer, forgive me…"

The gray-robed man quickly raised his hand, indicating for him to keep silent.

The shopkeeper froze. Then he heard someone shouting curses on the second floor, like a mad dog, all of it filthy language unsuitable for the ear. After a few breaths, a woman with her clothes in disarray burst out of the private room upstairs and called wildly for help, but she was caught by the two strapping men who came out after her and pulled her back into the room by the hair.

Next came a few dull thuds, and the woman's voice weakened, gradually becoming inaudible.

Downstairs, there was a deathly silence. Very soon, a customer stood up to settle his bill and leave. The rest followed suit. The gray-clothed man thought this was strange. He turned to the shopkeeper. "There's about to be a death upstairs. Why doesn't the shop report it to the authorities?"

The shopkeeper, looking miserable, gave an alas and haltingly said, "Sir, you aren't aware, in Taizhou City, there are some things that can be controlled, and some things, they really can't be controlled."

The gray-robed man understood. He took a step and headed upstairs. The shopkeeper panicked, immediately reaching out to block his way. "No! You can't go up!"

The man's back had at some point limbered up. He shot him a lofty glance. That look was very cold, like an icy pool or a frozen cavern, utterly cowing. It instantly nailed the shopkeeper fast in place. The man brushed aside the obstructing arm, went right upstairs, and came up to the private room. The two strong men guarding the door had heard what was happening downstairs and disdainfully cast their gazes over him. "Mind your own business. Anyone tactful would get out of the way in a hurry. You can't afford to offend the person in there."

"Oh?" The gray-robed man raised his eyebrows and actually smiled. That smile was teasing and sly, as hard to fathom as his sudden movements. The two guards felt the world spin before their eyes. They didn't even see the moment he struck. Instantly, they felt a sharp pain in their midsections as each was kicked by that man and sent flying.

The trembling shopkeeper, as well as the customers in the main hall who had yet to leave, stood there watching two strapping men of over two hundred pounds sail up into midair, just like the unfortunate teapot from before, and drop straight down from the second floor!

When he was through, the turned-up corners of the man's lips had yet to drop. He dusted his sleeves and, speaking quietly to himself, he finished the statement he had previously left uncompleted: "Apart from my humble wife, there is no one in the world I can't afford to offend."

Having said this, he lifted his leg and kicked in the thin door of the private room.

A strong fragrance came right at him from inside the room.

The gray-robed man had been ready. He stepped aside, covering his nose and mouth with his sleeve. He looked all around, grabbed a teacup, and tossed it into the room, knocking open the tightly shut window. When the draft had blown away the remnants of the fragrance, he strolled into the private room, which was a scene of chaos.

The woman had fallen unconscious. There was only a dissolute young lordling in the room, his clothes disheveled, lying on top of the woman, thrusting rapidly, with obscene language coming out of his mouth, all his ugliness revealed. He even looked somewhat deranged. A noise as loud as that of the door being kicked in actually hadn't disturbed him.

There was a copper incense burner on the tea table with smoke gently wafting up. The gray-robed man held his nose and walked over. He removed the lid of the incense burner. Inside it remained a fingernail-sized chunk of autumn night white slowly dissolving. He splashed half a cup of leftover tea onto it to douse the rest of the flames, then went around the table and pushed the frenzied lordling aside with his foot. He poured some cold tea on him from a pot. "Wake up."

The lordling moaned and groaned, struggling interminably. Sadly, the gray-robed man's foot was on his chest, and he was extremely weak. He could only flail his limbs like a turtle that had been flipped onto its back. Seeing this, the gray-robed man knew he wouldn't come to his senses in a hurry. His eyes turned; he thought up a cheap trick.

Not long after, all of Taizhou City turned out in full force. In a grand occasion comparable to the Lantern Festival, countless people came when they heard the news, crowding in front of the Baiyuan Tea Shop to watch the fun. They saw the window of a certain private room on the second floor wide open, and a man as skinny as a bean pole hanging out, his hands tied, suspended naked in midair. But he was neither humiliated nor struggling. Rather, he was randomly calling out filthy language unfit to be heard, even announcing the name of his own family. Calling out to a little lady who might have been anywhere, he boasted that he was the young master of the Taizhou prefect's family, and if she only consented to him, he guaranteed that she would enjoy inexhaustible glory and wealth in the future.

The prefect took bribes and bent the law. His family was bossy and arrogant. This was no secret among the people of Taizhou, it was just that no one had dared in broad daylight under the blue sky to make irresponsible remarks about that "blue sky." But today's scene was like a thunderclap right to the ear, a flash of lightning cleaving the night. It ignited the long-accumulated grievances of the people.

This matter quickly reached the ears of Taizhou's prefect, Huang Ruofei. After hanging for two hours, Young Master Huang was at last rescued by the late-coming bailiffs. Ridiculous to say, as soon as Young Master Huang was brought down, he collapsed into a faint. A doctor was called to examine him, and it turned out that the cause of his illness wasn't shock or a chill, it was that overuse of drugs had caused excessive discharge, leading to renal weakness.

The lead bailiff ferreted out the shopkeeper and loudly interrogated him about who had committed this crime. But before he could move on to threats of torture, the shopkeeper, the waiters, and a crowd of spectating teashop customers spoke with one voice: "The Blessed Travelers Inn!"

The bailiff was bewildered. "What?"

The shopkeeper, trembling, said, "Before he left, he said that if officials came to arrest him, they were asked to go to the Blessed Travelers Inn. He is w-waiting there for you, sirs."

The bailiffs exchanged blank looks. It wasn't that they had never seen people turn themselves in, but they had never seen someone commit a crime, then leave a message for the authorities in this way—as if he weren't waiting for them to come arrest him but glorifying his own position, asking them to come invite him to the law courts.

"Let's go," the lead bailiff said with a wave of the hand, gritting his teeth. "To the Blessed Travelers Inn!"

A big team of men and horses charged mightily toward the

Blessed Travelers Inn two streets away, with a big crowd of gawking people following after them. It was simply a farce. At the inn, the gray-robed man was indeed as good as his word. He really was in the main hall. He didn't say anything extra, and he didn't fight. He urbanely went with them.

It was getting toward evening. Under normal circumstances, the prefecture's office would have been closed by now, but tonight, it was all lit up. The bailiffs expended a great deal of effort to disperse the gathered people. Huang Ruofei walked out of the rear hall with his face grim. He ordered the main doors closed, took his seat at the judge's desk, knocked heavily with his judge's block. He started off with a display of severity. "Who is the accused? Why does he not kneel upon seeing me?!"

The gray-robed man standing trial stood in the hall with his hands behind his back. Now he awarded Prefect Huang a direct look. Had the tea shop's keeper been present, perhaps he would have cried out in surprise. Using some unknown means, his face no longer had the lean and waxen look of a person weathered by time. His always slightly stooped shoulders had stretched out. From his features, it seemed as if clumsy makeup had been washed away, revealing his original faultless handsomeness. He was imposing and stern, and even stood nearly a head taller than Lord Huang in his black felt cap and official's robe.

"Lord Prefect," he said, smiling, "you will know later that I do not kneel for your own good."

While Huang Ruofei was lax in his work, he wasn't an idiot. A commoner wouldn't have dared to speak to him like this. This person had evidently come to make trouble for him. But who the hell knew whether this scoundrel was actually hiding his light or pretending to be more important than he was?

Thousands of thoughts instantly flitted through his mind. At last, he chose to dodge. Calmly, he said, "And just who are you, Your Excellency? I hope that you will indicate it clearly."

"There is no need for Your Honor to be in a hurry to ask," the gray-robed man said. "There are a few questions on which I would like to seek Your Honor's instruction. If you can answer, then naturally you will know who I am."

Huang Ruofei's heart trembled. He suddenly had a bad feeling.

"If I might be permitted to ask, Lord Huang, do you know the punishment for embezzling and taking bribes, for perverting the law and bending decisions?

"Do you know the punishment for conniving at the violence and quarreling of your servants, of protecting your only son in the evil conduct of rape and murder?

"Do you know the punishment for colluding with bandits and falsely claiming credit?

"Do you know the punishment for embezzling water control money, tax money, money made in the illegal trade of tea and salt, in countless amounts?

"The court's explicit order bans autumn night white, and only in Taizhou Prefecture under your jurisdiction are thousands of ounces smuggled at every turn, bringing in hundreds of thousands in profit, afflicting Jiangnan and Huainan. What punishment does that merit?"

A clatter. The judge's block rolled off the table. But no one dared to come forward to lift it. Huang Ruofei's face was ashen. Trembling, he pointed at him, and nearly spat out a mouthful of blood on the spot. "... Who the hell are you?!"

"I am the person sent by the court to pluck the official's cap off your head."

The gray-robed man took an ivory token from his sleeve and regarded him coldly. "My surname is Yan, currently holding the post of the Tianfu Army's representative. On the orders of the empress dowager and His Majesty, I am overseeing the investigation into the illegal trade of autumn night white in Taizhou Prefecture."

The Tianfu Army's representative... Yan Xiaohan!

The Feilong Guard that had once run rampant through the capital, now a minister of high standing and great authority as willed by the emperor. It was said that he came in and out of the palace's prohibited areas as if they were his own home, with nothing to impede him. Even the Duke of Jing had to yield to him somewhat.

While Yan Xiaohan did not set fire to homes, did not murder or plunder, did not seize men's wives and daughters, the cases handled by the Feilong Guard had all been major cases in which the blade would fall as soon as raised, in which blood would flow like a river. Because of this, he was often not known of by common people, but had achieved extreme notoriety in official circles, making people respect and fear him, wishing that they could avoid ever having anything to do with him.

Huang Ruofei clutched his chest, breathing heavily. The bailiffs, petty officials, aids, and others present were all silent as cicadas in winter. In unison, they knelt.

No one had ever thought that Young Master Huang would bring this King of the Underworld to the door!

Yan Xiaohan strolled up in front of Huang Ruofei. His speech was not without derision. "Lord Huang, if not for the recommendation of Young Master Huang, you and I would not have met so soon."

When forced to an impasse, a person would perhaps kneel and acknowledge his loss, and maybe he would throw caution to the wind and attempt a desperate struggle. Had Huang Ruofei not been bold and ruthless, he wouldn't have been capable of deceiving his superiors and deluding his subordinates like this. Eyes fixed on Yan Xiaohan, standing in the hall alone, he thought of something, and suddenly began to laugh grimly. "Since Lord Yan has come to Taizhou, do not be in a hurry to leave. Allow me to fulfill my duties as host to the fullest—"

Yan Xiaohan's wrist moved slightly. Under cover of his sleeve, a dagger slid into his palm.

Huang Ruofei shouted: "Men! Take him!"

Suddenly, the sound of urgent hoofbeats came from outside. It sounded as though there were many people. Yan Xiaohan suddenly met Huang Ruofei's grim and bitter gaze. His heart immediately lurched. The reason he had changed his appearance and come incognito in plain clothes, covering his tracks, rather than openly inspecting Jiangnan, was that he was afraid of startling that viper Huang Ruofei.

Huang Ruofei had married one of his children to a child of He Qi, Jiangnan's military commissioner. Since Emperor Changzhi's new policy, the power and influence of the military commissioners had grown by the day, especially in the south. Yan Xiaohan had schemed to catch Huang Ruofei unprepared, to avoid him colluding with He Qi, acting in desperation like a trapped animal. But today's encounter with Young Master Huang at the tea shop, tricking Huang Ruofei into bringing him to the prefecture office, was entirely the conception of a moment. How could Huang Ruofei have been aware in advance, and how had he found reinforcements at this critical juncture?

The whinnies of horses were close to his ears. Yan Xiaohan didn't have time to think much. He leapt and instantly flitted beside Huang Ruofei. The dagger in his hand, like a viper's tongue, lightly touched the side of Prefect Huang's neck.

The next moment, the main gate of Tainzhou's prefecture office were opened from outside.

"No one move!"

"Who dares to act blindly?!"

Two voices spoke at once. A white-socked black horse entered without resistance, instantly speeding in front of the hall, followed closely by a team of fully armored warriors, who quickly surrounded the law court.

Only the leader wasn't wearing armor, but when he reined in his horse and stopped, no one dared to think of resisting again.

Everyone present, including Huang Ruofei and Yan Xiaohan, who had seized Huang Ruofei, was dumbfounded.

"Jingyuan?" he whispered.

"It would appear I have come just in time." Fu Shen nodded slightly to the dumbfounded Huang Ruofei. Urbanely, he said, "I heard that Prefect Huang was unwilling to have his hands tied and await capture. It was on my way, so I came to help Lord Huang along. Right, as for the subordinate you sent with a letter to He Qi, I've brought him back, returning him to his rightful owner. No need to thank me."

Huang Ruofei was speechless.

What was the Duke of Jing doing here, too?!

"Men, arrest Huang Ruofei and all his accomplices. Take them into custody to await trial." Fu Shen made a gesture at the guard behind him and jumped off his horse. The guard following him immediately came forward to press Huang Ruofei to the ground and tie his hands behind his back. Fu Shen, meanwhile, walked toward Yan Xiaohan. With a slight smile, he extended a hand to him. "All right, Lord Yan, put down the weapon."

Yan Xiaohan put the dagger back into his sleeve, and Fu Shen led him out from behind the desk by the hand. While Yan Xiaohan did his best to control himself, the corners of his mouth still turned irresistibly up. He cast a sidelong glance at the Duke of Jing. "'On my way?'"

Fu Shen put a hand on his shoulder, leaned over, and laughed. "I was in a hurry to see you. I went out of my way to pick up my wife."

The two of them had left the capital together. Yan Xiaohan had gone under orders to investigate Huang Ruofei's corruption, while Fu Shen ought right now to have been at Taizhou's Jinghai military barracks, only arriving somewhat later. Unexpectedly, when Yan Xiaohan had made a last-moment plan of action, as soon as he left the inn, Fu Shen arrived immediately after. He had come just in time, ultimately succeeding in putting on a performance of "the mantis stalks the cicada, not knowing that the oriole is behind."

The two of them left the prefecture office hand-in-hand. A carriage was waiting outside the gate. At first, Yan Xiaohan was bewildered. Then, seeing Fu Shen betray no surprise, he got in without a word of demur. As soon as the carriage curtain fell, the mighty Duke of Jing was held down and kissed. Affection between the two of them had become natural, but this time it was a little different. The narrow carriage soon warmed into a steamer. Fu Shen undid the strip of cloth Yan Xiaohan was using to keep his bun in place and impatiently pulled at his black hair, which slid like flowing water.

Yan Xiaohan said indistinctly, "Hm?"

"Only a feeling." Fu Shen tucked a lock of hair behind his ear. "Lord Yan, you are unusually clingy today."

Yan Xiaohan's arms tightly encircled Fu Shen, unwilling to let go no matter what. With justice on his side, he said, "While investigating today, I accidentally got dosed with autumn night white. I'm having an attack. What can I do?"

Fu Shen laughed in spite of himself. "This again? I don't have a second back for you to snap."

Yan Xiaohan gently sucked at the side of his neck, one hand naughtily slipping into his clothes. "I think this back of yours is just right, general…"

Fooling around was one thing, but there wasn't even room in the carriage to turn around. Yan Xiaohan naturally couldn't put Fu Shen to the trouble in this narrow space, and the road was bumpy; they couldn't do anything. It had been days since the two of them had seen each other. They seized this fleeting opportunity to be idle and cozy up. It seemed like a kind of ritual of supporting each other with all they had.

When the carriage stopped, Yan Xiaohan lifted the curtain and saw right in front of him the reflections of lanterns in water. The night wind was cool, the stars banded the sky, the colorful lanterns at the riverside bobbed in the water. Pleasure boats came and went along the river. The lingering strains of strings and woodwinds curled upward. It was a scene of rare bustle and prosperity.

"This…"

"Have you been so busy you forgot the date?" Fu Shen made an inviting gesture and led him to board a pleasure boat moored at the shore. The boatman said, "Gentlemen, take your seats." His pole touched down, and the little boat drifted to the center of the river. Yan Xiaohan sat inside the boat. He glanced over the carefully prepared tea, fruit, and pastries on the table. In spite of himself, he laughed softly. He took Fu Shen's hand. "I didn't forget. How could I forget?"

When he had bought the food and drinks at the tea shop, he had been figuring that Fu Shen would only reach Taizhou City very late. While they couldn't raise their wine cups and wander together, at least they would be in time for the tail end of Qixi. But Fu Shen's actions were always outside his expectations.

The autumn night was clear, the crescent moon curved. The resplendent river of the heavens lay across the night sky. As the pleasure boat moved to the center of the river, Fu Shen raised his head to watch the sky. Yan Xiaohan lay with his head pillowed in his lap, mind wandering. After a while, Fu Shen suddenly looked down and covered his eyes. "Why are you staring at me instead of staring at the stars?"

Through the gaps between his fingers, Yan Xiaohan saw the raised corners of his lips. He candidly said, "You're handsome."

There was a warm touch on his forehead, light as a dragonfly skimming the water. With a smile in his voice, Fu Shen said into his ear, "More handsome than you?"

Yan Xiaohan was at a loss for words, struck dumb by his sweet words. Fu Shen still wouldn't behave. He reached out and caressed the base of his ear. "Hey, you're blushing. You're still so bad at taking praise."

As they spoke, the sound of the pipa came over the water. Strings and woodwinds were clear and melodious. Perhaps because the two boats were close, the singing that came to them on the night wind was unusually clear, sweet and melodious. The song was to the tune of "Magpie Bridge Immortal."

The wutong's first leaves appear, the osmanthus shoots have just emerged, the lotuses in the pool are ever so slightly wilted.

*In the pleasure house, a girl threads a needle, and the moon appears
like a platter of jade, its light trickling down.
Spiders spin busily but magpies loiter, the cowherd is weary and the
weaver-girl tired, thinking only of their long-held tryst.
A year has passed in the human world, but in the heavens, only a
night has gone.* [1]

The lyrics were a little girl's lyrics, but hearing them now,
they were peculiarly touching.

Yan Xiaohan suddenly remembered some past events that he
did not like to bring up. It was only after many years of partings
that he and Fu Shen had won themselves this night of worldly
desires. He wasn't a sentimental person given to wallowing in the
past, but while the past was gone, some secret agonies were still
buried deep in his memories. Though time had smoothed the
wounds, he still knew perfectly well where they were.

When a person had once felt bone-deep pain, it was hard to
forget, no matter how carefree he might be.

He opened his mouth, about to speak, but suddenly Fu Shen
stuck an icy candy into his mouth. Sweetness and the scent of
osmanthus spread over his lips and teeth—it was one of those
osmanthus candies he was always thinking of.

Strange to say, when Yan Xiaohan had been alone in Jinling,
he had found all the osmanthus candy in Jiangnan, but not one
had had the flavor he had wanted; but now in the one Fu Shen
had given him, plainly bought casually by the road, he tasted
long absent but familiar sweetness.

"Is it sweet?" Fu Shen asked.

"Yes." Yan Xiaohan caught his hand and laced their finger
together. "But not as sweet as you."

Fu Shen bent his head and kissed his lips. He laughed. The
laughter flitted over the hair at his temples and was carried away
by the breeze on the river, floating with the water toward the
depth of the starry night.

The sorrow of separation in this world was so painful, but

there were always those who would cross the vast river of stars, race over vast expanses of mountains and river, just for a tiny drop of sweetness.

It does not matter that fleeting time is always slyly substituting, that when you look back, the present moment will have become the past.

In this moment, it is the pleasant night on which the two stars meet, a tryst as perfect as a dream.

---

1. "The Wutong's First Leaves Appear," to the tune of "Magpie Bridge Immortal," by Yan Rui, a poet and prostitute of the Southern Song Dynasty.

Extra 5 - Final Reunion

Zero

Somber countryside, half the sky reflecting red from bloodshed. Wind rustled the grass, revealing the broken arrows and corpses all over the ground. He was carried on the bloody wind, lightly flitting over the vast grasslands beyond the Wall, coming to that man's side.

An armor-piercing arrow stuck out of his chest, the head of the arrow buried deep in his heart. Blood had dyed the white collar beneath his armor red. His chest was only weakly rising and falling. He didn't have long to live.

His visage was concealed under his helmet and the blood and grime. Because he was over forty and spent much of his time at the border, signs of age marked his face, and his temples were grizzled, but from the deep lines of his features, his appearance in his prime could still be discerned.

He knelt beside that man, wanting to wipe away the stains on his face, but the hand he extended, like empty air, passed right through his body—only then did he remember that he was a wandering ghost outside the world, dead for he didn't know how long.

367

The gravely injured, dying man seemed to sense something. His eyes opened slightly. His pupils reflected the sky that seemed dyed with blood, and also held a scarcely visible figure.

When the man saw him, he was stunned, as if he didn't dare to believe it. Then he was relieved. His lips even curved into what might have been called a gentle arc. He whispered, "At last I see you again...

"Do you still..." His unfocused pupils were fixed on that wraithlike man. His voice was extremely soft, almost a mumble. "... recognize me?"

He didn't know what to say, so he raised a hand to gently "touch" his cheek.

The touch was plainly illusory, but an icy breeze seemed to waft over his temple. Laboriously, the man raised a hand and hollowly held the image hanging in midair, as if clutching his final obsession before death. "We've been apart seven years... Zhongyan, forgive me, I've made you wait again."

He shook his head and opened his mouth to say something, but he didn't make a sound. From the movements of his lips, it was: "Don't die."

The man laughed, but the light in his eyes was gradually dimming. "I couldn't protect you, and I couldn't protect the northern frontier. Living would be worthless. There's nothing to regret if I die.

"When we meet in the underworld, don't disdain me for being useless. In the future, I will no longer be a prince, only devote myself to loving you... all right?"

Black clouds blew toward them from the distant horizon. Raindrops fell, passing through his insubstantial, transparent body and falling on that man's face, like a drizzle of icy tears, washing away the blood and dirt on his face.

The hand went limp and dropped, softly falling at his side.

"Don't die..." At last he heard himself force a hoarse sound from his throat. "Don't die, A-Feng..."

ONE

"A-Feng…"

"Awake? Someone next to him stood up and loudly said, "Call a doctor here!"

Fu Tingxin was pulled back to the land of the living by pain. He raised his eyelids with difficulty. White walls and lamplight, the faint odor of disinfectant, and a profusion of voices rapidly engulfed his senses. All at once, he stepped out of dreams and into the mortal world, and was instantly so surrounded by noise that he wanted to be unconscious again.

He blinked, rapidly adjusting to the lights and images in his line of sight. Sensation began to return to all parts of his body. He tried to bend his index finger, gradually recovering control over his body. At the same time, he began taking notice of the things and people around him—all these movements and reactions seemed to be natural and practiced, as if they were an instinct honed over many years and carved into his bones.

The next moment, a tall young man opened the door and strode into the hospital room, followed by a series of trotting doctors and nurses. Hearing movement, Fu Tingxin abruptly looked up and unexpectedly met his eyes.

Though he was much younger, and his hairstyle and clothing were all different, he still couldn't fail to recognize him. This was a visage that had only appeared in his dreams.

The illusory patter of rain came once again to his ears. The accompanying despair and pain were so real, like water bursting its banks and instantly rising above his head, the flood of it so powerful that Fu Tingxin almost forgot how to breathe. His emotions wavered sharply, and the world spun before his eyes. The monitoring devices at the head of the bed immediately beeped in warning. The man had been nailed in place by his look. Now the sound called back his soul. There was no time to think carefully over his loss of self-possession just now. He hurriedly charged over to the hospital bed. "What's wrong?"

Before he could finish speaking, Fu Tingxin suddenly looked up, cold sweat sheeting off him, and grabbed his hand.

The IV needle and Band-Aid were torn off and went flying together, causing a spatter of tiny bloodstains that fell like plum blossom petals on the white sheet. But Fu Tingxin seemed not to feel the pain. He clutched his hand, the veins on the back of his hand popping up. Blood flowed to his cuff, but he, undaunted, continued trying to sit up in bed. "A-Feng…"

A doctor quickly said, "Hold him down! Don't let him flail around!"

The man seemed lean and lanky, but he was very strong. Hearing the doctor, he quickly pressed Fu Tingxin back into bed. Only his movements weren't gentle. When he bent down and leaned close, Fu Tingxin saw his bloodshot eyes behind the lenses of his glasses. That gaze was full of anger, just like the great strength holding down his shoulders. It even seemed sinister.

Gritting his teeth, he quietly asked, "Who are you calling for?"

Fu Tingxin was stupefied by his question.

Perhaps because he was angry, the man's voice was trembling. Fu Tingxin inexplicably thought that he was about to cry at any moment.

"Who is 'A-Feng?' Do you know that you nearly died? And you won't stop going on about him!"

TWO

After a period of busy confusion, the hospital room was at last restored to tranquility.

Fu Tingxin lay ramrod straight on the hospital bed with an IV drip in his arm, bandages around his head, and a cast on his leg. He looked wretched, and he was turning his head disobediently to sneak a glance at his figure standing at the window. Groaning, he said, "Don't stand there like you're being punished. Are you still angry? I have amnesia and everything…"

"You—" The man was tongue-tied from anger. As soon as he turned and met his not-quite-smiling gaze, his bristling fur softened. After a long hesitation, he finally said, "I'm not angry."

"Right, right, you're not angry," said Fu Tingxin. "Then aren't you getting tired of standing there? Sit down and rest, have some water. Don't be angry."

"…"

Fu Tingxin had been injured in an explosion and sustained a concussion. He had only woken up after three days in a coma. While examining him earlier, the doctor had discovered that there was a problem with his memory. He absolutely couldn't remember any of the past, or his own friends and family, even his own identity. This was commonly known as "amnesia."

But unlike other people, he said that while in a coma, he had had a dream. In the dream, he was a general called Fu Tingxin. After dying on the battlefield, his spirit had roamed the grasslands beyond the Wall for seven years. Then there was another war on the grasslands. The country he belonged to was defeated, and the commander-in-chief of its forces—the "A-Feng" he kept calling for—had his chest pierced by an enemy arrow. On the point of death, he had seen Fu Tingxin.

"The person I saw in my dream was the third son of the emperor. His title was 'Prince Su,' surname 'Sun,' given name 'Luo.' When his mother was pregnant with him, she saw the Buddha tie a necklace of jade and pearl around his neck, so she chose the 'luo' character from 'jade and pearl necklace' for his name. To ask for the Buddha's protection, she also gave him a baby name, 'A-Feng,' as a tribute." Fu Tingxin, staring at him, asked, "And you… friend, may I ask your name?"

Sun Luo was briefly silent.

"Sun Luo. The 'Luo' from 'jade and pearl necklace.'" He gave a dry cough. In a clumsy attempt at denial, he added, "I don't have a nickname."

"All right, then you don't have a nickname. Why did you have to squeeze me so hard?" Fu Tingxin recalled the last words of the person in the dream and said with a fake smile, "From how you're fretting, if I didn't know better, I'd have thought I'd been cheating on you…"

Sun Luo very much wanted to rush forward and put a hand over his mouth. "You have amnesia. Why do you still have so much to say?!"

Fu Tingxin was just bored and teasing him for fun. But he had just woken up, and his energy was low. A few sentences exhausted his mental vitality. As he spoke, his upper and lower eyelids fought, and his voice weakened. "You sit there, I'm going to sleep for a little bit."

"Okay." Sun Luo went to close the door to the hospital room and sat in the chair beside the bed, even pulled the cover up for him. "Sleep, I'll keep an eye on your IV."

The better part of Fu Tingxin's consciousness had already sunk into chaos, but for some reason, in the midst of his drowsy haze, he suddenly said, indistinct and quiet, "Don't leave."

It was like a heavy hammer slamming against some soft place in his heart. Sun Luo stared at his fast asleep, worn-out face, zoning out for a long time, then at last answered him.

"I'm not leaving." He bent his head and gently kissed the bruised needle mark on Fu Tingxin's right arm. Quietly and solemnly, he said, "In the future, I won't leave again."

THREE

Fu Tingxin slept for several days without regard for night and day. During this time, Sun Luo stayed by his side. When he was awake, he narrated the background of the Fu family to him, and their own past, using the times when Fu Tingxin was asleep to take care of all his own work. Not taking a step from his side for so many days, sleeping without taking off his clothes—Fu Tingxin wasn't stupid. In the life he had lived in his dream, he and "His Highness Prince Su" had only been short the status of husband and wife. He was very well aware of Sun Luo's behavior when he liked a person.

Such tender care, undertaking all this without complaint. He had to be in love with him. He hadn't run away.

According to what Sun Luo said, the Sun and Fu families had a long-established friendship. The Suns were in politics, the Fus in the military. The two of them had grown up together, were model childhood friends who could have worn the same pair of pants. They had loved each other dearly from kindergarten all the way to high school. After graduating high school, Sun Luo had tested into a top domestic university, while Fu Tingxin had gone to join the army.

The Sun family was a big clan, with fierce infighting among its factions. Sun Luo had no plans to go into politics and had gone the path of business. He had started his own business in university. After graduation, his company had joined his uncle's Taihe Conglomerate, and he had become a board member of the conglomerate. Fu Tingxin, meanwhile, three years after joining the army, had been chosen to enter a certain special brigade in the northwest region.

A few days ago, there had been sudden peril while the team was abroad conducting a secret mission. Fu Tingxin had been caught in an explosion. He had been seriously injured and fallen into a coma, then was urgently sent back to the country for treatment. When Sun Luo heard the news from his family, he nearly went out of his mind with worry. He tossed aside his work and traveled through the night to the northwest region, and, concerned that the medical standards there wouldn't be good, he called in a connection to have him transferred to an army hospital in the capital. As long as Fu Tingxin was comatose, he stayed in the hospital.

But he hadn't expected that when Fu Tingxin survived by the skin of his teeth and returned to the human world, he would have forgotten him.

Actually, you couldn't have called it forgetting. He could

recognize Sun Luo's face, could say his name, but Sun Luo didn't have the nickname "A-Feng." After all, Fu Tingxin's reactions while comatose had left him with a grudge. The attachment formed to a person in a dream couldn't be applied to him, an outsider.

Those years full of childishness and youth had all been stolen, fruitlessly leaving behind two grown men weathered by life, separated by a big blank space, looking at each other with nothing to say to each other.

FOUR

That evening, two special visitors came to the hospital. Sun Luo went out to take a phone call and waited at the elevator door for a while. It wasn't long before he saw a little sprout not even as tall as his legs were long jump out of the elevator and affectionately cry, "Uncle Sun!"

"Hey." Sun Luo bent down and picked him up. He held him in his arms and weighed him, then put on a rare smile. "You've gotten taller, and you're heavier than before."

He looked down at the child who came out afterward. He hadn't expected him to come as well. When their eyes met, the child greeted him very calmly. "Third Uncle."

Sun Luo was an elder. Even if he had misgivings, he couldn't show them on his face, so he nodded to him and said to the driver who followed after, "I'll take the children over."

The driver was an old man from the Fu family and naturally recognized Sun Luo. He smiled reservedly at him and conscientiously went to wait in the corridor. Carrying one child and leading the other by the hand, Sun Luo returned to the hospital room. Fu Tingxin was just leaning against the headboard, solving a Rubik's cube. He was used to using guns. His hands were extremely swift, the long, slender fingers flying, almost leaving a blur. The little sprout Sun Luo was holding saw him and immedi-

ately started squirming to get down. He cried out crisply,
"Second Uncle!"

"Hey, who's here?" Fu Tingxin dropped the Rubik's cube and
smilingly opened his arms, ready to hug him.

But Sun Luo gently put the child beside him and instructed,
"Careful, don't jar your injuries."

"Second Uncle, my dad says you have amnesia," the little
sprout said, his black grape-like eyes round and glistening as he
looked at him. "Do you not know who I am?"

Though Fu Tingxin couldn't remember the past, in his
dream, he had seen this child grow up. He hadn't thought that
this little thing would know what "amnesia" was. All smiles, he
said, "How could I not know who you are? Second Uncle could
forget anyone, but I still couldn't forget our Xiao Shen."

But when Fu Shen heard this, he didn't display any happiness. Instead, his eyebrows drooped, and he sighed, seeming very
troubled.

"What is it, baby?" said Fu Tingxin.

Tears appeared in Fu Shen's eyes. He turned his head and
said, hurt, to the child standing at the foot of the bed, "Gege, my
Second Uncle really does have amnesia."

Fu Tingxin exchanged a dismayed look with Sun Luo.

The other child quickly walked over, took a handkerchief
from his pocket, and wiped Fu Shen's face, very properly saying
in consolation, "He knows who you are. Didn't he call you Xiao
Shen?"

Glumly, Fu Shen said, "But he wasn't like this before. He
always called me 'dolt.'"

Fu Tingxin was silent.

Sun Luo, shaking, covered his mouth and turned away.

Fu Tingxin hadn't had much contact with this nephew of his.
He had only spent half a month joining him in wild games the
year before last on a visit home. At the time, there hadn't been
this other child with him yet. Fu Shen had been very close to

him. To tease him, Fu Tingxin had often called him "dolt." Unexpectedly, this little sprout still remembered it to this day.

Sighing with emotion, Fu Tingxin said, "I see I wasn't wrong about you…"

The other child was a little older than Fu Shen, his future handsome features already distinguishable from the childish face, but he was extremely gentle and patient with their dolt. Holding his little hand, he said, "Dolt doesn't sound nice. Xiao Shen sounds nice."

Fu Shen reciprocated. Softly, he said, "Your name also sounds nice."

Fu Tingxin was unbearably entertained by the two of them. Smiling, he asked Sun Luo, "Whose child is this?"

Sun Luo's gaze flickered undetectably over that child. As if nothing were the matter, he said, "He's my nephew. His name is Yan Xiaohan. He attends the same elementary school as Xiao Shen."

As soon as Fu Tingxin heard the surname, he knew there was some story behind this and tactfully didn't say anything. He teased the two children a while longer, saw that it was getting late, then urged Sun Luo to send the two of them back.

Sun Luo led one with each hand and took them downstairs. But when he returned to the hospital room, he saw Fu Tingxin staring out the window at the setting sun, lost in thought.

During his illness, he had lost a lot of weight. Only a thin layer of skin and flesh remained wrapping his bones. But the lines of his face seemed to have been carved with a knife, increasingly sharp and proud.

This appearance belonged to a completely different person from the teenager in Sun Luo's memories.

He stood amid the twilight, for the first time in his life truly comprehending the meaning of "regret."

He didn't know whether Fu Tingxin's lost memories could be recovered, but the time he had missed out on because of a momentary wrong decision could never be recovered.

Fu Tingxin's ears were very sharp. Though he was lost in thought, he quickly noticed Sun Luo. He turned in his hospital bed. "Have you sent them off? Come over here and rest."

Sun Luo shut the door and sat down at the bedside. "Yan Xiaohan is my second brother's illegitimate child. His mother's position is very complicated. I couldn't explain it in a hurry. His mother died last year, and that was when my second brother took him in. He didn't change his surname. I figure he isn't planning on having him inherit family property in the future. If you think he…"

"I think he's pretty nice," Fu Tingxin interrupted him and casually said, "Fu Shen is still so young. He's in no rush to make connections. He can play with anyone he likes. Don't overthink it."

"Right," said Sun Luo.

Fu Tingxin glanced at him, then said, "And it's pretty nice to have a childhood friend grow up with you. See how long I've been in the hospital, and you've been doing all the running around for me. Where are my own brothers?"

The lenses of his glasses were a little reflective. They screened his eyes. But Fu Tingxin clearly sensed that there was a moment when Sun Luo dodged.

No.

Sun Luo dropped his eyelids, avoiding his gaze. In his heart, he silently said, *We aren't childhood friends, and I've never taken you for a mere 'brother.'*

FIVE

Between his concussion and injured leg, Fu Tingxin spent three months in the hospital before obtaining permission to be discharged. Unfortunately, his amnesia had yet to be cured. Naturally he also couldn't remain in the army. Before he left the hospital, his superior came to visit him. The two of them spent a morning talking in the hospital room, and afterward Fu Tingxin had Sun Luo submit his application to be discharged from the army, entirely shedding his uniform.

He was taken back by Sun Luo to the latter's apartment. No one in the Fu family demonstrated any surprise or resistance about this. Fu Tingxin languidly lay on the soft, clean double bed in the guest bedroom, listening to Sun Luo say: "Your injuries still need some time to heal. It's not safe for you to live alone. If you stay here, it will be convenient for me to take care of you. Don't be a stranger."

Fu Tingxin nodded while inwardly laughing: "Fine, go on pretending, I'll see how long you can keep it up."

Fu Tingxin had only lost his memories, not his intellect. He had seen all of Sun Luo's attentiveness. Most likely this person did have designs on him. But according to Sun Luo's description, the two of them were undiluted, 24 karat gold good brothers, with harmonious fraternal love between them, without the slightest bit of overstepping.

Fu Tingxin had nearly believed that he was secretly in love with him and didn't dare to say it, but on the day he'd chatted with the brigade captain, he had happened to hear the captain mention that before, while he was serving in the army, in order to avoid receiving special treatment, he hadn't called his family for many years, or sent them letters. Fu Tingxin thought this was a little strange. After following up a little, he learned that while in the army, he had never mentioned his family background, and he had certainly never brought up his "good brother" Sun Luo to anyone.

He kept an eye out, and when his older brother Fu Tingzhong came to visit, he questioned him closely and finally found out that he had cut off contact with Sun Luo after joining the army. His family thought at the time that the two of them had broken off all relations.

This didn't make sense. Sun Luo acted like he owed him from a past lifetime. If there had been no conflict between the two of them, he couldn't have withstood not having contact with Fu Tingxin for many years.

Separated seven years, with no news passing between them, but he could arrive in the northwest immediately upon learning that Fu Tingxin had been wounded; you couldn't say that this devotion wasn't profound. Under these circumstances, how could the two of them have broken up? If not for this unexpected disaster, would Sun Luo never have contacted him while he was serving in the army?

Fu Tingxin's mind was full of ideas. He concocted a handful of melodramatic plots for himself, remembered various experiences from his dream, and spent a good while conjecturing in confusion, until Sun Luo came to knock on his door and tell him to come eat. Then he cleaned up his thoughts and raised his voice: "Come in."

Sun Luo opened the door and came in. He was dressed in the simplest white shirt and suit pants, extremely tall and upright, extremely handsome. He didn't wear glasses at home. Without obstruction, his features instantly became sharp. But the gaze that fell on Fu Tingxin was very gentle. "Get up. The weather is nice today, how about I take you downstairs for a walk after dinner?"

Hearing him talk like he was humoring a child, Fu Tingxin felt inclined to playfulness. He reached out his arms and whined, "I can't get up."

A little ridiculously, Sun Luo walked over and pulled him out of bed. Fu Tingxin raised his upper body, swaying, in the direction of his pull. As soon as Sun Luo loosened his grip, he bonelessly slid back down onto the pillow.

Fu Tingxin was deliberately acting shameless. Sun Luo indulgently pulled him up again. This time, before Fu Tingxin could fall, he pulled him into his arms, encircling his back so he couldn't get away, but unexpectedly, Fu Tingxin, like a giant panda that had finally latched onto its zookeeper's leg, threw himself at him with a flail and wouldn't get up no matter what.

The two of them ended up tangled together. Finally, Sun Luo simply carried him out over his shoulder and only put him down at the top of the stairs—because there was a housekeeper downstairs.

The housekeeper actually hadn't noticed the two of them fooling around upstairs, only told Sun Luo while laying out the food, "Sir, your phone just rang. I think you have a call."

Fu Tingxin sat at the table drinking soup, occasionally sneaking glances from the corner of his eye at Sun Luo, taking a phone call by the window. Hearing him use a completely different cold tone to speak to the person at the other end, a previously unthought-of guess emerged in his mind.

Was it possible that Sun Luo thought he was homophobic, and that was why he didn't dare to contact him, and even when he had amnesia only dared to tell him that they were childhood friends?

Could it be that... he had already confessed his feelings before Fu Tingxin had lost his memories?

So was it too late for him to show Sun Luo a one-hundred-eighty-degree turnaround?

SIX

By August, Fu Tingxin's wounds were mostly healed. He was so idle staying home that mushrooms were about to start growing on him. Seeing how bored he was, and that he couldn't remember anything, Sun Luo was worried that being cooped up would make him sick. It just happened that the conglomerate was holding a charity banquet at the end of the month. The chairman was out of the country this year and had asked him to deliver a speech in his stead. Sun Luo thought that Fu Tingxin was bored anyway. Therefore, he painstakingly dressed him up and took him to the banquet to watch the fun.

Fu Tingxin was a military man. Even having lost his memory, the habits he had developed during the course of many years in the army hadn't changed. Wearing a high-fashion suit, his bearing was compelling. He seemed more like the boss than Sun Luo. When they walked in shoulder to shoulder, they attracted quite a few gazes. After they had gone by, the guests gathered in clutches of two or three to make private guesses about his identity.

Apart from being one of the Taihe Conglomerate's board members, Sun Luo also had the enormous Sun family standing behind him. Though he had done all he could to be low-key, it was still hard to avoid people determined to make connections. He made his way haltingly. From time to time, a person jumped up to exchange greetings with him. Fu Tingxin waited for him very patiently. Seeing Sun Luo frown with slight impatience, he put a hand on his shoulder and quietly cajoled, "Don't get mad, what do you want to eat? Can I go get something for you?"

It was different with someone to feel for him. The clouds immediately cleared from Sun Luo's face. He turned his head and murmured something to him, probably complaining that there were too many people, so Fu Tingxin switched places with him, walking on the outside himself, deflecting some lines of sight for him with his body. The two of them were of similar height, in an intimate posture. Just like this, as if no one else was around, they entered the venue. From behind, someone called, "Director Sun?"

The two of them turned their heads in the direction of the voice and saw a lanky young man standing behind the back of a chair, a smile on his face, so handsome as to be rather ostentatious, but not seeming frivolous; rather, there was an unexpected affability about him. Sun Luo knew him quite well. He voluntarily shook hands with him. "President Ye."

Ye Zheng shook hands with him and released him. His eyes fell on Fu Tingxin beside him. He raised one eyebrow high. "Whoa. With that manner, are you interested in joining the entertainment circle's recruitment?"

Sun Luo's face immediately looked as dark as if brushed with ashes from the bottom of a pan. Fu Tingxin thought nothing of it. He readily extended a hand toward Ye Zheng and said, smiling, "Hello, my surname is Fu, a retired soldier, currently President Sun's bodyguard. I served in the mess squad before, but I've never specialized in literary or artistic pursuits."

Ye Zheng froze. Then he shook hands with him, laughing heartily. "Xihua Entertainment, Ye Zheng."

"He's joking. This is my childhood friend Fu Tingxin. He was injured recently and hasn't fully recovered yet. He's currently convalescing." After finishing making the introduction to Ye Zheng, Sun Luo said to Fu Tingxin, "This is Xihua's second young master. His sister-in-law Sun Qingning is my cousin. He's a relation."

Fu Tingxin nodded. He seemed to have become accustomed to the Sun family's enormous network of relationship by marriage. Ye Zheng expressed concern for the condition of his injuries. Hearing that he had memory problems caused by a concussion, he immediately slapped the back of his chair. "What a coincidence. It's like this, in a bit I'll introduce you to a person, Hengrui's Director Huo, Huo Mingjun, you must have heard of him? His partner Xie Guan had amnesia from a concussion when he was young. I heard it was cured last year. Lao Huo found many neurological experts to consult. You guys can chat later, maybe he can help with Mr. Fu's injury."

Where Fu Tingxin's condition was concerned, Sun Luo didn't dare to miss out on any opportunity. The banquet began, and he hurriedly went up on stage to deliver a brief speech. As soon as he stepped down, he went right to the lounge. By coincidence, Xie Guan had been invited to attend tonight, and Huo Mingjun had come along. When Sun Luo came in, everyone had already been introduced at Ye Zheng's arrangement and had been talking enthusiastically for a while.

Though Taihe had competed in business with Hengrui, it was unrelated to Sun Luo's focus; there was no antagonism between the two parties. Sun Luo had never met Huo Mingjun in person, only heard that he had a severe and cold disposition, a major player with courage and finesse. But meeting him today, he was nowhere near as unapproachable as he had imagined; perhaps it was because he was in a relationship.

Xie Guan didn't put on any airs. He told Fu Tingxin everything he could think of, then said, "I think the reason I was able to recover my memories was that I fell again afterward. Though it sounds ridiculous, apparently many people only recover their memories after hitting their heads. Don't you fret, maybe it will resolve itself in a few days."

Fu Tingxin nodded, carelessly raising a wineglass. He considered, then quietly said, "I'm not fretting myself, it's mostly Sun Luo. He's under a lot of stress. This is about to become a mental disorder for him."

Xie Guan had more than common sensitivity. He immediately noticed something off about his words and tentatively asked, "You and Mr. Sun…"

"Haven't reached the step you and Director Huo have," Fu Tingxin said.

There was a great deal of information contained in this sentence. Xie Guan smiled understandingly. Fu Tingxin stood and put his wineglass on a small counter, said, "I'm stepping out to the restroom."

The ballroom's restrooms were reached by going out and walking to the other end of the corridor. Fu Tingxin, one hand in his pocket, sauntered over the soft carpet, considering his dialogue with Xie Guan just now.

Xie Guan said that when he had fallen from a stage, he had dreamed of past events. This automatically made Fu Tingxin remember the dream of grandeur he'd had while in a coma— had that really been just a dream?

He became lost in thought and stood at the sink washing his hands for a rather long time. Not far, the stall next to him opened. The man who walked out had been drawn by the sound of water. While passing by, he happened to glance into the mirror. After taking a few steps forward, he suddenly stopped in his tracks and said in astonishment, "Tingxin?"

Fu Tingxin turned his head at the sound and found an unfamiliar face. He knew that this was likely an acquaintance he had met before. But he couldn't remember who this was. He could only brace himself and ask in feigned surprise, maintaining politeness, "Hello, you are…"

"You don't remember me?" A trace of disappointment flickered over the man's face. He said, "I'm Qiu Ming, we sat by each other in high school. You forgot?"

Fu Tingxin had a sudden realization. "Just look at my memory. Forgive me, I didn't recognize you just now—you've changed a lot."

Qiu Ming was twenty-four or -five. His face could be described as fair and delicate, but to Fu Tingxin's eyes, it was a little uncoordinated: the bridge of the nose too high, the chin too sharp, the double eyelids seeming cut. His whole face was very stiff when he smiled. There was no doubt he'd had plastic surgery. So when he said this, Qiu Ming didn't notice anything wrong. He continued smilingly, "I was nothing to look at then, it's no wonder you don't remember. But I haven't forgotten you. You were the most handsome boy in school, the man of everyone's dreams. Many of your classmates had crushes on you."

Fu Tingxin didn't like hearing this very much. He raised his eyebrows. "Really? I don't recall."

"Really. But you were always hanging around Sun Luo. You didn't spend much time with your classmates." Qiu Ming took a step closer. His cologne drifted over faintly. "Did you come with him today, too? I heard that you went into the army after graduating. You're still in contact with him after all these years. You two really are devoted."

"Yes." Fu Tingxin imperceptibly put distance between them and perfunctorily said, "Everyone was busy after graduation, and while I was in the army, it was inconvenient to communicate with the outside world. Are you in the entertainment circle now?"

Qiu Ming laughed unnaturally and vaguely said, "I suppose. Are you... on leave now?"

Fu Tingxin said, "I've been discharged."

Qiu Ming's expression became somewhat more fervent. "Are you planning to go into business?"

He came closer and closer. Fu Tingxin didn't know whether this person was being overly familiar or had some other intentions. After a brief pause, he answered, "I'm unemployed, currently living off someone else."

"You have a partner?" Qiu Ming froze. "Male or female? Who?"

Fu Tingxin nearly choked. "Could it be male?"

"Fair enough," said Qiu Ming. "To get away from me, you didn't even go to university but ran off to join the army instead. I thought you liked Sun Luo, but it turns out you're straight."

Fu Tingxin was all at sea. He didn't quite understand what he was saying.

The footsteps of the person outside the restroom stopped abruptly.

SEVEN

Sun Luo didn't remember how he silently left the restroom door, or how he got to the garden outside the ballroom. At any rate, when he came back to himself, he had smoked half the cigarette in his hand.

These past few months, because Fu Tingxin was living with him and was ill, he had simply stopped smoking. But at one strong shock, he couldn't resist smoking again.

Concerning the past, he had in fact not told Fu Tingxin the truth.

Sun Luo had discovered around his second year of middle school that he had been born gay, but he hadn't told anyone about it, including his best friend Fu Tingxin. But the two of them were always together, and Fu Tingxin was truly dazzling.

While he had done all he could to control himself and stay within proper norms, he couldn't avoid falling for his straight friend, had even done stupid things like secretly throwing away love letters other people sent to Fu Tingxin.

Fu Tingxin was proud and independent. While his grades were bad, he was handsome and good-natured. He was especially good to Sun Luo, even more considerate than the couples in their class. There were always people in class making jokes about them. He remembered that Qiu Ming had sat at the table behind Fu Tingxin's then and often said sourly to him, "Fu-ge is really good to you."

He ought to have noticed the clues, but he hadn't thoroughly analyzed his own feelings then and wasn't in the mood to pay attention to Qiu Ming. Until the second semester of his third year in high school, the crush was like an inferno constantly scorching his heart. Sun Luo bore it patiently and rationally, in comparison to his peers, but finally he couldn't hold back his own feelings. He wrote the affection filling his heart into a short letter and stuck it into Fu Tingxin's notebook.

The next evening, after getting out of class, Sun Luo had gone to the gym as usual to meet Fu Tingxin. When he came to the changing room door and was just about to knock, he suddenly heard a boy say: "... Are you really sure? I hear it's very hard being a soldier. Even if you only go to a second-rate school, it'll still beat going into the army."

"Give it up. If I don't go, what else can I do? If he wants to hit on me, even if I go to a vocational college, he can still follow me there," Fu Tingxin answered irritably. "Maybe I can't afford to offend him, but does that mean I can't hide from him?"

Then from inside the room came the sound of tearing paper. Fu Tingxin furiously kicked a trashcan and uttered a rare profanity: "What are these things? Fuck!"

It was like a clap of thunder exploding in his ears. Before the cluster of flowers in his heart could fully bloom, they were suddenly met head-on with fierce wind and rain.

Half a minute later, Sun Luo silently turned and left the gym, not waiting to go with Fu Tingxin. He returned home missing his soul. The whole way, he thought of him saying, "If I don't go, what else can I do?"

He realized in surprise that all these years, Fu Tingxin had been his only intimate friend, that he had even sometimes treated him as his personal possession, unwilling to share him with others. The two of them had gone to the same kindergarten, the same elementary school, middle school. With Fu Tingxin's grades, he shouldn't have been able to attend a key school. It was because Sun Luo had been planning to test a little worse, insisting on going to the same school as him, that Fu Tingxin, afraid of injuring his prospects, had used his family connections to force his way into the same class as him.

This stubborn possessiveness, perhaps Fu Tingxin was aware of it, but he had never complained about it, had even poured his attention onto him unstintingly. It was precisely because of his indulgence that Sun Luo had developed his unrealistic admiration.

Before today, Fu Tingxin had never mentioned wanting to join the army to him, not one word.

Sun Luo examined his conscience. Throwing everything aside to test into a vocational college with Fu Tingxin was something he would do.

It turned out that without knowing it, he had forced Fu Tingxin to go to such lengths—so that he wanted to flee to a distant place, get far away from him.

Soon after, Fu Tingxin passed the physical examination. Before joining the army, he took a whole crowd of people to the food stalls to eat skewers and drink. Everyone chattered animatedly into the night. At last, only Sun Luo, about to take the university entrance exams, was left clear-headed. On the way home, he stared at Fu Tingxin the whole way in the taxi and ultimately did nothing, safely returning him home.

After graduating high school, Sun Luo changed his contact

information and address, deliberately avoided information related to Fu Tingxin. There were thousands of miles between the two of them. They hadn't corresponded.

He had spent over a decade being stubborn. Finally, that night, he learned to let go.

But in his heart, how could he ever let go of that person?

The bone-deep love and despair hadn't been worn away by time. Instead, they had only become more deeply carved within him, into his marrow. Since then, Sun Luo had encountered no other person who could move his heart. As good as Fu Tingxin had been to him before, that was how much it hurt to have that stripped away. The memories were repeatedly traced over, every stroke and image growing with his flesh and blood. He couldn't have forgotten even if he'd wanted to.

By chance, Fu Tingxin had once again returned to his side. He had lost his memories, but his disposition hadn't changed. His tone when he spoke to Sun Luo had the same transcendent familiarity as in the past. This simply seemed like a heaven-sent opportunity. Fu Tingxin's memories were a sheet of white paper. It was up to him, who knew the truth, to paint them in.

But Sun Luo didn't dare to mention any topics related to "being gay" in front of him, didn't even dare to reveal a single trace of his own feelings—perhaps because the possibility of being knocked out of his beautiful dream was too painful. Once bitten, twice shy; he didn't want to experience that a second time.

Sun Luo had had very little contact with his high school classmates over the years. He had completely forgotten that a minor character like Qiu Ming had ever existed in their lives. But today he had unexpectedly heard an account completely different from the circumstances back then.

How could Fu Tingxin have joined the army because of Qiu Ming?

EIGHT

The night of the charity banquet, Fu Tingxin picked up Sun Luo from the little garden, where he had been bitten all over by mosquitoes. Neither of them mentioned the encounter in the restroom. Fu Tingxin hadn't taken it to heart, Sun Luo had too much on his mind. After this, everything was as usual. The wind calmed and the waves quieted. Only bit by bit, Fu Tingxin found that Sun Luo was a little strange.

Of course, it wasn't a bad kind of strange.

When he had just been injured, Sun Luo had treated him meticulously, but he had always maintained propriety, as if there was an uncrossable "thirty-eighth parallel" between the two of them. But since returning, the physical contact between the two of them had become increasingly clingy. Sun Luo seemed to have spent many years accumulating patience, which he poured out unstintingly onto him, joining him in seeking medical treatment, exercise and rehabilitation, as if a crack had opened slightly in a tightly sealed clamshell, letting gentle light trickle in to illuminate the whole room.

Fu Tingxin was no pure-hearted gentleman above worldly desires. It was impossible for him to be unaware of these thoughts, and he certainly couldn't remain unmoved.

After a few more days, Sun Luo at last came to a decision. He invited an old classmate for a meal.

He hadn't been in contact with his high school classmates for a long time, and the ones who had been on best terms with Fu Tingxin had left the country or settled down in other parts of it. Sun Luo put in several days of work and finally only got in contact with a second-generation rich kid running a company in the capital. His company was in another part of the city. In a show of good faith, Sun Luo deliberately faced the midday traffic to get there.

He had gone out during the midday break. By the time the old classmate came downstairs, lunchtime had passed. The two of them didn't have a formal meal. They just found a coffee shop and sat down for a chat.

The old classmate was friendly enough toward him. It must have been on Fu Tingxin's account. "Has Lao Fu been doing pretty well lately? If you hadn't contacted me, I wouldn't have known that he was in the hospital. I'll go and look in on him sometime."

"His external injuries have healed." Sun Luo raised a hand and pointed at his temple. "But the blood clot in his head hasn't resolved. He still can't remember the past."

His old classmate said consolingly, "Don't fret. This will take time to treat. It may get better on its own one day."

Sun Luo nodded, said, "I wanted to see you so I could ask about something. You were on good terms with him in the past. Do you know why he joined the army?"

"You were the one on best terms with him. We just played basketball and hung out. I never heard him say why," the old classmate said. "Can you give me a hint?"

Sun Luo said, "Do you still remember Qiu Ming?"

"Qiu Ming? Who?" The old classmate racked his brain recalling for ages. "… Oh, you mean that little pretty boy who sat behind the two of you. I remember.

"Isn't Qiu Ming's father Qiu Yongshan? That miraculous 'retail king' from the aughts. Qiu Ming wouldn't have gotten into our school otherwise. But I think he went bankrupt later, dropped his wife and child and went to America to dodge his creditors. He was even on the list of old debtors last year." The old classmate slapped his leg. "Now that you mention him, I recall something. A buddy of mine said Qiu Ming had been chasing Lao Fu, pretty obviously, often bringing him water and stuff and all that, liked him so much he was nearly possessed. I heard he even picked the lock and snuck into the teacher's office to go through the applications, trying to apply to the same university as him. I don't know whether that's true. Didn't Lao Fu ever tell you?"

Sun Luo clutched the handle of his cup and shook his head.

"Fair enough. Lao Fu thought of nothing but you back then. He probably didn't tell you because he didn't want this trifle to impact your university entrance exam results," the old classmate said, laughing. "I suppose you don't know this. When you stole and threw away a love letter to Lao Fu, he happened to see it, so later when others sent him things, he quietly took care of it behind your back. Back then, the whole basketball team tore up love letters and ate chocolate for him. Hahaha…"

Sun Luo was dumbfounded.

The old classmate said, "He really was perfect toward you. The two of us often smoked next to that garbage bin behind the gym. You never saw it. He smoked a cigarette as if he were thieving, never dared to wear his jacket, and when he had finished smoking, he'd stand in the wind for ten minutes. He was afraid you'd smell it on him."

Sun Luo was taken by surprise. These words struck old hidden wounds in his heart. For a time, he was lost in thought, blank. The old classmate was still speaking with emotion: "Suddenly it's been so many years, and you've been the one doing everything to look after him now that he's been injured. Lao Fu was right to care for you before. That's good. It's not easy being brothers for so many years."

Sun Luo nodded automatically. The old classmate saw that his mind was wandering, so he tapped his cup with his spoon and called him back to himself. "President Sun, coming all this way to see me, what was it you wanted to ask? Did you specifically want me to recall the vanished years of your youth?"

"I'm finished asking." Sun Luo gave a dry cough and apologized somewhat awkwardly. "Forgive me, I've taken up so much of your time."

The old classmate stared at him uncomprehendingly for a while. Finally, he couldn't resist laughing. "All right. As long as you know what you're doing."

The two of them said goodbye at the door. The old classmate watched Sun Luo drive onto the main road. He took a cigarette from his pocket. Thinking of something, he clicked his tongue and thought in pleasure at another's misfortune, *I always said that kid Sun Luo's expression wasn't right when he looked at him. Lao Fu didn't believe me. Now I suppose he's going to get himself fucked. It's what he deserves.*

NINE

As to what was going on with that dialogue back then, apart from Fu Tingxin, perhaps no one could give him a definite answer. But that was no longer important. The ill feeling and the stone that had weighed on his heart for many years instantly lost their oppressive weight. Sun Luo thought his heart was light enough to float away.

He only wanted to get home as soon as possible, embrace the person he had pushed away himself.

Sun Luo drove back to his villa as if pursued by murderers the whole way. He didn't find Fu Tingxin in the living room. He searched the upstairs and downstairs, and finally found him sleeping on a sofa in the media room. Light and shadow alternated on the screen. The movie had played to the end. A song rose slowly in time to the subtitles—

The one in my dreams, that familiar face
You are the warmth I have waited for.
The familiar feeling between us,
Love is about to awaken.
Through the years of joy and sorrow, only love is an eternal myth.
Neither of us has forgotten the ancient, ancient promise.
Your tears turn to butterflies filling the sky.
With love beneath their wings, two hearts fly free together.[1]

This was a movie from over a decade ago. The two of them had seen it together when it had been in theaters. It had been popular everywhere at the time, the adolescent memory of a generation. From the prelude of the ending theme, Sun Luo could still sing along.

He stood still in the darkened media room and listened to the whole song. His roiling emotions slowly calmed. Sun Luo could somewhat understand Fu Tingxin's reason for rewatching this movie. Though he was always laughing, never saying anything, who was really willing to be a wraith from another world, without origin or destination?

He sighed silently in his heart, picked up a blanket, and carefully covered Fu Tingxin.

His movements were almost silent, but Fu Tingxin had been awake from the moment he had come in. Now, seeing him draw near, he instantly developed a mischievous urge. He reached out and grabbed Sun Luo's wrist and swept out with his foot, tripping him up. Sun Luo lost his balance and fell right into his arms.

Sun Luo just managed to brace himself against the back of the couch. He was nearly scared to death. "Stop fooling around! What if I fell on you?!"

Fu Tingxin laughed at the success of his scheme. He carelessly raised a hand and gently slapped him on the back. "It's sturdy, a fall wouldn't break it."

"That still won't do, your fractures have just healed…"

His words gradually faded away under Fu Tingxin's smiling gaze. The warmth in his palms seeped through the thin shirt to scorch his skin. It wandered along his nerves and muscles, burning him so that half his body went numb. But in his chest, countless beautiful notions formed against the wind. His thoughts and feelings ran wild everywhere, as if he had opened a zoo.

Raising his head, Fu Tingxin could see his low-hanging, long eyelashes, the glasses on his straight nose, his beautifully shaped eyes screened by the lenses. Moved by some feeling, he reached out to take off the glasses. The two of them could smell each other's breath. The tips of their noses nearly touched. The position was a little excessively intimate.

Dry, rough fingers lightly brushed against the corner of his eye. His eyelashes, like startled butterflies, flapped their wings in a flurry at his fingertips. Fu Tingxin's throat moved. Irresistibly, he pulled him down and pecked at his tightly pursed, thin lips.

This touch was very soft, the force like that of the brush of a feather, but Sun Luo seemed to have been burned by a hot iron. He immediately jumped off him and staggered several steps back, nearly falling onto the carpet.

The tenderness in Fu Tingxin's eyes froze.

He was briefly stunned, then at last slowly blinked. As calmly as he could, he asked, "… Do you hate me?"

Sun Luo was completely stupefied. Hearing Fu Tingxin's question, he shook his head automatically without thinking about it. Fu Tingxin continued: "Then what…"

Before he could finish, Sun Luo, in a shaking voice, hoarsely asked, "Don't you hate me…?'

"Huh?" Fu Tingxin asked, bewildered. "Why would I hate you?"

The lovely eyes that had lost the screen of glasses suddenly reddened. He seemed to be once again cutting out his heart and basely offering it up in both hands, presenting it to be stepped on. Struggling, he said, "I'm… gay."

"Obviously." Fu Tingxin had really had enough of his mental circuit. "So am I. Or else what do you think I'm doing?"

"…"

Fu Tingxin got up off the couch, wanting to go over to wheedle him, but seeing Sun Luo with his head hanging, the cuffs of his shirt shaking slightly, as if he were distraught from a shock, he thought he had better drop it. "Calm down. Your brain isn't working. We'll talk again when you've thought things through."

Then he turned, ready to leave. Unexpectedly, Sun Luo suddenly threw himself at him from behind, wrapping his arms tightly around him as if catching a thief. "You can't go!"

Had he been someone else, Fu Tingxin would have thrown

him over his shoulder. But when Sun Luo threw himself at him, he only went rigid, then stood still where he was. "Oh? What's wrong?"

Sun Luo was a few centimeters taller than him. His lips were just at his ear. Without warning, a warm, shaky kiss fell behind Fu Tingxin's ear. "I don't need to think... I like you, I've liked you for many years..."

Fu Tingxin's heart beat wildly, but he said, "Really? And you still said we were friends."

"I didn't dare to tell you the truth." Sun Luo buried his head against the juncture of his shoulder and neck, wrapping his arms around his chest. He whispered, "I thought you hated gay people."

Fu Tingxin sighed, freed up an arm, and covered the back of his hand. He turned his head and asked, "Was it something I did before that made you misunderstand?"

Sun Luo didn't answer. In a very small voice, he gave an *mhm*.

From this syllable, Fu Tingxin picked out a sense of deep grievance. He felt a little helpless, and he also felt his heart become unbearably soft. By temperament he didn't bother explaining things, did whatever he liked, but Sun Luo wasn't someone else, so he only thought about it, considered his wording, and said, "I don't remember what happened before, but if it were you, I might not understand, but I definitely wouldn't hate you."

It was as if a sword suspended high up had finally fallen, but it didn't stab anyone. Instead, with a quiet whistle, it slipped seamlessly into a sheath.

Sun Luo was letting everything go in one ear and out the other. He didn't care what Fu Tingxin said, as long as he answered. For a time he was immersed in the sudden tenderness and contentment. In his complacency, he suddenly thought, why hadn't he gone to Fu Tingxin to seek confirmation back then?

Why not hear his answer with his own ears? Even if what he said was a refusal, it would still be better than seven years of pain and torment because he thought he couldn't be wrong, seven years of lengthy separation.

Why hadn't he dared to believe that as good as this person was, he would never hurt him?

"Kiss me again." He pulled Fu Tingxin's face toward his own, urgently seeking tenderness and consolation in his lips. He said again, "I like you. I've liked you for a long time."

"What a coincidence." Fu Tingxin met his lips. "I've also liked you for a long time."

"Hm?"

"Since our last lifetime."

TEN

Fu Tingxin was incapable of being idle. After a few months of recovery, having succeeded in turning himself gay, he thought that his physiological and psychological health had both been restored, so he started planning to find himself something to do.

Sun Luo listened to a big heap of grandiose plans, then said, restrained and gentle, "Why don't you come work at my company?"

Fu Tingxin said, "I only have a high school diploma, I can't do anything. I can only be your driver."

Sun Luo agreed at once. "All right, no problem. You can be my 'secretary' if you like."

"I was really wrong about you," Fu Tingxin said sighing. "Do you want to close the office door…"

Sun Luo threw himself at him and stopped his mouth.

From that day on, Director Sun began to live a pleasant life in which his driver took him to work in the morning, his driver brought him food in the afternoon, and his driver warmed his bed at night.

Sadly, after a few days of this, Fu Tingxin quit his job in disgust.

Sun Luo lay in his lap and asked, whining, "Why? Is your boss not handsome enough, or is your salary not high enough?"

"Where have you ever seen a boss who will only get out of the car after a kiss from his driver?" Fu Tingxin ridiculed. "President Sun, that's called workplace sexual harassment."

Fu Tingxin's memories weren't coming back all at once like Xie Guan's. He was slowly remembering things, a bit at a time. Though at first it was a little confused, fundamentally he was no different from an ordinary person now.

The second year that the two of them were together, Fu Tingxin contacted some retired comrades-in-arms, and they jointly opened a hotpot restaurant. Their former training base had been in the northwest. They were deeply attached to that location. After an inspection, they signed a contract with local herdsmen to supply grasslands beef and mutton directly to the capital. Later still, the hotpot restaurant's business gradually expanded. They even opened a restaurant across from the Taihe Conglomerate.

The day the new restaurant opened happened to be Sun Luo's birthday. He hadn't remembered it himself, but in order to support Fu Tingxin, he specifically invited some friends from senior management to eat hotpot.

Midway, Fu Tingxin knocked on the door of the private room and came in. Some servers filed in carrying luxurious fruit bowls and cake, singing "Happy Birthday."

Everyone began to shout at once.

Fu Tingxin was dressed in a shirt and pants, his figure tall and straight, aggressively manly. He openly walked over to hug Sun Luo and kiss him, and said, "Happy birthday."

It had long been a half-public secret that the two of them were together, they had just never been so brazen in front of outsiders. Sun Luo felt a little embarrassed. The tips of his ears turned faintly red. But his eyes held an unrestrainable smile. "Thank you, we'll enjoy it together."

The servers began to distribute slices of cake. Sun Luo also had a saucer in his hand, with an imperfect but still reasonably complete frosting flower on it. Fu Tingxin, smiling, said, "Try it? I just squeezed it out myself with a pastry bag."

Once he said this, never mind a poor outward appearance, even if this flower had been made of plastic, Sun Luo could still have chewed and swallowed it without batting an eye—

"Hm?"

His teeth had been hurt by something hidden in the flower.

Fu Tingxin kindly passed him a paper napkin. Sun Luo covered his mouth and turned aside. A gleaming ring fell into his palm, cushioned by the paper napkin.

Sun Luo was amazed.

The whole crowd of immaculately dressed elite businessmen in the private room had absolutely no shame, without exception. They began to clap and cheer and whistle. "Say yes! Say yes! Say yes!"

Fu Tingxin pulled out a paper napkin and wiped the ring clean. He took Sun Luo's faintly trembling left hand, hanging at his side, but he didn't proceed according to script. Instead, he regarded him and with a slight smile asked, "Is there something you'd like to say to me?"

The moment their eyes met, Sun Luo suddenly understood what he meant. A promise a long time coming came naturally to his lips.

Like fortune blessing the mind, and like a channel forming naturally when the water comes.

"I love you—

"All my life, through all our lives, I will love only you."

The ring was neither loose nor tight. It fit snugly at the base of his finger.

This time, the red thread that had been torn was at last tied into a knot, binding together lovers who had missed their destiny, to the end of this life, never to let go, never to part.

---

1. Lyrics from "Beautiful Myth," one of the themes of the 2005 Hong Kong movie "The Myth."

GLOSSARY

Ren Miao | 任淼 | *noun* | rén miǎo

The characters of Fu Shen's name are 傅深, with the radicals 亻 and 氵, while Ren Miao is 任 (with the radical 亻) 淼 (made up of three 水, the full form of 氵).

Legend of the fish and geese | 鱼雁传书 | *noun* | yú yàn chuán shū

An ancient proverb based on the legend that the god of Yellow River, Hebo, exchanged letters with Ge Xuan from the Three Kingdoms era using koi fish as messengers. The legend of the geese originated from the Emperor Wu of Han, who shot down a goose to send a message back to his home country while being held captive by the Huns.

Adobe kang | 土炕 | *noun* | tǔ kàng

A traditional heated platform bed often found in the Northern regions of China, where winter is often colder than the Southern regions. The kang space is often built with bricks or clay and is designed to retain heat within the household.

Chang'an | 长安 | *noun* | cháng ān

Now known as the city of Xi'an in China, Chang'an was a prosperous ancient city throughout Dynastic China and served as the nation's capital for nearly 800 years. While historic Chang'an had relocated several times throughout the ages, it was generally near the center of Guanzhong and Xi'an. Two of the most powerful dynasties in Chinese history, Western Han and Tang, settled in Chang'an as their capital city.